ANSWERED PRAYERS
The Adventures of Joe Geezre

KAW TRILOGY
VOL. I

Printed in the United States of America

ISBN 0-9632098-0-9

Library of Congress Catalog Card Number:
91-91537

First Edition, 1992

Cover illustration: sculpture by Ed Root,
photograph Copyright by Jon Blumb, 1988; courtesy
Kansas Grassroots Art Association

This book is printed on archival-quality paper which meets
the guidelines for performance and durability of the
Committee on Production Guidelines for Book Longevity
of the Council on Library Resources.

REGILDING PRESS
13920 262nd ST.
LAWRENCE, KANSAS 66044

for
BARBARA HAWKINS

The author gratefully acknowledges the following people who provided archival material and assisted in editing and manuscript preparation: T. Watson Bogaard, Irish Jones, Pam LeRow, Jane Malin, Paula Malone, Lucille Marino, Lynn Porter, Melissa Ryckert, William Sharp, Thomas Swearingen, and Barbara Watkins.

1

The Fruitbats

Did you ever when you were walking along, thinking deep thoughts, did you ever get words in your head and say them over and over? I did. As I walked up the hill one bright springtime day I kept saying *I'm a retired virgin.* After a few repetitions the words made twisted sense. *I'm a virgin who retired. To retire is to go to bed. To go to bed is to leave Virginia. A professional virgin who hung it up.* And so forth. Nuts. Inside my head. When I was a kid nobody told me I was a virgin. Back then I thought virgins were female, like the Virgin Mary. I'm sixty-two, now. I'm retired. I have lots of time to walk the streets of River City and think about things. I never had a car either.

I'm trying to cross the boulevard through a gang of goofs wearing medieval cloaks. Many in the gang wear black robes (looking very much like fruitbats). The marshals attempting to control them wear black robes with yellow and purple and green hoods, like condors and vultures. Some fruitbats conceal champagne bottles under their wings, while others pose for photographs. Some are dazed—as if they're surprised to be here. Beneath their batcloaks I see spike-heeled shoes, bare feet, trendy running shoes, rubber chicken feet. I am nauseated knowing that any one of these imitation medievalists might be the graffiti artist, Penis Boy.

As the bats await their turn to swoop down the hill and gobble sheepskin I peer into faces wondering if any of them have found wisdom. Down the boulevard, next door to where I live, stands the old library building and carved in stone above its entrance is *Whoso Findeth Wisdom Findeth Life.* Wisdom. Life. These fruitbats are plenty alive, but they don't look very wise. Maybe the wise ones graduated last year. That's it! These are the dumb ones, fifth-year seniors, holdovers. Happy with that realization I work my way through the throng, going home to Flattop, the habitat of retired folks which lies anchored between the chapel and the old library. As I lift a weary foot stepping onto *terra firma* the flash of an aneurism blossoms in my starboard earhole. I feel bright pain. The sky goes black. I stumble. All I can see is a bloody field of red behind a pulsing yellow hexagon. A honeycomb as large as the sky. I hear the inane babble of fruitbats. Or is it the buzzing of bees? Intense pain surges through my neck extending down my right side. Brain explosion, paralysis. I am dying. I am light-headed and happy. Floating. This is death. I'm a standing dead man. I should pray. I should try to pray.

"Jesus, Harry! You hit the old man in the head!"

I sink to my knees giving thanks for that human voice. That fruitbat's voice. Hooray for Harry! Thank God he hit me! I can take hits. I can take blows. Hit me again, Harry! Harry has hit me and I'm happy because that means my brain isn't running out my ear. It means I'm alive. I blink to see sunlight through this vale of tears. I feel a burning lump the size of a monkey's fist and grasp it and hold it close to my eyes. Like Satan giving birth to Sin, I have plucked the bad lump from my brain. It feels knurled and hard like a walnut. It is clear, the color of mucus. Then to my eternal relief and delight I recognize it to be nothing more sinister than a plastic champagne cork. If ever there was an evil object, I hold it in my hand. Plastic cork. The boy mutters, "He's coming to."

I clutch my cork as he helps me to my feet.

"Are you all right?" he asks.

I grip his arm and squeeze hard, trying to inflict pain. "Geezre," I say, "I'm all right. I'm Joe Geezre."

The kid blinks at me, his moist mouth open. "Are you sure?"

"I know who I am! Just let me wobble on down to the chapel, crawl across the parking lot, put an icepack on my earhole, lie down and listen to my Mussolini tapes." I brush back my hair to show the fruitbat where I was hit. My wound. My earhole. "No ear at all," I say, grinning. "Not here, get it? No ear!"

He fears a lawsuit. "I didn't do that!"

"Of course you didn't. You don't have the gumption. This here ear was shot off in the Korean War."

"Which war?" his girlfriend asks, swooping close in her batcape.

"The Crimean," I say.

"Yeah," she says. "I'm a history major."

Her breath sparks my interest. I size her up. Weak eyes. Flat nose. Pink nostrils. Sharp teeth. Maybe I'll release my virginity to her, fall down, play dead, and let her give me the kiss of life. She blinks and informs me, "That was the war to end all wars. Pretty naive, wasn't it?"

I shift the plastic cork to my left hand so I can shake with her, gripping her lily-white longer than she wants me to. "Geezre," I say, "Joe Geezre. I live right down the street here. Fifth door on the right. Flit by sometime." I release her hand to brush hair over my earhole, making myself look normal. Another champagne cannon explodes and like any combat infantryman I hit the dirt.

His head throbbing, his eyes bleary, Joe Geezre quits the sidewalk and cleaves to the green grass. He skirts the Battleship, dips behind the Flagship, and passes the chapel. He crosses her gangplank and opens the hatch of the Aircraft Carrier. The Mothball Fleet, he calls it. He mails himself postcards addressed: Capt. Joseph Geezre, USS Flattop, The

Great American Desert. None of his postcards ever arrive, but he takes their misadventure philosophically. *Lost at sea*, he says. *A message in a bottle.*

He pads down the hallway, opens his salon door, enters, and pours himself a tumbler of buttermilk. His apartment is decorated in the scheme of a bachelor who believes that his surroundings embody spiritual meaning. There is a *faux* zebra skin hanging on the wall. Also hanging on the wall are large photographs of Taj Mahal and a horse named Comanche. The horse wears tack from the Seventh Cavalry—Custer's command. Joe Geezre forged Custer's signature on the photograph—*Wish you were here! Gen. Geo. Armstrong Custer.* A retired professor, Joe's next-door neighbor, offered to buy Comanche's photograph if Joe could certify its authenticity. Joe laughed at him saying, "Woolie, Old Chap, don't fall for that fallacy. Nothing is authentic." To prove his point Joe took a shrivelled wand of bones from the crack between his sofa cushions and shook it, like a witch's finger, under Professor Woolheater's nose. "This chain of bones, Woolie, is Comanche's authentic tailbone!" Joe used the tailbone to point across the street at the museum of natural history, the place where he'd worked twenty-six years. "I saw it come out of the rear end of Custer's horse, I *know* it's authentic. But how could I prove it? And who would give a penny for this mummified tailbone of the horse that survived the Battle of the Little Big Horn? Authentic? Nothing is authentic but yourself, Woolie."

Joe Geezre sips buttermilk. He is alone. "Mannie," he commands snapping his fingers, "Put on a cut of Mantovani! Or a cut of sirloin!" The dark apartment is silent. There is no manservant Mannie. Joe takes the plastic cork from his pocket and peers through it at the overhead light. He turns it, fracturing the light. "Comanche wasn't Custer's horse," he says. "But thousands of fruitbats flown from here to Four Corners think he was, so that makes it somewhat true."

Joe worked as a preparator in the museum. Before that he was a private in the army. As a preparator he skinned birds, polished bones, and went on expeditions to dig up fossilized sea turtles. He painted the dioramas. He designed displays. His supervisor urged him to study museum taxidermy but Joe replied in his skewed manner, "Taxidermy, Dr. Smoot, is a dead end."

As an undergraduate Joe majored in art. He haunts the library where he wanders the stacks repeating in his head the phrase, *My mind to me a kingdom is.* Unlike his brother who lives across the river, Joe fancies himself an intellectual. Everett, his twin, owns Geezre Plumbing Co. Everett Geezre's recreations are gardening and fishing the river for flatheads. His wife founded the River City Humane Society, and Everett has a photographic memory, "Not a blessing," he says, "in my line of work. I've looked down several thousand plugged stools and I am cursed with the vivid memory of every one!" Everett collects gossip. He never forgets an overheard remark, a magnetic note on a refrigerator or a sideways, mid-afternoon, housewifely-sleepy, bedroom look. He is incredibly handsome and sexy. Ask any woman in River City. He smokes thin cigarillos. He has wide shoulders, curly black hair, a stork tattooed on his thick arm, seven children, and two ears.

Joe, on the other hand, is gaunt, unattractive, and tall. He has close-set eyes, long stringy blond hair, and one ear. Joe could have stayed in the family house when he retired. He'd lived in two rooms of it off-and-on all his life, but instead he chose to move to the heart of the campus, a three-minute walk from the main library and the art museum, across the street from the anthropology museum, across the street from the natural history museum. *If there is intellectual life in Kansas I'm anchored in the middle of it!* he wrote in his journal. He is one minute from the chapel.

As a boy he followed his yellow dog down Hogtown Creek to where it joins the river. He explored the river up to Lakeview and beyond. He's seen washpots boiled over backyard fires. He's tramped around Bismark Grove and Gridley Hill where hippies farmed marijuana. He saw the hippies convene a nude wedding. He's seen falling stars, the *aurora borealis*, fire, rain, and floods on the river. He's been a lone outdoorsman—hunting, fishing, trapping, skinning—broiling his meat over campfire coals—but when he retired he quit the woods to seek wisdom in lectures, films, and *The Harvard Classics*. Acknowledging the fact that leaving college without a degree imprinted his psyche with a medallion of inferiority, he vowed to learn in retirement all the things he hadn't bothered to learn before. In order to gain life he vowed to find wisdom, so he gave away his basketball tickets and bought a notebook. Wearing a crisp white yachtsman's cap he attended plays, concerts, exhibitions, and poetry readings. He became known to the students as Walkman, and they ran rumors about him: *Walkman knew Ezra Pound. Walkman shot lions with Papa.*

His phone rings and he touches it lightly, afraid he is being called to task. Hesitantly, he lifts the receiver. "Hello?"

The caller is his brother. "Joe! Whatcha doing?"

"Thinking."

"Thinking?"

"Stinking. Sitting here thinking and stinking. Nursing my headache. I got shot in the head."

"Meet me at the statue of the gay guys."

"I have a headache."

"I'm taking you on a job. A job you'll like!"

Everett cuts through campus in his Geezre Plumbing van. He stops at the traffic kiosk, winks at the woman wearing a blue blazer, and says: "Big trouble! Chancellor's House!"

"What's wrong?" the woman asks.

"Boiler in the basement blew!" He flips her a snappy salute, clenching the cigarillo in his astonishingly white teeth. "Won't flush!"

Joe says, "Watch the place, Mannie. Anybody calls—tell 'em I'm out!" He runs to stand on the curb teetering, flapping his arms. When Everett stops for him he squawks, "Whatcha want, Everett! Whatcha want, Everett!"

"C'mon, Polly Parrot, get in the goddamned van and I'll tell you what I want. I'm on a high-dollar job out west, see? I'm in the basement and I hear people upstairs trying to keep their voices calm, but they're plenty excited. Seems they're waiting for a famous writer. I figure you'd like a piece of this action!"

"Famous writer? What's her name?"

"Her?"

"Ah, Everett! You're not liberated—"

"This writer's a man."

"How do you know?"

"They kept saying, *He don't like this* and *He don't like that.* Seems he's a finicky sonofabitch."

"What's his name?"

Everett grimaces, dropping cigar ash on his shirtfront as he turns the van hard, squealing his tires around the fountain. "Chivas."

"That's a brand of scotch."

"Maybe so, but that's his name."

I wonder who the writer is. I check my pocket to make sure I have enough pens and pencils, feeling rather fat-and-happy sitting high in the van watching Everett turn sharp corners. He runs a stop sign. Maybe I've finally plugged my cord into the proper literary socket. In my campaign to gain wisdom I have come to resent professors who, when I ask questions, look off in space as if a geek like me couldn't understand their deconstructions. Many of them don't have the sense to close a door. One professor used to come home in the middle of winter, unlock his door, go inside, and forget to close it. The landlord had to install a closer or the prof would have frozen to death. That's the kind of stories floating around this town. River Citians love nutty professor stories, like the one about the guy who smokes his pipe upside down or the woman who puts diapers on her car so it won't spot the driveway. I, on the other hand, am beginning to wise up. Having retired from base biology I shall never again turn a ravenous pack of *dermestid* beetles loose on a stack of bear bones, and I'll never again remove a dead snake from the live-snake display case. That's the new guy's job. It's a darned sight easier to pull skinny than push it, as I learned helping

Everett grind out clogged sewers, humping boxes of sewer rod while he sat on a milk crate feeding those connecting rods through his grinder, a cigarillo glowing under his nose to anesthetize his olfactory sensibilities. Sewers stink.

The high-dollar job is a bathroom addition. Everett takes me through the vestibule to show me a bronze bust of Harry Truman. "There," he says, winking, "look at that! They've got a million-dollar house, you'd bet your ass they're Republicans, and right here in the entrance they've got a big busted Harry Truman!" In the adjoining room a woman's oil portrait tells me whose house I'm in. I've heard Phoebe Jones read her poetry at the Glass Eye. In the room with her portrait there's a grand piano. On a shelf above the piano are several other busteds: a white marble busted Beethoven and a pewter busted Margaret Thatcher looking over Beethoven's shoulder, keeping a wary eye on Truman.

"So what's wrong with being a rich Democrat?" I ask, my feet sinking into a Persian.

"I wasn't finding fault with these people, Joe."

"Are they nuts?"

"I never said they were nuts."

"Plumbers aren't supposed to enter by the front door."

"They've got *new* money, Joe. They haven't worked out the details."

"Seems like a good way to get their busteds stolen."

"Maybe. But they want people to see them."

"They're nuts."

"This way to the job." Giving me a hurt look, Everett leads me to the stairs. He has been subcontracted to install fixtures in the new bathroom. The toilet and lavatory were routine for him, as was the base for the shower. All that remains is a wooden crate decorated with numerous French shipping tags. Someone has painted on it with a broad brush, BE DAY DON'T DROP.

Everett attacks the crate with a screwdriver, prying it apart. "Read me some of them French instructions," he says, and I grasp his reason for bringing me along. I read French fluently, if not accurately. "Let's see—*Il faux que vous mettrez votre pied sur le nord et petite chose.*"

"What's it mean?"

"It is necessary," I translate, "to use common sense in the putting together of this small thing."

"Uhmm."

We have barely gotten the bidet freed from its cage when the famous writer walks in on us. There is no mistaking him. He wears a Cerulean blue velvet suit and a rumpled cream yellow necktie with blue dots. He is small and puffy, middle-aged, with thin hair. Cherub-like. I can tell by the way he cocks his big head he's a genius. He has come to size up the plumbers, to gather material about our blue-collar condition. Everett ignores him, but I stare. He stands quietly, like an elf, in the space where the shower will go. He watches Everett with warm affection, admiration.

"Five-eighths copper nipple," Everett tells me in his full-dress surgeon's tone. He flicks a light to his propane torch—BANG—it erupts a six-inch flame. I hand him the nipple. He cleans it, positions it on a length of pipe, and sweats the union. The writer watches from his shower stall as Everett works the pipe on down, sweating on a ninety-degree elbow and a reducing T. Then the writer says, "I don't understand. What makes the silver stuff flow where you want it to?"

Everett, in his macho swagger, lights a fresh cigarillo from the blazing torch. "Flux!"

The writer looks at Everett as if he doubts it and says, "I need to go—and I don't think I can wait until you get this room finished!"

Everett lifts the bidet and sets it in front of the writer, trapping him in the shower stall. "Use this BE DAY."

Not to be outdone, the chubby Elf unzips his fly. To my everlasting shock and horror I watch him pull out his apparatus and aim it at the bidet.

Everett says, "No! Don't piss in that!" And he hastily moves the bidet aside. The writer, smirking, thinking he has done something funny, leaves us and saunters down the hall.

"Don't worry about that fairy faucet wetting his pants," Everett says, "they's five bathrooms in this house! You want to stand around in my way or you want to go eavesdrop on the literary gossip?"

I grin.

"Here. Take this plumb-bob to the kitchen. Stand beside the boiler. They'll be in the den and you can hear them through the ventilator. If the cook asks what you're doing tell her you're bobbing the plumb."

"Plumb pudding!"

"I knew you'd like this job. My brother the intellectual."

I go looking for the kitchen.

"Waitaminute," he mumbles, "take this too. It'll make you look professional." He hands me his assemblage of copper pipe that looks more like abstract sculpture than plumbing. I easily find the kitchen by following my nose.

Nothing makes a kitchen more authentic than the smell of burning onions, and nothing makes a house more homey than an authentic kitchen. I ask the cook, a thin Black man, where the boiler is and he opens a closet for me. I go in, turn on the light, and close the door. I unroll the string from Everett's plumb bob. Then I take a stepstool from its hook and step up so I can hold the string to the ceiling and my earhole to the ventilator grate. From the adjoining room I hear the Elf laughing. His high-pitched voice rises and falls uneasily. I hear a woman say, "You actually witnessed their executions?"

"Yes. It was an excruciating experience. I'd gotten to know them quite well."

"Are you working on a new book?"

"*Ask Me.*"

"Are you working on a new book?"

He laughs, pleased with himself. His laugh has an aftertaste, a way of lingering. He says, "*Ask Me No Questions.* That's the title."

"Is it a murder book?"

"Oh—no, no, no, no, no-ooh! It's a gossip book about the rich and famous. Silly little predicaments they find themselves in. Like—a man on his knees frantically washing hotel sheets at three in the morning—and all he has for soap is one of those hotel slivers—"

Someone asks, "Why would he be doing that?"

After a pause the writer replies, "*Ask Me No Questions.* Maybe it has something to do with sex."

"Say," a man's voice, "we had one out at the lake. A couple parked. Their car rolled in the lake."

"Drown them?" the writer asks, his tone revealing that he doesn't care.

"No. The water was three feet deep. They waded ashore."

"Oh," the writer says, his voice sliding down to register his disappointment. "Why didn't they use the brake?"

"Because," the storyteller says, savoring the punch line, "their legs weren't long enough!"

I hear the Elf laugh, but I don't think he's amused.

The woman tries to laugh heartily, imitating him, but she chokes and coughs. She speaks again, and I recognize her voice. She is Phoebe Jones. "How do you like being back in Kansas?"

"It's a place with its own charm," he says. "I have lots of friends here. Whenever I get stale I travel for inspiration."

There is a long pause. Phoebe asks, "Can I fix you another margarita?"

He says, "I want a jigger of tequila, just straight."

Someone coughs.

"Here," someone says.

Someone else says, "Isn't tequila supposed to have a worm in it?"

The Elf must have lifted his glass to make a toast because he says slowly and deliberately, "More tears are shed over answered prayers than unanswered ones, according to Saint Teresa."

I brace myself, standing atop the rickety stool, swaying, wondering what Saint Teresa meant by that. Then Everett opens the closet door.

"Well?" he gestures.

I get down. "What do you want?"

"Those damned onions are driving me nuts," he says. "Let's go eat!"

I know what that means—a dangerous drive to El Chico Cafe for cheese-and-onion enchiladas. El Chico doesn't have a liquor license, but Cowboy looks the other way if you carry in a brown bag. I tell Everett to stop for a bottle of tequila.

"Tequila? Joe, you don't drink."

"Well," I say, "now that I'm retired I might try something new." So Everett stops at the Bald Eagle and asks the bartender to lend him two shot glasses. She is Judy, his sometimes girlfriend. Of course May, his wife, doesn't know.

"You want to *borrow* two shot glasses? Two *empty* shot glasses?"

"Yeah. That's right," he says. "Please."

She grimaces. "Look, Everett. You don't lend out plumbing tools. I don't lend out bartending tools. No empty glasses."

"Two shots of tequila," he says, elbowing me and saying with his eyes, *Put the glass in your pocket.*

When Judy turns to pour the shots I see Everett gazing at the back of her tight jeans. He's been that way since childhood. He gets a dreamy, far-away look on his face. His eyebrows arch. The planes under his eyes stretch serene. His nostrils flare. Any taxidermist would want to mount a study of my brother erect.

I think about Rosealyn, Everett's youngest daughter who lives in Mississippi. She and I are tremendous pen pals. She writes me news of her daughter and son and Hub, the computer man.

"Here, Boys!" Judy says, "don't swallow the glasses!"

Everett lifts his and says, "To Joe Geezre's retirement!"

I drink mine. It brings tears to my eyes. "Put a little money aside," I say. "You can retire. Provide. Provide."

"Bub," he says tossing off his tequila, "I'll die pulling Ridgid-Kollmann up some professor's basement steps."

"Don't make jokes," I say. "Death is always at your elbow." Everett backs off because he knows I've heard Chinese bugles. He leaves Judy a tip, we waft out with her

shot glasses and drive to a place Everett calls the Drunk
People's Liquor Store where I buy a bottle of tequila. Sure
enough, the clerk is stumble-thumb drunk.   Then Everett
wheels us to El Chico Cafe.   As we take our places in his
booth something hairy, black, and larger than a tarantula chases
a brace of cockroaches up the velvet matador.   Cowboy takes
our order, and Everett pours two shots of tequila.

Cowboy is the only Anglo restaurateur in North River
City. His beautiful wife, Candelaria Maldonado, was waiting
tables the day he crawled out of a boxcar and followed his nose
to her father's cafe. Cowboy's black trousers were slept in and
his cowboy shirt with its mother-of-pearl snaps showed the gray
dust of Portland cement when he walked into Candelaria's life
grinning as if he wore silver spurs, a pearl-handled revolver,
and a sombrero across his shoulders. She fed him free. Her
father soon retired, and Candelaria and Cowboy ran the place.
She cooked. He waited tables thumping across the plank floors
in his Texas boots. When Candelaria died, her adult life barely
begun, the grieving Cowboy dug himself deep into a
Pentecostal sect. He decorated the walls with religious mottoes
and pictures of Jesus. He ran El Chico single handed.
Business fell off. A few sand rats like Everett keep him going
despite his roaches, despite his bad cooking, despite his six-
item menu. El Chico Cafe became a holy place filled with the
smell of scorched food and the sound of bootheels on oaken
floors.

"Here's to luck in Vegas," I say.

"Here's to onions, melted cheese, and cornmeal," Everett
replies. He drinks his shot, grinning. He says, "I'll make a
killing on this high-falutin job. The lady asked to see my union
card. She don't want scabs in her house because her old man's
gonna run for governor on the Democratic ticket."

I toast. "Here's to her old man," I say. "I hope he wins!"

"He'll win. He's got a busted Harry Truman."

"Sure." I like Everett's *joie de vivre*. "And," I say, proud
of my wit, "he's also got a big-busted Margaret Thatcher!"

"If Margaret Thatcher was an American would she be a
Democrat?"

Cowboy comes to eavesdrop. *Who's cooking our food?*
"Sure she would. She's just a commoner, folks like you and
me. The Queen's the Republican." Cowboy leans too close
and Everett offers him a shot of tequila.

"No, no," Cowboy says, his gold tooth flashing.

"Okay," Everett says, "that leaves more for us."

Unaccustomed to drinking, I feel a swirl of warm
sensations. The cockroaches are considerate enough to stay out
of sight when Cowboy sets laden plates before us. *Hot plates.*
Steam rises. Cheese runs like lava. There is ample grease.
Curled tortilla ends protrude from thick sauce like culverts on
a red-dirt Georgia road. There is the heavy smell of lard and
Mexican pepper, but Everett doesn't notice the lard. I'm
certainly not going to tell the vegetarian there's hogfat in
Cowboy's frijoles.

"Oops, hide the booze, Joe. Here comes the judge."

I gaze at the somber man walking our way.

Everett nods to him and says softly to me, "You wander
into his courtroom and he'll put your ass under the jail. I saw
how he operates. Some goofball got charged with cutting
marijuana. *Bring the guilty sonofabitch in and let's give him a
fair trial.*"

"Kangaroo court?" I say, loud enough for the judge to
hear. The tequila has loosened my tongue and given me a
devil-may-care sense of humor. I recognize the judge, having
seen him relaxing with lawn darts.

"Nah." Everett lowers his voice as the judge wiggles into
the booth opposite us. "He's okay. Pretends to nap during the
testimony, but he sees everything. That dope cutter hung
himself. Judge simply gave him twenty feet of rope. Hemp.
Five years for five-fingered grass."

The judge studies a greasy menu. When Cowboy comes
with his pad of guest checks and asks, "Are you ready to
order?" the judge points at the El Chico special. Then he
unrolls his silverware, sips his water, folds his hands, and
stares at the back wall. I'm fascinated by his thin nose, his
quiet dignity, his poker face. There are many questions I want
to ask him such as if he saw us drinking tequila in an

unlicensed Anglo Mexican restaurant, breaking the law, would he as a judge be obliged to arrest us? Judge, do you ever break the law? Do you have a radar detector in your Mercedes? After twenty years of hearing torts and misdemeanors, felonies, double-binds, pigeon drops, castrations, divorces, homicides, insurance frauds; how deeply do you pity the human heart? Who pities you? Who judges the judge? I open my notebook and write: *Read the Book of Judges. Were they judges in the modern sense?*

"After lunch we'll hook up that BE DAY. Won't take us twenty minutes," Everett says. "I'm curious to see how it flushes." Flush is Everett's favorite word. The sign on his van reads, *Geezre Plumbing—In Our Business a Flush Beats a Full House.*

"What will you play in Vegas?" I ask. "Craps?"

Everett flexes his arm to make his stork hop in a mating display. "I dunno. I'll see what Madame Leontyne advises. Maybe she'll get it right this time."

Cowboy brings us a plate of hot tortillas. "Anything to drink besides water?" he asks, knowing full well we have tequila.

"Water's fine," Everett replies, taking out one of his thin cigarillos and torching it. The judge turns his distant gaze on Everett and Everett quickly puts out the cigar. I wonder if the judge knows that we know that he's a judge.

I pull my enchiladas apart. "Remember," I say, "Madame Leontyne didn't get it right last time."

"No, she didn't. She talks numbers and I don't play numbers. So I told her *Give me information I can use.* She said, *Find a dealer with removables. Left and right.*"

"Like me!" I say, brushing back my hair to display my earhole, my hand cupped beside my face like an ear. The judge looks at my earhole, but it doesn't shock him because he's seen much worse—autopsies, eviscerations, abortions. "Find a dealer whose ear's been removed."

"They have complete dealers in Vegas. I couldn't find any dealers with any removable parts except some bald guys with rugs. Then I saw a blackjack dealer, beautiful redhead wearing a pair of jumbo falsies. I lost a grand betting on her sure thing—a dealer with left and right removables!"

I wonder if the judge hears our conversation. I don't think he is listening because he seems to be working out a judicial problem in his head. He sips icewater waiting for his special. A coal train passes. A cockroach runs down the matador's blade. I write in my book so I won't forget it, *Cockroaches in the bullring.* I also write, *Coal from Montana?* Suddenly Everett leaps up. I figure he wants a toothpick. *Sonofabitch!* he yells, running out the front door. The word *sonofabitch* has only one meaning in his dictionary. It's a customer who didn't pay the bill. I hear Everett starting his van and I know there will be hot pursuit in North River City. The judge seems to have heard no *sonofabitch*. He is sedate. But he's a sleight-of-hand artist because the icewater in his glass has turned amber. I smell the distinct odor of scotch. Everett's scream of *sonofabitch* gave the judge the opportunity to filch a bottle from his pocket, twirl off the cap, slosh two fingers into his icewater, and drop the bottle to his crotch. *Good move, Judge!*

I turn to face him. He reluctantly meets my eyes. I smile and say, "My brother." I jerk my thumb toward the front door. "Spotted a flake who owes him money."

The judge doesn't respond.

"Say, you're a judge, aren't you?" I ask, trying to warm him up. The tequila has made me cocky.

"Yes, I am."

"Well," I ask, "how does it stand, legally, for my brother to yell *sonofabitch* in a public place?"

"I don't object," the judge says, "but he'd better not yell it in a crowded theatre."

"What if he's in *Oklahoma!* sold out, and it's his role to run on stage and yell, *Sonofabitch!*"

"There's no *Sonofabitch* in *Oklahoma!*"

"Well maybe there's one in *South Pacific* or *Picnic*, it's all musical comedy."

The judge takes a long pull from his icewater. Cowboy brings his plate of special, and the judge picks at it tentatively, eating the crust. His scotch hasn't had time to perk up his appetite. I've observed one of Cowboy's shortcomings, his service is too prompt. People need time to settle into their seats, look at the dusty cactus pictures, read a few religious slogans, anticipate the hot food, work up a supply of saliva. But Cowboy brings the food too soon. It makes you suspect it was already cooked. It makes you think he might have a microwave oven.

"There are many other words he could have yelled," I say. "Dirty, obscene words." I name a few body fluids to prove my point.

"Drop it!" the judge says, spitting a mouthful of special into his napkin. "Just drop it!"

"What about lower forms of life? I'm curious about the legality of words. Snot-fly!"

"If you don't mind, I'm trying to eat!"

"Yeah," I say. "I considered running for judge but I don't know how to read Latin. Do you wear a black cape?"

"Robe. I wear a robe."

"Is that fair? I mean, phlegm-eater, could the kangaroo in leg-irons wear a robe?"

The judge stands. No bottle falls from his lap. He throws his napkin onto the special and stalks to the cash register. Cowboy gives his automatic question, "Was everything all right?"

The judge pulls out his billfold.

"Farewell, Judge!" I sing out thinking we might be friends some day. I wish I hadn't intruded on his privacy because he seems like a nice man. And now he's upset. As Judge scoots out the door I slip into his booth and run my palm along the bench. There it is, where it has to be, his silver flask. I confiscate it, thinking I'll return it to him some day with my apologies.

Cowboy comes to wipe tables. "What!" he says, "the judge didn't eat his food!"

"Nope. He urgently had to go with Everett."

"With Everett?"

"Yeah. The judge is up for re-election, and Everett swings several thousand votes."

"He does?"

"Sure. Through his customers and through the Catholic church. He only works for Democrats. He networks them on his computer. Sends out a newsletter."

"Is that right . . . ?" Cowboy says slowly, drawing it out in a long speculation. He sits opposite me.

"See how it goes? The judge wants Everett to deliver him some votes."

Cowboy nods wisely. I like the story I'm putting together. It makes Everett and the judge more interesting. "You've got a serious roach problem here, Cowboy. Get some boric acid and hedgeapples and take out the garbage twice a day. A week of that action and the vermin will go elsewhere for lunch."

Everett comes in swaggering, so I know he's collected a few bucks from the deadbeat. I rub my palm across the top of my head which tells him in the language of our childhood scams, *Go along with this*! I ask him, "Everything work out okay with the judge?"

Everett looks to me for his cue. I nod slightly.

"Oh yeah," he says, "no problem."

"Will he play ball?"

"Yeah."

"Good," I say.

Cowboy gets up to give Everett his seat. "Your food got cold, Mr. Geezre," he says. He's never called Everett *mister* before. "Let me warm it up." He whisks Everett's plate off to the kitchen.

"What's this all about?" Everett asks.

"I told him you're a politician."

"Politician?"

"Yeah, like Maggy Thatcher. Who did you chase down?"

"Fraternity girl. Her stool gagged and she said she'd get the sisters to kick in on the bill, but she forgot to put my check in the mail."

"So what happened?"

"I chased her to Lady Godiva's. Seems she's the entertainment committee. She's thowing a party with male strippers. The sisters will come in buses. Sisters like a little fun. Can't blame 'em."

Although Everett has explained this situation with earnest conviction, I know he doesn't understand it. He thinks the fruitbat's sorority sisters are nuns. I ask him, "Did she pay you?"

"Nah. But she will. She promised."

That's my twin, a killer with housewives who pour bacon grease down their sinks—an optimist. I show the flask and say, "Judge left this."

Everett grins. Cowboy returns with his plate of enchiladas and Everett says, "You can bet there's no worm in that!" Cowboy thinks he's talking about the food. He stomps back to his kitchen in a funk as I fill Everett's glass with legal scotch.

"Why are you drinking tequila? I've never seen you drink?"

"The famous writer gave me the idea."

"Why's he famous?"

"Because everybody knows him. He wrote a book about two guys who killed a farm family."

"Bastards!" Everett mutters. I could have predicted his reaction because he has an all-encompassing affection for farmers. He would be happy on a farm—if it weren't for slaughterhouses. Oxymoron. Many people who saw him smoking his cigar while devouring a plate of cheese and onions would think him a carnivore, but many people can be mistaken. Many people whose stools block up won't admit they caused the stoppage. They prefer to blame the equipment, the weather conditions, or their in-laws.

His head buzzing with tequila, Joe declines Everett's invitation to see how the bidet flushes. He tells Everett he'll walk back to his apartment.

The river separates North River City from River City, and the river bridge has a walkway for pedestrians and bicyclists. Joe enjoys crossing it. Fresh air has cleared his head, and he stops to look downstream at the island. Gulls are flying above the river and pigeons sit on the roof of city hall. Joe looks at the smooth, curved brink of riverwater slipping over the dam. *Water. Water. Water. Water.* He leans on the mayor's rail half-hypnotized, mesmerized. He has never visited Madame Leontyne. He decides that's the next new thing he will do this day. *I'll ask her what the future holds.* Somewhere in the back of his mind swims the notion that fortunetellers are prostitutes. *Hold my palm. Feel the bumps on my head. Footwashing. Gimme that old-time religion. Baptizing in the river. I want somebody to touch me, build me an ear, fix this tequila tingle in my brain.* He looks down to see a man in a boat glide beneath him toward the lip of the dam. The man looks up at Joe, smiling, puzzled about something. Then the boat drops away, its stern rising perpendicular before it vanishes. "Oh God! Help that man!" Joe screams. There is nobody on the bridge to hear him. Joe is in the middle of the bridge where he can't see the foot of the dam. He can only see the brink of curving water and beyond it the foam-flecked pool. He can't see whether the man is battered, swimming, or submerged. He runs toward city hall. *Tell someone! Tell someone!* When he gets to the end of the bridge he encounters a knot of people pointing at the churning water below the dam. He can't see what they can see. Winded, he clings to the rail, hugs it, and vomits. His eyes are closed. His head spins. *I might be on the rail of the Queen Mary with a trifling touch of seasickness. And the ship sails on. I hope that guy made it.* But there's a heavy sickness in Joe's heart telling him the guy didn't make it. He walks toward town seeking a bar.

Joe Geezre takes the glass from his pocket. "I brought my own," he tells the bartender, "fill it up."

"With what?"

"Tequila. I just saw a man go over the dam. I don't think he made it."

The bartender asks, "Why didn't you help him?"

"What could I do?" Joe feels guilty for not helping the man.

The bartender looks hard toward the river as if he can see through the brick wall. A man down the bar says, "Damned fool. What was he doing out there?"

"Fishing. He was in a boat."

"The boat went over the dam?"

"Yes. I saw fishing equipment in it. I think. I only got a glimpse. I think I saw a lacy green net and a galvanized, lead-colored, gray minnow bucket. A pewter bucket, dull bright in the sun. A pewter bucket of Margaret Thatcher."

When the bartender hears *Margaret Thatcher* he looks hard at Joe. Joe lifts the glass to the light, sights through it, and asks politely, "Where's my worm?"

"Worm's in mescal, not tequila."

"I had my heart set on a little worm."

The critic says, "Damned fool. Who'd eat fish out of that river? It's full of pesticides, herbicides, silt, sewage." He wears a khaki jacket with shooting patches on the arms. Joe looks at the shooter, knowing him. Joe lifts his glass and says, "Here's to Maggy Thatcher. There's something delightfully handsome about that woman." He drinks the shot and says to the shooter, "My brother catches big catfish, cuts them into steaks, fries them, freezes them, and eats them. He's burped your sewer quite a few times. Go see him. He'll pop a catfish steak into his microwave and serve you up a delicious meal."

"What about the lead, zinc, and chlordane?"

"Shooter!" Joe says, "there's a spiritual component to fish! Whatsamatter? You wanna live forever?"

"The river stinks. It's dirty and it stinks!"

"Okay," Joe says, holding his palms toward the shooter to fend him off. "You're right. It was his own damned fault. He's responsible. We're not to blame. The river stinks." He moves down the bar, away from the shooter.

"Walkman," the shooter says to the bartender. "He's some kind of a poet."

A well-dressed man says, "So's every other crackpot in River City. We should put a head tax on 'em. A *per poeta* tax. A poll tax. Make 'em go the courthouse every month and pay a dollar."

"Why?"

"To see how many of 'em are committed and how many ought to be committed!"

"Well—" the bartender shrugs. "Whether or not you charge poets a buck seems immaterial. It won't change anything."

"I don't give a damn what you think might be immaterial! I say tax every writer. Newspaper hacks. Computer programmers. Greeting card wits. Genealogists. Housewives writing romances. University professors trying to climb Tarzan's vine. All of 'em!" The man stands, jams his Royals cap onto his head, and marches out to his Triumph Spitfire.

"Who was he?" an Indian woman asks. A movie still of Humphrey Bogart evaluates her from the back bar. The dead actor is staring into her soul. She doesn't flinch.

"He waited tables here when this was a coffee house. Then he went to law school. Now he's trying to sell real estate."

"What's he got against writers?"

"They're like cobras and mongooses, realtors and writers. I've seen it time and again. Want another draw?"

"Yeah." She hefts a briefcase to the bar and opens it, turning it so the bartender can see her merchandise. "Indian beadwork," she says. "Handmade. Turquoise rings, bracelets, see anything you like? Kachina dolls?"

"Wow! You've got a whole store here."

"Yeah. I was gonna open a store, but the deal fell through."

"Where did you get this stuff?" The bartender takes a silver ring in the shape of a bear paw and tries it on.

"I go around reservations. Trade shows. Here. Put my card on the wall back there." She hands him a business card.

"How much for this ring?" he asks, reading her business card.

"Run me a tab. Fifty bucks. I mean, how much does a glass of beer cost you? Twenty-five cents? And you sell it for seventy-five. So that's a third. What's a third of fifty? Sixteen, seventeen dollars."

"Yeah but what did this ring cost you?"

"About that. But I've had it a long time. Prices go up."

"Okay, Mary Thunder," the bartender says, snugging the bearpaw onto his finger. You got a deal!"

Joe meanders. His mind feels soft, fuzzy. He holds up his glass to show the bartender it's empty. Then he looks into Mary Thunder's briefcase trying to see her merchandise while keeping enough distance to avoid her sales pitch. The briefcase is lined with purple satin and the objects in it are red and black and silver and turquoise blue. He sees carvings of white bone and the polished black tips of buffalo horn. *Ivory and horn*, he thinks, *there's something fetching about ivory and horn*. Mary Thunder smiles at him. Her dark skin is smooth. Her teeth are ivory. Her eyes are deep, as black as buffalo horn. "Come look," she tells him. "Look for free. C'mere. I won't bite."

There is no sign on Madame Leontyne's house which is so close to the sale barn that she can hear the cows moo. A red chicken escaped the barn and she captured him with a handful of corn. She tied a leather thong around his leg and hobbled him to her clothesline where she feeds him oats and waters him in the crisper drawer of her dead refrigerator. He walks cocky, stiff-legged, scratching dirt and shaking his hackles. His cherry-red cockscomb hangs heavy to one side, rich and vile like Elvis' pompadour.

Madame Leontyne's fortune-telling salon is not listed in the yellow pages. She runs a tiny ad in the *Trader*. Joe finds her front door permanently barricaded by the dead refrigerator, so he picks his way through her side yard between parked cars where he encounters the chicken. Joe knocks at the back screen door. The madame, a large woman, answers his knock.

"I'm Everett's brother," he says.

"Come in." She leads him through her kitchen to the living room. "Why did you come here?"

"I want to know some things."

"What kind of things?"

Joe waves his hand vaguely. "Whoso Findeth Wisdom Findeth Life."

Madame Leontyne frowns and says, "I answer questions for twenty dollars an hour."

Joe grips his billfold and Madame Leontyne points at her wall clock as if to say, *There's the clock. Look at it!* She says, "I'll get some tea." He hands her a twenty-dollar bill.

"Do you read tea leaves?" he asks. *How did she know I like tea?*

"I don't read soggy leaves, sweaty palms, or balls." She goes to the kitchen and returns immediately with two steaming cups.

"That was quick. You must've had the water boiling?"

"Sit at the table. Sometimes the cards help people relax."

A young woman enters the room. She wears a too-large Jayhawk sweatshirt and extra-tight acid jeans. As she passes the card table Madame Leontyne hands her the bill which she folds three times and tucks into her hip pocket. A knowing look passes between the women. The younger goes out through the kitchen and while Joe dunks his teabag he hears her starting one of the cars.

"You're not used to drinking," Madame Leontyne says. "While your tea cools go in there and wash your face and hands. Freshen up. There's a sweet cake of Ivory soap and a roll of paper towels."

In order to get to the bathroom Joe passes through a bedroom which is furnished with a dresser, an oval mirror, and a double bed. On the bed is a chenille bedspread decorated with an enormous blue peacock. The bed looks soft. Each feather of the peacock's tail is an eye looking at Joe. He mixes the hot and cold water then rolls up his sleeves to wash his face. He rinses his mouth and sits on the toilet to unlace his shoes. He takes off his socks and stands at the lavatory to wash each foot in the mild, warm water. He dries each foot with a paper towel and goes to tea feeling tipsy yet refreshed. He sits at the card table. "I'm ready."

"First drink your tea. Relax. I'll deal through the cards. When I lay down a card tell me the number and suit." She lays down the three of diamonds. Joe names it. Then she turns it over and he sees that she's using Temptations, cards of naked women. She plays out the whole deck, face up, then face down. She watches him intently, shuffles the cards, bounces them, and puts them into their box. "Ask your questions," she says.

"Will Everett go to Las Vegas?"

"Yes."

"Will he win any money?"

"No. But he'll see cheap Wayne Newton."

"Who's that?"

"You know who *Wayne Newton* is!"

"A man went over the dam in a fishing boat."

"Yes."

"Is he all right?"

"The odds of surviving the plunge are fifty-fifty."

"Are you an odds maker?"

"Yes."

"Well— About the man?"

Madame Leontyne almost imperceptibly shakes her head.

"Who was that girl?"

"What girl?"

"The girl just here."

"She's not a girl. She's my daughter."

"There's a famous writer in town. Who is he?"

"I don't read."

"Then how can you answer questions?"

"I watch television. My husband eats dirt and tells me things."

"I won't tell you what I thought when you gave your *daughter* my money."

"I know your nasty thoughts. This ain't what you paid for. Don't argue. Ask questions."

"Do you pray?"

"That's my business."

"Am I a virgin?"

"Yes."

"Why am I a virgin?"

"That's the way you want to be."

"Will I die a virgin?"

"You'll be a virgin when you leave my house."

"What's in the store?"

"In the store?"

"What's my future?"

"Now we get down to the tacks made of brass. There's an honest woman in your future. She has a moustache and, people say, a heart made of gold."

Joe yawns.

"Come on. You want to take a nap?"

"I hadn't planned on sleeping."

"Then why did you wash your feet?"

She grips Joe's hand and stands, leading him to the bedroom. She turns down the peacock bedspread and the top sheet. She fluffs the pillow. "Here, I'll go out and close the door, Joe. Take off your clothes and get in bed right, like a gentlemen. Don't worry. Nobody will come in." Joe undresses. He slips between the cool sheets and hugs the pillow. He dreams about gentle rain and the red chicken fleeing the livestock auction. Men and boys chase the cock which eludes them by flying over fences as easily as jets fly over rivers. Joe dreams about pink women, and he dreams about a silver mine studded with turquoise nuggets. He dreams about buffalo ivory and buffalo horn.

Joe is half awake. Disconnected thoughts trouble him. He remembers cleaning bear bones for a Canadian professor. *Bare bones.* He feels himself drifting. *Polish them bare bones. Them hip bones!* He remembers asking where he should take the Canadian to lunch—on his birthday—hundreds of miles from home. Someone said, *Take him to the Red Lion.*

No sign announced the Red Lion. Joe had its address on a scrap of paper. He'd been told that going there was like visiting a speakeasy. He found a curtained storefront window which contained a plaster lion, or perhaps it was a concrete yard ornament, painted Chinese red. To the right of the window was an unmarked door. Joe went into an ordinary cafe. On his left he saw a counter with stools. On his right was a row of booths. The Red Lion could have been any shotgun cafe in any American town. There was a cash register, a refrigerated pie cabinet, a stainless steel coffee urn, and a bearded, angry-eyed proprietor wearing a scarlet chef's hat. The proprietor wore a red kerchief knotted around his neck. He stared balefully at Joe. The dream becomes a nightmare. The man slams the flat of his butcher's knife on the counter. "Darling! You want the special!" he roars.

Joe falls easily to the conclusion that the man in the chef's hat is the Red Lion, but Joe doesn't know who *Darling* is. The cafe is crowded. *Darling* might be one of the customers or the weary waitress who moves among them filling coffee cups. Joe realizes that everyone has stopped eating. Everyone is watching him.

"Order up, Darling! You want the special!" the Lion screams. Joe, unaware that he is *Darling*, scans a menu board. The Lion slashes air with his knife. *It's good food and it's cheap but you'd better get the special.* Joe recalls that advice. *Free refills on the drinks.* Then Joe realizes he is part of a drama. He is being used by the Red Lion to entertain his lunch crowd. Joe is the Dutchman, the outsider, the immigrant. Raw meat. He reads a sign on the wall—*Please don't tell anyone about the lion! Remember it's your seat. We have no time for strangers.*

Humankind's instinct of self-preservation prompts Joe to speak for himself and his guest. *We'll take the special.* The regulars resume eating. The play is over. Joe and the Canadian are served. *A man sticks to his messmates.* The phrase comes to Joe and fills him with a dirty desire for a dialect-laden Dutchman to fall into the ant lion's trap and stand there ignorant, confused, badgered. *Darling! You want the special!* Joe smirks, knowing when it happens he will be an insider. He has been initiated. He has bought his club card. That realization makes the Red Lion dream a double nightmare. *Harmless prank, Officer. We pushed over the widow's privy, and she was in it, ha, ha, ha!*

When I awoke I saw long rays of sun through Madame Leontyne's curtains. A cup of tea, some questions, and a nap for twenty dollars. *I'm still a virgin on the verge.* I got up and dressed. I washed my face again, but not my feet, fingercombed hair down over my earhole, and opened the bedroom door. Madame Leontyne lay sprawled across her sofa. She was a full-figured woman.

"Did you have a nice nap?" she asked.

"Very nice. I'm refreshed. But I had a bad dream."

"Dreams!" She lifted her eyes as if to say my ignorance was a burden. "Tell Everett to come here before he goes to Vegas."

"Why? He'll lose no matter how he bets."

"Yeah." She gave me a conspiratorial wink.

"What are you going to do with that chicken?" I asked. "Are you going to eat him?"

"Eat Preacher! Hell no, he's my agent."

In my youth I'd seen people boil chickens in iron pots. I knew Madame was fattening Preacher for such a feast. Maybe I could soften her heart, persuade her to let Preacher live. So I issued an invitation. I said, "There's a joint in town that makes its own beer. Sort of up-scale. High dollar. A place to be seen. Let's go there for a glass of local and a plate of special?" I spoke quickly on automatic pilot, like a shy schoolboy.

"Is this a date? You're asking me for a date? I'm a married woman!"

"That's okay. I'm a virgin."

She stroked her jaw with her forefinger, thinking about it.

I said, "I don't have a car, so we can have some fun walking."

She frowned at the notion of walking. Remembering the cars parked outside, I wondered if her bulk had worn them all out. She shook her head. "If my husband caught us he'd whip out his machete and split your head like a cantaloupe."

I carry a three-bladed pocketknife, but I didn't show it to Madame. I went out through the kitchen and softly closed the screen door. Preacher stood on his tiptoes. When he arched his neck and flapped his wings mightily I fondled my knife thinking I would cut his leather thong. I would set him free. I liked the notion of Preacher flying over backyard fences, crowing in new territory, dominating the landscape. But cutting the thong would deprive Madame of her husband. And her property. Here he was protected. He was fed. Watered. He had a good life. For all I knew he was a virgin. Just because he wore bright feathers, that didn't prove anything. Like me for instance. I shook my limp hair until it fell at a rakish angle. When Preacher charged me, running twiddle-thumbs along his spurs, I jumped up, clicked my heels, flapped my arms mightily, and ran. I felt Madame watching me out her kitchen window. I hoped she wouldn't cook Preacher, but I'd seen a lean, praying mantis hunger in her eyes.

The sun was setting and I felt lonely. It would have been fun—just once—to sit in the Brewery amid chattering fruitbats and hear them say again and again, "This beer is *so* good! It's made right here!" *All beer is made someplace. Why's this place any better than St. Louis or Memphis?* But no. I wouldn't ask them that question because I knew the answer. Inside/outside. We're insiders here. We know who we are. I felt the immigrant chill of being alone in a new world.

As I walked up Tenth Street looking for a vine the daylight faded. A spring rain had fallen while I slept, making the pavement warm and dewy under the lights. Children with broomsticks trooped ahead of me slashing limbs off little trees. The crabapples branched about four feet up and the clever children slashed off their arms, the right and the left, leaving spiked saplings doomed to blight and failure. Breaking the trees made the children happy. Happy children. I asked them where they were going and they said they were headed for the movies. Maybe they'd never seen anything beautiful. Maybe their homes were broken. Maybe their sisters were pregnant. Nevertheless it's hard to love a mean-spirited kid who smashes crabs that are just standing there trying to look right.

I followed the kids, maybe hoping to teach them. But I was afraid of what they might say. *I hate trees.* Where would that leave me? Madame Leontyne told me not to argue. She told me to ask questions. *Why did you smash that tree?* But I knew the answer. When I was twelve, in the months of grief after my mother died, I might have smashed it myself. *What's so special about one tree, Walkman? Haven't you seen dinosaurs? Bulldozers? Forest fires? Volcano Mt. St. Helen's? This is a violent world we live in, Walkman, and you'd better get with the program!*

At Massachusetts Street I stood outside a bar feeling quite forlorn. There was a fresh, warm, cool, springtime balminess in the air. The first nighthawks of the season were dipping like boomerangs. I smelled beer and cigarettes, hot popcorn from the movie houses. Then I saw Mary Thunder coming toward me lugging her briefcase of silver and turquoise, beads and feathers, bone and horn. Her hair was woven into thick braids that hung almost to her waist. Downy owl feathers were tucked into her braids.

"Did you go find out about that river man?" she asked me.

"No. I went and got my fortune told."

"Was it okay?"

"Sure. I invited the fortuneteller to drink beer with me, but she turned me down."

"Don't invite me. I've got a belly full of beer. My feet hurt, and the bus to Topeka leaves at two a.m."

"The bus station is that way," I pointed to the direction she had come from.

"I'm looking for a place to hide. You got any cigarettes?"

"No."

"I've got credit at the Pentimento Bar, but I can't buy cigarettes with it. Just beer."

"Where are you going to hide?"

"Man, you expect me to tell my secrets?"

"I'll bet you don't have a place."

She set the heavy case on the sidewalk, between her moccasins. "I'll trade you two beads for a pack of Salems."

I gazed at her in the glow of the lights. A nighthawk swooped low, almost touching her head, framing itself behind her like a feathered head-dress. She was short and plump. The skin of her face was smooth, tight, and clear. She looked like she would make a good fortuneteller. I'd been kicked off the dating tightrope and instinct told me to climb right back up there. I had to ask Mary Thunder for a date or else I'd never walk the high wire. And with her I had leverage because she was broke and wanted to smoke.

"Okay," I said. "Some peace-pipe. But I don't want two beads. I want conversation. Come in this bar with me and I'll buy you a pack of cigarettes."

"Oh, Baby! You are silver-tongued!" She shook her head.

"C'mon. Why not?"

"Because this is when people go crazy. Trouble starts. I've gotta stay out of bars."

I looked across the street and spotted the Joke Shop. "Wait here," I said. I went to the Joke Shop and bought a pack of Salems. I gave them to her.

She said, "Okay. Follow. When I go in some dark place you wait until nobody's looking and follow."

I watched her slide the pack of cigarettes into her jeans-jacket pocket, heft her briefcase of valuables, and begin walking aimlessly down the street. *Goodbye Salems*, I said to nobody. I followed her through the park and past the rock castle. She crossed the street and worked her way to the back of the retirement highrise. After a few minutes I went around the retirement highrise until I came to the fenced trash area where I heard the sound of a pebble on metal. Three taps. Then silence. I entered the trash compound and found her hiding behind a steel dumpster, leaning against the board fence. I sat beside her.

"None of these retired people come out after dark," she explained. "They're afraid. And the janitors only work eight to five."

"Yeah," I said, relieved and grateful to have a date. I guess it was my first date. Maybe I had come close before. I'd gone a few places with women. But I'd never come right out and invited them—except Rosealyn. This was my first real date, and I was sitting in a trash corral.

"Where's your car?"

"Oh," I said. "I don't have a car. I don't know how to drive."

"What kind of work do you do?"

"Nothing."

"Well, you can't afford a car if you don't do nothing."

I shifted my feet trying to get comfortable. She no longer had her briefcase.

"You got a light?" she asked.

"No. I don't smoke."

"What kind of a guy are you? You don't know how to drive. You don't smoke. You ain't got no matches."

"Rub two sticks together," I snapped.

"I could. I could make a fire with flintrocks if I had to, but that takes too long. Go over to the store and get some fire."

"You mean, you want to stay here and keep an eye on your store."

"Maybe. Hey, what's your name?"

"Joe."

"Okay, Joe. You're a nice guy. I don't mean it like I'm ordering you around, but it would be good if you brought us some fire."

I stood up. "Will you be here when I get back?"

"Do you want me to?"

"Sure. I said I wanted conversation."

"Then I'll be here. I mean, just because I'm a Native American that don't mean I'd cheat you out of a damn pack of cigarettes. Besides, you don't smoke."

When I returned to the garbage corral I spotted the glow of Mary's cigarette. I wiggled in beside her. "How did you get it lit?" I asked.

"Oh, I found a match in my pocket. Forgot about it."

I gave her the BiC lighter. "Here. I have no use for this. Okay. Let's talk."

"What do you want to talk about?"

"Well," I said, "I'm sixty-two years old. You must be half that. That's ninety-three years between us. And we never talked before. There should be some conversation material in ninety-three years of living."

"I was born on a reservation at Jump, Oklahoma. I came here to school at the Indian college. Now I travel around Native American art shows and crafts shows. All over. North Dakota to Texas. New Mexico. Everywhere."

"So, you made the jewelry in the briefcase?"

"That stuff I bought. It'll sell okay. It's paintings and drawings and sculptures that you can't sell."

"Why not?"

"Don't talk about it. I spent too much time already trying to figure it out."

"Do you know that horse Comanche? After the Native Americans left Little Big Horn he was standing there. Wounded but alive. Everything else was dead. Soldiers, Native Americans, horses."

"Custer got Siouxed!"

"I've got his tailbone."

"Gimme a sip of that stuff."

"What stuff?"

"I see that bulge in your pocket. I see the shape of it."

I'd forgotten the judge's flask. I handed it to Mary. She sipped from it and held onto it. She said, "Try to sell Custer's tailbone. See what you get."

"Not Custer's. Comanche's."

"I was going to open a shop. The Eagle Feather. But my deal fell through. Where's your house?"

"On the hill. I worked there, in the museum."

"In the museum?"

"In the Aircraft Carrier."

Mary said, "I like this menthol. It gives me a buzz."

I didn't reply to that so after a few minutes she asked, "You really don't want no beads or nothing?"

"No." I showed my bare fingers. "No ornamentation."

"Well try something new."

"No thanks."

"Maybe I'm crazy, but I feel sort of safe with you. Like you're not gonna rip me off."

"My fortuneteller said I would meet an honest woman."

"Anybody can tell fortunes. Just make up some bullshit."

We sat still, without talking, for a long time. I put my head back against the cedar boards and looked at stars and dark windows in the old folks' highrise. Cliffdwellers. They were quiet, all asleep or dead or watching TV. Their garbage smelled clean. I imagined they washed their sardine cans before putting them in the trash. Mother always did that. She said it kept the house fresh. I thought about the quiet people. Some of them were grandparents, no doubt. I had enough age to be a grandparent, but I didn't feel old, I felt like a kid sitting out in the trash fort playing house with an Indian girl. Fifty years ago, alone in the woods, I played the same game. Mary handed me her cigarette and I took a puff from it. I coughed and she said *Sssshhttt!* putting her hand over my mouth, forcing me to breathe through my nose. That made my eyes sting. Then I was bleary eyed. All the stars had haloes. I think I kissed her palm because it was right on my mouth. She put her arm around me and hugged me up close. I didn't know what to do with my feet. They were jammed up under the dumpster. Mary tried to kiss my face but it didn't work. She said, "What's the matter?" I said I couldn't get comfortable. She said that was because I was a tall stringbean and she was a little butterball. Then she locked her arms around my neck and kissed me hard on the mouth and I didn't know what to do. *I'm having a date!* was the phrase in my head. Repeating, repeating, *This is great! I'm having a date!*

Mary said, "Man, you don't know how to kiss. Let's go." She got up and lifted a garbage sack out of the dumpster. The walk back to the bus station would be painful for her sore feet, so I went to the store and called a taxi.

I bought Mary's ticket to Topeka and left her sitting in the waiting room where nobody would steal her garbage sack. Outside I waved goodbye through the glass. Then I motioned for her to come out.

"What do you want?"

"I want you to come back to River City sometime," I said. "I want to show you my fake zebra skin, my genuine hula skirt, Comanche's tailbone."

"I'm afraid I'll break your heart."

I couldn't think of a reasonable reply to that so I said, "You're trash! I saw you smoking cigarettes in Trash City!"

"Yeah!" She smiled. "You got that right! You were in there too, Trashman!"

"Give me your phone number?"

"You think about that. I'm a heap of trouble, Joe. Tomorrow if you really want to call me you can get my number. Bogart put my card up on the wall."

Did she think the bartender was Bogart? "Okay," I said, "I'll think about it. Maybe I'll give you a call."

"Okay. Maybe I'll answer. Hey, why is it every time I say something you turn your head like a bird?"

"No ear, Trash," I said, turning my right side to her. I swept back my hair.

"My God!" she said, "You ain't got no ear!"

The generous taxi driver offered me a ride and I said to myself, *Why not? Relax and be lazy.* I got in the back seat and stretched out my legs and let him give me a slow ride up the hill to the U.S.S. Flattop where there was no coxswain to pipe me aboard. All the folks were asleep. The carved stone owl on the old library hooted softly to the smaller stone owl on the museum. The moon had come up and was keeping them awake. The chapel stood pretty in the moonlight. A fat skunk with four kittens made her way down Lilac Lane sniffing the curb. I went inside and locked out the world.

2

The Prayer Book

Joe awoke to the tapping of Woolheater on his door. It was late, almost ten o'clock, and Joe remembered drinking tequila. His head throbbed and his sour stomach clenched. His mouth was dry and stale. Woolheater wanted Joe to go to breakfast with him.

In the few weeks Joe had lived at Flattop Woolheater had taken him to every breakfast restaurant in River City. Woolheater was a widower who hadn't learned to cook. He and Joe disembarked in the port side parking lot and got into Woolheater's big blue Chrysler. The old boat was running on worn-out shock absorbers, and Joe got seasick as she yawed, pitched, and rolled through a nasty chop on Tennessee Street.

"What's wrong?" Woolheater asked, "You're pale?"

"Perhaps a touch of *mal de mer*. This buggy moves in more than one circuit."

Misunderstanding Joe's remark, Woolheater replied, "Yeah, I bought it new. Keep it tuned up. Keep good rubber on it."

Joe looked out the side window as they lurched along at twenty miles per hour.

Woolheater was a retired professor of genetics. His new occupation was flirting with waitresses. He gave them big tips—all of them—the one at Duck's who owned a monkey, the one at Lowbrow whose girlfriend was locked up for bad checks, and especially the one at Big Flag who told him jokes in the hope he would leave her his fortune.

Woolheater said, "You look like you were up late."

"Yeah. I met a woman in the dumpster at the old folks' home."

"Woman?"

"Indian woman."

"Did you ever eat an Indian taco?"

Joe, fighting down a surge of nausea, shook his head.

"Fried dough. Then they pour on spiced buffalo meat, tomatoes, onions, cheese—make a big pile, as big as your cap!"

"Sounds horrible!" Joe said. "Where are you taking me?"

"Thought we'd try the Big Flag. I'm feeling patriotic."

"Yeah," Joe murmured. "Look, if that waitress is there, the one who tells dirty jokes—"

"Sarah?"

"Yeah. Don't let Sarah get graphic at this early hour, eh? I'm a bit queasy."

"Hung over?"

"Nah. It's this car of yours. Makes me sick to ride in it."

"Hung over! Tell me about your Indian maiden?"

"Just drive. If you order hot cakes, get them on a separate dish from your eggs."

"Say, you do have a tender tummy!" Woolheater parked under the enormous American flag in a handicapped slot. A healthy seventy-three, he could walk across town. He and Joe had walked together to the Hippie Market for loaves of seven-grain bread and they'd walked to Louisiana Street for frozen yogurt, but when Woolheater drove to the Big Flag he always parked in the handicapped slot because he'd never noticed the wheelchair symbol painted on the asphalt.

As they entered the restaurant he said to Joe, "You should learn to drive. Could come in handy. I saw on TV a boy was flying with his dad. His dad passed out and the boy landed the plane."

"Whadda'ya mean, Woolie? We're gonna be swishing along the street and you're gonna die so I can take the controls, rip the wheel out of your clenched fist?"

"What if I had the flu. You could drive down to the drugstore and pick up my prescription."

"I could walk."

They claimed a booth in Sarah's territory. As she poured coffee she asked, "Did you hear about the guy who thought his pecker was a squirrel?"

Joe quickly went to the restroom. He washed his face, dried it on the roller towel, and stared at the wall where someone had written, *Penis Boy is Coming.*

"Weary, weary, weary," Joe muttered. "I'm weary of this one. It's vulgar, it's sacrilegious, *and* it's a threat."

He returned to the booth to bury his nose in coffee fumes. *Woolie was married, so he isn't a virgin. He's old enough to retire from sex yet he buys women's attention because he's as horny as a billy.* Joe looked at the geriatric geneticist wondering how many mouse cadavers he had carved in his day. The bifocal moons of Woolheater's glasses were milky white when they caught the light. When they caught his flesh tones they bulged like bags under his eyes. *When will you stop, Woolie? When will you stop being Preacher?*

"So?" Joe said, savoring his first sip of coffee, "did Sarah tell you a good joke?"

Woolheater smiled.

"Woolie, if you had the chance, I mean if the right woman came along, would you marry again?"

Woolheater shrugged. "My kids wouldn't like it. They think I'm still married to their mother. But I'll tell you, Joe, for the right woman—"

"Then why don't you seek wisdom?"

"What do you mean?"

"I mean, you spend all your time on coffee-dates with waitresses who could be your daughters! Why don't you chase women your own age? Flattop is full of 'em! There's seven widows aboard!"

"Ah, Joe. She really hit you, didn't she?"

"Who?"

Woolheater held the fingers of his left hand behind his head, like feathers, and patted his mouth moaning, *ooooh!,*

breaking the sound into a war whoop, *wou! wou! wou! wou!*
"You have an upset stomach. You snap at me about my young
women. She hit you hard."

"Who?"

"Who! Who! You sound like a damned tree full of owls.
That Indian maiden you cuddled in the dumpster!"

Joe slumped as Sarah approached with Woolheater's runny
eggs. "Hi, Joe," she said. "You look like something the cats
drug in."

Woolheater repeated his Indian war whoop for Sarah. "Joe
had a hard night. Buffalo girl."

Sarah stood close to Woolheater, casually pressing her
knee against his leg. He patted her bare leg just below the hem
of her skirt.

Joe blinked and stared out at traffic. Then he heard a
familiar voice. It was the Elf's voice. Joe sat up and spotted
him in the adjacent booth. Joe eavesdropped: "Well he's
much *older* than me," the Elf said. "And of course we're
different *kinds* of writers. Different techniques entirely. I find
it curious that the old queen would be living here. Y'know, he
had a fortress in New York and a bodyguard of street toughs.
If you'll pardon one blunt question, what does a man of his low
sophistication *do* in this town?"

"He leads an active life, I'm told. He writes letters to the
Journal about mistreated dogs. So, in his way, he's soft
hearted. We can swing past his house on the way to Madame
Leontyne's if you want to see where he lives?"

"Yes. I'd like that. I don't mean to belittle your town.
It's nice."

"It's quite a town."

"I'm taking notes."

"Does that mean you'll write about us?" Phoebe Jones
asked.

"Sort of *Tiny Town in Middle-America*?"

"Yes! We have a lake, an organ factory, a university, easy
access to Menninger's, a short drive to Leavenworth—if you
have friends in maximum security. Civil War history, hippies
in the sixties, eagles on the river—"

"Slow down!" the writer said. "I take mental notes and I'm good at it, but you're talking way too fast for me."

Joe watched Sarah pour coffee into the writer's cup. She obviously didn't recognize her famous guest.   Joe heard Phoebe Jones say, "Maybe we could arrange a literary shoot-out between you and the Old Man. Like Dodge City, *This town ain't big enough for the both of us!*"

"Wild west!"

"It would make great publicity."

The Elf laughed and said, "Oh, I'd be no match for him—in a BAM-BAM contest. But it's an intriguing idea."

Someone in the Elf's booth said, "Yesterday a man drifted down the river—I guess he'd been fishing or something—he drifted over the dam."

"And there's that couple who rolled into the lake," the Elf said, "this is a watery place for being in the middle of— I suppose you've had some brutal murders?"

"An old packrat was beaten to death for his money. His house was stacked full of newspapers."

"You wonder about people who hoard newspapers—"

"And there was the pizza murder, down by the river. The killers ate pizza while they cut up the corpse."

"The river runs through it all. Why?"

"North River City is built on the flood plain. Good gardens there. It used to flood, before the levee—"

"And there was a train wreck at Dead Man's Curve, coming into town. And we have the Indian college."

"You certainly have variety," the Elf said. "I want to see it all."

"The Land of Oz Tattoo Parlor," Phoebe said.

The Elf laughed, saying, "I'll buy you a black rose or a red spider. Tattoos are the rage in London. And what about this fortuneteller?"

"She's absolutely frightening."

"Spooky. She knows everything!"

"Does she feel the bumps on your head?"

"No."

"Good. I'm sensitive about my head. I have a large one."

Three men and a woman got up from the booth and walked to the cash register and pastry case. One of the men, the Elf, wore a white straw hat with a downturned brim. He wore dark glasses like a movie star trying to be visible, yet concealed. Joe nudged Woolheater. "See that little guy in the hat? He's a famous writer."

Woolheater turned to look. "Nah," he said, wiping his chin with his napkin, "he's too short. I've seen the famous writer buying garlic. He's tall. Wears a hat. You're right about the hat, but he's tall."

"You're thinking about the Old Man," Joe said. "This little one's the challenger, a bulldog. He'll chew up that Old Man."

"You have quite a palate for literature, Joe."

"I've attended some literary events. I heard the Old Man read. He specializes in being shocking and sacrilegious."

"You're quite religious, aren't you, Joe?"

"I don't go to church. When I was a kid my mother took me every Sunday. Look at that guy! He's a little bulldog with fire in his eye."

"Little bulldog! Ha, that's a lot of bull. I did some work on the genetics of bulldogs. They're interesting. Famous writers, well I don't know. And now we have two of 'em? I'd say one was enough."

A woman waiting to be seated recognized the short celebrity. Her jaw dropped as she tugged her husband's sleeve. The Elf, feeling her stare, ducked behind Phoebe and made for the door.

Joe said, "Leave your tip! I want to follow that puppy!"

Woolheater was slow counting his change because he wanted Sarah to see he'd paid for his eggs with a large bill. Then he became entangled in the revolving door. By the time he and Joe made it outside the Elf and his entourage had disappeared.

When he returned to Flattop Joe checked his mail. There was a free issue of *Modern Maturity*, an invitation to join an old-folks club, and a fat letter from Mississippi. He put the letter in his pocket and the magazine in the trash. He changed to Rockports before departing on an aimless walk which eventually took him below the dam where fire department rescue boats and private boats were searching the river. After selecting a convenient place to sit on dry sand, above the gravel, he took off his shoes and grooved the sand with his heels, watching the boats. Children drawn to the search had waded out to the island, but nobody fished in the pool below the dam. An airplane droned overhead. Joe thought it might belong to Captain America, the retired navy pilot. He watched the glint of sunlight on the water. He watched clouds. The airplane banked steeply. He wondered if it might be assisting the search. He opened his notebook, selected a pencil from his pocket collection, and wrote—*Insofar as the body isn't found the man isn't dead. Habeas Corpus. Find book on St. Teresa.* Then he opened the letter from Mississippi. He snuggled his toes into the sand.

> Dear Uncle Joe,
> How do you like retirement? Write me a full description of your new apartment. Mom said it's large and well decorated. I want to see it but not a photograph! I want to see it for real. Don't tell Mom and Dad about this letter. I feel guilty because I write you so often and I haven't written them in weeks. Mrs. Mason, my neighbor, told me this story. I hope you like it. When her sons were young she went to watch them every week play softball and an old man fell in love with her. She still has bewitching eyes! The old man was a moonshiner. Every ball game he would drive up in his old ratty truck come sit by her and breathe whiskey breath in her face and say, "I've got a watermelon for you in my truck." She told all this in a deep southern voice. She is married to a rich lawyer who works all the time and leaves her home to embroider in front of the TV. Anyway I am now fascinated by her. I keep seeing her young and with eyes flashing in the hot night while a moonshiner tries

to seduce her with watermelons! Take care, and write
if you get work.

> Love,
> Rosealyn

Joe reverently buried the letter in the sand. He felt an urge
to cross the bridge and go to Everett's shop, so he laced on his
shoes and walked up past city hall. Pedestrians leaning on the
mayor rail looked at the brown water. *It's an agricultural
river*, Joe thought. *It drains farmland, laden with silt.* The
airplane, having completed its business, flew away. *I guess it
wasn't part of the search.*

Everett's plumbing shop lies close behind the levee. Next-
door to the shop is the rent house Everett owns. Joe thought
Everett might be at his shop, but it was shut and locked.
Everett's fishing boat was parked between the shop and the rent
house. The boat was also locked, and when Joe touched the
lock Everett's new tenant came out. He eyed Joe suspiciously
and said, "Plumber's not here."

"Yeah," Joe said. "He's my brother."

"He asked me to watch his shop." The man spoke with a
British accent.

"I want to take his boat to the river."

"The boat's locked."

Joe knew the man didn't believe he was Everett's brother.
"We're twins," Joe said. "But we look nothing alike. He's
short and thick and dark and handsome whereas I'm tall and
blond and skinny."

The man, also tall and blond, wet his lips as if he wanted
to make a truce—or call the police. Joe turned away, in his
mind hearing the man tell Everett, *I caught a vagabond casing
your boat for theft.* Joe walked to the street, saying in his
mind—*I am a thief. Deep down a real thief which explains my
knack for seeing things invisible.   Details other people
overlook. The unlocked door. The bolt not thrown. The way
a man shifts his eyes. Wild animal droppings. Toothmarks on
a gnawed stick. The shape of smoke coming from a chimney.
The color frijoles turn, dusty gray, when they've been heated*

*too long. The way people insinuate themselves into a circle of
warmth. How many strokes did the naked bride brush her
hair? The groom was thin, bony like me. His skin was dusky,
the color of frijoles cooked too long. A breeze rattled
cottonwood leaves. The naked couple stood in the shade
holding hands. After the ceremony they wanted to stay with
their friends rather than wander the garden alone. I wonder if
they're still married. I wonder if they have children. I wonder
if some fruitbat bride, overdressed in white, posing at the
chapel, is their daughter. It's possible. River City's a fertile
place. Fruitbats fly to fruit. Fruit flies like a banana. Some
fruitbats stole an anatomy cadaver, took it to the campus pond,
laid it out on a beach towel. Put sunglasses on it. Very grim.
I was at the pond when a child drowned. I am a thief, a thief
deep down. The old taxidermist said, "I keep Dyche's stuff
stuffed. Some of it's a century old. Those walruses. The polar
bears. That moose, for instance." He repaired Comanche and
tossed out the old tailbone. It's unique. One-of-a-kind. I think
I'll go over to El Chico Cafe and see if Everett's having lunch.
I could call his answering service, but that's twenty-five cents.
Thou shalt not waste twenty-five cents. I shall walk along the
levee and see what I see.*

Joe found Everett sitting alone in his booth at El Chico
Cafe. Joe asked, "Where's your helper?"

"He's sick. I'm leaving for Vegas in the morning."

"Have you consulted Madame Leontyne?"

"She said the same damned thing. Find a dealer who has
removables. What the hell could that mean?"

"Gobbledygook. You'll lose anyway. Might as well lose
with *panache*."

Everett ruefully licked brown sauce off his fingers.

"Did you get that bidet installed?"

"Yeah."

"How does it flush?"

"Up, Joe. The bitch flushes up. I don't care. If the
contractor's happy I'm happy."

"Did he pay you?"

"Damned straight he paid me. I'm on my way to Vegas. I need the money."

"I need your boat. You don't mind if I use it to look for that missing man?"

Everett handed Joe two keys. "This one's to the shop. This one's to the boat. The motor and gas tank are in the shop. And the paddles and life jackets."

"Who's your new renter," Joe asked.

"His wife's a nurse. A bombshell. He's looking for work."

"What kind of work?"

"You tell me and we'll both know. I can't understand a bloody word he says."

"He got all over me when I touched your boat."

"Good for him. Maybe I won't jump his rent."

"Has that judge been in?"

"Nah. He's not a serious eater. I mean, Cowboy ain't named a calf after him. What's this between you and the judge?"

"I want to know him," Joe said. "Maybe I could get a job cutting his grass, or something. Get to know him that way."

"What the hell for?"

Cowboy came from the kitchen and asked Joe if he wanted the special. Joe nodded saying, "*Bueno*." To Everett he said, "I have an idea the judge is wise due to all the judging he's done." Then Joe heard *Walkman* float across the room. It came from a table of four fruitbats. He selfconsciously fluffed his thin hair to cover his earhole, pretending to yell, *Prostitute! I cut it off for a prostitute. You fruitbats only know five things: Van Gogh's ear, Marilyn's mole, Washington's false teeth, Hitler's testicle, and*—he couldn't think of the fifth.

"Prostitute?" Everett said.

"Huh?"

"Why did you say prostitute?"

"I didn't say prostitute. I was thinking it, but I didn't say it."

"Oh. Why were you thinking it?"

"Van Gogh. He cut off his ear for a prostitute. That's the fruitbat story."

"Fruitbat?"

"Yeah. But in fact he sent it to his brother Theo."

"I've wondered about us, Joe. Our names don't match. Twins' names ought to match. Everett and Joe don't."

"Joseph. Everett and Joseph. They match. When we were babies Dad was sitting beside the bed. He was holding you. Mom was holding me. He said, *What will we name these boys?* Mom said he could name the one he was holding and she would name the one she was holding."

"He cut off his ear and sent it to his brother?"

"Sorry. I can't give you mine. It's long gone."

"If you don't mind talking about it Joe, tell me this. Can you hear anything out of that?"

"Huh?"

"I said can you hear—"

Joe shook his head.

"Y'know, Joe. To be twins, we're not very much alike, are we?"

"We're fraternal twins, Everett. Not identical. We didn't come out of the same egg."

"Birds come out of eggs, Joe. Not people."

Cowboy refilled Everett's water glass, dripping icewater onto Everett's plate.

"*Cuidado, Muchacho,*" Everett said, lighting a cigarillo from the one burning in the ashtray. He asked Joe, "How will you put the boat in the water? I don't have time to fiddle around with it."

"There's a way where there's a will," Joe said. "I presume you'll see Wayne Newton in Vegas?"

"Not if I can help it." Everett backhanded a cockroach, slamming it into the crevice between table and wall.

The Englishman's name was Graham. When he heard me unlocking Everett's boat he emerged from his little green house. In response to my pointed questions he grudgingly confirmed what Everett had told me. His wife was a nurse. They'd come to River City because she got a job in the hospital. He was looking for work. Back home they'd lived in a town called Hull where he'd done a bit of clerical work. I told him why I was unlocking the boat and he took a keen interest, helping me mount the outboard engine and connect the gas tank. Then he went into his house for a jug of water. "Fortunately," he said, "my Ford has a trailer ball." He backed his car to the trailer and connected it. This was done without any conversation. And he knew where the boat ramp was. It didn't take us ten minutes to tow the trailer to the ramp and launch Everett's boat. "Well?" he commented when she floated free. He obviously wanted to join me.

"Well—" I said, "we can motor around and look. Freelance. Unless the authorities tell us to go to some particular place." Graham sat up front staring at the water while I steered, hugging the north bank. When I got to the dam I crossed over and drifted down as far as the sewage factory. Then I crossed and went up again. That was the pattern other boats were following. Around and around we went like circus elephants. Graham didn't talk. We stayed out several hours and he made no observations. I asked him what kind of work he was looking for and he said, "Anything." I asked how his wife liked her job at the hospital and he said, "Fine." I said, "Look at that tree where the beavers gnawed off the bark." He looked, but he didn't say anything. Maybe he didn't believe in beavers, like beavers were a joke we Americans played on immigrants. Badger pull. I asked for a swig from his water jug and he handed it to me without speaking. Then we hauled the boat out of the river and returned it to Everett's shop.

I knew Graham was late to pick up his wife by the way he kept checking his watch, and as soon as he got the trailer unhooked from his car he drove away in a cloud of dust. I felt bad about making him late. If he'd said something we could have come in an hour earlier. *Englishman with lockjaw!* I secured everything and relaxed in the shade. *It's hard being a stranger*, I thought. *I'll wait here and apologize to his wife for*

*making him late. Graham certainly isn't lazy, but he has a
dreamy, melancholy nature. He'll have to overcome that to get
a United States job, and he'll have to occasionally say
something.* I wondered what his wife was like, picturing her
as a blonde with a white-rose complexion. Maybe that's a
British nurse image burned on my brain from WWII movies.
Bombshell!

When Graham and his wife pulled into the driveway, not
trusting Graham with the speaking role, I introduced myself.
I told her about Graham helping me search the river and I said
that to repay him I would take them to dinner. I had already
sniffed their kitchen window, so I knew there was no kidney
simmering on the range.

"Pinkie," she said. "It's a silly name, but I'm rather stuck
with it."

"Pinkie, I'll take you to a place called the Palm Tree for
calamari and whatever else the waiter recommends." She
obviously liked food. She bathed me in the warmth of her
smile.

"Come inside, Joe," she said. "Graham will brew tea
while I dress."

We went in the house and that was the last I saw of her for
an hour, but I heard many gallons of bath water running
through the pipes. I sat at the small kitchen table and watched
Graham make tea. I stubbornly refused to talk. After a long
time, after the milk and sugar had been stirred, he asked,
"What line do you follow?"

I told him about polishing bones. He nodded and said, "As
a boy I had an interest in natural science."

Yes, I thought, *I'll bet you collected birds' eggs when you
were a little English boy. You'd like my job, but they've
already hired someone.*

Pinkie twirled into the kitchen snug like a bobbin of blue
silk. She glowed. Pink, fresh powdered. Lipstick, rouge,
curls—all wrapped nicely in a blue satin dress. She wore a pair
of high heels. No, she wanted no tea. It was Graham's turn

at the bath. I took her all in, delighted to be alone with her while Graham bathed. Later it would be fun to watch her eat.

"Tell me about yourself, Joe."

I told her I was retired and didn't own a car. I told her I was a bachelor. I told her about seeing the man go over the dam. Unlike Graham, she didn't mind talking. She told me she and Graham couldn't have children. If they'd had a child they would have raised it in England, but since they were footloose, and since nurses' wages are quite better in the U.S., they'd decided to come over here. I wondered why they couldn't have a baby. She looked perfect for childbearing and Graham seemed to be a good specimen. He didn't talk much, but that shouldn't be a hindrance. She lit an English cigarette and inhaled deeply.

"Everett," I said, "my brother, y'know, he smokes too much. He's always sucking a cigarillo."

"I'm going to quit," Pinkie said. "I only do it out of frustration."

"You're a nurse."

"I should know better, eh? But I don't smoke while on duty. I certainly wouldn't smoke if I got pregnant."

That's good. Think of the baby.

She smiled. Something private passed between us. Something I'd never felt before. I thought about Woolie and his waitress girlfriends. I thought about genetics. Maybe Woolie could tell me some genetic reason why Pinkie and Graham failed to make a baby. I thought about cocky Preacher. I thought about soft Mary Thunder. I didn't feel special with Mary Thunder, but I did with Pinkie. Then a graphic idea slammed into my head. What if I helped her get pregnant? Wouldn't that be wonderful! But I didn't let the idea linger. I hitched it out on the clothesline with Preacher. *No, you're not free to fly around, Old Crowbait, no sir! Stand there amid the rusty cars and crow for oats.* I knew a few things, but I didn't know why Pinkie made me feel so warm and happy.

Aside from Everett and May and Woolheater, Graham and Pinkie were the first visitors to my new apartment. I didn't invite them fishing for compliments, nevertheless it made me feel good to see their reaction. Pinkie called the apartment lavish and palatial. That made me feel guilty for wasting two bedrooms on one person, especially since I'd had a peek into her tiny house. But her situation was temporary, I told myself. Graham would find a job and they could afford a bigger place. He immediately spotted my zebra rug as false and, like a true gentleman, he didn't contradict Pinkie when she gushed on and on about how lovely it was.

I served my guests orange juice. Pinkie took the Hawaiian skirt off its bulldog and stepped into it, pulling tight the strings. She kicked off her shoes and danced a hula. My skirt was authentic and Pinkie's dance was authentic. I wished she weren't wearing her blue dress. Nothing but grass! I excused myself for a cool shower, Burmashave, and change of clothes.

I splashed on cologne and a good dose of foot powder because with all the walking I do I have to be quite conscious of foot protection. I always buy good shoes. I pulled on socks to hold the powder tight and I checked my hair in the mirror. I wear it long to hide my earhole, but it had grown too long and tickled my neck. I had postponed getting a haircut because I dreaded the barber. Always lurking behind his questions was the insinuation that people on The Hill don't work very hard, not as hard as barbers, for instance. Pinkie looked like she would be a good barber. She was comfortable in conversation. And Graham's long hair appeared to have been cut at home.

I put on new black shoes, new black trousers, and the new royal blue tuxedo shirt with ruffles. Suspenders. I topped off my ensemble with the new satin-lapelled jacket. This was the first time I'd worn the fancy clothes since my retirement dinner. I gently lifted the black fedora from its box and tried it on. I would have worn it if Graham had worn a hat, but he preferred to go hatless. Like the Beatles.

When I entered the livingroom Pinkie sat up straighter. She smiled. Graham stood, his trousers baggy at his knees, his tweed jacket sagging at the join. *Hey*, I felt like saying, *don't look so shocked! I don't dress this fancy all the time.* I certainly had no intention of changing my lifestyle. I had donned the duds merely to treat Pinkie and Graham to a nice meal, give them a welcome to River City. Then I would get back into blue jeans and flannel shirts. "I bought this monkey suit for one occasion. My retirement dinner!"

"You look so—" Pinkie said, giggling, "Good!" Tears came in her eyes.

Graham, as usual, didn't say much. But I saw by his hurt-hound-dog look that my splendid clothes made him feel shabby and unemployed. "Tralaa-la!" I yelled, leaping, clicking my heels. "This isn't Joe Geezre you see before you! This here is merely a male model, a movable mannequin. This wardrobe, Graham, is the one I've selected for your debut in River City society! Come into the bedroom. Excuse us, Pinkie." I grabbed Graham's arm and hustled him into the bedroom where I shucked the monkeysuit. "Take your clothes off," I told him severely. "We're the same size. Close enough. You shall wear these duds. They'll match Pinkie's dress," I tugged off his jacket.

"But what will *you* wear?" he asked, gripping his belt buckle, reluctant to remove his pants.

"Yours! It's an American custom. Potlatch. You visit my house. I give you new clothes."

"Is this a joke? Did you make a bet?"

"No joke. Welcome to America! Out of those trousers!" It didn't take me five minutes to get Graham dressed. I put my fedora on his head and when I presented him to Pinkie she really laughed, her eyes dancing merrily. I could tell she loved him. Pinkie and Graham made a perfect sapphire-blue weddingcake couple. *Who knows*, I thought, *we might bump into somebody important at the Palm Tree. Some entrepreneur who'll give Graham a job.* We went down the stairs and exited by the port side to the parking lot. I got in their backseat and said, "Just so there's no misunderstanding about this, I'm buying dinner. Let there be no fighting over the bill."

They nodded, settling in contentedly as I directed Graham on a tour of The Hill telling him and Pinkie the names of the buildings. Graham was a good driver. I had no doubt Pinkie was a good nurse. "How are your patients?" I asked her.

"Huh?"

"How are your patients? At the hospital?"

"Oh. They're sick. Some might pull through. Put up your window so I can light a cigarette, Gigi."

Graham rolled up the window.

I stretched my arms across the back of the seat, my knees stuck up in the air. I slumped, indulging myself in bad posture, and I gloated feeling really good. Pinkie was totally relaxed to have talked about her patients so irreverently. She talked like I was a member of the family. None of that professional formality you would expect. Just down-to-earth wisecracks. It felt great to be wearing Graham's baggy suit. I daydreamed about his jacket and trousers—how they'd roamed around Hull in the fog. I wondered how many times they'd lingered in Shakespeare's pub for a glass of bitter beer and a pig's foot on a bun. Crumpets. Clotted cream.

"Graham," I said, "this Palm Tree is a place in which to see and be seen. Movers and Shakers, y'know. If I spot any hiring agents I'll introduce you."

He nodded, catching my eye in the rearview. Pinkie smoothed his collar. They looked glamorous, Graham and Pinkie, like movie stars.

I chose the smoking section for Pinkie. The waiter, to my surprise, was a dent who worked part time in the museum. He was a nice kid. I'd always wanted to watch English people drink gin, so I asked for some. The dent looked puzzled, like he never expected to see Joe Geezre guzzle. I said as a joke, "Certainly not cotton gins. English gins!"

"How's that?"

I looked to Pinkie for help. She said, "Gin and vermouth in a glass with an olive." She held up three fingers. "One for each of us."

"Martinis?"

"Of course," I said. "I just couldn't remember their name, Martinis!"

While we waited for our drinks I scouted the room, seeing nobody I knew. Pinkie and Graham sat close together, and I admired their good looks. I was glad I hadn't taken them to El Chico Cafe to suffer Cowboy's hard-heeled morality. This place was perfect for us. We had three rounds of martinis, then *calamari*, then broiled salmon with garlic and capers. The waiter touted dessert. Pinkie shook her head and said, "Toosh!" pointing to her empty glass. We had martinis for dessert. I felt woozy. Through the shimmering maze of faces I spotted the judge sitting with his back to us. I hadn't recognized him until he turned to pick up something from the floor. I caught the eye of his waiter and fingered him over. "The Judge needs a clean fork," I said. "And what's he drinking?"

"Scotch and water."

"Buy him another one, on my bill," I said, "and his pretty wife. Get her something of her choice."

"Judge?" Graham asked, looking at me like I was somebody important.

"Yeah. Friend of mine. But I don't reckon he's hiring. I reckon he already has a bailiff. But maybe not. You'd make a good bailiff, Graham!"

I got up and went to the judge's table. His wife, half his age, wore lots of diamonds, or zircon cubes, you can't be sure. "Hullo, Judge," I said. I had picked up a bit of Pinkie's British accent and Graham's baggy tweeds helped me act British. The martinis helped too. The judge didn't remember me.

"Hello?" he said. He was nervous, maybe a bit afraid.

I offered his wife my hand saying, "Captain Joseph Geezre, Madame." She put up her hand to shake, but I bowed low and kissed it. "I'm delighted to meet you," I said. I remarked to the judge, "My friends over there are English. She's a nurse at the hospital. He's looking for work. Do you have any openings at the courthouse? He'd make you a dandy bailiff. British accent, y'know."

The judge shook his head. "No, Captain Geezre. Not at the moment. But I'll keep him in mind." He gazed somewhat hungrily at Graham, maybe dreaming of Graham in a powdered wig yelling, *Hear ye! Hear ye! Hear ye! River City Court is open according to law! Honourable Judge Judge presiding!*

I bowed. The judge nodded. His wife smiled. She had a sharp face like Margot Fonteyn.

I returned to our table. Graham and Pinkie stood. The three of us lifted our glasses to the Judges. Mrs. Judge waved back. Then I paid the bill and Pinkie said, "Let's go look in some shops!" So we walked all the way to the courthouse and back, looking in every window. Pinkie tickled me the way she said funny things. We went in the Opera for popcorn and then we strolled past the Brewery to let the swells gaze upon us. Having no place else to go we walked to the bridge and leaned against a fresh breeze, watching the streetlights flicker on.

"Our house is down there, beyond those trees," Graham said, pointing it out to Pinkie.

"I know where we live," she said. "Behind the levee."

A few boats still made the circle.

"It makes me sad," she said, "watching those boats. Sad because I know what they're looking for."

"Yes. Sad."

"Want to take the boat out tomorrow?"

"Sure. Let's take her out. Those batterboards there, see? They raise the level of the river."

"Why?"

"To put water through the turbines. Generate electricity."

Graham looked down. The breeze caught his fedora and blew it into the river. It floated over the dam. Pinkie laughed. Graham shook his hair loose, glad to be rid of the hat, and I looked down the front of Pinkie's dress. Titties. I realized we were all quite drunk. We went to their house, leaving the Ford to collect parking tickets. Pinkie walked between Graham and me rocking on her high heels while he and I held her steady, like bookends, but of course I was older than Graham by some thirty-odd years.

She made me a pallet on the livingroom floor. Then she closed their bedroom door and we turned in. But no door could muffle the embarrassing sounds of their matrimony. I dressed and crept into the starlight. Having no way of locking their door from the outside, I pulled it snug and left it unlocked hoping they would be safe there in the dark, shut behind two doors, clinging together, making sounds I'd never heard before. I struck out in Graham's old tweeds feeling shaky but clearheaded. I saw stars and ruby red tail lights. I felt the keys to Everett's shop and the key to my Flattop cabin rubbing together in my pocket.

As I crossed the bridge, above the roar of water rushing through the millrace, I wondered who might be bedded down there. I'd seen Hat Woman recently. Joey or Trasheater might be there, I thought, and maybe Venus Lady.

The upwardly mobile were still whooping it up as I passed the Brewery, keeping to the dark side of the street. I hit my stride and cut over to Illinois Street because that's an easy climb up the hill. It's a gradual incline, and you can eat a greasy Joe's for fuel. I cruised onto the campus, steamed past the union, and docked myself at the wharf. The exercise had circulated my blood. I felt good, savoring my delightful evening with Pinkie and Graham. In the mind of this retired virgin, this bachelor, there was no doubt that when the morning sun broke over Everett's plumbing shop, warming the east side of his little rent house, Pinkie would be pregnant.

A six-inch square of cloth had blown against the hatch and stuck there. I knew what it was. Fruitbats fornicate year round, but springtime, after graduation, is their nuptial season, and I'd seen quite a few such cloth squares recently. They are wrapped around throwing rice. I looked across at the chapel sitting dark in the shadows of pine trees. It was deserted, so I paid it a call opening the door rather timidly, thinking that if I went in and sat for a few moments I might draw some inspiration from the atmosphere. I don't think I was actually praying. I think I was merely thinking. I didn't speak aloud. I didn't move my lips. I didn't form my thoughts into complete sentences. But I held the distinct notion in my mind that Pinkie deserved to have a baby. It didn't occur to me that if she got pregnant she would cross the Atlantic to bear her child in England. That thought came later. I couldn't see the beautiful windows because they require sunshine to illuminate them. The

pew was hard, and I speculated it was intentionally so to keep
people from staying too long. I sat there thinking about the
poor man slipping over the dam. I had had much too much to
drink. I swayed.

A middle-aged woman entered the chapel. She walked
purposefully down the aisle and stepped onto the dais, where
there was a pulpit. Behind the pulpit an altar shelf supported
an open Bible and the woman went to it, her manner so direct
that I couldn't help watching her. She took a spiral notebook
from the altar shelf, walked to the front pew, sat down, took a
pen from her purse, clicked it, and began writing. She was so
much at ease that I guessed her to be a beadle. I wanted to ask
her advice about praying. *Does a prayer have to be spoken to
be valid? Does a prayer have to be addressed to God? This
chapel has a carved-stone cross on its gable, so must a valid
prayer prayed in here be addressed to the Christian God? Not
the humanists' marshmallow god nor the mongrel god of some
rinkydinky offshoot monkey religion?* I hadn't yet had time to
get a book on St. Teresa.

After she'd spent several minutes writing the woman
clicked the retractor of her pen, stood up, smoothed her skirt,
and replaced the notebook on the altar shelf. Then she came
down the aisle toward me. Her eyes were bright and gentle.
She had brown hair which curled softly around her face. She
was well dressed, wearing a bit of lipstick and some eye
shadow. *Fifty*, I thought, *she's about fifty*. I held my palms
together in the prayer position, for no good reason, and I raised
them to her, nodding slightly like a Russian, but she chose not
to acknowledge me. I had seen her before. I couldn't
remember where. Maybe it was in the library or the bookstore
or the cafeteria.

She'd been gone perhaps ten minutes when I stood to
stamp the stiffness from my knees. No one else had come into
the chapel. I smoothed out Graham's tweeds as best I could,
walked up the aisle, stepped onto the dais, and crept around the
altar. The spiral notebook lay beside the Bible. Someone had

written on its cover, PRAYER BOOK PLEASE DO NOT THROW AWAY. I opened the book to its last entry and read:

Dear God,
Bob is very much a concern, but not my #1 concern at the moment. Grades, money, and Tara paying off the phone bill are pressing matters. Yet BOB STILL MEANS MUCH TO ME. Please have me receive a response to the package I sent him by early next month. As for Jennifer, I have such a petty, jealous, cat-woman feeling towards her. Even though I realize this, I still want her to envy me, think that I'm attractive, etc. I don't dislike her, she is a very cheery person. But I want her to envy me. As of the time being, I please ask of you that these things become a reality: Tara pays the phone bill. Bob responds. I succeed in school. Money is secure. Please. Make me able to concentrate, not think mind game thoughts. Thank you. Love, Kimberly.

I closed the prayer book, put it back on the shelf, and walked out of the chapel, my head buzzing like a bee hive. I crossed the parking lot, crossed the gangplank, opened the hatch, and went to my cabin. I undressed and hung Graham's tweeds on a wooden hanger. Then I crawled in bed, but I couldn't fall asleep. *Kimberly is too old to be a fruitbat, yet she prayed to succeed in school. And she has a cat woman feeling toward Jennifer? She wants Tara to pay the phone bill! Are these the things people pray for? If Kimberly's prayers are answered will she or Bob or Tara or Jennifer shed tears over them?* I set the alarm so I could get downtown and pay the meter before the parking police ticketed Graham's car. Then I would go shake Graham out of bed and take him to search the river. I thought about Preacher and Madame Leontyne and Everett's blackjack dealer with the removables and Woolie rubbing Sarah's leg just below the bottom of her skirt. I thought about the handsome boat sliding over the dam and I thought about Mary Thunder, but mainly I thought about

Kimberly needing a response from Bob and needing Tara to pay the phone bill.

3

Bulldog

My alarm clock rattled my brains early. I made a quick breakfast and hustled to feed the parking meter. When I arrived at Pinkie and Graham's house I found Everett tossing pipes into his van. He should have been halfway to the airport, and I said as much.

"You've got to finish the goddamn job, Joe! When you hustle your ass for a living, out in the goddamn real world, you've got to finish the goddamn job!"

"You said you were paid."

"True. But the goddamn contractor called me back. I ran a goddamn cold line to that goddamn BE DAY. Seems they want a hot and a cold supply. Seems they want to mix hot and cold so they'll have goddamn *warm* water. You ever hear such crap?"

"No."

"If I had a good brother he'd help me finish this goddamn job!"

"Well—I sort of promised I'd search the river some more."

Everett, sensing a moral imperative, snapped, "Promised who! Who goddamnit did you promise?"

"I agreed to go out with the Englishman."

Everett walked to the door of the green house and battered it with his knuckles. The door swung open. "Hey!" Everett yelled, "Anybody home?"

Out came a sleepy "Hullo?" from Graham.

"I'm taking Joe on a job! Be back in an hour!"

"Yes," Graham said.

Everett nodded, pulling the door shut. "No problem, Joe. He's still asleep. I'll T-in above the washing machine, run along the joist, up beside the cold line. We'll be outta there in an hour."

When we arrived at the job Everett didn't waste time showing me Phoebe's busteds. We entered by way of the basement door and got cranking. We did everything from below then went up to the bathroom to connect to the bidet. But the bathroom was occupied, its door locked. Everett paced the hallway smoking cigarillos and staring at his watch. He had tickets for a noon flight. May was no doubt at home dressed, her bags packed, holding a sack of catfish sandwiches and a thermos of hot coffee. Unable to watch him sweat it out, I said, "Leave me your wrenches, the torch, some solder, and pipe. I'll connect it up. Go on to Vegas!"

"How will you get back across town?"

I shrugged and gave him a salute. If he didn't know after sixty-two years that his twin brother was a famous walker, he'd never know. "Don't worry about me," I said, "I'll walk. Go on. Go to The Stars. If you see Wayne Newton tell him hello."

Everett ran to his van and I followed to get the tools I needed. As he handed me wrenches Everett said, "They weren't removable! My own goddam stupidity kept me from seeing the truth. Madame Leontyne sent me to the right dealer but I was too damned dumb to know it."

"How's that? I mean—if she sent you to the right dealer—"

Everett shook his head wisely. He said, "I was too busy looking at the dealer's titties. I should have looked at her shoe."

"Shoe?"

"The shoe, Joe! The shoe! Removable. Left and right. How many decks are in a shoe?"

"I have no earthly idea what you're talking about," I said.

"The blackjack dealer's shoe! If I can find out how many decks are in there, I can multiply by that! I can memorize the cards as they come out. I can use my goddam memory, for once in my life, I can *use* it!"

I didn't know what he was talking about, but whatever it was it made him happy. I wished him luck and went upstairs to wait for the bathroom door to open. Out came the bulldog, wearing a red robe. His hair was slicked back and he had a white towel around his neck—boxer style, like a knockout king headed for the ring. "Hello?" he said. "What brings you back? The bathroom's all finished."

"I need to connect one more pipe," I said. "It'll only take a minute."

"There's no hurry. I've had my bath. Will you drink a glass of orange juice? Say yes and I'll watch you work."

"Sure," I said. "Why not? Yes!"

"That's the spirit," he said. "Vodka *mit*?"

"What?"

"*Mit*'s German. Of course you want vodka with your orange juice?"

"Of course."

While he was gone I pulled the pipe from below and lined it up. It needed an adapter sweated on because the adapter was too big to pass up through the hole in the floor. I cut the pipe to length and cleaned it. I was cooling my heels when the bulldog returned with our orange juice.

"Oh, good," he said. "I've had that on my mind. It's like magic, the way the solder flows in there. Your friend was quite cryptic. I suppose it's a guild secret—"

"My brother," I said. "My *twin* brother, is a plumber. They're cryptic people, y'know. Plumbers. Steer clear of plumbers."

"Then what the devil are you?" he said, gazing fondly into my earhole.

"Oh, me? I'm just helping him out so he won't be late getting to The Stars."

Bulldog handed me juice saying, "You speak strange dialogue, my lovely."

"I'm retired, see," I said. I almost added that I was a retired virgin in the sense that if one retires from being a virgin one doesn't have to be a virgin anymore. "This stuff I'm doing here is child's play. I was a museum preparator. That's a skilled job. I mean, a preparator has to do a little bit of everything—drawing, painting, welding, carpentry, sculpture."

"Let me try it, if it's child's play. I've always wanted to plumb."

I took a few minutes to give him instructions. Then I turned him loose. He made a good union, maybe. It looked good. I turned off the torch and while everything cooled down we stood there drinking orange juice. He broke wind and eyeballed me closely, like he was sizing me up for a role in a play. Then I connected the adapter to the mixing valve. "Now we test it," I said.

"How?"

"You stay here so you can yell if it sprays. I'll go down in the basement and turn it on."

He was happy as a kid with the responsibility, and the suspense. I went below to open the valve. There was silence in the bathroom. *She held!* I certainly didn't want to cut out a bad union and start all over. I ran upstairs to tell him the good news.

"C'mon!" he said. "Come in to breakfast. I need you to verify how handsomely I sweated that union!"

"Handsome is as handsome does," I said. "That's Gospel. Three or four years' work and you might be a plumber."

He unleashed one of his extensive growling laughs. "C'mon in to breakfast. Have you had breakfast?"

I thought it best to be sly, so I shook my head. I stuck out my hand and said, "Geezre's the name."

He played it coy asking, "Do you know who I am?"

I played him coy right back. I said, "You're Bulldog."

"Bulldog who?"

"Bulldog Drummond."

I knew that would toss him into a fit of barking laughter. And it did. The cook fried us some link sausage with grilled tomatoes and square eggs. Bulldog refilled our juice glasses pumping me for information about River City, and I knew why. He was writing a book on our town. He asked about Agnes the Frog and all that endangered species stuff and the town's water supply and the landfill like he was from Mars shopping to buy a town. He asked about the unfortunate man stuck in a dry-hole privy. He was particularly interested in the town's famous writer, so I told him everything I knew about the Old Man. "He's a cutup," I said. "I've seen him in his yard throwing a Bowie knife. He's fierce, grunting and muttering insults to his imaginary foe. He dynamites paint cans. Blows hell out of them. He's dangerous—heavily armed."

"Delightful! Have you read his work?"

"Nah. I've seen him read it, but it doesn't excite me." *Like you, he's getting by on his looks!* I thought, but I didn't say it. Bulldog grinned, liking it that I wasn't a fan of the competition. In came Phoebe Jones, and Bulldog introduced us. Recognizing me as Walkman, she was a bit shaken to find a town character sitting at her breakfast table. The obsequious cook greeted her. She ordered tomato juice and he hustled his butt to get it. I thought he was the most interesting person in the house. Straight from England, skinny butt, lilting Afro-British accent. *How much does a Democrat pay for such a prestige cook?* I wondered.

"Joe Geezre taught me to solder," Bulldog said proudly. "I made a good union, and it didn't leak!"

"Wonderful." Phoebe bent over to peck him on the cheek. There was not an ounce of enthusiasm in her *wonderful*. She didn't know I'd heard her read poems in the Glass Eye. I could've quoted her lines back to her, but that wouldn't serve the cause of friendship. Her poems were about abortion and you could tell they were all true. *Whimpering autobiography! Where's the art?* Skinhead yelled, *She's just talking about her own damn self!* He couldn't start a revolution, so he walked out in a huff. Skinhead was against abortion.

"Well, the bidet is fixed," I said. "My job here is finished." I wadded my napkin and tossed it onto the table like you're supposed to and stood up. If I'd had a silver bullet I would have left it for a tip.

Phoebe said, "You're a *plumber*?"

"No, no," Bulldog said. "He's not a plumber. *I* had to help him fix it!"

"That's right, Little Friend," I said, bowing to Bulldog. "I'm not a plumber, I'm a poet."

"Oh?" Phoebe looked hard at me.

"I haven't written any poems, but I'm taking notes. By the way, I heard you read at the Glass Eye."

"Oh, really?" She smiled, like I might have some sense after all. "What did you think of my poems?"

"They were good."

She warmed as if life, after all, might be worth living. I searched the cockles of my heart to see if I was being truthful with her. "What's your opinion of the proposed head tax on poets?" I asked.

She shrugged, pretending to know what I was talking about and said, "Suits me. I mean, if you want quality you pay for it. What kind of poems will you write when you get around to it?"

"Religious poems."

"Who's your favorite poet?"

"*Hark! Hark! The dogs bark. The beggars are coming to town. Some in rags, some in tags, and one in a velvet gown.* For me, that one has stood the test of time."

"But it's not religious—"

"Think about it," I said.

"Doggerel—"

"So what? Who cares if it has some puppy dogs in it. What's wrong with a few puppy dogs?"

Phoebe and Bulldog exchanged looks. He said, with emphasis, "But one in a velvet gown—"

"Right on!" I yelled. "Back to childhood! How would a child see it? A new plush velvet gown trimmed with fur or an old cast-off faded thing, the kind a beggar might find in a ditch?"

Bulldog smiled. He recited, "*The dogs bark, but the caravan moves on.*"

"That's the stuff!" I yelled. "The old stuff! Back, back in time!"

"Too much emphasis on childhood," Phoebe said. "A woman's sole obligation is to her talent, not some nonexistent children."

Bulldog, sensing that Phoebe was becoming unhappy with me, opened a new topic. "Joe knows River City's famous writer."

"Big deal!" Phoebe responded.

"I've heard gossip about Methusela, that's all. And I was kidding about wanting to be a poet."

"If you're not a plumber and you're kidding about being a poet, then what the hell are you?"

"Sixty-two years old," I said, heading for the door.

"That's your age." She followed me. "You're quite childish, telling someone your age. What do you do? Why do you walk all the time? Where do you live? Are you homeless? I have extra bedrooms. Maybe you'd like to stay here a few days—"

I turned my mutilated side to her. "You can buy a busted Truman and you can buy a busted Thatcher. But you can't buy a busted Geezre!"

"Are you trying especially to piss me off!"

"Look, Phoebe. I *said* I like your poems. I'm not accustomed to having vodka *mit* for breakfast. I'm not accustomed to being grilled like a tomato. Thanks for the square eggs."

As I walked out of the room Bulldog followed me, hissing in my ear, "Ease up, Joe. She's the Peggy Guggenheim of Kansas! You could get a grant!"

I grabbed the torch, wrenches, and a long piece of left-over pipe. As I went out the basement door I heard an upstairs window flung open. Hearing a dog growl, I looked up into the happy eyes of Bulldog. He had his chin thrust out and his teeth bared, growling at me as fiercely as he could. He gave me a tentative, delicate little wave. I smiled thinking, *He's a child and I'm a child. I came to play at his house and we played too hard, got too tired, and quarreled. His mother sent me home.*

He looks like he might have a Teddy under his arm. I saluted him, lifting the copper pipe like a drum major's baton as he blew me a kiss. I marched up the driveway singing the Army Hymn. From next door a real dog barked. Bulldog joined in, yapping from the window.

As I marched along the boulevard I daydreamed of the literary shootout that will occur between Bulldog and Methusela on the Opera stage. Each will have a table—stage left and stage right. Each will have a carafe of water and an empty glass. The house will be sold out. A ticket—if you could buy one—would cost a paperhanger's armpit and the fast crowd will overflow from Kansas City and Beaumont; Atchison and Topeka. Like at any championship fight, swells will parade in fur coats, rhinestone tiaras, false eyelashes, tattoos. Phoebe's cook will handle Bulldog, massaging his neck, whispering over his shoulder, *You can take him, Kid. You can take him!* Penis Boy will manage Methusela, reminding him of his accessories concealed under the table. *Here's your electric cattle prod, your bull cane, your Bowie knife.* Methusela will speak extemporaneously claiming to be Bulldog's bastard father at which insult Bulldog will crawl across the stage barking *Mommy! Mommy!* Like professional wrestlers, Bulldog and Methusela will grapple through their choreography exchanging insults—*Faggot! Junkie! Artsie-Fartsie Son-of-a-Dog!* The crowd will froth into a frenzy and you can guess the finale. From fifteen paces Methusela plugs Bulldog in the heart with his Bowie knife. I hope I can get tickets! I want to take Woolie and Everett and Pinkie and Graham. Back to the wreck shop. Of course Bulldog will rig his piano-wire garrote to behead Methusela. And they'll both wear fedoras to keep the dreadful glare of publicity out of their sensitive eyes and as with all good dramas none of the principals survive. Gore. Lots of flowers will be thrown, just like a bullfight opera. Sure, the River City Opera Singer will be there to rise spontaneously third row center and sing something appropriate from *Madame Butterfly.*

When Joe got home he checked his mail.   There was a letter from his niece and a note from the apartment manager. He put Rosealyn's letter, unopened, on the table and read the photocopied note which was addressed to all tenants:

Dear *Mr. Geezre*,
This is to advise you that Ms. Melanie Moore, a student in psychology, is working on a research project concerning our home(s). She wants to see how we "fit together" and live as a community. I hope you will find time to "assist" her with her interviews, questionnaires, etc.
                    Thanks, Manager

Joe balled the note and tossed it in the trash. He stripped to his underwear and socks, went to the bedroom, and crawled between the sheets.   Bulldog's vodka had given him a headache.

When he was half asleep he heard someone knocking on his door. Above the knocking he heard Woolheater's voice yelling, "Joe! Emergency! Open up!"

Could be a fire, Joe thought, swinging his socks onto the carpet. *Could be we're sinking. All hands on deck! All hands on deck!* He opened the door and Woolheater burst in without invitation. "Joe, what have you done?"

"Oh, I ran a hot water line to a bidet. I angered a distinguished poet. I drank vodka for breakfast. Why?"

"Are you drunk?"

"Half-and-half, I suppose. I was in bed. Almost asleep. And it's not even noon yet."

"A policeman is looking for you."

"Policeman?"

"Detective. Someone told him I knew you better than anybody here, so he pumped me with questions: Had you ever been in trouble with the law. Had you expressed any cuckoo political beliefs. Were you a stable individual—"

"Well?"

Woolheater shrugged. "Joe, I had to tell the truth."

"Good."

"I told him you've been sleeping in dumpsters with Indian women. Told him you have the crazy idea this building is an aircraft carrier. You think we're all sailors."

"Woolie!"

"Just kidding. I told him you were a sane, nice old fellow. What did you do, Joe?"

"Nothing!"

"His name's Bradley. He'll be back. Have you done a crime?"

"No!"

"If you haven't done any crime you have nothing to fear." Woolheater shook hands solemnly, like it was goodbye forever. He turned and walked down the hall. Joe closed his door, got back in bed, and lay there reviewing his sins. *I'm not a licensed plumber, but I plumbed for Phoebe Jones. I'm not a licensed exterminator, but I told Cowboy how to handle his roach problem. When I took Everett's boat on the river maybe I interfered with police work? I lifted Comanche's tailbone from the trashcan, but that was long ago, and besides, the horse was dead.* He got out of bed, looked up the number of the police department, and dialed it. While the phone rang he heard another knock on his door. He hung up and answered it. The knocker was Detective Bradley.

"Come in, Bradley," Joe said, knowing the man by his sunglasses and wide shoulders. "Geezre. Joe Geezre." He held out his hand. Bradley showed his badge. "Sit down?"

The big man chose to sit on Joe's new sofa, directly beneath the *faux* zebra skin. He could have made a polite remark about the zebra skin or the grass skirt on the coffee table, but he didn't. He said nothing, waiting for Joe to ask what he wanted. Joe sat across the coffee table in a padded chair and said nothing. Minutes passed. Bradley shifted his feet, took off his sunglasses, and said, "Mr. Geezre, this isn't getting us anywhere."

"Where do you want to go?" Joe replied.

"You've been harassing a judge. Why?"

"The judge! You mean the judge thinks I'm harassing him?"

"Yes. What has he done to anger you? Have you disagreed with his verdicts?"

"Of course not. He has a lean, weary look about him. Tired and sad. I figure he's seen ten tons of human misery. I want to be friends with him. Get to know him."

"Why?"

"I'm seeking wisdom."

Bradley's eyes settled on the grass skirt. By the way it lay on the coffee table anyone could see that it had been recently worn. He looked at Joe as if he thought Joe had worn it. "If that's your interest, why did you tell the owner of El Chico Cafe the judge was making a deal with your brother for votes?"

"That's hearsay, officer. I'm ashamed of you."

"Would you do anything to harm the judge?"

"Absolutely not. I'm sorry if he got that impression. I had a brief conversation with him. Introduced myself to his charming wife. Bought them a drink—"

"You weren't invited to their table."

"The Palm Tree is a public place! What's the big deal? Does the judge have enemies?"

"Any judge worth the name has enemies." Bradley stood. "So, Mr. Geezre, stay away from him."

Joe followed Bradley to the door. After closing it behind the detective he went to the kitchen, took two aspirins, and went back to bed.

But there was no sleeping for Joe Geezre. He tossed. *Restraining order* came into his mind and revolved there. He thought about Rosealyn's unopened letter. He wondered if Kimberly had visited the chapel to write another entry in the prayer book. *Yes, a judge can issue a restraining order.* He'd forgotten about Graham and the river and the boat and the missing man. He got up, put on his coffee pot, hung his grass skirt on its bulldog, and moved Rosealyn's letter to the mantle above the gas-logs fireplace. He propped it up so he could see it from across the room. He would leave it there in expectation, unread, until the mood was right. While the coffee perked he got out his vacuum and cleaned the livingroom carpet then sat at the telephone table to drink a cup of coffee black with two lumps of sugar and make his calls. He called the police department to ask if the missing man had been found. He was told that the police couldn't release that information so he called the *Journal* and learned that the man had not been found. Then he looked up Graham's number. He called to apologize for being late. Graham said he wasn't inconvenienced, but he told Joe to return his jacket and trousers because he needed them for an interview. The new clothes Joe gave him were, in his opinion, too flashy for everyday wear. They wouldn't make a good impression on a personnel manager.

Joe sipped coffee thinking that so far it had been a dreary day. He phoned the Pentimento Bar and asked for Mary's number. The bartender gave it to him, along with a sleazy remark. Joe dialed Mary's number but there was no answer. He dialed Phoebe Jones' number and the cook answered. "I'd like to speak to Bulldog Drummond," Joe said.

"Is this who I think it is?" the cook asked.

"Joe Geezre."

"You got out of here not a minute too soon. Someone flushed a toilet and everything flooded."

"Tell Phoebe I'm on my way right now to fix it."

"That is not good because she called a real plumber. The house is a mess. Everybody left but me."

"Tell Bulldog to call Joe Geezre. I have something important to tell him." Joe hung up the receiver and sat looking at the black telephone for a long time. It was an old desk model. Solid. Heavy. With white space beneath the dial wheel. The numbers and letters were black—printed on the white space. Spots of brass gleamed inside each finger hole where the black enamel had worn off, and fingernails had scratched a trail through the black numbers. Joe phoned Woolheater, inviting him for coffee.

Joe told Woolheater about his morning's visit to install the bidet. He didn't mention the fact that the water line broke.

"Hey!" he yelled. He grabbed the phone and dialed Phoebe's number. Her cook answered again.

"Hey, this is Joe Geezre!"

"Still nobody here, Mr. Geezre. Just me."

"The water that leaked. Was it hot or cold?"

"What do you mean?"

"I mean was it hot water or was it cold water?"

"Man, it was very cold water. It went everywhere!"

"Thanks," Joe hung up. Woolheater refilled their cups and Joe said, "At least it wasn't my line. It was Everett's line. That's some relief."

"Having a bad day, Joe?"

"So far." Joe told Woolheater about the tweed jacket and trousers, confessing his disappointment that he couldn't keep Graham's old suit. He also told Woolheater about seeing brown-haired Kimberly in the chapel and reading her prayer. Woolheater laced his fingers across his paunch, nodded sagely, and said, "It's retirement, Joe. Retirement's driving you nuts. You get a crush on a judge. You get a crush on an Indian woman. You get a crush on a devout brown-haired woman. You even get a crush on another man's clothes! You're lonely. You don't have any kids telling you not to, so why don't you get yourself a woman?"

"It's that simple, is it?"

"Look back over your life. Remember when you've had a bed partner how smooth the road was?"

"I've never had a bed partner, Woolie. I'm a virgin."

"How can it be? To be crass, what about libido?"

"My twin brother got it all. While we were swimming around in the womb the libido settled over to his side and he absorbed it. He's chased women all his life."

"And you're a virgin?"

"That's what I said."

"Well, well, well—"

"A well is a dark hole in the ground. Frequently has water at the bottom."

"Captain Joseph Geezre, I don't know what to say. Maybe you're falling in love with love. Do you think you could handle a woman? To sleep with and get up and eat breakfast with?"

"Ah," Joe said, spreading his hands, "and now we get down to the tacks made of brass."

"Clever phrase."

"I learned it from my fortuneteller. When my brother enlightened me about sex he didn't mention breakfast."

"Then he's a poor one to give advice."

"Maybe so. I've let him do my share of the lovemaking. Maybe he's bungled the job!"

"He never told you about the old double bind?"

"Double bind?"

"When you think you're taking advantage of a woman and suddenly realize that you're taking care of her. You rock along like that for a while until it becomes apparent that she's actually taking care of you. That's when a man like your brother would take off looking for another woman."

"What would a man like you do?"

"Joe, don't worry about me. Worry about you."

Joe smiled, thinking, *Here's advice from a man who would have bought Gen. Geo. Custer's autograph if I'd said it was authentic.* He looked at the photographs of Comanche and Taj Mahal. Then his eye caught Rosealyn's letter propped on the mantle. *It's Pinkie*, he thought, *that's why I crave Graham's old tweeds. How many times have they walked beside Pinkie, their arm around her, down the streets of Hull? How many times has she pressed out their wrinkles on a rickety English ironing board?* "Let's start a business, Woolie. Give ourselves something to do."

"Okay. What kind of business?"

"Liquor store. We'll call it Two Old Boys' Liquor Store."

"Nah. You'd drink up the profits." He tried to leave but stood there befuddled as if he'd forgotten something.

"There's no need to tip me, Woolie. I didn't tell dirty jokes or let you fondle my leg."

Woolheater scowled, walked to the door, and said, "I'll bet they lock you up, Joe. You're an irritating old sonofabitch!"

Joe hung a don't disturb sign on his doorknob and settled
into his chair beside the north window to recuperate and look
out at the world. He could see the south side of Whoso
Findeth Wisdom Findeth Life, and if he leaned close to the
window he could see the towered museum. A black iron fence
separated Flattop's berth from the street which mounted the
hill. Joe watched a woman climbing the hill. Her legs flashed
beyond the black fence. She kept a strong, purposeful pace but
Joe noted that she wore thin-soled shoes—bad for walking.
Halfway up the hill she slowed and stepped over to the fence.
Gripping it to steady herself, she stood there catching her
breath. She looked up at Flattop, raised her eyes to Joe's
window, and saw him watching her. He waved. She
considered waving but thought better of it and turned away.
He recognized her as Kimberly, the woman he'd seen in the
chapel, the woman with bright eyes and soft hair. Knowing
she was being observed, she stepped off bravely. *She's going
to the chapel of love*, he thought. *I could catch her there.* He
reclined his chair another notch and closed his eyes. *Maybe
it's hanging out with Woolie that's making me as horny as he
is, always thinking about women.*

He slept until his phone rang. When he lifted the receiver
he heard a high-pitched dog's bark. He barked back. The dog
on the other end growled. Joe held silent. Then the dog said,
"This is Bulldog returning your call."

"Thanks," Joe said. "I hear a pipe broke after I left."

"Not ours, Joe. Not the one we put in. I ran downstairs
and turned off the water saving Phoebe *extensive* water
damage."

"Good work. Sorry I got crosswise with Phoebe. I didn't
mean to offend her. She's so damned pushy."

"Say no more. So, what's going on with you?"

"I'm nursing a wounded ego. My brother's out of town,
and I seem to have taken on his complex burdens. Bulldog,
I'm more naive than you might think. What's up with you?"

"We drove out to see where the guy spent the night in the
toilet."

"Well, are you going to visit Methusela?"

"Methusela?"

"The Old Man. Your competition. Famous writer."

"I put a message on his phone but he hasn't called back. I left an open invitation. I mean, I invited myself openly, but he hasn't responded. You want to get together for a drink?"

"No more booze for me, Bulldog. It scrambles my brains, makes me act crazy."

"Of course. Well—I'd like to talk with you sometime. You have access to some information I need."

"You're writing a book."

"*Ask Me No Questions—*"

"And I'll tell you no lies. Look, if you put my friends in your book they will make a darned good story."

"Oh really? Tell me about them?"

"Do you like to walk?"

"It's okay."

"Meet me at the chapel. An hour before dusk, about seven o'clock. It's across the street from the natural history museum."

"Okay. I'll get Phoebe to take me there. She knows where everything is."

"Don't bring her."

"Sure, sure."

"You know a man's missing in the river, presumed drowned?"

"Yes."

"Don't wear your fancy pants. We'll go look for him."

"At dusk?"

"Everybody else is looking in the daytime. We'll look at night. Wear comfortable shoes." Joe hung up and closed his eyes. He remembered overhearing Phoebe tell Bulldog, "On our way to Madame Leontyne's—" *I wonder what Bulldog asked Madame Leontyne? I wonder if her daughter was there to fold his twenty?*

Joe awoke in time to catch the radio news. After listening to it he took a shower. Then he prepared supper: corned-beef hash, a bowl of instant rice, and a pouch of frozen lima beans. The beans were from Everett's garden of the previous summer.

He poured himself a glass of milk and cut two thick slices of twelve-grain hippie bread—made from sunflower seeds etc.

Remembering the sign on his doorknob, he decided to go public. Clipped to it was a note: *When it's convenient I'd like to talk with you. Sincerely, Melanie Moore.* "Nice to hear from a lady," he said. He remembered the name. Melanie was the psychological fruitbat who wanted to study the "fitting together" of old folks in the Mothball Fleet. He thought about her while eating his supper. He washed the dishes, brushed his teeth, and sat at his phone table to write:

Dear Ms. Melanie Moore,
I'm new here (relatively) and probably have little to add to your research. But I will be delighted to talk. Knock anytime. If I'm home I'll answer the door. Sincerely, Capt. Joseph Geezre, U.S.S. Flattop, The Great American Desert.
P.S. If I'm not here leave a message with Mannie.

He pulled tape off a roll and went out in his undershorts to stick the note securely to his door. He put on jeans, a lightweight shirt, good socks, and dry walking shoes. He made sure he had his billfold and keys. When he sat down to wait for Bulldog it was five-fifty. *I can't sit here for an hour and ten minutes. Think I'll take a walk.* He stepped out at a rapid pace but was unable to pass the chapel without looking in. A group of like-minded Christians sat near the door, praying in hushed tones. Joe went behind the altar and casually opened the prayer book, looking for a recent Kimberly prayer, but there was only the one he'd already seen. He read it through, then opened the book at random to read a fruitbat's prayer: *I praise my Father, our God, for my time in this chapel—it is a place in a storm.* He turned to another page: *My new problem is that I am dating a non-Christian (agnostic) man. He tries to understand but he needs proof. I can only give him proof by my example.* Another page: *What a neat blessing it is to see what everyone writes in this book—I just encourage those that read this to go ahead and write something down because it blesses those that read it.* Another page: *Tim, Let's meet to pray. I know we have a lot in common!*

He closed the book, put it back in its place, tiptoed out the back door, and hit his stride. Some fruitbats who met his eyes smiled shyly, as if they feared being photographed with Walkman. He cruised past the belltower and down the grassy incline where dogs chased frisbees. A white sycamore glowed majestically as he circled it, druid fashion, counterclockwise. He walked to the fast-food street, bought a cup of yogurt, and went back by the library to check out a three-volume edition of *The Complete Works of Saint Teresa.*

Bulldog came early to sniff. He got Joe's address from campus information and instead of waiting at the chapel he went to Joe's apartment and read Joe's note to Melanie. Then he snooped aft. He sniffed his way down to A deck and promenaded up to the bow reading names off doors, chatting with the people he met, getting a feel for Flattop. He returned to the poop deck and tapped on Joe's door.

"Come in?"

"It's not dusk yet. I'm early."

"Would you like a cup of tea?"

"Tea's always nice." Striding across the livingroom and turning abruptly, Bulldog sat on the sofa. "You have a nice place, Joe. Very cozy."

"I've never traveled, except with the army. My decor is more worldly than I am— Grass skirt— Zebra rug—"

"Who's Melanie?"

"A dent who wants to interview us old coots. Maybe she's writing a term paper."

Joe went around the kitchen divider to put on tea water. He said, "That's not a real zebra skin."

"Looks real enough to me."

"I bought it at Pier 1, in case you're an animal lover. I wouldn't want to offend you."

"Are *you* an animal lover?"

Joe centered the pan on the burner and returned to the livingroom. "I used to be a hunter. Now I'm too soft-hearted to shoot anything."

"I knew you'd have a soft spot in your heart for something—" Bulldog flirted, making his eyes twinkle.

"Women. Sometimes I see a woman and my heart melts. Makes me want to cry. Look here—" Joe pointed out the north window, "see that sidewalk? Today a woman came walking up there, God knows where she'd come from, this is a steep hill. She was fifty-ish, a little soft around the middle, soft breasts, soft brown hair—paper shoes—and I'd read her prayers so I knew how pressed she was, how lonely, frightened. How much she wanted to be attractive. She was out of breath. It broke my heart, seeing her like that."

"You read her prayers?" Bulldog's high-pitched voice drilled with interest.

"Yeah. And there's Pinkie, a nurse recently arrived from England. She and her husband are poor. They want to have a baby, but Pinkie can't get pregnant. And there's Mary Thunder, a Native American woman who walks around carrying fifty pounds of Indian jewelry."

"And let's not forget Melanie Moore."

Joe heard the water boil over and fizz the burner. He ran into the kitchen. "Regular or herbal?"

"Herbal. Unless you've got gin?"

"I'm fresh out."

Joe prepared two cups and carried them into the livingroom. He set them on the brass table. "I got this table at Pier 1," he said.

"Nice, Joe. Real nice." Bulldog stirred his tea and gazed around the room, taking everything in. He saw the *Complete Works of Saint Teresa*.

It's all phony, Joe was tempted to say. *Everything here is phony except the grass skirt and Comanche's tailbone.* But he didn't mention the tailbone because he didn't want to go through the motions of explaining it.

"You like Taj?" Bulldog asked.

"Very much. Sometimes I get little phrases in my mind and they spin around there, forever and forever, and it makes me think I might be crazy. Then I ask Mannie to play a Taj album—to bring me back to sanity."

"I met Taj at a party."

"Have you ever been in love?"

"Why, Joe! We hardly know one another!"

"I never have been—all my life. Until the last few days. Now I'm falling in love with every woman I see."

"Once you acquire the habit of falling in love you will find it happens quite often and means less and less. But I'll bet you didn't fall in love with Phoebe—"

"Lucky for me I got out of her house when I did. I was verging on the verge." *I'm a virgin. No. I'm not going to tell anyone else! It sounds phony, coming from an old man like me.*

"Good tea, Joe. Who are your interesting friends?"

"First you'll meet the Englishman. The boat's at his house."

They finished their tea and struck out down the hill toward town. *Mutt and Jeff*, Joe thought, *but which was the short one, Mutt or Jeff?* He decided to ask Bulldog no trivial questions. He cut down his pace, nevertheless it was hard for Bulldog to keep up. They walked through town and stopped on the bridge overlooking the dam. "This was a natural waterfall in the old days," Joe said. "It was harnessed for power—to run a barbed-wire factory and a flour mill. And there was a windmill back up the hill, to grind wheat."

"Uh huh."

Bulldog wasn't interested in windmills.

"There are holes washed out along the foot of the dam there. That's where we'll look for the man's body."

Bulldog nodded. A truck passed close beside them and Joe cautioned, "Hold onto your hat. I lost a good fedora here."

They crossed the bridge and walked to Graham and Pinkie's place. The Ford car wasn't there so Joe assumed Graham had gone to pick Pinkie up from work. He and Bulldog sat on their porch.

"I'm a writer," Bulldog said, swinging his feet.

"I know."

"Have you read anything of mine?"

"No."

"Do you want to?"

Joe was slow to reply. Finally he said, "Of course, but later. I wouldn't want to read it at a time when you knew I was reading it."

"What does Graham do?"

"He's looking for work. I think he should get a job in a bookstore. British accents sound good in bookstores. Let's get the boat ready." He unlocked the shop and put paddles into the boat along with the life jackets, the gas can, and Everett's heavily-weighted snag line. Bulldog took an interest in the snag line. Joe said, "Highly illegal, for catfish. But we're not after catfish."

"Is this going to be an act of love?" There was a note of playful sarcasm in Bulldog's voice.

Joe turned sharply to face him. "It's something I have to do!" he snapped. "I know where the holes are. Nobody else does, except my brother, and he's in Vegas!"

Bulldog smiled. A film of sweat glistened on his forehead. Joe thought, *Need a drink, eh? Now you're getting something to write about!*

"You know the holes because you fish them illegally?"

Joe nodded. "I have a drop of outlaw blood. I could be a thief, if I set my heart to it."

Graham and Pinkie arrived and parked beside their house. Joe introduced his companion as Mr. Bulldog Drummond, and they took it in stride. Joe said, "I forgot your suit, Graham. I'll bring it tomorrow."

"Let's get it this evening, please. I have an employment interview in the morning."

"Where?"

Graham cut his eyes self-consciously at Bulldog and said softly, "The dogfood factory."

"I'll buy you a new suit. Swap it for the old one?"

Graham shook his head. "I'd rather have the old one. It's my wedding suit."

Pinkie had gone into her house. She reappeared at the side door to beckon Joe. He went to the door and she pulled him inside, slipping her arms around his waist, hugging him up close. "Darling," she said. "Such a sweet man! You are a four-star, All-American aphrodisiac! One evening with you. Five martinis. And something absolutely wonderful happened!"

"What?"

"I got a bun in the oven, Joe! Thanks!"

"I didn't do anything."

"Oh, Joe, you did. You did." She pulled his face down and gave him a warm kiss full on the mouth. *I'm having another date, and it's nothing like the first one!* Joe thought about the possibility of Graham catching him in Pinkie's arms. He pushed her away gently, opened the side door, and stumbled out into the glow of twilight, spinning.

Graham was a totally different man than he'd been the day before. He took charge, ordering Bulldog around as if he were a seaman recruit. At the river he told Bulldog where to stand and how to hold the rope. He backed down the ramp until the trailer was submerged then tapped the brakes letting inertia carry the boat onto the muddy water where she floated like a lotus. While Graham drove up the ramp Joe remarked to Bulldog, "Nothing like a little encouragement, a job interview, to get a guy's spirits up, eh?"

Graham said, "I'll drive the boat this time, Joe. You get in the front. You get in the middle, Mr. Bulldog."

"Call me Bully Beef," the short man said. "*Boeuf-sur-le-Toit.* I can't believe we're going to sea with no grog." He got into the boat and sat where he was told.

"Go downstream," Joe said, "It's still too light for our purposes."

"What are our purposes?" Graham asked.

Bulldog, sitting primly like a good child, his knees together, leaned toward Graham to say, "We're going to do a bit of illegal fishing."

"Fishing, Joe?" Graham cranked the engine unsuccessfully. Joe told him how to prime it and count to twenty so it wouldn't flood. Graham finally got it started and motored away from the ramp. They met a boat coming in, having completed its search. Joe waved. He turned to tell Graham above the engine noise. "Take us downstream about a mile." But before they'd gone a mile, at a spot that caught his fancy, Joe said, "Okay! Stop! Take us to the bank." He threw a loop around a cottonwood root and the boat snubbed up in the current. "Here's what we're doing, Graham. I know some catfish holes up there. I doubt that anybody has checked them."

"Why all the secrecy?"

"If we go after dark we won't have to explain what we're doing. I've never had luck explaining myself to police. They make me nervous. Or I make them suspicious. I don't know exactly what happens, but it's never pleasant."

Bulldog snatched a frond of grass from the bank and chewed it farmer style. He gave Joe a penetrating look and asked, "Ever been in jail?"

"No."

"I have," Graham said. "There's a whole different society. Cigarettes are money. Friendship is fluid. And everybody wants out."

"What did you do?" Bulldog asked.

"In jail, or to get in jail?"

"Both."

"I was a bad boy. Thought I could steal without getting caught. Once I was in there—I learned bookkeeping. It was a very good opportunity for me."

Bulldog turned his attention to Joe and asked, "What's your plan?"

"We can't anchor at the dam, so I'll hold us in position with the engine. You'll be handling the snag line. When we are over a hole I'll tap Bulldog and Bulldog will tap you. Drop the snag straight down, right off the bow. Then pull it up in short jerks, about eight inches. We'll repeat that until we've searched all the holes."

"All right," Graham said, rehearsing Joe's instructions. A train moaned in the distance and the soft sound of water could be heard lapping the sides of the boat. Joe watched a flycatcher working from a twig. He remembered seeing this spot in the winter when the river was frozen.

"I lived in London several years," Bulldog remarked to Graham.

Graham nodded. "Now you live here?"

"Nooooooooooh. I live in New York."

"He's a writer," Joe explained. "Looking for material." He swept back his hair exposing his earhole. "Here's the New Yorker Bulldog sitting in the Kansas River with a one-eared American and an ex-con Englishman waiting for it to get dark so the police won't see us dragging the river! That should be something to write about!"

"Nah," Bulldog barked, "happens in New York every day."

To pass time I told Bulldog about the POW camp near where we sat. I described the rotting barracks buildings and the trees growing up through rusty army cots. The windowpanes had all been broken. That's where the *Deutsch* boys slept. It was an honor camp with no barbed wire, no guard towers, and the boys were sent out to work the wheat fields. In the evenings I visited them and tried to learn their language. *Kuck in der Küche für einen Kuchen.* I haven't gone there lately because it's a dead, sad place. Bulldog said he'd like to see it.

As I made my way to the stern Graham clamored forward and we met above Bulldog. The boat lurched. We grabbed one another like acrobats and danced awhile until things settled down. No doubt we would have amused anyone walking along the bank because we would have looked like a circus act: a little man crouched in a boat peering out from under his down-brimmed straw hat, the lenses of his glasses flashing merrily while two skinny guys, six-fivers, stood on each side of him holding one another's shoulders. It would have looked like

Graham and I were acrobats building a human tower for
Bulldog to climb and Bulldog was holding out for better wages.
That would be good. If we could get him standing on our
shoulders—if I could drive the boat with one foot—motoring
serenely up the river. Picture a tower like that! Picture the
skinny *Deutsch* boys sitting on the bank—our audience.

When he was seated in the bow Graham helped himself to
a cigar. He offered cigars to Bulldog and me, but we refused.
It delighted me to see him turn his back to us and light up, gray
smoke outlining his head against the water and weeds. *If only
he would wear a hat,* I thought, *he would look like an actor.*
"Lend him your hat, Bulldog. Don't you think it would be an
improvement?"

Bulldog, graceful, very much at ease in the boat, went
forward and pressed his hat firmly onto Graham's shaggy
crown. "Captain Geezre thinks you should wear this. It gives
us something interesting to look at."

Without turning, Graham acknowledged us with a cloud of
gray smoke. I wondered if English people gave cigars on the
birth of their children.

I remembered walking along the river trail in wintertime
with snow covering everything. The river was frozen. A tree
which had eroded into the river lay near the bank, submerged,
several of its roots sticking up through the sheet of ice which
was moving downstream slowly, almost imperceptibly. In fact
I wouldn't have known the ice was moving if I hadn't heard the
tree roots ripping it. After the ice ripped, tension would slowly
build again with the ice crust pushing the roots back, back,
back—like a catapult being cocked. The roots were strong and
flexible. Then inevitably came the moment when the ice could
no longer resist the strain—and it would rip again filling the air
with shards of flying ice. Ice chunks the size of my hand
skated across the frozen river to collide with pieces that had
been flung before them. They caromed off one another making
a pattern like ploughed ground—furrows and rows. *It was right
here where we're tied,* I thought, *this is where the roots were
shooting ice to Kingdom Come. I stood here an hour watching
the show.*

"What are you thinking about?" Bulldog asked me.

"Ice," I said. "Frozen water."

"Me too. In a glass with some gin."

Graham turned to tell Bulldog, "Don't go drinking with Joe. He doesn't know the meaning of moderation." He smiled, intending it as a compliment. *Call me a rummy and a ginsop too, what cares I for praise?*

"Okay, Men!" I tried to make my voice grim, like a commando leader. I primed the engine and counted, whispering, "Fire up, Baby!" as Graham untied the bow and fended us off the bank. He had obviously spent some time with boats. The engine started—to my relief—and I stood us out in the middle of the river and turned upstream. The sound of the engine was low. Night was falling. Bulldog's phosphorescent hat glowed in the half light, and Graham's dark hair hung menacingly beneath it. We could have been alligator poachers in a remote Louisiana parish—or a South American lake. Nobody on the bank would know who we were or what we were after. Bandits.

"If," Graham said, turning so his words would carry back to me, "just if—we happen to find the man's body. What's our plan?"

"Simple," I said. "We yell for the police."

"There won't be a problem for us then, being there?"

"Of course not. The river's public."

"In that case why are we being so damned secretive!"

"Because we *won't* find anything. It's only a notion I got in my head. It's easier for me to act on it than to forget it."

"Yes. But if you told it to the police you could go out in their boat and show them the places?" Graham wasn't being pushy, I could tell. He merely wanted to get the facts straight for his book.

"I'd rather be with you guys," I said. "Quite honestly, I'm acting like a kid. I've always been this way. I can't outgrow it."

Graham turned to nod. He gave me a tight smile. Maybe we're all kids when we go out in boats. It grew darker. There would be a glow at the dam from streetlights on the bridge. But downstream it was plenty dark.

"Can you see where you're going?"

"Well enough," I replied. "If we run aground we push off. If we hit the bank we bounce off. This is a safe river."

"Joe," Bulldog patted my knee. "It's my understanding we're looking for a man who's dead as the result of boating on this river. Is that correct?"

"Yeah, sure. But we're not going over the dam like he did. We're *below* the dam!"

"Just as long as you know what we're doing."

"I don't know what we're doing. But I know where we're going."

As we neared the dam I kept the commando motif in mind. Go in. Do the job. Get out. I used low throttle to hold the boat against the current. No water was coming over the dam. That meant the floodgates had been closed upstream. But water routed through the generators sluiced out making a nasty side current. I looked up at batterboards propped against the force of the river. They were as big as barn doors. If one broke loose it would smash us like snails. I maneuvered into position and tapped the dog. He passed the message, and Graham dropped the snag line. In the dim light I saw that he'd tied the end of it to his wrist.

"No!" I said. "Get it off your wrist!"

He turned a quizzical look at me.

"There's monster catfish in there! You don't want to be personally connected to one!"

He nodded, quickly untying the knot.

"Bulldog, that's a vision we'd never forget, eh, Graham dragged under by a killer fish. Your hat floating in his ripple. Write about that!"

"Don't worry about my writing, Joe. Just drive the boat!"

It was a job keeping the boat straight in the shifty current. But having handled her before for Everett—at night—I knew where the holes were relative to landmarks on the dam. I moved Graham from hole to hole. He patiently dropped the snag line many times.   Then I shut off the engine and we drifted out of there.

"Feel better, Joe? I mean, we went and looked."

"Yeah, I suppose."

Graham lit a fresh cigar.   Again he offered cigars to Bulldog and me. This time we accepted. Bulldog took his hat back. His hair was thin, so maybe the top of his head was getting chilly. We drifted sideways down the river, glowing our cheroots to amaze the heathens. We drifted past the boat ramp, which was marked by a street light, and Graham said, "How far are you planning to go?"

"Kansas City," I said.   "Then St. Louis.   On to New Orleans, if you want gumbo?"

There were no houses or lights.   No heathens.   In this stretch the river flowed wide and slow.   Stars were out. Except for us and the boat, the world was empty. The cigar smoke addled my brain. I heard owls hooting in the trees and beavers gnawing sticks on the banks, but I didn't feel obliged to give the boys a nature lecture.

"Start the engine and take me home, Joe. I have an interview tomorrow morning."

I primed the engine and asked, "What's the job?"

"Dunno. I'll do anything except taste it. I definitely will not work in the tasting division!" When he said that I saw by the glow of his cigar that he had deferred to Bulldog, like maybe he thought Bulldog ate dogfood.

I fussed with the engine several minutes before the cranky thing would start. We got Everett's boat locked up properly, and Pinkie was not to be seen. *Maybe she's already gone to bed,* I thought, *or maybe she's taking one of her marathon baths.* Graham gave Bulldog and me a ride back to Flattop so he could collect his jacket and trousers. Bulldog called Phoebe to come get him. He and I sat out on the redwood bench. He was middleaged, several years younger than me. We watched dents, and to me they seemed incredibly young. To them we were surplus men sitting on a park bench. I wondered what Bulldog was thinking about, but I didn't ask. When Phoebe picked him up I knew she was full of questions, but I knew

Bulldog wouldn't be giving out any answers. I'd felt him clam up. He was ruminating, meditating, digesting the day's catch so he could put it in his book. I went into my place to make a cup of tea and read Rosealyn's letter.

———————————

Dear Uncle Joe,

Greetings from the Land Time Forgot! We are all fine. Hub wants to buy a fishing boat, a small one, so we'll fit in with the natives. I say what the heck, I've got curtains, you can have a boat. The kids are fine. They talk like they were born here. Maybe I do too, I can't hear myself! Thanks for the check. I used it to take them to the BIG CITY for pizza and a movie. I told them the whole day was a present from their Uncle Joe.

My usual passion for gardening has taken control and I've cultivated everything in sight. Now the pine trees are dumping yellow dust on it all. I trapped a black butterfly yesterday. A strange cat is hanging around our house. He is friends with Kitty. In this place one has no choice in pets or vegetation. Things persist or perish according to some larger scheme. This would be a good place to catalogue mushrooms. There are a thousand varieties in the "hollow" behind our house.

Last week, an overcast late afternoon, I heard horsehoofs outside and when I looked out it was a man sitting backwards, bareback, on a horse with big blue tassels on its ears, walking down the street. He had on a tophat. I watched him til he was out of sight and for some reason he made me think of you. I had to write and tell you. I transplanted a bunch of geraniums around the birdbath and some animal came up out of the ground and piled dirt all over them. It's like Mississippi is a place where they send you to find out if you can take it. I have fits and insist we move but only half-heartedly. I'm not so certain this animal

wouldn't follow us to San Francisco and dig up my
flowers there. When we first moved here it seemed I
was forever being pursued by a swarm of black flies.
Anymore it's simply bird calls. Keep an eye on Mom
and Dad for me. Write me quick. I need news from
the outside world. I need a vacation!

Love, Rosealyn

Joe made supper. He fried garlic in olive oil, pounded a
chicken breast flat, and swirled it in the skillet. He boiled
frozen corn from Everett's garden, then he opened a can of
cranberry sauce. He poured himself a large glass of milk. His
dinner carefully arranged at the counter, he pulled up a
barstool, tuned his radio to a jazz station, and stared at the
livingroom wondering what was needed to complete its
decoration. *Something red.* He thought about the bedrooms,
each of which was furnished with half a set of twin beds, and
he decided to invite Rosealyn. She would need some sort of
dresser in her bedroom. And he would buy himself a bathrobe
for her visit. Having a female guest, he couldn't continue to
walk around in his underwear. But he'd already accumulated
too many things. The bathroom was cluttered. He would
empty out the medicine cabinet to make room for Rosealyn's
necessities. Why would a man, wearing a tophat, riding
bareback backwards on a horse with blue tassels make her think
of him? There was only a mattress on the spare bed. He
needed a cover for it and some sheets, a pillow case, a pillow,
blankets and a bedspread. Where could a person find a nice
chenille? They sell them in the south. When you drive the
roads through red-clay cuts where the valleys are full of
sweetgums and the hills are fuzzy with pines you'll sometimes
come upon a raw wooden house with eight or ten chenille
bedspreads hung out for sale. *Fresh eggs for sale. Machine
quilting.* Maybe he could send Rosealyn money for one. He
remembered taking her on river walks when she was nine or
ten, when she claimed to be a dancer. She would run ahead on
the trail, stop, turn quickly, and run back as if that were
dancing or an exercise for dancers. She was never coy.

Whenever they came upon decayed animals she helped him pick them apart with sticks. *Like big chopsticks, see, Joe? We won't have to touch anything.* He showed her how the parts fitted together and he showed her the difference between stomach and intestines, liver and lungs—how muscles were attached to bones. They found a freshly killed gartersnake and sliced its belly open. *Snake guts!* she said, *yuckey!* They named the birds and trees. He didn't try to teach her the proper names but let her make up her own—*red bird, black bird, big duck, little duck, sticky tree, lacy tree.*

He wondered if Rosealyn had acquired the habit of watching television. Perhaps he could rent one, if she liked to watch it. *And what kind of food does she eat?* He sliced into the chicken and found it raw in the middle. He tossed it back for a second cooking. While he was standing he got paper to write his letter of invitation.

Dear Niece Rosealyn,

You needn't tell your mom you're here—for a few days. You can come to my place and relax and be anonymous. Walk. Tell me stories about Mississippi. I've fixed up the guest bedroom for you. Do you like television? I've made friends with the man down the hall, Professor Woolheater. He's an old-fashioned professor. By that I mean he's keen on explaining things. So if you have any biological questions I'll send you to him. And I'm attending a lot of films and lectures. There might be something interesting when you visit. As you probably know, Everett and May are off to Las Vegas. He has a new system to bet on blackjack. I hope he breaks the bank! Cowboy's still slinging Mexican hash, but it's not as good as it used to be. I think he takes it out of cans and heats it in a microwave. Speaking of microwaves— It seems I've become something of an aphrodisiac! I'll explain this when I see you. Do they still sell chenille bedspreads around the countryside? They did when I was through the south—twenty years ago. If so, do they make them locally or import them from Korea? If they are local made, and if you can ferret out this information, will they make designs to order? I'd really like a pair of chickens for twin beds. A rooster and a hen. If such a deal is possible let me know. I'll send money. I've seen a mother skunk and kittens around the outside of this apartment building (which is actually an aircraft carrier). You'll see when you visit. My supper (chicken breast *à la garlic*) is burning, so I'll sign off.

Love, Uncle Joe.

He washed dishes and tried to think of something red to put on the livingroom wall. He phoned Mary Thunder's number but got no answer. In the back of his mind he was thinking she might get him a big, bright Indian painting. He envisioned white tipis lit from inside with jaunty red handprints on them.

He fantasized the delightful prospect of taking Pinkie's baby for walks along the levee. He would buy a pram from the antique store. He would clean it up, give it a coat of black paint, oil the wheels, and tie some bright, dangling toys from the hood. *Boys are blue and girls are pink, so instead of painting the pram black I'll paint it pink or blue. I'll bet Pinkie has a girl. But I won't paint the darned thing pink until we see what she has.*

Joe was itchy. He paced his apartment, sore tempted to go see Pinkie. He phoned to ask for an invitation but got no answer. He pictured the phone ringing, and he wondered where she and Graham were. Then he remembered Pinkie saying she would quit smoking if she became pregnant. He remembered sitting in the chapel wishing she could get pregnant. He remembered her saying if she had a child she would want it to be born in England. He reviewed his knowledge of human reproduction and came up lacking, so he sauntered down the hall and knocked on Woolheater's door.

"Woolie, refresh me up on some biology?"

"Okay, Joe. This is Brazilian. Want a cup?"

Joe nodded, and Woolheater poured. His apartment was packed with mementos demonstrating what happens when a family's possessions are cooked down to fit into a retirement apartment. The walls were covered with photographs, diplomas, and children's certificates of achievement. Sandwiched between the certificates were Woolheater's various awards and between the awards were photographs of Woolheater's wife and children and ancestors. The livingroom was overloaded with Danish furniture. A large color television, the sound turned down, displayed stock market prices. On the counter were a six-slice toaster, a microwave oven, a blender, an electric coffee grinder, and a carved German breadbox with two kissing children on its lid. The radio, tuned to a classical station, played softly in the background. On other visits Woolheater showed Joe regiments of sterling silver, brigades of bone china, and armies of lead crystal. Woolheater's daughters and daughter-in-law were battling over the disposition of his wife's military treasures.

"Refresh you on what?"

"Human reproduction."

"Okay, Joe. I've read the literature, and I've had experience. Can you be specific with your question?"

"Is it possible for a woman to know when she's in the fertile part of her reproductive cycle?"

"Sure."

"Then—would she know, after coitus, say the next day, would she know if she'd gotten pregnant?"

"Indian woman, eh?"

"No, not Indian Woman! Englishwoman!"

"Ah, Joe. When you break out, you go East and West!"

"I haven't broken out. I'm merely asking for information."

"Is this why the detective was chasing you?"

Joe described his evening with Pinkie and Graham, including Pinkie's embrace the following morning. He repeated what she said when she hugged him.

"Sure, Joe. She knows. I don't know how she knows, but I wouldn't bet against her intuition. You're not in trouble, are you? I mean, there's no question of your being the father?"

"No. Of course not. Except I did pray for it."

"Then you must be proud of yourself, conjuring up this biological development."

"I'm afraid if she is pregnant she'll go back to England."

"Let her go and God bless her. How about a glass of Napoleon alongside that Brazilian?"

"Oh no, Woolie. I can't handle booze. Thanks for the info."

"Somehow I feel like I didn't tell you much."

Joe returned to his apartment for a jacket. He grabbed his flashlight in the hope of seeing skunks in the lilac bushes, then walked around the chapel, shining his light into the shrubbery. When he got to the chapel entrance he surprised Kimberly, who was leaving. "Hello, Kimberly," he said, shining the light so she would see his face in the darkness.

She stopped, pulled herself up straight, and stood still. She seemed frightened, as if she were considering whether or not she was, in fact, Kimberly. "I don't know you," she said.

"Remember? I waved to you from my apartment there, Flattop."

"Flattop?"

"Aircraft carrier. Apartments for retired faculty and staff."

"You're retired faculty?"

"Staff. Did Tara pay the phone bill?"

She shook her head. "There's been a misunderstanding. Turn that light off. At least take it off your face."

"It makes my nose big, doesn't it? Harsh light's unflattering. We can go in the chapel and sit down."

She shrugged. "Okay. But those benches aren't comfortable." She stood at the door, waiting for him to open it. He pulled the handpolished brass knob thinking, *She's of my generation. She knew I would open the door for her.* He followed her in. She sat on the last row and looked as if she wanted to cross her legs, but there wasn't room. He offered his hand saying, "Geezre. Joe Geezre." She held out her hand and he kissed it.

"Kimberly," she said, smiling. "You read my prayer?"

"Yes. Did Bob respond to the package?"

"Not yet."

"What's your last name, Kimberly?"

"Let's be informal. First names are enough."

"Do you remember me waving to you? You were walking up the hill, alongside the iron fence. You stopped for a breather, looked up, and our eyes met."

"Why were you shining the flashlight?"

"It's for skunks."

Kimberly glanced around the baseboards. She asked, "Do you write in the prayer book?"

"I haven't yet."

"Why not?"

"I'm afraid to. Saint Teresa said, or wrote, *More tears are shed over answered prayers than unanswered ones.* Of course that's a translation."

"Uh huh. She gives one pause— Tell me about Saint Teresa?"

"I can't. I got her books from the library, but I haven't had time to read them."

"But you have time to go out looking for skunks?"

"I was taking a walk. If I hadn't run into you I'd be across town by now. I'm quite a walker. Long legs."

"Do you know Melanie Moore?"

"She's a fruitbat. We haven't met, but we've exchanged squeaks."

"Tell me about her?"

"She's going to write a term paper about us old folks in Flattop."

"Why do you call the building Flattop?"

"Look at it sometime. It's flat on top."

"Why do you call Melanie a fruitbat?"

"Put out some apples, pears, bananas, and prunes. A few ripe peaches. Watch what she does! She a friend of yours?"

"She's my student. Really," the woman smiled, "I'm Paula Ramsay." She placed her fingertips softly on his wrist. "I'm a professor of psychology."

"Why did you sign your prayer Kimberly?"

"I didn't write that prayer.   I made a copy of it.   I've copied all these prayers to analyze them in terms of students' stress functions.   Then I'll write an article."

Her revelation made Joe uncomfortable.   He shifted his feet, realizing she'd asked him about Melanie Moore to verify that he lived in Flattop.   This crafty woman with the paper shoes wasn't as helpless as he'd thought.   "But," he asked, "don't you feel guilty, meddling with God?"

"God is free to do whatever It wants to do.   If I copy the prayers, how does that meddle?"

"I don't know.   It seems to."

"God, by definition, is meddle-proof."

"How?"

"It is all powerful, all knowing."

"Really?"

"Of course.   Are you a believer?"

"Probably not."

"So there.   You're as much a voyeur as I am.   Maybe more.   You've read the prayer book.   You've noticed its exhibitionistic tendencies.   All those entries aren't prayers. Lots of them are addressed to local people."

"Local rather than celestial?"

"Absolutely.   One hot Evangelist is using the prayer book as a dating exchange."

"What's wrong with that?"

"Nothing's wrong with it, Joe.   I don't make value judgments."

"Are you married? I mean, I'm single, myself. I was sort of wondering about you?"

"Five minutes ago you thought I was Kimberly, with Kimberly's multiple inane problems.   Now you want to start a courtship?"

"Are you?"

"No."

"I'm sixty-two."

Paula didn't reply.

"I'm a virgin."

Paula smiled.

Joe brandished his flashlight, "Let me walk you home?"

"I'm parked close."

"I'll walk you to your car."

"There's no need."

"Sometimes muggers lie behind the seat. You never see them."

"I always lock my car."

"Maybe he was in there when you locked it."

"Joe! For Crissakes!"

"Shsssst! Not in the church."

Paula got up, walked through the vestibule, and opened the heavy oak door for herself. She left the chapel with Joe beside her, shining his light in front of their feet. She went straight to her car, and her hand shook as she unlocked the door. When she opened it the interior light came on. Nevertheless, Joe used his flashlight to search behind the seat. "All okay," he said, "Nobody here."

"Thanks, Joe. You've managed to get me really scared!"

"Scared? I checked it out. It's safe."

She got in the car, slammed the door, and locked it. The window was up, so Joe couldn't tell her goodnight. He smiled, wig-wagging the light on his face. She reversed and he watched intently as she backed hard onto the curb, turned, and drove away. *She has a campus pass. That means she can park anywhere. So if she chose to walk up the hill she did it for exercise. If she wants to walk for exercise she needs better shoes.* He switched off the flashlight and hit his stride, eager for a brisk walk. As he rolled along he realized that Paula had the same mysterious thing Pinkie had. In her body. There was excitement. There was softness. Attraction. He walked with long strides knowing that every house he passed contained a phone book and Paula Ramsay's number was printed in each and every one of those books. *I'll send her some roses!* He looped north of the hospital, between it and the low-lying trailer park where a pack of dogs spotted him and followed at dog distance. He stooped, pretending to pick up rocks. The dogs stood their ground, stifflegged, barking, but they didn't follow him. *No. She wouldn't be in the phonebook. She*

*would have an unlisted number. Just as well. I never have any
luck with phones. Nobody's ever home when I call.*

When Joe got back to Flattop he tried Mary Thunder's
number. She answered. "Joe Geezre, remember?"

"Yeah, Joe. Sure. How you doing?"

"I want to talk about some art."

"Whose art?"

"I want to buy a picture for my apartment. Maybe you can
get me something?"

"Give me some idea what you like?"

"Something nice."

"Yeah. Nice. I'll bring you some slides sometime. You
got a projector?"

"No."

"Never mind. I know where I can steal one."

"When will you come?"

"Oh, Joe. Like, don't hold your breath. I'm
undependable. Were you telling the truth about that horse's
tailbone?"

"Yes."

"Well—I told my father about it. He's smart, my father.
College degree. He says the tailbone might be powerful. He
says he could do some good with it if he got his hands on it."

"Sure he could. It's strong medicine." He hung up and
pulled his tailbone out of the sofa. He put on a Taj Mahal
album and heated a cup of milk, tapping his leg with the
tailbone as if it were a riding crop, pretending to be Willie
Shoemaker. When he'd drunk the milk he turned out the lights
and lay on the sofa gripping the tailbone, hoping to dream a
vision. He slept, but when he awoke at midnight he
remembered no dreams. He undressed and went to bed.

4

The Haircut

I was awake when Woolie knocked, and I declined his
invitation because I was already in a hopped-up mood, feeling
like I'd had too much coffee. The air smelled of important
things happening—valuable time was passing—as I sat at my
phone table with a pen and paper to round up information. I
should tell Bulldog these tricks, if he wants to learn River City.
Call the reference desk at the library. Call city offices and
bounce around from one to another. Ask plenty of questions.
Call Mr. Man at the *Journal* to find out who's working the
beat. Call the information center on The Hill. Check the city
directory. Check Mr. Man at university archives. Walk.
Keep your eyes open. Talk to people on the street. Ask
questions. Read the free papers—the *Moon*—the want ads.
Hang out at the humane society to see what comes and goes.
Wash a sack of clothes at the Huge Man, carry it across town
and dry it at the Poor People's. When it's dry it's not heavy,
so take it to Jesus' Cleaners and dry it again. Have a brother
who's a shameless, nosy plumber. Ask more questions. Keep
your ears open. Carry political leaflets door-to-door. Help
somebody change a tire. Visit Madame Leontyne. Eat at the
nasty lunch counter. That's where I met Captain America who
showed me River City from the air—the sludge pits and the
salvage yards and the ball parks—the electric plant—the
dogfood factory—lovers' lane—cemeteries—everything. When

we flew over the chemical plant Captain America said, *That's where they make fertilizer. It's all chemical, no shit!* He laughed at his joke.

I located Paula Ramsay in the faculty-staff directory and memorized her address. I checked the city directory and, sure enough, she had no listing in it. *Unlisted number.* I knew where the judge lived. In the summer he likes to wear shorts, a Wolftrap teeshirt, running shoes, and a tennis visor. He and his wife play lawn darts. And they play croquet. I think that's nice. They never touch yard work. No trimming or mowing or raking, and especially no fertilizing. No shit. He maintains the dignity of being a judge. One night as I walked down his alley I saw him pacing his back yard, deep in thought. He's a man who thinks with his backbone. He was wearing his black robe and a white powdered wig. Scared the bejabbers out of me. I saw no instruments of torture, so he was probably benign, but it was too dark to be sure. He didn't see me, yet I felt scared and guilty, like a Peeping Tom.

I called Mr. Man at the *Journal* and requested information on the judge.

"What for," he asked. "What are you looking for?"

"He's an elected official. I voted for him last time. He's running again, so I want to see if he's doing a good job. Public trust and all that. Civic responsibility."

"You want my opinion?"

"That's why I called."

"I think he's doing a good job. Have you been on jury duty? That's the way to judge a judge."

"No. I try to get on juries but the attorneys never choose me. They think I'd be a problem. Y'know, corny or nitpicky or something. I ask them too many questions, but I can't help it. I'm a compulsive inquisitor."

"Well, the judge has an interesting case. You might go watch it. Form you own opinion. The case involves a business partnership in which there was some alleged embezzlement, an alleged death threat, and some alleged sleeping of one partner's alleged wife with the other alleged partner."

I thought about revealing to Mr. Man the fact that Detective Bradley told me to stay away from the judge. That would be a hot story. My civil liberties curtailed without due process. And what if the judge threw me out of his courtroom? *Habeas Corpus.* I'll bet I could beat that judge at croquet. I have a good eye and a steady hand. "Thanks," I said. "I'll go watch the trial. Maybe I'll write him up for the League of Women Voters."

I got dressed: thick socks, foot powder, dry shoes, and my captain's cap. I took my notebook, pencils, pens, chewing gum, and wristwatch. It was too early for a trial to be starting, so I cruised over to Madame Leontyne's place and caught her hanging clothes on the line. Preacher huffed along courting her fuzzy houseshoes. I sneaked up behind her and said with some authority, "It's a good thing you haven't put Preacher in the pot!"

She turned. Her hands were clean. She wore a red bandanna tied tight, the corners neatly tucked in. Preacher ran at me, defending her shoes. "Get back there, bird! I'll cassowary you!" I tucked up my arms like wings and got defensive, bending forward in my cockfighting stance.

"Joe Geezre! No refunds!"

"No?"

"I guess you want a quickie. Five minutes out at the clothesline. No tea, no cards, just some free questions?" She shook out a sheet, pinned one end, and ran it down the line. Then she pinned the other end and shook out the middle wrinkles. "Like, I have this friend who has this problem—"

"No. I came to check on Preacher. I'm the social worker from chicken welfare."

"You came here to rub it in about my wrong answer."

"Wrong answer?"

"I said Everett wouldn't win any money. Seems he got to Vegas about five o'clock, started playing blackjack, and won so much they ran him out of the casino."

I rocked back on my heels knowing Preacher would charge me if I let my guard down. "I don't suppose they let him keep the money?"

"Oh yeah. He retired. Gave me his sewer machine."

Preacher made a run at me, wings flapping. Madame Leontyne grabbed his leather thong. "Leave Joe alone," she scolded. "I guess I'll have to cut your spurs off. You could hurt somebody!" To me she said, "But with spurs he makes a good watchdog."

"Did Everett see Wayne Newton?"

"That's a question, Joe. No free questions! Want me to sic Preacher on you?"

"That's a question," I said leaping over the crisper drawer she'd set out as his water trough. "No free questions!"

"You're a screwball, Joe. Get off the property. Don't come back!"

She didn't mean it. I waved goodbye to Preacher and picked my way through her maze of parked cars. My brother was rich. I was happy. Everett could retire. He could buy his dream liquor store, sit on his butt, and smoke narcotic cigarillos. Preacher crowed. The old cock had a crush on Madame Leontyne's walkers.

I'd never been in a law enforcement building before, so it took me a while to find the right courtroom. The jail is in the same building. I wandered into a restricted area where a polite guard stepped square in my path. I knew my stringy hair irritated him, so I explained that I wore it long to hide my ears, only having the one. I could tell he had a good wisecrack on the tip of his tongue but was too professional to release it. I'd read his motto on the wall: River City Police—Firm But Fair. He turned me around and got me headed in the right direction. "The jail's that way, isn't it?" I asked, hooking my thumb like a hitchhiker.

"Yeah. But you don't want to go to jail, do you?"

"Maybe. What's for lunch?"

"Go to room twenty-one and fill out a form."

I rolled on past room twenty-one to the courtroom, picked an obscure seat in the corner, slumped down, pulled the cap over my eyes, and chewed gum. I opened my notebook and drew the chandelier, the flags, and the statue of Blind Justice. Twelve jurors filed in hesitantly, unsure of where they were supposed to sit. The bailiff came in, stood beside the bench, and said, *All rise!* I crouched up like a tall kid in school trying to look short. As the trial got underway I followed the testimony, but it wasn't the kind of story that interested me. The judge wrote notes to himself. Or maybe he was also drawing the chandelier, because he stared at it from time to time.

The trial rocked along until lunchtime and I'd pretty much made up my mind not to return after the lunch break. I was cruising down the hallway when the bailiff caught my elbow. "I'm the judge's bailiff," he said.

"Sure you are," I replied. "I saw you in the courtroom. You should grow a moustache."

"What?"

"A moustache. Go to the museum and check out photographs of city officials, turn of the century. There's an old bailiff who could be your grandpa. He has an enormous, sad, drooping moustache. Like a walrus."

"A moustache isn't in my job description."

"But," I said, warming to the notion, "the judge tries to look like a judge. The lawyers try to look rich. The plaintiff tries to look righteous. The defendant tries to look innocent. You might at least try to look like a bailiff."

"I *am* a bailiff! Come with me. The judge wants you in camera."

Walking beside the bailiff felt worse than being sent to the principal's office. We came to an anteroom between two locked doors and the bailiff stepped deftly behind me to pat me down, without any warning or permission. Then he used one of his many keys to unlock a door. He held it open for me. The judge, not wearing his robe, looked up when I entered. The bailiff stood firmly by the door. "Detective Bradley paid me a visit," I said.

"Oh?"

"He told me to keep away from you. But your courtroom is a public place. *A Certiorari!*"

"What's your interest here?"

"I thought I wanted to watch the trial."

"You *thought* you wanted to?"

"I'm not returning after lunch."

"Why not?"

"Because that defendant is guilty. You'll be able to figure that out."

"Oh? Why do you say he's guilty?"

"I went in his store once to buy a shirt. He had women working there, minimum wage. I could tell by the vulgar way he talked to them he would steal pennies off a dead man's eyes. He would sleep with his partner's wife, too, if he got the chance."

"Do you know anything material about this case?"

"Nope. This case interests me no *iota*. I came here to see you."

"Let's talk about that. Why do you want to see me?"

"Coincidence. Remember, we met at El Chico Cafe. I bought you and your charming wife drinks at the Palm Tree. Our paths seem destined to cross. Whoso Findeth Wisdom Findeth Life. I'm retired now, trying to find wisdom. You look like you have it."

"Oh." The judge's eyes softened, similar to the look on Phoebe Jones' face when I told her I liked her poems. Again I searched my heart to see if I was being truthful. Did I mean what I was saying, or was I merely buttering-up the judge? "What makes you think I have wisdom?"

"You've seen sixteen tons of human misery. Lust and greed and bickering. You've had to call the shots. You've been the parent to lots of childish adults."

"Let's say, for the sake of argument, I am wise. Then what?"

"I'll do you a favor sometime. Civic pride. I'll volunteer some of my time. Mow your grass."

"I appreciate your offer. What are you retired from?"

"Museum work. Preparator. The last thing I made was a couple of science kits for grade schools. Bones, bugs, rocks, fur—natural things the children can touch."

"I've seen you around town. You walk?"

"Nervous energy. And I don't have a car. So I walk wherever I go. I've often walked past your house."

"I know."

"If you ever need a croquet dummy I'll try to give you a decent game."

"Think you could, eh?"

"I said I'd try."

The judge looked at me brightly, as if he were a child who loved recess. He said, "This evening? Six o'clock?"

The bailiff rattled his key ring. I knew it was an unconscious tic he'd developed to irritate his wife. The judge offered his hand, and we shook. I made my way from the Bowels of Justice out into the sunlight of a beautiful spring day and spent a few minutes looking at a lump of sculpture beside the courthouse. *No taxes*, I thought, sneaking a free peek at the courthouse clock. *If I had a house or a car, I'd pay taxes here.* Then I checked out the sculpture again, but it didn't fire me up. The only sculpture that fires me up is Mr. Kabuki at the law building. Sometimes I eat lunch with him. He has angles like broken ice. He looks like he has a belly full of guts, like his muscles are securely connected to his bones.

I cruised across Massachusetts Street which is, of course, Main Street. The town was built by settlers from Massachusetts who laid it out so Massachusetts Street would terminate at the waterfall, a source of energy and an obstacle to navigation. Massachusetts Street and the navigable river coincide. A likely place to build a town. People used to be more logical than they are now.

Cruising on automatic pilot, I allowed it to take me where I was supposed to go. A place I'd never been before. I walked right in and sat down, delighted to try something new. I noticed lots of sweet smells, and I noticed the clatter. The radio was tuned to rock-and-roll. Of course I felt everyone's eyes on me. I picked up *House Beautiful* pretending to read an article until a trim woman finally came over and offered to help. I stood up and looked down at her. She was petite. "Yes," I said. "I'd like a consultation." She led the way to her chair, cranked it down to the low position, and gestured for me to sit. Beautiful eyes.

"If you don't mind," I said softly, "I'd prefer a private consultation?"

She thought about my request and said, "Sure." She led me to a supply closet in the back of Unisex, carrying her scissors and comb as if they were extensions to her hands. "Well," she said, "this should be private enough. Do you want a chair? I can bring you a folding chair?"

"No need." I took off my cap. "Let me explain my unique requirement. My hair is shaggy." I shook it to make it even shaggier. "I've noticed people staring at me. They stare at my hair. And this cap mashes it down. I think I'm beginning to look like a creep or something."

She nodded thoughtfully.

"I don't have a wife," I said, "or anybody else to advise me on personal details. I've recently been thinking, maybe my hair isn't right?"

"Yes," she said. "You're onto something. Why don't you let me cut it a bit shorter and style it. I'll smooth out the ends and give it some body. You should get a different kind of hat. Or no hat at all. You'd look good with no hat. Maybe a rough felt for when it's really cold. When it snows. Not a captain's cap. Definitely not a cap. Do you go to the football games?"

"Sometimes."

"Well, check the hats there. That's a good place to get ideas."

"Okay," I said, liking her firm approach. "But, there's something else—personal." I put my hand on her shoulder.

"Personal?" She backed a step away.

I lifted my hair and bent over to show her my missing ear. "See? I need to cover this up. That's why I wear long hair."

She tisked her tongue off her alveolar ridge in a way I hadn't heard in many years. She was a young woman, too. I wondered where she learned to tisk. Perhaps from her grandmother. She gnashed her scissors a few times—unconsciously—like a race driver revving his engine.

She put the end of her comb to her lips—deep in concentration. Then she said, "May I know your name?"

"Geezre. Joe Geezre."

"May I call you Joe?"

"Yes. Of course."

"Good. Call me Trish, Joe. This is bold. But you asked for a consultation, so that's what you'll get. Of course I'll start with a shampoo. And I'll want to match ph and get you on a good conditioner. I'll have to see you every week. Regular. I'm going to cut you off shorter. I'm going to darken you just a smidgen to give us some definition. And some body. I'm going to curl you under—like a pageboy. But just to the top of your ear here—and just across," she touched my head with the tip of her comb, "here! Like I say, it's bold."

"But that won't hide my earhole!"

"That's right, Joe. That's exactly right. Let's be bold. I promise you, when the hair is right the head will be right. A bit macho! Don't cover it up. Flaunt it! I know lots of guys who would go earless but they don't have the," lowering her voice to a husky, confidential register she put her face close to my earhole and said, "balls!" I suppose I flinched. She withdrew to a respectable distance and said, "Like getting a tattoo. Lots of people would get one, but they don't have the—"

"What's all this interest in tattoos?" I interrupted.

"People like to be naughty. I have one."

"Oh?" I scanned her arms.

She winked. "Intimate," she whispered.

I made the old familiar *tisk, tisk*, and said, "My brother has a stork tattoo."

"Stork, eh?"

"Yes. Standing on one leg holding a precious little bundle in its beak."

"Did it bring the precious bundle to your brother?"

"Seven times."

"See! Like crystals— Body marks are powerful. You have a wealth of power in this ear. Use it."

My gaze roamed the shelves where I counted eleven rolls of cheap white paper. There was a box of stool freshener. There was a mousetrap baited with peanut butter. There was a litre bottle of diet cola.

"Well?" she said. "What do you say to my proposal?"

"It would be bold," I said.

She patted my arm. "Trust me."

I trusted her to the chair in the public room where she tilted me back, mixed the hot and cold to perfection, and washed my head with expert hands. Firm but fair. I'd never felt such a wonderful sensation. It gave me lots of ideas. Then she straightened me up and started cutting. Perfume went up my nose. Someone changed the radio to the classical station. I half dozed. She patted me reassuringly and talked about her book of recipes. Between the acts she slipped out for a *cappuccino.* I was almost finished. As she combed me dry she leaned close and whispered into my earhole, "Leave that captain's hat where it is! I'll toss it in the trash. You don't need it. You are now one raunchy good-looking dude!" She gave out a deep-throated growl and her breath tickled me in a warm, interesting way.

As I paid the hefty tab she said, softly, "Only one pen in the pocket, Joe. A pocket full of pens is definitely not cool." I thanked her and wandered into the sunlight. My hair felt light and puffy, and my earhole was sensitive to the slightest breeze, even the breeze caused by my walking. At the corner I pulled a handful of pens and pencils from my shirt pocket and dropped them in a can. I began checking other men's shirts. If a man carried more than a pen/pencil set I found myself asking him, in my mind, *Why do you have all those spares and backups? Think you're on a desert island? Think there might be a pencil shortage? Gonna start writing your memoirs, Chicken Inspector?* And a dozen other snappy remarks. Trish had smarts. She was young and breezy and she groomed her sexuality out at arms' length where it could be enjoyed. She had hit my nail right on its head. Why carry around fifteen writing instruments? Why be insecure? Why not join the jaunty ones who say, "Gimme a light? You got the time? Got a pen on'ya?"

I decided to go through the middle of town and observe people's reactions. After a few blocks my step lightened and my spirit soared because I was getting gentle looks from strangers. *Money well spent* was the phrase that came into my mind. I played it over and over. *Money well spent.* I took myself to the Palm Tree, picked up a free paper, sat at the bar, and felt very much like a celebrity. Babe Ruth or Woodrow Wilson. *What's your grudge? Croquet with the judge. Money well spent. Pay the rent. On a dare. Cut my hair!* I winked at myself in the bar mirror, turning my head to the earless side, glancing at it casually. Not bad. It didn't look bad at all. In fact it looked quite respectable, like a Heidelberg duelling scar or an ear lost to frostbite during a polar expedition, a dash to the pole. I scanned the room to assure myself that my vanity went unobserved. That's when I spotted Paula Ramsay sitting alone at a table for two.

I touched the empty chair opposite her and moved it slightly before I spoke, indicating my desire to join her. She looked up. "Hi," I said. "Mind if I share your table?"

She didn't recognize me.

"Joe Geezre, remember?"

"Oh! Joe. Yes, of course."

Her *of course* sounded like of course she remembered me rather than *of course you may share my table.*

"Mind if I join you?"

"Uhm, sure. Why not?"

"Why not indeed." I pulled out the chair, careful not to jostle the table. "You didn't recognize me?"

"No."

"Have you been back to the chapel?"

"No."

I eased myself into the narrow space between the table and chair. I thought I caught a gypsy smile flirt across her lips.

"Did you find any skunks?" she asked.

"Only the two-legged variety. What are you having?"

"One of the specials. There are two. Fish and veal."

"You're having veal?"

"Yes. Do you think that's immoral?"

"No."

"You sounded critical."

"I didn't mean to."

"Ah," she said, sipping water, "you look different?"

I realized I'd been showing her my left side, my good ear. I shrugged, taking the silverware out of my napkin. The waiter came for my order and I said, "The special. Fish."

"Rice or potato?"

"Should be automatic," I said. "Rice with the fish, potato with the veal. Makes it easier on the cook."

"Well it's not that way. You can have your choice."

"Rice," I said. "Please." As I spoke to the waiter I turned my head so Paula would see my bad side. He jotted down my order and took off. "I had my hair cut by a woman. First time in sixty-two years."

She nodded.

"This is a dream come true, having lunch with you!"

"Oh, really?"

"Sure. I planned to ask for a date the next time I saw you. And if I didn't see you soon I was going to write a letter. Three-one-eight River Road, isn't it?"

She stared at me.

"How's that special?"

"So so."

"So. If I asked you for a date, would you accept? I don't have a car. We'd have to hoof it."

She looked at me thoughtfully and I knew she was thinking, *That's a coward's way of asking for a date. Built-in escape hatch.* She said, "I don't know. It depends on my plans. I might be busy."

"Are you usually busy?"

"Usually."

"What do you do besides write articles and teach?"

"I fly. I'm taking lessons."

"Soloed yet?"

"Oh yes."

"Do you know Captain America?"

"He's my instructor."

I drank some water to break the conversation and give her a chance to eat. I didn't want to make her talk so much her food got cold. I watched her sneak a couple of peeks at my ear. "I scared you, talking about a mugger in your backseat, didn't I?"

"You unnerved me."

"I'm sorry."

"Why did you do it?"

"I didn't mean to unnerve you. I realized after you drove away what had happened."

"It's easy to say you're sorry *now*. Why did you do it *then*? At night? When there were no people around?"

"I'm an old bachelor. I didn't realize talking about muggers would frighten you. Now I see how it looked. It looked like I was the mugger. I'm sorry. It seemed like a prudent thing to say, but it wasn't. How do you like my hairstyle?"

"It's nice," she said without looking.

"It's Unisex. One for all and all for one!"

She fidgeted.

"I hope you don't mind my barging in?"

"Certainly not."

The waiter brought my order and cleared up Paula's dishes. When he was gone I said, "Busy as you are with your job and learning to fly, I hope you'll find some time to walk with me."

"That might be nice. Where do you walk?"

"Everywhere." I tasted the fish. She eyed the dessert board. I made a bet she wouldn't allow herself any dessert. *Hunched up there in a little Cessna, chugging along at ninety miles an hour. That's no exercise.*

The waiter brought her check and asked if she wanted dessert. She firmly refused as she counted out his tip. I felt it in my bones that she didn't like me or my ear. It was goodbye forever. I remembered the girls in high school—at the dances. At the all-school picnic. She smiled insincerely and nodded.

"Happy trails," I said. "Whenever I see a shiny airplane I'll think it's you." As she walked out of the room I heard her thinking: *He knows my address. I'll put an extra lock on the door.* My fish was overcooked. I remembered seeing anti-veal ads in tony magazines. She'd no doubt seen the same ads. A photograph of a calf in a tiny pen. The caption read: *Veal Factory. This calf doesn't have room to turn around or lie down.* She was eating alone. She ordered the veal. If I hadn't showed up she would also have had Douglas County pie and coffee with cream and sugar. *She's an old bachelor just like me*, I thought. *Set in her ways.* I knew I'd made a bad impression. I paid for lunch and cruised out of the cafe, suspecting that my hole-revealing haircut was a harebrained idea. It certainly didn't impress Paula.

I let my feet do the walking and they took me to the river bridge where I leaned on the rail and watched two fire department boats working their way along opposite banks. The flow was still restricted. Water stood several feet below the top of the batterboards. Some freelance pornographer had drawn Fritz the Cat cartoons on the rail. I felt wind in my bad ear, but it was merely a tickle—something I would get used to. I crossed the bridge and walked the bicycle trail atop the levee, following it to my turn-off. I cut down to the fence, stepped over it, and tiptoed through a garden. Then I crossed the street at Everett's shop. Pinkie, dressed in her nurse's uniform, sat alone on her porch. The Ford was not in the driveway. I waved as I crossed her lawn, happy to see her. She sat in a brand new, cheap, aluminum folding chair. There was an identical one beside her. I chose to sit on the edge of the porch. "How's tricks?" I asked.

"What happened to your hair!"

"I got Unisexed. What do you think?"

She touched my bad ear. "My gawd, Joe, I didn't know about this. What happened?"

"Born that way. How about the haircut? What do you think?"

"Oh, Joe. I liked it long. Pardon me for saying so, but it looked sort of British. Especially when you wore Graham's trousers and jacket. You reminded me of an old boyfriend."

"Graham?"

"Someone else." She smiled mysteriously.

"Where is that chap?"

"He landed the dogfood job. He's a charmer, when he puts out effort."

"So he went for an interview and stayed to work?"

"They needed someone immediately."

"What's he doing?"

"He's around getting his papers in order. And his physical."

"But for the job, I mean. What's he doing?"

"Clerk. You know, counting boxes and filling out forms."

"Everett struck it rich in Las Vegas!"

"Oh my!" Pinkie was very pleased. I was gazing at Everett's shop, thinking he would sell it. Pinkie would have a new landlord.

"Why are you sitting here all dressed up?"

"Waiting for a taxi."

"I see. That will be a problem, won't it. One car, with you and Graham both working."

"I don't drive, so the taxi's fine for me." She leaned forward and looked me hard in the face. "Tell me about your ear."

"Everett got two ears. I got one. Roll of the dice."

"I distinctly see scars. Tell me?"

"It happened in the war. But it wasn't traumatic. No big deal."

"Tell me?"

"A Chinese shell landed close by. Took off my ear. Whizzzzzz. Within a day I was sewed up, ambulatory, walking all over the hospital ship. Remembering the sound of that Chinese shell, I strove to make myself useful. It was a navy ship, but all the medical people were army so I blended in, taking things here and there, helping load and unload patients. I prowled around wearing a big bandage over my ear. I hung out in her engine room, galley, gun batteries. I fell in love with her. I kissed her more than the sailors did."

"Why was that?"

"I'd heard Chinese bugles. They hadn't."

"And you didn't go back?"

"My unit sort of ceased to exist. On paper it was there, the same number. But none of the same people."

She put her fingertips on my earhole. "So what are you doing today, just taking a walk?"

I told her I had already visited my fortuneteller, visited the courthouse, and had lunch with a ladyfriend. She expressed interest in my ladyfriend, so I said, "A woman I met. A professor. It wasn't an arranged lunch. I happened to see her in the cafe and sat with her. We didn't hit it off."

"Hit it off— Did you want to?"

"She looks vulnerable, like she needs somebody."

"Ah, Joe. That's no way to select a sweetheart, because she looks vulnerable. She can probably fend for herself. You're now, I take it, between girlfriends?"

"She reminds me of you. Not her vulnerability. Her full-blown beauty."

"You flirt! Now I've gotten used to it, I must say— I like your hair. Do you crossdress?"

"What's that?"

"You know, wear women's clothes."

"No."

"Don't blush. Some men find a change pleasurable."

In a flash I remembered the pleasure of wearing Graham's clothes.

"Clothes are powerful, Joe. Hair is too. You dress down because you're tall. You try to blend in. But you could play it the other way. You could dress up."

"Huh?"

"Who bought that shocking blue outfit you wore to your retirement dinner?"

"I did. Nobody else buys my clothes."

Pinkie shifted in the aluminum chair and it squeaked. She wasn't tall enough for me to wear her clothes, I thought, picturing myself in her nurse's uniform. The skirt would strike above my knees, like a mini-skirt. I was too skinny to fill out the bosom properly.

"That retirement suit's awful, Joe."

"Awful?"

"For you it is. Take me along when you go shopping. I can pick something that will turn a few heads."

"Let's go! I have a social opportunity tonight with the judge, and I don't have a thing to wear."

"The judge!"

"It's not as important as it sounds. He almost locked me up."

"Oh, I'd love to go shopping with you, but—" she shrugged, curling her wrists to point her fingers back at herself, at her uniform.

"Call in sick."

"Joe, I won't *lie* for you. A judge, eh? What's the occasion?"

"Croquet."

"Oh my gawd, Joe, you've got to get into some decent clothes! Look. Remember our stroll down Main Street, window shopping?"

"Massachusetts."

"Yes. Remember the men's store, the little college shop with ducks in the window?"

"Decoys. They had neckties around their necks. Pretty dumb, eh?"

"Go there, Joe. And don't ask prices. The mannequin in the window swinging the golf club, buy his suit and tell the clerk to pick you a shirt and tie to match. No hat. If they have to cuff the trousers or make a few alterations, tell them you'll wait. Don't ask the price for that either. If they act snooty, be firm. Oh, I *wish* I could go with you! Be firm, Joe. And it will be done."

"I remember that golfer," I said. "He had a terrible stance. I'm a pretty good golfer."

"You're not buying him, Joe. You're buying his suit. Trust me. And *don't* help the clerk pick the tie."

"What if he picks one with ducks on it?"

"Ducks would look good. Are those the best shoes you have, Joe?"

"These are wonderful shoes! They're Red Wings. I *know* shoes!"

She reached out to smooth my hair, lightly caressing it.

I turned and leaned against a porch post so I could see her in profile. She gripped her purse and stood. "The thing I like about this country is yellow taxis. See over there, creeping along looking at house numbers, already I know it's a taxi and it's coming for me." She walked down the steps and gave me a tight hug. "I love your hair, Darling. I really do. Buy that suit! Now Graham and I are both working there'll be money for skylarking. We'll go to Kansas City and eat at fancy places!"

It felt strange for her to kiss me in the front yard, in the daylight, with the taxi coming. It made me feel like part of the family—an uncle or a brother.

I came out of The Gigolo Shop with the suit in one hand, shirts and ties in the other. But it hadn't been easy. The golfer's suit was too small for me and Gigolo didn't have it in a larger size. I told him my girlfriend admired the golfer. He fitted me in a suit which he said was so close to the golfer's that my girlfriend wouldn't know the difference. I asked him to pick the shirts and ties. He thought my shoes were bad, and he sent me next door for shoes. He called the shoestore owner to tell him what style of Florsheims I wanted. *Okay*, I thought, *this is one way to buy clothes, don't ask the price and don't pick them out.* I remembered Trish saying, *Bold, bold, bold! You are now one raunchy good-looking dude!* After buying the shoes I had the suit and two packages to carry. I headed for Flattop thinking Pinkie and Trish and Gigolo were conspiring to get me a girlfriend. I knew I wouldn't be able to do much walking in the new shoes, but it wasn't far to the Judges' house—over on Windmill Hill. While I cruised up to Flattop a lot of thoughts dropped into my head. One was this. If I'd been wearing the new suit, new shoes, and new haircut last night at the chapel would Paula have been afraid of me? Then a bigger thought dropped in on top of that one. I didn't care what Paula thought of me. I tried to befriend her. I told her I was sorry. I didn't care if she ate veal. I didn't care because it was Pinkie who made me feel good. I wanted a friendly girlfriend, a sweet one like Pinkie.

I was balancing the packages on my left arm leaning them against my door for support while fumbling my key into the lock when Fruitbat swooped down the hallway, young and fresh and pretty and businesslike. "Mr. Geezre! I'm glad I caught you! I'm Melanie Moore."

"Here," I said, "hold one of these while I open up. The key's in the hole, but if I turn it the door swings open and they'll fall."

She took two boxes. I swung the door open. "C'mon in. I've got to hang up this suit before it wrinkles."

"New suit, eh?"

"Yes. Sit down."

I went into my bedroom and hung up the suit. The shirts were folded around stiffeners, pinned securely, and wrapped in cellophane. I left them on the bed with the gimcrack Florsheims, returned to my guest, put on the kettle, and asked her, "What are you trying to learn?"

"Knowledge for the sake of knowledge."

"Okay," I said. "When the water boils we'll have tea. Do you want to ask questions?"

"Yes."

"Shoot."

"Why did you decide to live in this apartment building?"

"I worked across the street, so I've known Flattop for years. I used to look over here and wonder what these people were up to. I guess I thought they had a game room with pinochle, maybe a movie theatre, a Great Books Discussion Group, a blood bank, a political action committee, a weight room, Jacuzzis, barber shop—I was outside looking in."

"And do you still feel like an outsider? *Vis-à-vis* the other tenants?"

"Absolutely! How did you know?"

She shrugged as if to say she knew many things.

I said, "Most of these people are frightened. Except for Woolheater down the hall, they all run from me."

Melanie opened her notebook and clicked her ballpoint pen, making the sound Paula made when she copied Kimberly's prayer. Students are influenced by their teachers. I wondered if Melanie went so far as to use Paula's brand of pen. She wrote and said, "You mentioned you'd lived here a short while. Maybe that's why you feel like an outsider?"

"No, it's not a question of how long I've lived here. I'm an extrovert. Pushy. I'm not a bit shy about meeting people, but the tone of this place is retrograde, very defensive. Why do you think that is?"

Melanie used her radar to hear my water. She said, "Your water's hot." Only a fruitbat could have picked up the sound, imperceptible to human ears, of water spitting inside a brass kettle. I went to make tea. "These people," she said around the kitchen divider, "are warm and open, to me. Everybody has given me tea or coffee. And cookies. A nice man offered me brandy."

That would be Woolheater, I thought. *Lecherous old goat!* "India or herbal?" I asked. She didn't answer, so I used one bag to make two cups. *Cookies!* I never buy cookies. *My pantry was empty.* *No cake. No pie. No licorice whips.* I opened a can of fruit cocktail and put it into bowls. "Milk or lemon?" I asked around the corner. She didn't reply, so I put milk and sugar alongside, the way Graham did. I put the tea and fruit on a tray and took it into the livingroom. She was gone. I would have seen her if she'd left the apartment, unless she flew out the window. I set the tray on the low table and stood there, twiddling my thumbs. She was in one of the bedrooms, the bathroom, or the closet. *She's obviously bat-hanging in the closet.* I heard the toilet flush. *Not a bit shy*, I thought. *Helped herself to the john.* I stirred my tea. She returned and picked up the thread. "But I'm not blinded by their hospitality. Oh, fruit cocktail! How nice! I'm an

authority figure to them. So they try to please me." Her hands
were dry.

I looked at my mother's bowls stained by sixty years of
blackberries and cream. The economy fruit cocktail had
yellowish grapes instead of red-dyed cherries. It had lots of
pears and peaches which had been diced green so they would
remain firm, tasteless, and pale. I heard suave Woolie asking
her, *Would you take a bit of brandy alongside that Brazilian?*
Napoleon?

"Mr. Geezre, when you get to know these people you
won't feel like an outsider." She spoke with the professional
warmth of an anchor.

"Would you read someone else's prayers?" I asked.

"What do you *mean*?"

"If people wrote their prayers in a book, and if that book
were in a public place, would you read it?"

She sipped tea and pointed toward the west. "The chapel?"
she asked.

"Yes."

She smiled, sliding back in my overstuffed chair.
Completely relaxed. "Is it white with black stripes or black
with white stripes?"

"It's fake," I said. "Pier 1."

"Joe, can you keep a secret?"

I nodded like a fool.

"My psych class has nine members. One of them invented
the prayer book. He passed his notebook around class and we
all wrote prayers in it. He put it in the chapel and told
Professor Ramsay it was there. She thinks it's real. Piltdown
Man. She'll publish an article about it. Don't ever tell."

"I know Professor Ramsay."

"Yes. She told me."

I wondered if Paula had told Melanie about my ear.
Melanie gave no indication of having noticed it. I felt vain. I
asked, "How will an article based on a bogus book contribute
to knowledge?"

"Who's to say prayers we wrote in mayhem are less
authentic than prayers other students wrote in the chapel?"

While trying to absorb that question I said, "But if she publishes the article, and if the prayer book is a hoax, that will make her look foolish."

Melanie gave me a wise, mischievous look.

I grinned and immediately regretted the grin, but I couldn't reverse it. It was a compromise. Melanie had tricked me into grinning with her, like a conspirator. She glanced at her watch. Her glance was cool and premeditated. "Oh! I'm late!" She scooped up her notebook, beamed me a dazzling smile, and flitted out the door. I wondered if she, like Miss America, put Vaseline on her teeth so her lips would spread easily into a sparkling, self-assured smile. She was gone. She used my john without asking, she hinted for batfood and left it untouched, and she drew me into a conspiracy. Quite a haul for fifteen minutes. But her greatest insult was that she had recorded a false version of me in her database. She had given me no opportunity to explain myself. I didn't trust her glib powers of observation to get me right because I'm not a glib man. I'm a complicated man. I phoned Paula Ramsay's office. "This is Joe Geezre, chap with one ear, your luncheon companion."

"Yes."

"Meet me in the chapel, Toots. I have something important to say."

"I'm very busy."

"It won't take a minute. And you can pick the time. Any time."

"I'm sorry, Joe."

"I'd rather tell you there. It would be appropriate." There was silence while I gave her time to reconsider. In the silence I thought, *It sounds like I'm planning to propose matrimony.*

Then she said, "I'm sorry. Joe. I don't have time to go to the chapel."

"Okay. I'll tell you on the phone. Don't publish anything about that prayer book. Your students wrote it."

"Did Melanie tell you that?"

I held my silence.

"Of course she did. Joe, I read those prayers as they evolved, from day to day, and I told my class about them. I asked the class to debate the question: What would be the difference if the book had been composed as a class project versus its being composed by a semi-anonymous group in the chapel? Classroom setting versus chapel setting. Group of peer students versus anonymous individuals, *etcetera*."

"Okay," I said. "Melanie lied. I thought it was fair to warn you."

"Thanks, Joe. Thanks for trying to protect me. But I'll muddle along taking care of myself."

I felt like a white willow limb floating down the river. A limb the beavers had gnawed the bark off. A nude, spongy, useless limb. I took the tray to the kitchen, washed the cups, and put stretch plastic over Melanie's fruit cocktail. I stuck it in the refrigerator thinking, *She knew all along she wasn't going to eat this stuff.* I unwrapped my new shirts and like any fussy bachelor I saved all the pins.

Geishas take short steps because their skirts are tight. I took short steps because my gizmo Florsheims were as hard as rocks under my feet, their thin, hard-leather soles hitting the sidewalk *clack* like dominoes and their leather tassels flipping up and down with my every step. I carried a bundle of hothouse daisies wrapped in green florists' paper. My shortened pace, new clothes, Unisex haircut, and handful of daisies made me a new person. None of the fruitbats recognized me as Walkman. To them I looked like an overdressed English professor on his way to teach *The Prelude*. I wore one pen, a good one, in my coat pocket, a quiet gray tie, and a new shirt itchy around the collar.

Mrs. Judge's dancing eyes told me my outfit was a hit. I passed muster. I bowed, handing her the daisies. Her entryway was parquet wood in diamonds with a white marble border and my leather soles clicked on the wood like tap shoes. The walls were panelled oak. I followed Mrs. Judge into a large room which had a cathedral-beamed ceiling and enormous

windows overlooking the back yard. A black piano hovered in
the room, floating like a manta ray. White rugs lay scattered
across the blue carpet. Chunks of coral. Hero, Mrs. Judge's
Pekinese, snorted and stood his ground, making me walk
around him as the judge and I shook hands. Judge made three
gins and tonics, put them on a tray, and carried them to the
rock garden. Mrs. Judge and I followed. She wore beige
trousers, a white blouse, and no bra. No sooner were we
seated than Hero scratched the screen wanting out. I've never
been able to get friendly with a Pekinese, but Hero stuck out
his tongue and grinned at me like he was willing. Mrs. Judge
opened the screen for him. He trotted past me to pee.

"Mr. Geezre, Judge tells me you've recently retired?"

"Yes. Quite recently."

"Are you finding enough to do—to occupy your time?"

"Nonstop."

Judge settled into his stony-faced courtroom pose and I
scrunched down in my chair trying to capture his somber tone.
Mrs. Judge asked, "What was your profession—before you
retired?"

"Ah," I uttered, feeling Hero's baleful stare directed at my
new Floor-shines, knowing then how Madame Leontyne's shoes
felt when Preacher scolded them for being shapeless and
unresponsive. "I was an exhibits technician. Something like
a window dresser. You've seen Gigolo's window? Duck
decoys wearing neckties, an adult male human mannequin
taking a golf swing— I made scenes for the museum of natural
history."

"There are some good ones in the museum. I go there
often."

"Thank you. I didn't do them all."

"So now you're retired—"

I wondered if she was in on the secret. Detective Bradley,
the bailiff, and the judge were. They knew I was the
suspicious character who had spooked the judge making him
fear me as the man in the crowd who would step forward and
plug him. *I'm your greatest fan, Judge! I love you! Bam!*
Or, *You gave the farm to my brother! Here's your probate,*

Crowbait! Bam! An ingrown guy like me recently evicted from his Gothic museum might go looking for a judge to kill. "Now that I'm retired? Well, I'm striving to crawl beyond the material, the pseudo-physical. I'm investigating Saint Teresa. Religious ecstacy. Mysticism. I want to fly."

"How delightful! Do you do psychedelics?"

Hero caught my eye, trying to stare me down. Judge pretended not to have heard what she said.

"I experimented with tequila."

"Mescal is the one that works. Tequila's for drunks who get high just yelling out the word: *tequila!* Sometimes I yell *tequila!*"

"Oh?"

"I can't sit still," she said. "I can't spend all day contemplating my navel. That's my question. How do you get outside the limitations of self?"

"I walk. You wouldn't believe it from these silly shoes, but I walk eight or ten miles a day." I saw her eyes flicker when she recognized me as Walkman. I pictured her contemplating her navel, sitting crosslegged, her breasts sweet and heavy like ripe peaches. She leaned over, snapped her fingers, and said, "Hero, here!"

Judge said, "Mr. Geezre and I are going to play a round. Care to join us?"

"No. I'll watch."

"You're welcome to join in."

"No, thanks."

Judge had laid out the course. His zoysia grass was freshly cut. There were no loose clippings. Undoubtedly it had been vacuumed. He invited me to inspect the course while he nipped into the potting shed and put on his golf shoes, so I walked across his lawn reading the green, feeling very much like a blue-tailed fly in the land of leaping spiders. Judge, of course, knew the lay of his land like the back of his hand. The spiked shoes wouldn't help his game. They were an intimidation factor. Psychological warfare. But I'm a scratch golfer on the green. I reached for an intimidator of my own by asking, "Want to play for anything?"

"Eh?"

"Make it interesting. Play for something?"

"Money?"

"Of course."

"Not legal in Kansas," he said, smiling. I knew then he would beat me for nothing. *Don't beat me, Boss! I didn't do nothing!* I saw how the cards fell, remembering the Red Lion. Mrs. Judge had by this time gotten Hero into her lap. She would sit and watch us. I—an excellent croquet player—would play well, but not well enough to win. Judge, having whupped me, would be able to relax and trust me. I've seen it hundreds of times. Children bond to one another. Make ties. But first they have to whip or be whupped. It's not far back to the wreck shop. The judge's paradise was connected to the Red Lion's web by a spider's thread, and people are more akin to arachnids than they like to admit. Everett knows the big-fish holes below the dam as well as Judge knows the mantraps under the daisies. I glanced at the patio and saw Mrs. Judge arranging my daisies in a crystal vaise, neck-deep in clear water. She would, no doubt, drop an aspirin in to keep them fresh.

We played a fine-textured game in which I was never absolutely for-certain sure why I was losing. Was I losing to win Judge's heart or was I losing because Judge made better shots? Was it his home advantage or was I hustling him, setting him up for a re-match? I couldn't tell. He whupped me. I apologized for not giving him a better game, but he was happy. He'd had all the game he wanted.

I thought we would sit around, sip on the gintonics, and talk about crocuses, but Hero needed walking. Like any dog, he wanted to walk the streets and trace his race. Mrs. Judge stifled a mock-yawn, so I said goodbye.

"Wait," Judge said. "Hero and I will keep you company."

"Sure," I said, hoping for some conversation. Two blocks with a Pekinese might take twenty minutes. Judge gave me the silent treatment. Hero strained at his leash. I wanted to ask Judge what he thought of my new suit, but that question would have been inappropriate. I wanted to talk about his fear that I was his assassin, but I knew better. I'd learned from my mugger chat with Paula that folks don't want to discuss their fears with the agent of those fears.

Hero pulled hard, constricting his windpipe. He wheezed. I checked the muscles in Judge's jaw and saw that he was relaxed. He was having fun, as long as I didn't ask questions. I held my silence as we hobbled along; me constrained by my nasty shoes; Hero constrained by his leash; Judge constrained by Hero. We three boys were bonded, struggling, and content with our lot.

When Joe returned to his apartment he promptly took off the new shoes, wiped them top and bottom with a damp cloth, and stowed them under his bunk. He had taken only a sip of the gin-and-tonic, but its taste lingered. He brushed his teeth. As he brushed he recounted his alcoholic experiences. After drinking tequila at El Chico Cafe he pressed the judge boisterously, causing him to abandon his lunch. After more tequila in the Pentimento he staggered to Madame Leontyne's salon where she, seeing his condition, put him to bed to sleep it off. After drinking martinis at the Palm Tree he went to the Judges' table and drunkenly introduced himself, kissing Mrs. Judge's hand. And after drinking orange juice vodka *mit* with Bulldog he pressed Phoebe Jones so far that she said, *Are you trying to piss me off?* He brushed, rinsed, brushed, rinsed, and said to the mirror, "You can't handle the sauce, Skipper. Better stick to tea and crumpets!"

He went into his kitchen to make himself a cup of tea, and he wrote on his memory pad, *Mannie, Check the possibility of getting good China tea. Crumpets.* He carried a myth from his boyhood that China tea was fortified with opium. *The original Coca-Cola had cocaine*, he thought, *every fruitbat knows that.* He remembered Mrs. Judge asking, *Do you do psychedelics?* Not take, swallow, smoke, injest, inject, absorb, use, resort to, employ, rely upon, but *do*. She had used the short, direct, druggy verb. He wondered where she learned it. Perhaps from public radio, trashy magazines, or bridge-party gossip. Perhaps she, herself, *did* drugs. Maybe she employed a physician pusher. Valium. Percodan. Stranger things have happened. He remembered her saying she contemplated her navel. Maybe she wore yellow silk pajamas, sat crosslegged, puffed a long pipe, intoned *hummm-ah, hummm-ah, hummm-ah,* and mentally followed the turns of her navel the way a sea spider crawls deeper and deeper into a shell. The phone rang. It was Bulldog saying, "Hi, Baby. Tell me all about your sweet self."

"I had my hair styled. It's bold. I bought a new suit. New shoes. I was interviewed by a fruitbat. I became entangled with a psychologist. I lost a croquet match to a judge. My brother broke the bank at Las Vegas. Now I'm shopping for opium tea. Got any?"

"Joe, don't talk so fast. I'd need a tape recorder—which I never use—to get everything you say."

"Okay, I'll speak slowly. What—have—you—been-doing?"

Bulldog replied, "I—called—Methusela—again—but—have—had—no—luck—arranging—an—interview."

"Why—do—you—want—to—interview—him?"

"Because, Joe, if I'm going to profile your town I need something catchy about your famous writer. He's a hook to hang the story on. Besides, he's famous for being interviewed. Everybody interviews him."

"I'll bet he tells them all the same things—"

"Of course. You wouldn't expect him to invent new stories for every kid journalist, wet behind the ears—"

"But you're not a kid, Bulldog. He's afraid you might chew his chitterlings."

"Nah. I'd take it easy on the old man."

"Okay. Let me suggest something. Why not be different? Why not observe him secretly, like a commando. Sneak in. Do what you're there to do. Sneak out. He'll never know he was hit."

"Great, Joe! I'll put you in charge of my disguise. Change my voice and make me tall!"

"It's possible. C'mon over and let's kick it around."

Bulldog sighed, picturing himself tall with a different voice. "I can't. Phoebe is having a do. I'm her centerpiece."

"*Do*, eh? Noun or verb?"

"Adverb, adjective, proposition, Baby. I'll think about your suggestion and give you a call. *Ciao!*"

"A chow," Joe said, as Bulldog's receiver clicked, "is one mean breed of canine!" He added a rousing growl and bark. He wondered how Graham had fared on his first day at the dogfood factory. He remembered Pinkie's face. *One thing about booze; it gets the job done. If I were crocked I could stagger to the chapel, kneel down, press my palms together, and say, Dear Lord, I pray that Pinkie grow increasingly heavy with child. Amen.* He poured scalding water on a once-used teabag. He said aloud, "There! I thought a prayer all the way through!" He heard a soft knock.

Joe, fearing a Heavenly Guest, opened his door cautiously. When he saw Mary Thunder he relaxed and swung it wide. A man stood beside her. Mary held a case which was obviously heavy. The man carried a large, fringed leather bag over his shoulder. The leather was smooth, almost white, and Joe recognized it as natural buckskin.

"Hello, Joe. I brought some Indian pictures." Mary came into the apartment and set her case on the floor. It wasn't her treasury of silver, bone, and turquoise. It was a slide projector. "I'd like you to meet my father."

Joe gestured the man inside and closed the door. "Tea?" he asked.

"Coffee," Mary's father said. "Strong."

"Make yourselves at home. Be right back," Joe skipped down the hall to knock on Woolheater's door. "Woolie! I have some guests who require strong coffee. Would you brew a stout pot?"

"How stout?"

"Remember buffalo nickels? Make it thick enough to float one." Joe knew what had reminded him of buffalo nickels. Mary's father's nose. The man wore a blue pinstripe suit, a white shirt with a frayed collar, a red necktie, and no braids, beads or feathers. But his face, like the face on the nickels, was unmistakably Indian.

"Good! I've been craving dangerous coffee. You can die from too much caution."

Joe said, "Bring it down when it's ready. You'll like these people."

"Who are they?"

"Native Americans. Woman and her father. Observe their genetic traits."

When Joe opened his door he caught the man staring contemptuously at his zebra skin. Mary had taken the projector from its case and was assembling it on the coffee table. She aimed at the wall of the bedroom, exactly where Joe wanted to put something red. Joe said, "My friend down the hall is making coffee. It won't take long."

Mary asked, "Does your friend buy art?"

In his ignorance Joe said, "Yes."

"Good. I'll hold the slide show. Maybe she'll buy something."

"My coffee-maker isn't a she. He's a wooly old ram."

"Ah." Mary brightened. She liked the idea of being the only woman in the group. "My father's name is Joe too."

"Joe Thunder," the man said, extending his hand.

Joe shook with him and said, "But surely your Native American name isn't Joe?"

"Joe Thunder is my *legal* name. I don't go for this Native American crap."

"Oh—"

"We've been Indians for three hundred years. I like being named after Christopher's mistake better than I like being named after Amerigo Vespucci. All us Injuns know who we are. This Native American crap is one big joke. But Mary, she has to be Native American, see?"

"Yeah, Joe. I have to be Native American because it's the new way. Can I use the bathroom?"

Joe pointed. He was certain he'd left the lid up, but it couldn't be helped. "So," he said to her father, "it's okay with you if I call you Indian?"

"Sure, Joe. Makes me glow. Think of all those Indian treaties, those Indian reservations, the Great State of Indiana! You don't think they'll change Indiana to Native Americana, do you! They'd have to re-print the road maps!" He laughed, delighted with his observation. He winked at Joe and asked, "Know what a merkin is?"

Joe shook his head.

"A citizen of Amurika!" Joe Thunder laughed again. "You wouldn't want to be called a Native Merkin, would you? Mary has pictures. He fondly patted his leather pouch, "I have the *genuine* stuff right here."

"What's wrong with my zebra skin?"

"Wrong continent. And it isn't real."

"I *know* it's not *real*. That keeps the animals' rights people from cutting off my head."

"You could have some bad dreams with that ugly thing. Broken bones."

Joe unhooked the false skin and rolled it up. He stuffed it under the sofa.

"That's worse! Don't put it where you can't see it! Get rid of it!"

Joe tugged it out and took it to Woolheater's apartment. "Woolie," he said, "can I leave this here awhile?"

"Sure, Joe. You having the humane society in?"

"Don't ask. How's the coffee coming?"

"Two shakes of a lamb's tail."

"Bring it on down."

When Joe returned Indian Joe was closing the blinds against the twilight. Mary had plugged in the projector. She flashed a commercial slide of Mt. Rushmore on the wall and used it to focus.

"Thanks for getting that zebra out of here," Indian Joe said. "I appreciate it."

Mary, satisfied with the focus, turned off the machine. Woolheater discretely kicked the door and Joe opened it for him to bring in his coffee urn. Joe introduced Mary as *my Native American friend* and her father as *my Indian friend.* Woolheater took it in stride. He set down the urn saying, "I hope you folks like strong coffee. This stuff can walk and talk. It's out of diapers, off the teething ring. This stuff is adolescent!" Joe fetched cups, cream, and sugar. He turned off the lights and Mary showed slides. Joe remembered Madame Leontyne laying out her Temptation cards. With each card he'd been able to name the number and suite. But when she'd turned the cards over he couldn't bring himself to name the pictures on them. *Naked woman in chair drinking orange juice through a straw. Naked woman at the beach. Naked woman driving a Farmall tractor.* He stared at Mary's pictures of tipis, eagles, and Indians. Woolheater bravely attempted comments. "Ah, *that's* a nice one. Looks like a saucer flying through trees—what is it?"

"It's a hubcap. My brother painted it. He's wacky. He propped it up on some bricks and put straw in front of it. The hubcap came off a car. My grandmother's. She drove it to South Dakota every year. And the straw came out of a doll I had when I was a little girl. It was an Indian doll. I was an Indian girl."

"Uhm," Woolheater said. "Is it for sale?"

"Two hundred dollars."

"I'll buy it."

"No," Joe said. "That might be the one I want. Wait until we've seen them all."

"Bid the price up!" Mary said, giggling. She showed more slides. Joe chose a stalk of red hollyhocks for himself. Woolheater got the hubcap. Joe and Woolheater gave Mary checks, and Indian Joe poured more of Woolheater's oily black coffee.

Mary unplugged the projector, rolled the cord efficiently, and packed the machine away. Woolheater, captivated by Mary and her father, asked, "What's in the bag?"

"It's in the bag! It's in the bag!" Indian Joe chortled. "You want to see?"

"Sure."

"Well—sure. It's all ritual stuff. I'll perform an Indian ritual to seal the deal."

"Okay."

He took from his bag and unfolded an extremely thin, tightly woven Navajo rug. Joe didn't say so, but he thought, *That's exactly what I want to hang where the zebra skin was!* Indian Joe spread the rug and Mary sat on a corner, gesturing for Joe and Woolheater to join her. Indian Joe took a white-painted buffalo skull from the bag and placed it in the middle of the rug. He sat on the remaining corner and took out a stone pipe, the kind of pipe Joe had displayed in the museum opposite Custer's stuffed horse. He filled the pipe with tobacco saying, "Native grown tobacco. Very powerful. Like your coffee," he nodded an acknowledgement to Woolheater, "very strong. Very good."

Woolheater shrugged as if to say *It's nothing!*

Mary produced the BiC lighter and squeezed a flame out of it. She held the flame to the bowl while her father puffed. When the pipe fogged Indian Joe whispered a few words in his language and handed it to Joe. "Just take some smoke, say in your heart the truth, and give the pipe to Mary."

"Uhm," Joe grunted, holding back a cough. *May there be no smallpox in your bedroll*—he thought. He handed the pipe to Mary.

"That's a prayer, y'know," Mary said, "old Indians like my father, that's the way they pray."

So, Joe thought, *in the last hour I've prayed twice. And I prayed when the Chinese shot off my ear and I prayed when the fruitbat shot me in the earhole.* Mary smoked and handed the pipe to Woolheater. Indian Joe arranged bundles and pouches on the rug, but he didn't open them. The pipe made its way around the square again. No one spoke. A serene spirit, like a green owl, floated above them. Joe coveted his new picture. In his mind the dark shaft of hollyhocks became an Indian war lance festooned with bright red tassels, thrust into the ground. He looked at Mary thinking the skin across her cheeks was wonderfully smooth and tight. Her face would make a nice picture. Indian Joe said, "Mary tells me you have bones of Custer's horse—"

"Tailbone."

"The Indians left Yellowhair's horse alive because they were afraid to kill him. Some power he had. His tailbone still has that power, if it's authentic."

"It's authentic. No question," Joe said.

"How do you know?"

"Yeah," Woolheater said, "how can you prove it?"

"I was there," Joe said, "when the taxidermist repaired the horse. I saw him take it out and throw it in the trash. He said he didn't want it. Said he could do a better job with an iron rod."

"Yeah," Woolheater said, "But how do you know it was the *original* tailbone?"

"Because that's all history! Dyche rode the train to Ft. Riley. He skinned the dead horse, brought back the bones and the skin. Why would he put in a ringer tailbone when he had the real tailbone at hand?"

"May I see this object?" Indian Joe said.

Joe pulled it from the crack between the sofa cushions and handed it to him. He examined it closely. Then he asked, "You would smoke the pipe it's authentic?"

"You bet! It's Comanche's tailbone. But Comanche wasn't Custer's horse. Comanche belonged to Captain Keogh."

"Uhmmm—" He fondled the tailbone. "I won't harm it in any way," he said, "if you'll allow me to examine it privately?"

"You mean alone?" Joe asked.

"Yes."

"Sure. Take it in the spare bedroom." Joe ushered his guest to the bedroom. Indian Joe closed the door.

"Well," Mary said, putting her father's objects back into his bag, "he's so excited he forgot this stuff. He'll need it." She took the bag to him. "He'll be in there a couple of hours. What he did here was white man's ceremony. What he's doing in there is Indian stuff. We might as well send out for pizza."

"Quite an encounter," Woolheater said. "It's the meeting of two different worlds."

"No," Mary said, "it's all the same crazy world. My father went to college and got a master's in linguistics. I'm a high-school dropout. Crazy. Kick off your moccasins and relax. C'mon guys! Off with shoes!"

Joe and Woolheater obeyed.

"Does your door lock when it's closed?" Mary asked.

"Yes. Why?"

"Because I'm gonna send up a few smoke signals. Okay?"

Woolheater grinned. He knew what she was saying.

Mary fished a wrinkled cigarette from deep in her pack of Salems. She lit it and puffed. Then she handed it to Joe. He smoked and handed it to Woolheater. Around and around it went until it was ash. Then Mary held out her braids. Woven into her left braid was a red ribbon. Woven into her right braid was a green ribbon. "See?" She held her braids out like wings and droned her engine, flying around the room, "I'm an airplane. That's right! Look up some night. Airplanes have a red light on the left, a green light on the right, just like me!"

"Yeah!"

"You got anything sweet to drink?" she asked, landing on the rug.

Joe felt as disarmed as he had when Melanie asked him for a cookie. "This is a health-food house," he said. "Nothing here but raisins and nuts. Hippie bread and tofu."

"I've got a bottle of brandy," Woolheater said.

"Yip! Yip! Yip!"

Woolheater went to get his brandy. Joe wondered if Mary had noticed his new hair style. His missing ear. He turned that side to her and pointed. "See this?"

"Yeah, Joe. Remember? You told me you didn't have no ear. No problem."

Woolheater returned with his bottle and three glasses.

"None for me," Joe said.

Mary and Woolheater drank shots. Joe dozed against the sofa. When Indian Joe finally came out of the bedroom he handed Joe the tailbone and thanked him. Joe, struggling to his feet, said, "It means infinitely more to you than it does to me. Keep it."

Indian Joe speared the bony wand into his deerskin pouch. "That's a good Navajo," Indian Joe said. "Put it where the zebra was. Non-verbal communication."

"Right," Joe said. "Absolutely!"

"C'mon, Mary. We gotta go."

Mary and Woolheater stood. She hefted the projector case.

"When will we get our pictures?" Woolheater asked.

She put down the case, opened it, picked out two slides, and held them to the light to make sure they were the right ones. She handed one to Woolheater and one to Joe. "You got 'em," she said.

Indian Joe opened the door. Mary followed him, lugging the case. "But Mary," Woolheater whimpered, "I mean, when are we going to get the real pictures?"

With a faraway patient look in her eyes Mary said, "'Splain life to him, Joe. How it is. How it really is."

5

Red Dress and Heels

Joe awoke to the drumming of a woodpecker on the window frame, not three feet from his head. He knew the woodpecker wasn't eating Flattop. It was broadcasting a mating call. Joe stood in the steamy shower trying to wash away the web of Mary Thunder's ceremonial smoke. He remembered Mrs. Judge asking, *Do you do drugs?* Now he could answer her, *Yes, Ma'am. An occasional spot of pot.* He dried his hair, fluffed it, and realized that Trish hadn't told him what kind of shampoo and conditioner to use. He wet his new hair until it stayed in place. He dressed, went into the kitchen to prepare breakfast, and wrote on his memory pad: *buy a bathrobe, buy shampoo and conditioner, write Judge thankyou note for croquet.* He was eating breakfast when Woolheater knocked.

Woolheater declined tea. He sat opposite Joe, watched him eat, and said, "I've offered brandy to lots of girls, Joe, but she's the first to accept. She's a honey."

"Mary?"

"Yes!"

"You've got a crush on Mary?"

"Joe, I never met such a fascinating woman. *I'm like an airplane, red on one side, green on the other!*"

"Maybe she's horny."

Woolheater bristled. "What the hell does that mean?"

"Well— Y'know— It's a common phrase."

"What's come over you, Mr. Geezre? One day you're asking dumb questions about human reproduction, the next day you're telling *me* about women."

"What would your children say if you hooked up with an Indian woman half your age?"

"Native American."

"Native American? They'd say *Native American*?"

"They wouldn't have a say, Joe. What do you think of that?"

"Profound."

"What did Mary mean, *Tell him the way life really is?*"

Joe put his plate in the sink and drew hot water. "She doesn't have any pictures."

"Really?"

"It's like that with Indians, Woolie. All they have is postcards—*Scenes from the Black Hills*. That's what makes Mary unreliable. That's why she drifts like a leaf on the water."

"What kind of leaf?"

"Sycamore."

"Why, Joe?"

"Manifest destiny."

"So. Will we see her again?"

"I don't know." Joe knelt and patted the rug. "I traded Comanche's tailbone for this old Navajo. It might be important to her, important enough that she'll come back and look at it from time to time."

Woolheater rubbed his hands briskly. "I'm going to breakfast."

"Do you want that zebra skin?"

"Sure. My carseat's threadbare. I can use it to sit on." Woolheater left. Joe cleaned up his kitchen. He phoned Everett's house. May answered inviting him over. As he laced up his shoes he pictured Woolheater driving his Chrysler, bouncing along on the phony black-and-white. He remembered Indian Joe saying, *Broken bones*. He went to Woolheater's apartment. "I changed my mind, Woolie, give me the zebra."

Woolheater handed Joe the rolled bundle. Joe carried it down the hill, cut through the student slums, and dropped it into a trash bin. Then he thought about a fruitbat scavenging it. He took it from the bin, unrolled it, ripped it in half, and tossed it back. "There! I've done my duty. Drive a stake through its heart!"

With no bundle to carry, Joe hit his stride. He stopped at Unisex and got Trish's prescription for hair conditioner. He cruised across the bridge. There were no boats on the river, but two men walked the shoreline. He quickened his pace, eager to see Everett.

"They strongarmed me, Joe. Didn't want to let me to leave with the money."

"Why didn't you call the police?"

"The police were already there."

"Uhmmm— Did you see Wayne Newton?"

"Would you goddammit shut up about Wayne Newton! I go break the bank and all you care about is Wayne Newton!"

"So, they kept the money?"

"Hell no they didn't keep the money. I played poker till they looked the other way—then I took off."

"You ran like a turkey!"

"Damned right. We rented a car and drove back. Figured they'd look for us at the airport."

"Where's the money?"

"I banked it, Joe. I'll pay IRS their bite off the top. Then it's Easy Street."

"Is that what you'll call the liquor store? Easy Street?"

"Who said anything about a liquor store? I didn't get rich to go to work!"

May came in, sleepy-eyed, to join them and Joe saw that the long drive had taken its toll. "Congratulations, May. Did you have fun in Vegas?"

"I saw a vulgar show. Everett tell you they tried to rob us?"

"Yeah."

"I'll never go back, Joe. It's too crazy. You want eggs? What happened to your hair?"

"I had it modernized so I won't look shabby and embarrass my rich brother, who, by the way, put in a leaky water line. Ms. Jones called a *real* plumber to fix it!"

Everett recoiled. "After forty years of plumbing my last job leaked?" He banged the table and laughed hard. He slapped his thigh as tears ran down his cheeks. "Joe, you need any money? Hold out your hand. C'mon, Bro, don't be shy! Hold out your hand!"

"No. I've got all I need."

"After we fill up on cholesterol, caffeine, sugar and salt, what else can we do on such a fine day? Smoke cigars? What do rich people do?"

Joe scratched his head. He heard May cracking eggs against the rim of a stainless steel bowl. He thought about Madame Leontyne, picturing her in a red bandanna, tight blue dress, and red lipstick—cranking a snake of sewer rod down someone's clogged drain. He thought about Mrs. Judge dressed in a warmup suit sitting crosslegged, her eyes closed, contemplating her navel to a Dylan tape. *Peaches.* He saw Mary Thunder flogging a Greyhound across Nevada and Paula Ramsay lecturing her class of psychology students, *ergo ego*, and Judge on his bench saying, *Overruled*, and Phoebe Jones in the sweat of composition biting the rubber off a yellow pencil. "Well—we could take out your boat and look for the man?"

"What's with you, Joe. Why do you keep looking for that man?"

"Because I was the last person to see him alive. I was on the bridge, right there above him. He looked up like he wanted to tell me something."

"Okay, Joe. After breakfast I'll take my line and check the holes."

"I already did."

———————

Pinkie heard them hooking the van to the boat trailer. She opened her side door. She wore a faded blue bathrobe. A sleep mask was pushed up on her forehead. "Joe! Hi."

"Hi." He waved.

"Graham wants to celebrate. But I don't get off until eight. I *can* get off at eight, if you want to?"

"Sure. Eight. That's great! Celebrate. How?"

"Dinner in Kansas City?"

Joe grinned.

"Did you buy that suit?"

"Yes I did."

"How does it look?"

"People don't laugh when they see me coming."

"Wear it tonight, Joe. Hey?"

"Yeah?"

"Call at eight-thirty. I'll tell you the plan." Pinkie withdrew.

Everett gave an appreciative whistle. "I see you've made a beachhead with the English."

"They're nice," Joe said. "Graham helped me search the river, so I took them to dinner."

Everett checked the gas can. He filled it before launching the boat. While Everett primed the engine Joe made himself comfortable on the middle seat. As they floated away from the ramp Everett said, "Four days and nobody's found him. That means he'll never be found."

"It won't hurt to look."

Everett turned downstream, pushing his boat faster than the current would have taken it. "I'll go down ten or twelve miles."

Joe nodded, understanding Everett's decision. Everett assumed the bloated body had risen and floated downstream. The day was warming. White egrets flew off sandbars as the boat approached them. Joe looked at the water and mused over Everett's good fortune. He thought about Everett's seven children. In his mind he named them, starting with Rosealyn. *The father of seven children can use a windfall. Windfall: a strong blow that knocks fruit to the ground. Good deal, unless you're a fruit*. The boat passed a neck of water trapping carp against the bank where they leaped and swirled, muddying the green water.

After an hour staring at water any notion of finding a dead man slipped from Joe's mind. His eyes were overpowered by the natural images of the river: glistening sunlight, driftwood, ribbed sandbars, the texture of eroded banks, lush vegetation, crayfish chimneys, birds, clouds, the changing wind. Everett shut off his engine. He lit a cigar and whistled through his teeth. He flexed his arm making the stork hop. They floated under a highway bridge. They floated past Hogtown Creek.

"What will you do with your money?"

"You didn't even ask how much I won."

"It's just a number. But I hope it's a big number."

The boat drifted, turning in the current.

"We're the only boat down here."

"Yeah."

"I'll set up college funds for the grandkids."

"Why did you give Madame Leontyne your Ridgid-Kollmann?"

"Did you want it?"

Joe made the sign of *certainly not*.

Everett smiled. "She's so full of crap, she needs it. You been talking to her?"

Joe nodded. "She showed me her bellybutton cards."

"She watches your eyes to see the ones you like. That way she knows which lies to tell you."

"If she lies, why do you pay her?"

"She doesn't lie. You *will* meet a woman. You *will* take a trip."

"I respect her Rhode Island red. He looks like he knows all there is to know."

"He doesn't know the edge of a knife."

"Does she have a daughter?"

Everett coughed and spit in the river. He said, "What can I do? I mean, what do you *do* all day long?"

"I cockadoodle do!" Joe flapped his wings.

"Well—I can't goof off. I'm too nervous."

"Buy some walking shoes."

Everett ignored Joe's remark. "So your goddamn water line broke, eh?"

"Nope. It was the cold line."

"Uhmmm. I've always heard a body floats after three days." Everett persuaded his engine to start. He turned in a large half-circle, lit a fresh cigarillo, and squinted against the glare.

"You can expand your garden. Plant more corn. Be a fulltime grandpa."

Everett nodded.

Joe felt the skin of his forehead beginning to burn. He knotted the corners of his handkerchief and wore it for a cap. The twins stared at the river, but they didn't merge. They were too close to understand one another. They didn't find what they were looking for.

When Joe got back to Flattop he opened his mailbox, took out a fat letter from Rosealyn, and hurried into his apartment. He hung out a don't disturb sign and made a pitcher of iced tea. Then he settled into the recliner and used his pocketknife to slice open the envelope.

Dear Joe,

Last night Bea Dean died. It is a ritual here, whenever somebody in the neighborhood dies, the others get together and send food. So I called Mrs. Mason to palaver on what to do. It was neighborhood opinion that because Bea Dean wouldn't speak to the rest of them but would talk to me it would be suitable for me to represent the rest of them in tending to the grieving family. Anyway it was in this capacity that I got some insights into the mysteries of Bea Dean.

At Mrs. Mason's house Mrs. Mason and her sister, a leathery old blonde, rehashed tales of Bea Dean. How she came from a rough family where the men were wild and two of them were shot and killed in fights over gambling. How Bea Dean had a redheaded sister who used to dance by herself, up and down the town streets, embarrassing all the other women. How Bea Dean herself didn't like women but was always fast to embrace men, that she had nothing to do with the neighbor women, except for me, and I didn't really count being an "outsider." That her husband adored her but she was mean to him. True, before she got sick I would lean over the fence and visit with Bea Dean who was a sharp mouthed cat. Her husband would sort of flutter around her sweetly smiling at her naughty jokes and she would smoke and fume at him. He seemed to love her however nasty she was. Anyway they decided that poor Bea Dean had come from a hard life and it was no wonder she was ill tempered bearing such a burden of grief.

Mrs. Mason and I went out and bought some bar-be-que, white bread, and coconut cake to take to the house. This is the first time I had been in Bea Dean's house, as ours was a fence friendship.

The house was very small and packed with food. The family was all going to the funeral home, so I offered to keep the babies. I was alone with the babies and all that food. Bea Dean's room was lined with bookcases full of Avon bottles which she had collected. There was no dust on them. Because Bea Dean had been very ill for quite a while and couldn't have cleaned house and would allow nobody in the house, I can only guess that her husband kept them dusted. It's easy for me to see her in bed with her oxygen tank and him slowly dusting the Avon bottles.

The walls of the living room were decorated with family photographs. There was a picture of Bea Dean young and beautiful and a picture of a thinfaced longnecked woman with bushy hair. I wondered if this was the redheaded sister. On top of another low bookshelf sat a ceramic cat studded with multicolored marbles. When turned on, the lamplight made the marbles glow. The room was humble, hadn't been painted in years, dark and closed but somehow charming. As if, however grim, there was an aspect of vision to Bea Dean's taste, a certain quality of calm, an appreciation for little glowing marbles.

Later Mrs. Mason told me she had gone to the funeral home to see Bea Dean. She said Bea looked beautiful, forty years younger, and her hair was so lovely, everybody was amazed. I remembered the time Bea Dean said to me, "It's the silent sow that gets the slop." As if she knew that, in the end, however bad her family was, and contrary herself, she would be buried beautiful.

Love, Rosealyn

P.S.   Don't be surprised when I turn up like a stray cat on your doorstep. Hub has a few days vacation coming. He said he would stay home and play with the kids for me to get away. But *when* he can arrange to get the days is another matter. R.

Joe assumed Rosealyn hadn't had time to receive his invitation. If she did turn up like a stray cat he would be ready for her. He had her phone number. He could have called her, but he decided to let things run their course. If she came to River City she could easily find Flattop.

He went shopping for a bathrobe and bed furnishings. He hung Indian Joe's rug. He swept and dusted. He scrubbed the toilet. He bought milk and bread, cereal and fruit.

When Bulldog dropped in he caught Joe inking his courtroom sketch of Blind Justice. "What's that?" he asked.

"A thankyou card for the judge."

Bulldog sized it up, "Joe, you can draw!"

"Of course."

"You're talented! Got any gin yet?"

"No. How about some iced tea?"

"Icetea we called it in New Orleans. I'd love some."

"Lemon *mit?*" Joe poured Bulldog a glass. "Why are you on the prowl?"

"Research.   You said you'd help me get close to Methusela."

Joe carefully plugged the stopper into the ink bottle. "How do you like my new rug? I got rid of that zebra. Wrong continent."

"I said nothing, Joe, but zebras are nigger taste. Where'd you get this?"

"Indian powwow last night. Barter. Peace pipe. That sort of thing."

"Back to Methusela?"

"How's the icetea? Authentic?"

"Excellent, Joe. One of the best iceteas I've ever had. Back to the Old Man—"

"Okay. We start by asking why he avoids you. Tell me every reason you can think of."

"One. He has something to hide. Two. He fears I might be boring. Three. He's jealous of my success. Four. There's nothing in it for him."

Joe tapped his forehead. "Now you are getting down to the tacks made of brass. There's nothing in it for him! What's his nature?"

"He's a renegade. Iconoclast."

"Let's make him an offer. What do you have that he wants?"

Bulldog squeezed a wedge of lemon. He rolled his eyes, stared at the ceiling, wet his lips and flipped his hand to his cheek. "Big P might tempt old Crawdaddy out of his hole."

"Big P?"

Bulldog leaned forward and whispered, "I could put together a deal wherein he and I would interact pictorially. Photo op. Actually, Joe, I don't know how much this impacts upon you, but he and I are paddling back-to-back in the old literary canoe, and I have a bigger paddle."

"How's that?"

"Subject matter. Audience. Money. Everything."

"Robot."

"Huh?"

"Send in a robot. Not my original idea which was to disguise you as someone else— Like you say, your height— Voice— Too hard. He has defenses, right? What can we use to breach his defenses? A robot!" Joe pointed at himself.

"You?"

"My thoughts exactly."

"I could wire you, Joe."

"If he caught on, I'd be dead meat."

"A plugged nickel!" Bulldog liked his metaphor. "He'd beat you to a pulp with his walking stick!" He chuckled. "Right, Joe. You're tall as a tree, your voice is as deep as a well. He'd never guess you're me."

"Dogs! Methusela loves dogs! I'll tell him I represent River City Dogfood and I'll give him a lifetime supply if he'll endorse our product. Stands to reason a photogenic man will have photogenic dogs. I'll bring my cameraman."

"Who's your cameraman?"

"Graham. English accent for ink."

"Ink, Joe? To sign a contract!"

"Octopus ink. Graham will need a grip to send out for coffee and Joe's. You, Grip!"

"Me? I thought we decided—"

"Hippety-hop. Red wig. Elevator shoes—"

Bulldog pursed his lips, smiling. "I like this idea except for one little thing. It's too complicated."

Joe sipped tea.

"After dark, Joe. We go to his house carrying a wooden horse and a bottle of vodka. We knock on his door. We say we happened to be in the neighborhood, thought we'd be neighborly. Have a few drinks, break the ice. Tonight."

"Tonight I'm going to Kansas City."

"See? Nothing works with Methusela!"

"Make it up. You're a writer, just make it up."

"I can't *make it up*, Joe. It doesn't work like that."

"How does it work?"

"Everything I write is true. Deep down, it's all true." Bulldog stood, preparing to leave. "I'm famous for inventing the non-fiction novel. Most non-fiction is false, Joe. But the non-fiction *novel* is true. You can't invent the truth."

"That sounds like Zen."

Bulldog nodded. "There is that which is true and there is that which is *really* true. It's my job to point out the difference."

"Where are you going?"

"To get the accident report on your friend over the dam."

"Why?"

"He's part of the story. Maybe he has a wife. Children."

"That scares me, Bulldog. For some dumb reason that scares me."

"Why?"

"It's an invasion of his privacy."

"You tried to gouge his flesh with steel hooks—"

"But I don't want to know personal things about him."

"The name of the game, Joe. With a little digging I'll know why he went over the dam. He was awake. Alert. The water was swift, but calm. I'll find the answer."

It was a long time until eight-thirty, so Joe accompanied Bulldog out of Flattop. They parted at the chapel, each on his own mission. Joe headed west. He sailed to Judge's house, dropped the thank-you card in the mailbox, circled the golf course, and came home. He read Rosealyn's letter again. *It's the silent sow that gets the slop.* Then he showered, shaved, and dressed for dinner.

I brushed out my hair, put on the new suit, and wondered what the plan was. If Pinkie and Graham were picking me up I could wear my Florsheims, but if I walked to their place I would wear good shoes. At eight-thirty I phoned Pinkie. She was happy to hear from me, but then, with a hesitant tone, she said, "Joe, if it's not too much, could you walk over here?"

"Sure. I never mind walking."

"Good. Uhm— There's something a bit unusual. Promise you won't be shocked?"

"Okay."

"Graham can't drive. You don't mind driving, do you?"

"I can't drive. You'll have to."

"Oh," she said. "*I* certainly can't drive. I've tried it, but driving makes me nervous."

"Why can't Graham do it?"

"A long story. I'll put him on."

"Hullo, Joe. You won't mind driving my car?"

"I'd be happy to except for one thing, I've never driven a car in my life."

"All Americans drive!"

"All but me."

"Why not you?"

"I never learned."

"But you drove the boat?"

"That's because I learned how to drive a boat."

"The Ford's automatic. All you do is steer, press the gas feed, and brake."

"I don't have a license."

"Tush, Boy. One uses a driving license to cash checks. Mosey over here."

"Mosey?"

"Yes."

"Why don't *you* drive?"

"I've made reservations in your name at the Savoy. I'll pay the bill. We'll have plenty of those little martinis!"

"I'm not going to drink, Graham. I have bad brains for it."

"Not drink?"

"No. I'll watch you."

"Right. You're driving."

I laced on a pair of comfortable Red Wings, tucked the Florsheims under my arm, and struck out. The sky was cloudy and a strong southerly wind kicked the treetops. It would be full dark when I got to North River City. I was nervous about Graham's insistence that I drive, and I resented his bossing me. As I walked I grew more and more defensive about my automotive history. Everett began scheming to buy a car when we were fifteen. He and I saved our money, and when we were seventeen we bought one. We each paid half. The purpose of the car was to get girls and Everett tried to teach me to drive, but I was afraid I would wreck it. Subconsciously I didn't want to compete with my handsome brother in a game I was certain to lose. After a few months I sold him my half and managed to get along nicely afoot. I vowed never to drive. But on this day as I walked down the hill I marveled at how fast my life was changing. Against my will, I was becoming attracted to women. Against my will, I would drive a car to Kansas City.

When I got to South Park I waved to a wedding party at the bandstand. At Gigolo's window I paused to chat with the golfer. His feet were wrong. I told him to level his stance and get his head down. I asked him if he'd ever been to the Savoy. *Great seafood, Joe. Good bar. Good Bloody Marys.*

I walked on to the river bridge and paused at Fritz the Phallic Feline to stare at water running between the batterboards. I wondered if Bulldog had learned the drowned man's name. Surely he had. Bulldog knew his way around police stations. He had witnessed executions. While I stared at the water and listened to its hollow roar I thought about Bulldog bulldogging Methusela. That project seemed a vanity. Bulldog had been refused an interview. His pride was bruised. His bruises were paltry compared to those of the man who went over the dam. Then I realized I was thinking of the man as drowned. Previously I had told myself he would live until his body was found. But now I was thinking he was dead and his body would never be found. Funny how the mind works. Funny how life works. Who would believe a jakeleg plumber could go to Las Vegas and get rich? Madame Leontyne didn't. Would Bulldog put me in his River City book? Would he satirize my missing ear? Would he describe the awkward way I swing my arms when I walk? The fact that I'm a virgin? Everything human seemed at that moment to be nothing more than a colossal vanity. Comparing the living and the dead—the dead grow thin and the living grow vain. Could I drive Graham's car? I resolved to give it a try. I was vain enough for that. First the dead grow fat. Then they grow thin.

Their house was dark, except for a light glowing in the kitchen. The wooden porch rang beneath my feet, making my knock unnecessary. Pinkie opened the door. "Come in," she said, her voice thrilling me.

"It's dark in here," I said.

"Your eyes will adjust. What's in the box, chocolates?"

"My fancy shoes."

"Oh, goody! Come to the light. The suit looks super! You look *wonderful*, Joe. Here, I'll bring a chair for you." She put a straight chair where the light seeped in from the kitchen.

"Where's Graham?"

"Putting on his face." She brought a chair for herself. "Joe?"

"Yes."

"I mentioned cross dressing. Remember?"

"Yes," I said, struggling with a shoelace. Pinkie leaned over and gave me a warm kiss on the cheek. I felt as if I should compliment her on the dress, but I couldn't see much of it other than its color. It was blue. "Cross dressing?" I said.

"Yes."

"Graham is dressed up like a woman?"

"Give him five minutes. That's why we waited for dark, so the people across the street won't see him get in the car."

"Okay," I said, as if it were necessary for me to approve.

"And that's why he can't drive. Because of the heels. If he took them off he'd ruin his stockings."

"He's wearing high heels?"

"Yes."

"But he's six-five already?"

"Yes," she said in admiration. "He's quite tall when he gets dressed up!"

"Why?"

"Because he likes it. Joe, understand this. Graham's not a pansy. Not a bit. He merely likes to wear women's clothes and paint the town. You'll be our escort. He can't do the voice, so you'll have to order and pay the check. And the reservations are in your name. But he can do everything else. The makeup. The walk. I promise nobody will know."

"Did he shave his moustache?"

"Of course."

I had managed to get my fancy shoes tied. I set my good shoes together, by the wall, so nobody would trip on them.

"Now don't feel silly when you see him. He's himself. I mean, he's not *mental*. I'll go out, get in the backseat, and hold a cloth over the dome light. You'll drive, and Graham will sit beside you and tell you how to do it. All you do is steer."

"And start and stop. I have three things to do. Start, steer, stop. And *park*. I certainly can't park."

"You can, Joe. You can do it."

I heard the bathroom door open. That meant Graham was entering. I heard the sound of a tall man wearing high heels. He stood in the doorway. His dress was red. I stood up, as I'd been taught from childhood. "Graham?"

"What do you think, Joe?" He lifted his arms and turned. He held a small purse. "What do you think?" He towered above me.

"You look like a woman—"

"Thank you. Are you ready for the bright lights?" He sounded like a man, like himself.

"Graham, I really don't know how to drive."

"Don't worry. I'll talk you through it. It's turnpike all the way. Can you handle—" he indicated himself, "this?"

"No problem, Buddy. But the driving scares me." My heart raced. The idea of driving was tantalizing. If the trip had been cancelled at that moment I would have been keenly disappointed.

"Suitcase!" Pinkie said. "I'll get it." She went through the doorway, toward the bedroom.

"My male clothes," Graham said. "If we get in a pinch I can change back."

"Why?" I asked.

"Why go to the moon? Why work forty hours a week counting dogfood? It's difficult to explain. Does it bother you?"

"No," I said, wondering if it did. "I'm seeking wisdom. Whoso Findeth Wisdom Findeth Life."

"That's a darned good motto, Joe."

Pinkie returned carrying a small suitcase. "I'll take this," she said, "give me time to get in the car before you come out."

Graham and I crossed the dark porch and I held his hand while he negotiated the steps, but I didn't open the car door for him. We got in the car and sat there a minute as if we were waiting for something to happen. Then Graham opened his purse and took out a key. He put it in the ignition. "The shifter's in park. So that's fine. That's the gas feed, that's the brake. Okay. Push the gas feed slightly, let it up, and turn the key."

I did as I was told. It took me a few minutes to get the feel of the accelerator and the engine speed. Graham switched on the headlights for me.

"Now. Put your foot on the brake, and move the shifter to R."

I did.

"Now touch the gas feed lightly, tap it, so she rolls back a few feet."

I did.

"Now turn the wheel. Turn the wheel. Now the brake. Now shifter to D. Now touch the gas feed. Now turn the wheel—"

We drove slowly onto the street. I circled the block three times, and Graham pronounced me fit for traffic. I drove along the busy street learning how to use the turn indicators. Then I made a nervous stop at the toll booth to pick up our ticket. From there we had clear sailing all the way to Kansas City. Graham sat close beside me, and I kept my eyes on the road. It seemed like Graham was a man sitting there. He talked just as he had talked before. He told us about his day at work.

Pinkie lounged on the back seat. I couldn't be sure from what I saw in the mirror, but it looked as if she had put her

feet up on the seat and was leaning against the door, half sitting
half lying. She looked extremely cozy and comfortable. She
had lowered the window about half an inch, and her cigarette
smoke, when she exhaled, rose like a gauze curtain flat and
smooth as it flowed out. She radiated contentment. She was
at ease cruising along with an ignorant driver and her husband
dressed like a woman. I didn't talk, but she and Graham kept
up a steady stream of chat in their routine way—with single
words—and grunts—as if I were deaf. I pretended to be their
chauffeur. Their man. But I wondered who I would be when
we got to the Savoy. I would pretend Pinkie was my date and
Graham was her sister. Our chaperone.

Graham said, "I can buy the product at discount."

"Maybe we'll get a pooch."

"What kind?"

"What kind, Joe?"

I relaxed, and the car slowed down. I had to remember to
keep my foot firm on the gas feed. I considered my reply, then
I said, "Go to the humane society for an old doggie that has
already chewed up someone else's furniture."

"Which dog?"

"Watchdog? Do you think we need a watchdog?"

"No. Don't get a dog that stands around and barks. I hate
barking dogs."

"That's because you walk. Why do you walk so much,
Joe?"

"I *told* you, I don't own a car. I don't even know how to
drive!"

"Pekinese," Pinkie said. "They're cute."

"Judges have a Pekinese named Hero," I said. And we
chatted like that and rolled along as if we'd been in the car
forever. I completely forgot that Graham was wearing a dress.
Then some time later I forgot that Graham was Graham. I
thought he was Pinkie's sister. I felt virile and protective, like
Preacher clucking over those fuzzy shoes.

Graham told me the street address of the restaurant but
he'd never been there so we had to drive around looking for it.
After we located it we had to find an easy place for me to park.

That meant a long walk with Graham in his heels and me in my tight Florsheims. Pinkie had better shoes than either of us. We walked through the warm night air breathing the smell of roasting coffee. "Gigi," Graham said. "Remember G for Graham."

"You're Gigi?"

"If you need to get my attention, say Gigi. We'll all read our menus. Pinkie and I will tell you what we want, and you'll order for us. If they have it, I'll get lobster. Plain steamed lobster. And a bottle of Liebfraumilch. A couple of martinis before. You select the appetizer, Joe."

The prospect of ordering dinner for him and Pinkie was more frightening to me than the prospect of learning to drive. I tried to hold his instructions in my head. "Run through it again," I said. "I've never eaten in a lobster place."

"Easy," Pinkie said. "We walk in. Tell the *maître d'* your name. He leads us to our table. When the waiter comes order three martinis."

"The Bloody Marys are especially good," I said. "But I'm not drinking. I'm driving."

"Okay. Fine. I'll tell you what to do. Graham can just sit there and look pretty."

Why not? I thought, *Who says he can't look pretty? Who says a plumber can't go to Las Vegas and get rich?* We played it straight and got seated. None of us had been there before, so we had a lot of historic things to look at in a place that was already old when Harry and Bess ate there. I ordered two Bloody Marys and an iced tea for myself. Graham and Pinkie gushed over the drinks.

"How did you know they were so good, Joe?"

"A golfer told me. Those guys know their booze."

"I'll say!"

No one at the other tables paid us any attention. I excused myself, wanting to wander around the large, crowded room so I could observe Graham from a distance. I did that, and from across the room he was very attractive. He wore a black wig, red lipstick, and a high, firm bosom. Pinkie was lighting a cigarette while Gigi stared at infinity as if she were bored.

Very tall and sophisticated. I could tell he was getting his money's worth. They didn't see me cross to the bar where I caught them in the mirror. It was interesting because they didn't know they were being watched. When they got up and went to the ladies' room all the men at the bar checked them out and waiters carrying trays of steaming food stepped aside. Gigi was so tall everyone admired her.

"Yes, Sir?" the bartender said, cocking a sly eyebrow at me.

"Nothing, thanks. I wanted to inspect the bar. It's historic, I assume?"

"Yes it is, Sir." His nametag said Thom.

"You make an excellent Bloody Mary, Thom."

"Thank you, Sir."

"How's your martini?"

"Oh, Sir. One man's martini is never another man's martini. How do you drink yours?"

"My lady friends are English. Think you could make martinis to their liking?"

"Tanqueray up, easy on the vermouth, two olives. I've never had an Englisher complain about that—"

"Good. Two of them." I watched him swing as gracefully as a caged orangutan. He knew exactly where all his things were and he worked with a flourish, dash, and twinkle. I remembered Red Lion slashing the air. This was a different world. Here was no special. Here were no free refills. No insult here. This was a suitable place to bring ladies. I paid the barman, stuffed a bill into his tips jar, and carefully worked my way back to our table, a martini in each hand, walking stiff and important like Cary Grant. I passed a table of randy conventioneers who stood making a ribald toast, and at the next table I found myself staring into the eyes of Mrs. Judge. She and Judge sat with another couple. She recognized me. I smiled. Having a full glass in each hand, I bowed like a gentleman.

"Captain Geezre!" she exclaimed, bringing her palms together in applause.

I smiled at my friends the Judges. Judge stood, and the man beside him stood also. "Captain Geezre, I'd like you to meet Judge and Mrs. Lebow," Judge said.

I set the martinis on their table and shook hands with Judge Lebow. Mrs. Lebow didn't offer her hand. I reached for Mrs. Judge's hand and kissed it. She managed to blush. "What a pleasant surprise," she said.

"How's Hero?"

"Hero is just peachy! Are you alone? Join us?"

"No," I said, picking up the drinks. "I'm with friends. They're English. I got Thom to make martinis to their taste."

"Ah. Two olives!"

"I can't hide that part of his recipe. But the rest is secret."

"Uhmm—they look wonderful."

"Nice meeting you," I bowed again and fled to our table wondering if there was a law against cross dressing. I wondered if there was a law against impersonating a ship's captain. I wondered if there was a law against a man going into a ladies' room. *Surely they have privacy stalls*, I thought. *Surely he won't be found out. He didn't go in there to pee.*

When my ladies returned I helped each with her chair and saw Judge staring at us. "Try these martinis," I said. "I had them special made. Remember the judge at the Palm Tree? He's here."

"Oh damn!" Graham said under his breath.

"Don't worry. He didn't get a good look at you."

Pinkie said, "Skip ordering, Joe. Let's go!"

"No," I said. "Don't beat feet. I'm buying you a platter of oysters on the half shell. They're a mild aphrodisiac. Don't worry. Mrs. Judge didn't remember me when I kissed her hand at the Palm Tree because she ignores people until the second meeting. That way she doesn't clog her head with useless information."

"She's looking straight at me!"

"Don't let it spoil our evening. What do you think of those martinis?"

Pinkie sipped. "Marvelous, Joe! The best I've ever tasted!"

"Oh damn!" Graham said. I followed his eyes to see Judge making his way to our table. As Judge approached he smiled at me affectionately. He'd whupped me, so we were tight. I stood up. Introductions were in order.

"Judge," I said, "I'd like you to meet my British friends, Pinkie and Gigi."

"Delighted to meet you," he said, smiling. "Captain Geezre, you were with British friends when I saw you at the Palm Tree. Quite the Anglophile, eh?"

I nodded. *Anglophile, Anglophobe? Which is which?*

"I've never managed to get a decent martini in this place. Tell me how you did it?"

Pinkie lifted her glass, sipped, and said, spreading her accent thick, "They are marvelous, Your Honor!"

"Okay," I said. "But don't tell anyone else. Tanqueray up, easy on the vermouth, two olives. Thom does the rest. It's all in the wrist. Go to the bar and deal with Thom directly. Never let a waiter get between you and the bartender." I winked.

"Thanks, Captain." Judge patted my shoulder. He hadn't an inkling that Gigi was Graham. I ordered oysters and steamed lobsters, which I'd never eaten before, but I figured I could take any animal apart. We had a marvelous time making jokes and cracking crustaceans. Pinkie and Gigi, as was their tradition, drank martinis for dessert. Then Gigi discreetly opened her little purse and slipped me a large bill. We made our way to the door. I paid the check. When we were safely on the street Pinkie said, "That's what I call a celebration!" She hugged me, and Graham gave me a great big, sisterly hug. "Can you handle the drive back, Joe?" she asked. I assured her I could. I oozed confidence. She stood waiting for me to unlock the car. "Good," she said, "because I want Gigi in the backseat with me!"

They got in the backseat and I rehearsed the starting procedure. A car had parked in front of me, so I had to reverse a bit in order to turn. Getting no help from the backseat, I fumbled my way through the dark streets until I stumbled onto the turnpike entrance. Then it was easy. I cruised along. The car ran well. I hoped she wouldn't have a blowout. All was quiet in the backseat. I stole a glance and saw Graham and Pinkie snuggled like sisters, cheek-to-cheek with their eyes closed. *That's good,* I thought. *The lipstick will muffle the noise.* I drove on like an experienced chauffeur, having fun despite the fact that while we ate lobsters I entertained the fantasy that on the way home Graham might sit in the backseat and let Pinkie ride up front with me.

I parked in their driveway and, although it was quite late, Pinkie took the precaution of holding the cloth over the light while Graham and I got out. I helped him up the steps. Pinkie insisted that we finish off the evening with coffee so we sat in the kitchen behind pulled curtains. Graham took off his shoes. I asked him if he'd had a good time.

"Wonderful," he said, "simply wonderful!" I saw Pinkie, who had changed into a robe, carrying a stack of quilts to the front room. I didn't object. We three settled around the small table nursing cups of coffee. There was no conversation. We all seemed to go deep within ourselves. Gigi's lipstick was smeared, and he had taken off his wig. Pinkie passed the coffeepot over my cup. "Want me to warm that up?" she asked.

"Just scare it," I said, not knowing exactly what I meant. It was something I'd heard the Big Flag waitress say, *Just scare it, huh?* as she slopped hot coffee into my cup. *Jumpstart my heart.* That's what Woolie told her when she poured his. I liked being in Pinkie and Gigi's circle of warmth, amid the silly idea that they were women and I was their Preacher. Maybe they were the fuzzy shoes of an Amazonian washerwoman hanging boxcars against the stars.

We finished our coffee and said our goodnights. When their bedroom door closed I mussed up the pallet and slipped out. Remembering my shoes, I went back in to get them. It had started. I give credit to the oysters. I changed shoes sitting on the edge of the porch and walked away feeling rich. Pinkie and Graham were like family. Judge and Mrs. Judge were like friends. I could have been a socialite years ago if someone had told me to cut my hair and buy a brown suit, which proves the old saying, clothes make the man.

There was no traffic on the bridge. I looked for Fritz in the artificial light and felt the dampness kicked up by the cascade at the foot of the dam. The smell of woodsmoke rose from a campfire under the bridge, and a lantern glowed downstream at the edge of the sandbar, belonging to someone who had set out a line for catfish. It was the first sign of fishermen I'd seen since the man went over the damn. A police car cruised by, checking me out. The officer was young with long sideburns. I had some advice for him. *Walk the street like your ancestors, Flatfoot.* He was a kid. I figured he wouldn't know the term.

As I tucked the shoebox under my arm and resumed walking I tried to guess how old I was. The number I came up with was twelve. I was a twelve-year-old boy walking through River City at three o'clock in the morning. Sixty-two minus twelve leaves fifty. Wherever those fifty years went, Pinkie had resurrected them. She had run my clock back half a century. There used to be canoes for rent on the river. She would be a good date to take out in a canoe. Good natured. Confident. She wore lovely perfume. She would like seeing Japanese lanterns on the water. She would enjoy a bonfire. She would wear a little heart-shaped locket on a gold chain. Pink gold. White shoulders. I didn't even know her real name.

As I opened the hatch warm air came out carrying the blended smells from several kitchens. There was some cabbage in there, pound cake, steamed carrots. I unlocked my apartment and crept inside. Tired. I took the brown suit off, tossed it on a chair, and crawled between cool sheets.

Woolie caught me sound asleep at eight o'clock. When I heard his knock I thought he might be Rosealyn turning up like a stray cat, so I answered the door in my new robe.

"No thanks, Woolie," I said. "I was out late. I'm not ready for breakfast." I went back to bed and lay there thinking about snow. I remembered walking the woods two days after a late snowfall when the twigs were full of sap. The snow had melted the previous day and then re-frozen during the night making a crust strong enough to walk on. The ice crust undulated in graceful curves, shining like a skating rink. The rattlesnakes under it were dormant, but turkeys, squirrels, rabbits, and owls were alert—moving, hiding, feeding, making it a perfect day for Rosealyn to have been here. Away from the Mississippi flies, away from Hub and the kids, she could have skated with me through the trees. If she came now what would I have to show her? Pinkie? Pinkie was thirty-two, twenty years older than me. Too old for me. And Pinkie was married.

I knew Rosealyn would save the best Mississippi stories to tell me in person. Hub's transgressions. The sins of the priest. Maybe we could take out Everett's boat and putt around. Take binoculars and look at ducks all day. Maybe then I could tell her I was in love with a married woman thirty years younger than me whose husband wears dresses. *Let's see you top that one, Rosealyn! Life certainly has its quirks, eh?* Then a new awareness sifted down covering my brain reminding me that I knew how to drive a car! I could buy one and zip around town if I wanted to. I could drive to Mississippi. At about the time I was ruminating on those car thoughts Woolie, making his way to breakfast, ran into a parked car. Fortunately the car he hit was empty because his heavy Chrysler demolished it. Woolie was taken to the hospital. His car was hauled to the car jail. But I didn't learn about it until later.

Another knock at the door. I already had on my robe, so I meandered over to answer it. Bulldog stood in a blue seersucker holding his panama in front of his chest looking for all the world like a New Orleans undertaker.

"It's ten o'clock, Joe. You're not awake yet?"

"I'm awake. I'm just not awake," I said. "Come in. Icetea? I'll have hot tea, myself."

"Hot tea is fine," he said, hovering in the kitchen while I made it. I used loose leaves, China style, and a preheated pot. Some leaves swirled up in our cups to join hands like skydivers. As always, I looked for meaning. I found myself reading Bulldog's fortune. "You will enjoy a long and happy life, if your parachute opens."

"Thanks, Joe. That's as good as I got from River City's phony fortuneteller."

"Madame Leontyne?"

He nodded. "Phoebe worships the old fraud."

"You're skeptical?"

"I gave her easy questions. She got them all wrong."

"Yes, but did you see her cock?"

"Honey, I've been seeing cocks all my life."

I put our cups on the counter and pulled up two barstools. "I don't have any cookies," I said. "How about some fruit? There's some dandy fruit chilling in the refrigerator."

"No thanks. Relax. You're a better host when you don't try so hard. Read my leaves."

I leaned over so I wouldn't have to disturb his cup. "Looks to me like an iris. Not the flower. An opening, like the iris in a camera."

"Or an eye?"

"Yes. A camera or an eye. Your future will be visual. Maybe a big publicity shot. Maybe you'll hit the front pages. I'll confirm this with Madame Leontyne."

"What's so hot about Madame Leontyne?"

"She told Everett how to play blackjack. He followed her advice and broke the bank."

"Phoebe is having a fling with a fireman. Madame Leontyne was able to describe him, down to the size of his suspenders."

I smiled thinking Madame Leontyne's daughter probably fed her the information. "I asked Madame Leontyne about you. She didn't know a thing."

"Of course not. I'm clean, Joe. Clean and pure!"

I put in milk and sugar *à la Graham*. As I stirred I asked, "Did you ever encounter the situation of a man who wears women's clothes?"

Bulldog rolled his eyes, toyed with his fingertips, and said. "Oh dear. One does hear of such things, Honey. I know lots and lots of people, so I hear many things. There are nightclub acts of female impersonation. Why?"

"I wonder how serious it is."

"Serious isn't a word that comes to mind. It's not serious."

"I know a married man who does it."

"I'll put him in my book."

I was shocked until I saw Bulldog's twinkling eyes. I said, "Everett won't have to install any more French fixtures in *nouveau riche* bathrooms. Put that in your book."

"Oh sure. I'm devoting a whole chapter to Everett."

"He gave Madame Leontyne his Ridgid-Kollmann. It's his idea of a joke."

Bulldog tucked up his feet like a child and twirled on his barstool. He looked at the grass skirt hanging from his namesake, but he didn't know the hanger was a bulldog. It could have been a common nail, a screw, or a clothespin for all he knew. "Did Phoebe's bathroom get fixed up okay?" I asked.

"Yeah. New wallpaper. Everything's fine."

"I told Everett his water line broke, not ours."

"Ours! You told him I helped you?"

"Why not? He's rich now. He doesn't care if there was scab labor on the job."

"I don't relish being called a scab. I didn't get paid."

"Speaking of pay, Graham found work. Now he and Pinkie have plenty of money."

"Good. Are you going on the river?"

I shook my head. "I've abandoned the search."

"Oh—" He sounded disappointed. "That's too bad."

"What do you care?"

"That's why I came to see you, to tell you I'm meeting Phil's wife for lunch."

"Who's Phil?"

"Phil's the man who drowned."

We sat quietly drinking our tea. Bulldog told me I'd had
the right idea about Methusela. Just make it up. Bulldog had
hired a researcher to collect all Methusela's old interviews.
Bulldog would regurgitate the reviews in his River City book.
That would be that. He was through with Methusela. Now he
was looking for stories about hippies. I described the nude
wedding I'd seen. The head hippie was still alive, so I told
Bulldog where to find him. He would tell stories about his
friends throwing bedsprings on a bonfire and Safeway chickens
on the bedsprings. Called it the Big Eat. They were too
stoned to take off the shrink-plastic, whereupon the plastic
melted, dripped onto the coals, and flared up like skyrockets.
He would tell about hippies stealing their friend's corpse and
taking it to the Big Eat for cremation. They underestimated the
amount of rags and walnut slabs required. Of course they got
their walnut slabs from the sawmill that made gunstocks. That
was a tenet of hippiedom, ironic recycling. L.S.D. There
were lots of hippie stories, and I by no means knew them all.
But Bulldog would find them because he had a keen nose for
the bizarre, the offbeat, the Man in the Privy.

I showered and dressed. Bulldog was meeting Phil's wife
at the Tin Can, a place I avoided, but Bulldog didn't know our
town. It was the best he could do. We found her at the
counter, swinging her foot. I suggested we sit by the window
so I could keep an eye on the courthouse. She was an
attractive young woman, but something about her reminded me
of Melanie Moore, the fruitbat psychologist. Something about
her was too self-contained and competent. Too calculating.
Cold.

Bulldog built us up by saying we'd searched for her
husband. He told her I'd been out lots of times, so it looked
like she was predisposed to like me. *Or else,* I thought,
predisposed to think I'm a ghoul. Bulldog had considered that
possibility. I didn't for a minute overlook his strangeness or
his intelligence—like when he toyed with the sharp hooks of the

snag line and asked, *Is this going to be an act of love?* He saw the soft underbelly of things.

Phil's wife believed her husband to be dead. She made that quite clear. She told us Phil was an insurance salesman who had been transferred here from Omaha. They had no children. It was Phil's first time to take his boat on the river. Bulldog nodded sympathetically and asked hard questions, earning his name. He wrote no notes. He allowed her to tell it her way, but sometimes he interrupted her to pin down details.

Phil's insurance policy paid double if he died in an accident. The local office was willing to settle, but the head office observed that nobody knew for sure that Phil was in the boat when it went over the dam. The boat had been recovered along with some of Phil's fishing equipment. But his shoes or clothing hadn't been found. Bulldog pursed his lips, waiting for me to tell the woman that I was her eyewitness.

"Do you have a photograph of your husband?" I asked.

The widow unsnapped her billfold and handed it to me. The man who looked up was smiling as if he expected to catch Moby Dick and live forever. I closed the green-leather billfold. It was new. The brass snap was untarnished. I brought it across and pressed its pin into its hole, feeling a stiff click. My eyes watered. I watched a dent painstakingly tie his dog to a parking meter. New dog. New leash. New experience. The waitress brought our food. I returned the billfold to the widow who interrupted her recital of Phil's life to stare at something in her Greek salad. I asked Bulldog for a copy of the accident report. "Here," the widow said. "I have it." She took a paper from her purse without seeing the fat tears that blurred my vision. According to the report there was no witness to Phil's trip over the dam. People below the dam reacted to a boat crashing down, but none of them saw a man in it. Nobody had seen the lonely man who looked up to me.

I lost my appetite for Tin Can food. It wasn't as good as it once was. At that moment nothing was as good as it once was. I looked hard at the young woman trying to read grief in

her eyes, but I saw none. Consternation. Impatience.
Righteous indignation. But no grief. She knew who Bulldog
was. She'd probably seen him on television talk shows. She'd
seen his pictures in *Parade*. She asked him what her rights
might be concerning the publication of her story and she made
a point of saying that she was friendly with a good lawyer. I
thought, *I saw your husband moments before he died. I could
give you that dubious gift.* But something in her kept me from
speaking. I pulled my food apart. The crusted cheese was the
turtle's shell and I was the crawfish picking at the turtle's soft,
fleshy parts. As I ate out the rice, mushrooms, and florets of
broccoli I decided to go to the police.

"Thank you for searching the river," she said. "I wish you
were successful."

I wish you had found my husband. Habeas corpus.

Bulldog looked at me. He was wondering why I didn't tell
her. He watched me closely, holding his tongue.

"You asked what Phil was like, deep down. He was a
loner. He liked to go out in his boat. You asked if he knew
the dam was there. If he knew it was dangerous. I went to
look at it. It's not high. A person wouldn't think going over
it, for sure, would kill you. I mean, it's not Niagara Falls.
It's not sky diving. It's more like eating wild mushrooms."

I was certain of my mushrooms. They were domestic and
overcooked. My tears had dried. I looked out the window
wondering if Phil carried an anchor in his fishing boat. Maybe
he carried an anchor with a cotton line and maybe he wrapped
the line around his foot in a seemingly accidental suicidal hitch.
When his body was found it could be argued that his foot had
become entangled in the fall. We're talking double indemnity
here—versus suicide. Double or nothing. My imagination
presented that notion so strongly that it seemed real, visual. I
closed my eyes tight and lowered my head. The dent looking
at me probably thought I was praying. The widow probably
thought I was praying, but I had already shifted my food. It's
unorthodox to pray over food after it has been shifted. I
concentrated, struggling, trying to recall what I saw from the

bridge, wondering what it was that made me know the man died. I couldn't capture it.

I left Bulldog to pay the check. Some mean thing inside me had kept me from telling the woman I was her witness. She would learn of it soon enough. If it took her a day to be notified, if her claim was delayed twenty-four hours, so what? She could wait one more day to be rich without grief. As I approached the police station a car drove by slowly. It was the kind of car that would be driven fast anywhere else. It was low-slung and black with an airfoil. If she'd had a couple of kids perhaps her motherhood would have melted my heart. If she'd cared that her husband was dead—that certainly would have melted my heart. But she just sat there and talked about her lawyer. She was like that fast car. *Keep off the grass.* I deliberately walked on it stepping down hard—*Keep off the grass!*—until I remembered the kids smashing crabapple trees. Then I took soft steps to the sidewalk. But what if she was brave? What if her grief was elsewhere than her eyes? What if she was too proud to show strangers her private thoughts? I entered the police station looking for a telephone. I called the Tin Can and got her. I hurriedly told her what I had seen from the bridge.

I wandered the halls hoping to bump into Judge or his bailiff or Detective Bradley—hungry for a friendly face. At the Firm But Fair window I made my business known and was ushered into a cubicle. The policeman who took my statement fretted that I had waited five days to make it. I told him I hadn't thought it necessary to make a report until I met the man's widow and learned that no one else had seen him in the boat. The policeman hinted I might be lying in her behalf. He remarked that it was a big coincidence for me to be standing on the bridge, looking down, at the exact moment the boat plunged over the brink. His illogical logic succeeded in making me doubt myself. On the grass I had resolved to keep my information from the woman. Let her find out in due course. As best she could. That would be soon enough for the likes of her. Then I crossed to the sidewalk, took three steps, and became seized with a panic to find a phone, call the Tin Can, and tell her my bit of ghoulish news. *How did you know it was him in the boat?* the policeman asked. *Because his wife showed me his photograph in her wallet,* I replied. *How do you know she's his wife? Especially since you didn't know him?* I gripped the desk and raised my voice. I said, "Let's keep this simple! I was on the bridge! I saw a boat go over the dam! There was a man in the boat! I saw his eyes! Who he was, I do not know!"

The policeman leaned back and exhaled as if he wasn't being paid enough to take my abuse. He didn't say anything because he was obviously waiting for someone. After a couple of minutes Detective Bradley joined us. Of course he remembered me. When the policeman told him the nature of my call, Bradley held a poker face. I wondered if he knew that the judge and I had become friends. He asked me to tell him what I'd seen there, looking down from the bridge, so I described the expression on the man's face. I mentioned the minnow bucket and the landing net. He asked where I had been prior to that and I told him I'd had lunch at El Chico Cafe with my brother. I added that I'd seen the judge there. He asked what I did after seeing the accident, and I told him I'd gone to the Pentimento Bar where I'd seen Mary Thunder, the seller of Indian jewelry. He asked more questions about the man in the boat, but I was blank. He asked if I'd ever been hypnotized. I hadn't, but I thought it was a swell idea. The policeman left the office and Detective Bradley hypnotized me by focusing my vision and counting backward. In the state of hypnosis I tried to suppress the urge to tell him that the man's pewter-colored minnow bucket reminded me of a pewter bust of Margaret Thatcher which in turn reminded me of a bronze bust of Harry Truman which in turn reminded me of a new, shiny copper pipe connected to a new bidet. Maybe I told him all those things or maybe I didn't. After the hypnosis I couldn't be sure.

"Thank you, Mr. Geezre."

I was sore tempted to tell him, *Judge and I played croquet. I can prove it. He has a wife named Mrs. Judge. She has a Pekinese named Hero.* But I said nothing. I slipped out of Firm But Fair feeling lucky to breathe fresh air.

It would be silly for me to pretend that every policeman in River City doesn't know me, because like it or not I'm a town character. Woolie asked the ambulance attendants to notify Walkman of his accident. The ambulance attendants broadcast that information on the police radio. As I waited for the light to change, crossing the street to the Can, a patrol car swerved to the curb, gathered me up, and gave me a ride to the hospital.

Woolie was swaddled in bed. He'd been to X-ray. He winked. I smiled at him and asked if he'd supervised the doctor.

"Joe," he said, "the seatbelt saved me. That little car I hit just crumpled. Like driving into a box of crackers."

"Why did you drive into it?"

"Geez, Joe. I guess I was picking my nose or something. I don't remember."

"Does your chest hurt?"

"It's taped, Joe. Tight. I told the kid doctor, *With cracked ribs you want to tape tight. For support.* Lucky I didn't collapse a lung. Got to watch out for pneumonia. At my age, I've got to be careful."

"I know you'll be careful. I'll see to it."

"And I've got to walk, Joe. I can't lie here and fluid up."

"Right."

"I told you to learn to drive. Damnit, Joe, you ought to listen to me sometime!"

Woolie had never snapped at me before. He'd never found fault with me. I almost replied, *Seems like you're the one who needs to learn to drive!* But I didn't because I knew he was uncomfortable. And he was embarrassed. I gripped his knobby knee and squeezed. "It's okay, Woolie. Now I know how to drive. I can help you out. Pick up your prescriptions."

"How—"

"I learned last night by driving some friends to Kansas City. But their car is automatic."

"Mine's automatic, Joe. And they tell me it's not hurt. They towed it to the wrecker yard, but it's okay."

"Back to the wreck shop."

"What?"

"They took it back to the wreck shop. That's an expression I use. Doesn't mean anything."

"If it doesn't mean anything why do you use it?"

"Because I'm not as logical as the monkeys I swing with. There's a passel of truth outside logic, Woolie, and don't you forget it!"

"Go get my car, Joe. Take it home. I'll feel better knowing it's where it belongs. There's my keys on the table."

"Who's your nurse?"

"I don't rate a nurse. I'm up for grabs, but nobody's grabbing!"

I went to the nurses' station looking for Pinkie Evans. I learned that her name wasn't Pinkie, it was Angela, and she worked on another floor. The duty nurse got her on the phone for me and I gave her Woolie's room number. I beat feet down to the lobby flower shop and bought Woolie a bouquet of cornflower blue carnations. I got back to his room before Pinkie, so I was on hand to introduce her to Woolie. The flowers matched her eyes.

"Pinkie, this is my friend Dr. Woolheater. Woolie, this is my friend Nurse Angela Evans." Pinkie reared back and looked up her nose at me for calling her Angela. But that was the name on her uniform. Above her nametag were three gold pins signifying meritorious service. I was proud of her. She held Woolie's hand and said, "Hullo, Dr. Woolheater. I'm happy to meet you."

He looked at me sharply when he heard her British accent. *Pregnant Englishwoman!* his naughty eyes snapped. "Nurse," he said, "Joe neglected to tell me you're so beautiful. And I detect you're British, aren't you?"

"Yes. What are you in for?"

"Couple of cracked ribs. Nothing serious."

She gave him a smile that would cure anybody. "I knew you weren't serious. This room's for hangnails and poison ivy."

He grinned. "Will you be my nurse?"

"No. I'm busy saving lives. But I'll pop in and see you from time to time. Bye, Joe. You were marvelous last night! Why did you leave before breakfast!" She swept out of the room.

Woolie grinned. He said, "Left before breakfast? You dog! She's pregnant, Joe. I saw it in her eyes."

"If she's pregnant it's none of my doing. I'm going to check on your car. Should I phone your children?"

"Not for this. The doctor said he'll release me tomorrow afternoon."

It took me an hour to walk to the car jail adjacent to the wreck shop. I loitered to study the place and make my plan. Nobody paid me any attention. A man came in, went to the counter, and ordered a headlight bucket for a Malibu. The parts puller went out to the yard to look for one. A pickup loaded with aluminum cans drove onto the scales. Then a thin fruitbat came in. She wore a tiny white two-piece outfit, and she stood on first one foot, then the other, impatiently waiting for the counterman to acknowledge her presence. Her shoulder blades fluttered like wings. He was talking on the telephone, writing down numbers. After a minute he said, "Yes, ma'am?"

"I want my car."

"Do you have the police release?"

She handed him a paper. He read it closely. "Driver's license?"

That's where they've got me, driver's license!

I cruised over to Everett's, told him my dilemma, and rode with him to the police station. I got a release, took it to the hospital for Woolie to sign, and then we stopped by to get May. Everett showed his license, picked up Woolie's car, and drove it to Flattop. I rode with May, following Everett. I asked if she'd seen Wayne Newton. May and I had always been friends. She liked to cook, and she invited me to Sunday dinner. Everett always prayed at Sunday dinner. When he prayed I bowed my head out of respect. Our mother died when we were twelve, and Everett stayed religious because of her. I didn't think it was fair that she died, so I got angry and never went to church again, except for Everett's wedding and the weddings of his kids. But during the last fifty years I've thought about religion, perhaps more than Everett has. Again I congratulated May on her new wealth. She acted like the money wouldn't mess up her soul. "You gonna get a new house?" I asked.

She scoffed. "I'm gonna try to hold onto the one we've got. Everett didn't win *that* much."

I watched her drive, trying to pick up pointers. She used the turn indicators to change lanes. She made it a point to slow down gradually rather than run up to the stoplights and hit the brakes hard, like Everett. She asked, "What have you heard from Rosealyn?" I told her the ordinary stuff. I didn't say Rosealyn might visit me.

"So," May said, "she didn't tell you about Hub?"

"No."

"Hub has MS."

"MS?"

"She called last night. She'll have to get a job. There aren't many jobs for her in Mississippi."

It didn't surprise me that Rosealyn hadn't told me the bad news. She would wait. She had never worked. She had no marketable skills. She was a mother with two kids.

When May stopped for a red light I said, "I need to take the driving test. Is it hard?"

She shrugged. "Nah. They give you a booklet. You memorize the rules. Then you take an eye test, a written test, and a driving test. I went through it with all the kids. Want me to help you?"

"Sure."

After Everett parked Woolie's car we gave him a ride home. Then May took me to the testing office. She went in and got me a booklet. We sat in the car and she quizzed me. Then I went inside to try the test. There were five clerks administering the tests. One of them was Madame Leontyne's daughter, looking sour and tired. I didn't think she would give me any breaks, but the office was run take-a-number and wait, so I could do nothing to get her or to avoid getting her. I took my chances in the lottery and drew a young man who passed me on the written and visual.

Then May let me drive her car and we went all over town. I practiced parking and backing up. When I drove to the testing office I wasn't a bit nervous.

It was after five when I got back to Flattop. I phoned Woolie to tell him his car was moored in its assigned slot, and I made plans to bring it to the hospital the next afternoon to fetch him.

My heart was heavy with Rosealyn's bad news. I set out a cold supper thinking Woolie had been lucky. Maybe Hub would be lucky too. After supper I went into Woolie's apartment and turned on his big-screen television wanting to sit there in the dark and watch pictures from around the world. I wanted to watch a documentary on the hazards of being old. I wanted to learn about a cure for MS, and although the television couldn't stop talking it refused to tell me anything I wanted to hear. I saw pictures of the moon that looked like all the other pictures I'd ever seen of the moon. I changed the channel and saw an old black-and-white newsreel of two locomotives crashing headon. I'll bet they smashed their headlight buckets! *Like driving into a box of crackers. Damn MS! Why does anybody have to have MS!*

I locked up Woolie's apartment and sauntered outside hoping to see a skunk or spy on a fruitbat wedding, but the chapel was deserted. *Skunks don't marry. They simply pair up and have puppies. But people aren't skunks.* The sunlight was still bright and falling at a good angle, so I went inside to look at the stained glass. I was alone. I saw the prayer book, but I wasn't tempted to read its recent entries. I was tempted to pray for Hub and Woolie and Rosealyn and Everett and May and Phil and his wife and Pinkie and Graham and Bulldog—so I didn't pray for anyone. The strongest argument against prayer is that there is no equity between the amount needed and the available supply. I wondered how Saint Teresa would have

countered that atheistic idea. My resolve weakened. I went to
the book and opened it to the blank page following the last
entry. I wrote,

> Dear Kimberly,
>   Forget the phone bill. Forget Bob and
> Jennifer. May I ask you a personal question? Are
> you a virgin? If you'd buy yourself some good
> walking shoes I'd take you on a tour of River City.
> I'd show you things you've never seen before.
>   Love, Joe.

Paula Ramsay. There she was. Surely she had been
watching me for some time before deciding to make her
presence known.

"Joe?"

"Hello."

"Am I intruding?"

"I just came to look at the glass."

"I hoped you would be here."

"Why?"

"Because I don't know your apartment number."

"It's on the mailbox."

"Oh."

"You were looking for me?"

"Sort of."

"Why?"

"Guilty conscience, I suppose. I was rude to you."

"Forget it. I'm rude all the time. Would you like a cup
of tea?"

"I'd love one."

I followed her down the aisle and walked her across the
parking lot onto the gangplank. I opened the hatch and held it
for her. She entered my apartment and sat on the sofa, a bit
tense I thought, while I made tea. I checked the refrigerator,
stared at the fruit cocktail, and decided to keep it for breakfast.
I hunted up my memory pad to write Mannie a note, *get some
cookies! Pronto!* I put milk and sugar in the tea without

asking her because I could tell she had a sweet tooth. I served
tea on my genuine hammered-brass table from India, via Pier
1. So far I had divested myself of one fake zebra skin and one
genuine tailbone.

"I hope you like milk and sugar?"

"That's fine."

"Whoso Findeth Wisdom Findeth Life."

"In spades. But I would expect you to say whoso findeth
Jesus findeth life."

"I'm not religious," I said.

"In a pig's eye!"

I thought it would be interesting to change the subject. I
said, "Got my driver's license today. Never had one before.
That's because when I was a teenager driving was all tangled
up with sex. Y'know. The automobile provided American
society with mobility, privacy, and a mark of status. Like a
codpiece or a cockscomb."

She nodded.

Merry widows. "Do you feel powerful when driving your
car? Do you feel like you're on top of something?"

"I usually feel like I'm late. Are you asking this because
I'm a psychologist?"

I nodded. I told her about the times Pinkie laid out pallets
for me. I told her about Pinkie saying I was a natural
aphrodisiac. She said Pinkie was an exhibitionist. My
presence excited her. I said that was the first time in sixty-two
years my presence had ever excited a woman, and Paula
laughed. Then, of all things, she asked what kind of shoes she
should buy. I got out several pairs to show her, tempted to ask
her about Graham's cross dressing and tempted to ask her about
my relationship with Everett—the way twins can be so different
that they actually become two distinct halves of one person—but
I didn't want to tax her generosity and milk her free
information. She slipped her bare feet into my walkers. I'd
felt a buzz of sensual gratification wearing Graham's old
English suit. I wondered what Paula was feeling through her
soles. She grinned, like a kid at Halloween. I figured she
would really grin if she found herself on the business end of a

Unisex shampoo. Warm water, sweet-smelling soap, and Trish's fingernails. I looked at her, holding that thought in mind. She had closed her eyes, no doubt wiggling her toes inside my shoes, and I began trusting her, thinking she was having a good time. I remembered kissing Mary Thunder in the trash corral. I looked into Paula's plain, open face and in my state of ignorance I thought I saw there the desire to be kissed. I remembered Pinkie's uniform with *Angela* on her full breast, tucked under the three golden service buttons—her eyes the color of the blue carnations. Paula's eyes weren't blue. They were closed. Her lips were parted. Maybe she wanted me to kiss her. Maybe being kissed was the farthest thing from her mind. I was ignorant. I wished I knew. First comes wisdom, then comes life. I looked at the Navajo rug behind Paula's face and followed a zigzag pattern of black lines through it, like a code—or a map. A mystery. In a moment she opened her eyes. She kicked off my shoes, put hers on, and said we would hit the walking trail together—soon—down along the river. I accompanied her to her car without naming all the folks who might be hiding in the backseat.

When she was safely out of the parking lot I went to my apartment and searched Saint Teresa looking for the phrase *More tears are shed.*

6

Icecream

The amorous woodpecker awoke Joe from a dream involving the loading dock outside a warehouse where there was a red stop sign in the shape of a tomato. Inside the warehouse were crates of tomato-shaped peaches. He rubbed his eyes and saw the woodpecker clinging to his window. *In a pig's eye!* Paula had told him. He visualized Paula's eye and its soft invitation thinking that perhaps Paula had a fetish for elderly one-eared gentlemen. At any rate, her chaste visit to his apartment had confirmed his virginal condition. *There's nothing like Saint Teresa to herd an old ram into the fold of virginity. All I want is for Pinkie to hug me tight and kiss me forever. Forever soft, forever chaste.* Joe got out of bed, planning his day. He knew Graham had left for work at seven o'clock and Pinkie wouldn't go until noon. And Woolheater would be released from the hospital in the afternoon. Joe wallowed in the pleasurable realization that he knew how to drive. Pinkie wouldn't have to hire a taxi. He would use Woolheater's car to take her to work.

He stood in the shower feeling shaky and drugged by Saint Teresa. He made his breakfast and vacuumed both apartments—to keep from calling Pinkie too early.

At nine o'clock, unable to wait any longer, he phoned her offering the ride. He hinted for tea, and she told him to wait an hour. In his nervousness he walked halfway to the golf course. While he walked he planned his lie. He would tell her about Paula's nighttime visit. He would truthfully say that Paula had given him an inviting look, but then he would exceed the truth and say he had accepted Paula's invitation. He would tell Pinkie he kissed Paula. Why? He didn't know why. He was sailing by dead reckoning, out of sight of land. He was playing courtship, a game he neglected to learn in high school. Because he didn't have the courage to kiss Pinkie he would tell her he had kissed another woman. Why? To watch her reaction in the hope that she would be jealous.

Sitting under the wheel of Woolheater's car, Joe lost his nerve. For courage he took out his billfold to examine his pristine driver's license which correctly stated his name and address and sex and height and weight and age and hair color. His hand shook as he attempted, first right-side-up and then upside-down, to push the key into the ignition. No one had ever told him not to flood a car, so he did. After much cranking he got the Chrysler started and sat there rehearsing his lie. He would tell Pinkie it was a bad kiss, an insincere invasion of Paula's privacy. And if Pinkie expressed curiosity or surprise he would confide, *I did it with my eyes shut pretending she was you!* And then Pinkie would open her arms, pull him to her soft breasts, and give him the mother's hug he needed. A haze of blue smoke enveloped Woolheater's car. Joe did not know how long he had been warming it. In Pinkie's arms two minutes or two hours were all the same. Joe shifted and backed out of the stall. He would drive fast or slow, it didn't matter. He would be early or late, it didn't matter. This was the first time he had ever driven alone and he was confident of his ability to get to Pinkie's house but he was frightened of what she would say when he confessed his flirtation with Paula. He shifted and rolled forward. Only then did he remember he'd always gotten seasick when Woolheater drove. He lowered the window for fresh air, crept to the intersection, and waited at the red tomato sign. Then carefully he ventured into the flow of traffic. *I know the difference between a tomato and a peach,* he said. *It's more than fuzzy skin.*

Joe saw his hometown anew, driving along her streets. The bridge looked tall and narrow with a smaller expanse of sky than there was when he walked it. The tires made a hissing noise on the pavement. The turn into Pinkie's street was difficult because oncoming cars didn't give him enough room. His palms were damp when he pulled into Pinkie's driveway. Wearing her nurse's uniform, she came out to admire his new car.

"Graham only just taught you to drive and now you have a car! You certainly work fast, Mr. Geezre!"

He grinned like a kid, standing beside the Chrysler, his knees shaking. "It's Woolheater's. I'm fetching him from the hospital."

"I know. Your cute friend with the gray moustache. Mr. Flirt."

"He's a geneticist."

"Hooray for him. Tea?"

Joe nodded. Pinkie had the pot pre-heated. "Unless you prefer coffee?" she said.

"No, no. I love tea. Woolie's the coffee man."

He sat at the small table. "Graham's off to the dogfood factory?"

"Yes. The dear made his own breakfast so I wouldn't have to get up. I worked late last night. A bit more money. What did you do?"

"I read Saint Teresa."

"You monk! Why don't you kick loose and have yourself some fun?" She emptied the pot, put in tea, and poured in hot water.

"I have fun. I have lots of friends—you, Graham, Woolie, the Judges, Everett and his family. Bulldog, he's a writer I'm helping round up information about the hippies."

She brought a second chair to the table and set it opposite him.

"Woolie says you're pretty. He's an expert."

"Joe, you melt a girl's heart!"

Joe tensed, thinking he might get kissed, but Pinkie turned to pick up cups and saucers. His plan of telling her about

Paula's visit flew out of his head. He had no script. "Why did you decide to be a nurse?"

"Not much choice, really. Why did you decide to be a preparator?"

"I wanted to work with my hands. Early in life I did a lot of hunting and trapping and fishing. Fishing is a form of trapping, you know. A fish hook is merely a baited snare. And I skinned animals, scaled fish, gathered wild fruit. I cooked over campfires. I dreamed of following the buffalo. I was full of that stuff. In love with dinosaurs."

"Do you like kids?"

"Oh yes indeed."

"But you never married?"

"No. I'm a virgin."

Pinkie didn't react to the news. She asked, "Your parents encouraged you to be a doctor?"

"No. Why?"

"Oh, your interests in animals, biology. There's frequently a connection."

"Our mother didn't encourage us to be anything. She died when we were twelve. Our dad was a plumber. Everett worked with Dad, to get money, to date girls. I spent a lot of time in the woods. Oh, I had to work too. I helped Dad from time to time, but I was basically a loner."

"And Everett raised a big family?"

"Seven kids. Sixteen grandchildren. Quite a few great-grandchildren. His youngest daughter lives in Mississippi." Joe fidgeted. "Her husband has MS."

Pinkie nodded. "Does she have children?"

"Two."

"Drink your tea."

"Of course MS doesn't scare you. You see sick people every day."

"That's my job. But I remind myself that most people aren't sick. And sick people get well. Death is—well—we'll all die eventually. I like it you're a monk."

Joe pushed his teacup aside to reach for her hand. *I'm not a monk, I'm a monkeyman!* He looked deep into her eyes.

"No," he said. "I'm not a monk! Not in a pig's eye!" He pulled her across the table and kissed her hard on the mouth.

"Joe! Jesus!" She slapped him.

"You've kissed me. Why can't I kiss you?"

"Not like that, Joe. I never kissed you like that!"

"What's a man to think? I mean, I don't know what I'm doing. I'm a virgin."

"Sure you are, Joe. Me too!"

"What did you expect? You made me a pallet outside your bedroom. A lot of thoughts went through my head."

"I shouldn't have done that. I'm sorry. Graham needed it."

"Graham has too darned many needs!"

Pinkie got up for a cigarette. She lit it and returned to her chair. After a few drags she sipped her tea. Joe held his ground, refusing to drink tea, refusing to smile.

"Joe, we're in the foothills of a quarrel."

"Yes. And I've never done it before."

"Damnit, Joe! Stop saying I've never done it! I never drove! I never fucked! I never quarreled! All I ever did was hunt and fish and read Saint Teresa!" When she finished yelling she was crying. Joe ran his fingers through his Unisex. He tasted the tea.

"You've gotten too close to me, Joe. I figured you to be homosexual. I thought our difficulty would come from you falling in love with Graham. But you're not that at all. You're merely a liar. You pretend to be stupid, but you know how to drive. You know how to kiss. You know what time Graham goes to work. Go, Liar. Walk back across town. Don't drive that car. Remember? You don't know how!"

Joe pulled the driver's license from his billfold and held it in the air. He raised his voice as loud as hers. "Here," he yelled. "Read this! Read every word of it. This is me. See my new haircut? Read the date. Yesterday's date. I only got the darned thing yesterday! I'm telling you the truth!"

She took the card and read it. After a moment she smiled through her tears. "You *are* a cute bastard. The way you turn your head to the left, showing off your bad ear."

"Lots of men would go earless, but they don't have the guts."

Pinkie snuffed out her cigarette and said, "I must wash off my face and put it back on. Before I do, kiss me."

After they kissed she went to the bathroom and stayed a long time. Joe spoke to her through the open doorway, "Are you going to let me take you to work?"

"I don't know. Why?"

"Because if you're not, I'd better call you a taxi."

"Joe, of course I want you to take me."

When Pinkie came out of the bathroom her makeup was repaired. She checked the range to see that all the burners were off. Then she led him out the side door and locked it. She said, "Let's sit in the new chairs until time to go. Let's breathe some fresh air and think about this."

"What is this?"

She led him around the corner and climbed the steps to the porch.

"This is the fact that you and I have an attraction. I'm married. If you're not married that's great for you. But I'm married."

"I never even thought about getting married. I mean it. I never even had a girlfriend."

"Okay, Joe." She unfolded the two chairs and set them apart, facing. She sat in one. "I'm going to tell Graham. He'll understand."

"Please don't tell him. I feel silly for grabbing you, being in love. I don't want anyone to know."

"All right then. It'll be our secret. I'm sorry I flirted with you. I didn't intend it in the way you thought. We'll be good friends now. Okay?"

"Yes. I want to be friends."

"Maybe Graham's cross dressing gave you the wrong idea."

"Maybe? Of course it did!"

"I'm sorry I said nasty things to you."

Joe shrugged. "Woolie thinks I'm frustrated because I'm retired. I've lost my interest in hunting and fishing. I have no job to go to."

"You're saying you fell in love with me out of boredom? That's not very flattering, Joe."

"Woolie said that. I didn't."

"Don't ever tell me another of Woolie's sayings, Joe. You can't hide behind Woolie anymore."

"I could say lots of my own things, sweet things, to you. But it wouldn't be right."

"No, it wouldn't be right. But I'm glad this happened. Now we understand one another. Now we can be great friends."

"You said if you had a baby it would be born in England. I want you to have a baby, but not if it drives you back to England." As he spoke Joe remembered Pinkie saying that she would quit smoking if she got pregnant.

"I said that? If a girl lives long enough she says many things. Graham and I have jobs. This house is cozy. We might get a dog. I could see us living right here. A little family of five or six brats. Uncle Joe gliding over the levee with his pockets full of sweets."

"Can you see that?"

"Easy."

"I think I could be a psychologist."

"Of course you could."

"You think so?"

"Of course. If I told Graham you'd kissed me I wouldn't be telling him to ease my conscience or to put him on warning."

"No?"

"I'd tell him for his benefit. Sex in the head, you know. Are you or are you not a psychologist?"

"I'm beginning to wise up."

"If you and I are going to be friends we can start by being wise."

"Yes. We're friends. If we go now we'll have time to get some frozen yogurt."

"Joe, you fuddyduddy! Isn't there someplace to get real icecream? I won't have you feeding my brats yogurt!"

Woolheater's car felt happy and balanced with the two of them in its front seat. It was old enough to have vent windows, and Joe turned them out like wings. At the first intersection he stopped, explaining to Pinkie, "I have to stop for tomato signs. It's the law."

"I suppose bananas are cautionary?"

"I step over bananas."

Joe drove across town to the icecream store where they both chose the tropical flavor. Then he drove north on Iowa Street, holding the wheel with one hand, holding his drippy cone with the other. Pinkie used both hands and several napkins to protect her uniform. She said, "It's the wind coming in that melts the icecream."

"Yeah," Joe said. "Life's a continual hardship, ain't it? This is the first time I've ever had tomato-peach icecream."

"It's not tomato-peach, it's Tahiti Beach."

"Okay."

Woolheater was pacing his room, forbidden to leave until the doctor signed his release papers. He grinned at Joe. "I have my walking shoes on, Joe. I'm ready to blow this joint."

"How about your ribs?"

"Tight, Joe. Tight. It hurts when I cough, so I don't cough. Your Brit hasn't been around."

"She just came to work. I brought her in your car."

"You drove okay?"

"It's easy, Woolie. That's why I never bothered to learn. I knew it was easy. Slide through bananas. Stop for tomatoes."

"Here, Joe, sign this paper and we're gone. You're my attending physician, aren't you?"

Through the lobby windows they saw a spring thunderstorm darkening the sky. Large, ominous raindrops spotted the sidewalk.

"I'll run for it. Pick you up here!"

Joe drove under the awning just as the cloud broke. He put the Chrysler in park and got out for Woolheater to drive, but Woolheater said his ribs hurt so Joe drove out into the thunderstorm and immediately had to stop because he couldn't see.

"Turn the wipers on, Joe! Don't you know anything?"

"Where are they?"

Woolheater groaned reaching across to flick the switch. "Lights too," he said. "For safety."

Joe grunted. "Did you have lunch?"

"I skipped it. Let's go to the Expensive Cafe."

Joe liked the food at the Expensive Cafe. Woolheater liked the waitresses there. Joe turned in that direction and drove carefully, avoiding bumps. Nevertheless Woolheater held his door handle and grimaced. "Easy, Joe! Take it easy!"

"It's not my driving, Woolie. You never rode on that side before. The driver can hang onto the wheel, but the passenger gets sloshed around. It's the springs or the tires or something."

"You're right, it's *something*!"

Joe parked in a handicapped slot right by the door. Woolheater said, "Can't park here. Don't you see the sign!"

"It never bothered you at the Big Flag!"

"What?"

"Aren't you handicapped?"

"Just a pain in my side, said Adam."

"Get out. I'll park in back and run through the rain."

Woolheater snugged his hat, wet his lips, and stepped out. He crowfooted to the door. Joe took his time finding a parking spot. The rain had slackened, and he was in no hurry, savoring the thought of Pinkie and the icecream cone. She'd had the foresight to pick up several napkins which she'd unfolded and placed in her lap before the icecream began to melt, using her purse to hold them in place. Joe would have thought of none of that, but Graham would have. If Graham didn't want to be a woman, why did he dress like one? He did it to deceive people. He was a practical joker. Bending people's perceptions. Like a magician. Joe was glad he'd kissed Pinkie, and he was glad she wouldn't tell Graham. He didn't lust for her, not the way Everett lusted for women. He merely wanted Pinkie to hug him from time to time and dance barefoot in his grass skirt. As the sun popped out a few drops of catspit continued to fall. Joe carefully locked the keys in the car and picked his way around puddles, keeping his shoes dry. He found Woolheater entertaining the waitresses, showing them his tape.

"Put your clothes on, Woolie. This is a public place!"

"I ordered tea for you."

"Thanks. What's the special?"

"Hamhock, beans, and cornbread. Funny how the Expensive Cafe serves poor folks food, eh?"

"Trendy's the chef. I want pink salmon, green spinach, amber tea, blue berries, and yellow sherbet. Ever eat at the Red Lion?"

Woolheater shrugged. "Once. Heartburn."

Joe spotted Trish sitting with two Unisex operators. He waved.

"Who's she?" Woolheater asked.

"One world. One sex. A political movement for human equality."

"And she's part of it? She's cute!"

"She is for a fact. She cut my hair. What do you think?"

"It's a definite improvement."

The rain had stopped by the time Joe and Woolheater returned to the parking lot. They were comfortable standing there, looking at fresh puddles, waiting for the locksmith.

"This is broken," Woolheater said, pointing at his bumper. "Broken clear through."

"It looks okay."

"Maybe it looks okay, but I'm gonna get it replaced. I need strong bumpers, the way I drive."

"Did you get a ticket?"

"Yes I did. Ticket, bumper, hospital, doctor, X-ray—that was one expensive nosepick!"

Trish and her friends walked by. She stopped to say hello and Joe introduced Woolheater who said, "I like Joe's new hairstyle."

"Thanks. Who does yours?"

"Barbershop."

"Uhmmm. Why are you boys hanging around the parking lot?"

"Joe locked my keys in the car," Woolheater said, smugly.

She opened her purse. "Here's my card. Call me for an appointment."

Woolheater slipped the card into his billfold saying, "We used to call it getting your ears lowered. You've gone beyond that. You remove the damned things!" He cut his eyes at Joe.

"Whatsamatter? Scared?" Trish replied.

Woolheater unbuttoned his shirt to show his ribs. "Look at this, Baby! You're looking at a he-man!"

"If you're squeamish about ears, I'll think of something else to cut off." Trish got in the car with her friends, waved, and drove away.

Woolheater said, "What kind of lie can we tell the locksmith, so we won't look foolish?"

"I guess he's heard them all."

"Well think, Joe. We're older than he is. We ought to be smarter."

The locksmith arrived and did his trick. Woolheater said he felt like driving around to shop for a new bumper. Joe took off. "I'll give you a ride home, Joe!"

"Thanks for lunch." Joe jogged across the street. He cut through an alley looking at things people had thrown out, following a route that would take him past the Judges' house. He imagined seeing young Mrs. Judge inside with Hero, playing the piano. Judge would be downtown courting. Joe wondered if she had checked the mail. If so, she had seen his thankyou note. Robins stalked earthworms on their lawn. A breeze stirred tree limbs shaking out drops of rainwater. Joe stood on the sidewalk, cocked his head like a robin, and imagined he heard the sweet notes of Mrs. Judge's piano. Then he stepped out for home to read Saint Teresa. As he walked he thought back on kissing Pinkie. He wanted to tell someone about his affection for her but he didn't know who to tell. He couldn't tell Everett or May or Woolheater or Bulldog

or Trish or Paula or Mrs. Judge. Certainly not Graham. Not
Gigolo or Fruitbat Melanie. Not Madame Leontyne or
Preacher, not Mary Thunder or Indian Joe. He stopped at the
campus pond to check the water. "Jug, jug, jug!" he croaked,
a lone bullfrog filling the space with his mating call. The
pond's surface was glassy. Somewhere in the trees a warbler
called. Then Preacher crowed as Madame Leontyne and all the
others swam toward Joe chanting, *Jug, jug, jug.* He looked at
their faces, counted noses, and realized that except for Everett
and May, they were all new friends. *What did I do for friends
a month ago, before I retired? I had none. I had family.
Rosealyn. I knew a few people at work, and the servers in the
cafeteria. The mailman. Now it seems like I know the whole
world, and they are all wonderful people! Even Phoebe Jones
and Phil's wife. And Pinkie!* He cruised toward Flattop
musing fondly on his froggy friends, Saint Teresa, and a
tumbler of cold buttermilk.

Joe read by his north window until the light faded. Then
he made a sandwich. After eating it he peeled and sectioned
two oranges so he could eat without moving his eyes from the
page. He put the oranges on the window ledge beside his right
hand, settled deep into his recliner, turned on the lamp, and
resumed reading looking for *More tears are shed.* He read
until he fell asleep. His last thought before sleeping was—*in a
search one is apt to find a different victim than intended—yes,
the searcher is the hunter and the sought is the prey.*

He awoke to someone knocking. He looked out the
window. Night had fallen. The book lay on his chest. He got
up slowly and padded to the door, his mind fuzzy as if he'd
been in another world.

"Hi, Joe!" Mary Thunder said. "Hold this. I've got to get
more stuff." She handed him a black-iron kettle. "It's hot.
Hold it by the handle!" The handle was a metal bail. Joe took
the kettle into the kitchen and hefted it to the range, but the
kettle's short legs kept it from settling straight, so he put it on
the counter. It smelled spicy, meaty, and good. He lifted the

lid and saw a reddish-brown stew with carrots, corn, and chunks of potato. "Uh-huh. You brought dinner," he said softly as if Mary were in the kitchen. A few minutes later she tapped at the door and he opened it again. She stood there holding two pictures, one in each hand. "Here's yours," she handed him the hollyhocks. "What do you think? Bargain? It's a Nikki Wildcat."

Joe turned the picture to the light. "It's much better than the slide. It's wonderful!" He held it in the blank place on the wall. "Perfect!"

"Yeah, well get a hammer and nail and you're in business. Wanna take Woolie's down to him?"

"I want to keep it here so I can study it." He propped Woolheater's picture on the counter. "I like it too. Hubcap with doll straw, eh?"

"Yeah. I told you, my brother painted it."

"Where did you get this stew?"

"Under the bridge. I guess the hobos were off hunting another dog. Native Americans used to eat dogmeat all the time, for vision."

"This is dog stew?"

"Maybe my father made it. Maybe he's giving it to you for the tailbone."

"I see. He wants his rug back. Okay. I didn't put any holes in it." Joe unfastened one end of the rug.

"No."

"Your father didn't send the dog stew for the rug?"

"Maybe."

"I thought so." Joe unfastened the other end. He handed it to Mary. "You'll take it to him?"

"If you tell me to. But only if you tell me to. He doesn't want you to think he's an Indian giver."

"Oh— I don't—"

"See. Where that idea came from is this. The old Indians gave land to white people because the old Indians didn't know you could own land. When they came back hunting for food the white people called them Indian givers. Just a big misunderstanding, like Columbus did when he bragged to everybody he'd found India."

"I want your father to have this rug."

"Okay."

Joe felt tired, as if he'd won a difficult argument. *It's the silent sow that gets the slop.* "Thanks for bringing the stew, and the pictures."

"Yeah. You looked surprised, like you never expected to see that picture—"

"I'm overwhelmed."

"Yeah. It's powerful the way that tailbone is."

"Sit down," Joe said.

"Sure. I'll spend the night with you."

"You can't do that."

"Why?"

"Because it wouldn't be right."

"Sure it would be right. If you want me to."

"No it wouldn't."

"Why?"

"Because I'm in love with another woman."

"Joe, you know that room my father went in?" She pointed. "There's a bed in it."

"Yes."

"Let me sleep there tonight, Joe. I got kicked."

"Kicked?"

"Out. Non-payment of rent."

"Where's your satchel of jewelry?"

"I sold it all."

"Do you have any more pictures you can sell?"

She smiled and patted his arm. "Don't start trying to think like a Native Merkin, Joe. You want some dog soup? It's good medicine."

"What kind of dog was it?"

"Sometimes he uses little Chinese-looking dogs. You know, us Native Americans came from China, not India."

"I had a sandwich a few minutes ago. I'm not hungry."

"Well I'll have a bowl."

They went into the kitchen and Joe handed Mary a bowl and spoon. "This bowl belonged to my mother," he said. "It was her wedding present."

"Crackers?"

"All I have is some fifty-grain hippie bread. How about that?"

"Sure, if that's all you've got." She took her food into the livingroom and ate while Joe used the rug clamps to hang her picture, temporarily, above the sofa. He sat in the overstuffed chair and looked at the shaft of hollyhocks and Mary's head. The stew smelled good. He was again struck by the symmetry of Mary's face. Her eyes were glossy black. Impenetrable. She held the spoon tight in her fist, like a child, and after each bite she licked it clean. She had a white scar at the corner of her mouth that curved up like a smile.

Mary took her bowl to the kitchen, washed it, and placed it upside-down in the drying rack. Then she picked up Woolheater's picture. "I'll see if he's home," she said. "You didn't say I could stay in that room?"

"Mary, I live alone. I couldn't sleep with a woman in here."

"What about that one you love?"

"She doesn't sleep here. She's married."

"You're too screwed up. Where's Woolie's wigwam?"

"That way. First door on the left."

"Tell me I can stay in your spare room?"

If he didn't allow her to stay with him she would spend the night with Woolheater, and Joe knew it. Jealousy made him say, "I'll prop the door so you can get back in. I might be asleep."

"Thanks, Joe."

"Woolie was in a wreck."

"No?"

"He broke three ribs. He'll be glad to see you."

"If you're asleep when I come back, goodnight, Joe."

Joe sorted through his junk mail. There was a note from the manager:

Would you like to have the outside doors to the
building locked? They would be opened with your
same key. It would be a little bit of bother coming
and going but it would be more security. Please write
"yes" or "no" on this note and place it in my mailbox.

Joe put the note aside. He stuck a fork between the door
and the jam, left the ventahood light on, and went to bed. But
he couldn't fall asleep for fretting over the manager's note.
Locking the outside door would be an inconvenience. He felt
safe. For that matter he could sleep with all the doors
unlocked. And whenever someone came to visit him, Bulldog
or Mary or Paula, they could get in. So he would vote no.
Then he thought about his shipmates, many of whom were
frightened. Best have the outside doors locked for their peace
of mind. Surely there would be a buzzer system so an
unexpected caller could ring to be let in. Why did all these
people, except Woolie, seem frightened? A cold realization
crept over Joe. Except for Woolie, they were all women and
he was the thing they were afraid of. Walkman. But now that
he had cut his hair and bought a brown suit maybe he would be
able to make friends with them. He resolved to stop carrying
his dirty clothes around town washing them here and drying
them there. He resolved to wash and dry his clothes in
Flattop's laundry room where he would meet the
women—folding shirts, matching socks.
    Although he had closed his bedroom door, Joe felt naked
and exposed. His feet hung off the bed moist and chilled. *I
could sleep in socks, I suppose.* He heard Mary return. He
rolled over, tucked up his knees, and caught his feet under the
blanket. The idea struck him that if Rosealyn arrived in the
morning, scratching on the door like a stray cat, she would find
Mary asleep in her bed. That thought ushered in a flock of
speculations and Joe realized he would never fall asleep. He
imagined the scene of Woolheater receiving his *Hubcap and
Straw*. The hubcap had hugged a wheel rolling up to a
reservation in South Dakota. The straw had been gathered by
the hand of an Indian woman, shaped, and stuffed into an

Indian doll. The violent slash of the hollyhock stalk looked like a war lance thrust into the ground, festooned with red bunting. *Does it look like an Indian lance to me because I know it was painted by an Indian woman? Does it look like hollyhocks to everyone else? What will Mary do with the rug? Is there a dog in the soup? I hope Hero didn't stray from Judge's mansion.* Then he thought about Pinkie's second kiss. Not the first one that had gotten him slapped but the second one she asked for. He thought about Mary Thunder lying asleep in his apartment keeping him awake. It wasn't desire for Mary Thunder that kept him awake. And Woolheater was no doubt lying awake because of the excitement of Mary's unexpected visit. Joe didn't hunger for women the way Woolheater did, the way Everett did. Joe distinguished a difference between himself and Woolheater and Everett. Then he remembered Pinkie's second kiss and he doubted his distinction. He would live with Pinkie and father her children, beyond doubt, if he weren't such an old man and if she weren't already married. He heard the sobbing of pigeons on the windowledge. It was the middle of the night. Pigeons should be asleep. The sobbing was the sound of Mary crying. But that couldn't be. A tough woman like Mary Thunder lying in a snug bed with a belly full of dog soup wouldn't cry in her sleep.

7

Membranes

When Joe awoke it was late. He put on his robe to venture from his bedroom and find that Mary and the rug were gone. She'd made her bed. He washed his face, brushed his teeth, and went into the kitchen to check the time, almost eight o'clock. There was no note from Mary. He assumed the dog soup was also gone, but when he opened the refrigerator he saw that she had rearranged the shelves making room for the black kettle. *Woolie must be dead or he would have hammered my door by now*, Joe thought. While his tea steeped he walked down the hall and tapped on Woolheater's door.

"Joe! Top of the morning to you!"

"You sound chipper."

"I'm faking it. Ribs bothered me most of the night. I couldn't turn over and get comfortable."

"If they're itching that means they're healing. How many quarters does it take to play these washing machines?"

"Nothing, Joe, they're free. That's another reason to lock the doors. And I don't like coming home to find junk stuffed under my door. Circulars and pizza ads. Anybody can come in here and walk the halls."

Joe rubbed his chin and said, "Okay. I'll vote to lock."

"You were wrong about not getting our pictures, weren't you, Joe?"

"I'm glad I was wrong. I admire your hubcap. What are your plans for lunch?"

"Nothing."

"Good. You're invited to my place."

"What time?"

"High noon."

"Joe?"

"Yeah?"

"Who got the best picture? You or me?"

"You did, Woolie. Yours has a story in it. Mine is just a stalk of red flowers."

"Yeah. That's what I think."

Joe tossed off a glass of orange juice and settled in to drink tea and read last evening's *Journal*. An article on homeless people made him regret the lukewarm hospitality he'd given Mary. He wished he'd said, *If you ever need a place to sleep you have one here.* He read the comics and the classified ads. Then he phoned Bulldog. Phoebe answered.

"Is Bulldog there?" Joe asked.

"Bulldog?"

"Yes. Famous writer. Ferocious. Thinks he's a dog."

"Is this Walkman?"

"Joseph Geezre, U.S.S. Flattop." Joe heard the receiver put down. He held the static line for several minutes.

"Hello, Joe?"

"Woof! Grrrrrrr. GRRRRRRRUH! Woof! Woof!"

"Joe, what's on your doggone mind?"

"I made a statement to the police. I guess Phil's wife told you?"

"Rachel."

"Rachel, huh? That's her name?"

"Yes."

"I was coming back to apologize to Rachel when the police nabbed me and took me to the hospital."

"Hospital? Are you okay?"

"GRRRRRRRUH! Woof! I got in a dogfight, Bulldog. Got my ear chewed off, but I'm all right. Do you have lunch plans?"

"No plans, Joe."

"Come to my place. Noon." Joe hung up feeling mischievous and frolicsome. He put the iron kettle into the oven. Then he made himself toast. He fried two eggs with sausage. After eating he washed his dishes and phoned Pinkie. Graham answered. "Hullo, Joe. Good to hear from you. Pinkie said you have a car—"

"Borrowed my neighbor's. Why aren't you at work? Nothing's wrong?"

"Nothing's wrong. I took the late shift so I can drive Pinkie. Want to say hullo?"

"Sure."

Pinkie came on the line and chatted a few minutes. She was warm and confidential, as if Graham weren't there. Joe recaptured the spirit of wind melting their icecream. Talking to her made him think of kites flying—the curve of strings against the sky. Remembering Woolheater's cornflower blue carnations, he promised Pinkie a visit. He went into the kitchen and stirred the soup, picked pieces of meat from it, and rinsed them under the faucet. They weren't cut into cubes like beefsteak nor were they ground like hamburger. They were random shreds, ragged and stringy as if they'd been cut off the bone with a flint knife. He tossed them into the kettle, returned the kettle to the oven, and lowered the heat. He made a pitcher of iced tea then mixed a batch of biscuits, put a fresh cloth on the dining table, and set it for three. At eleven-fifteen everything was ready. He looked up Judge's number. Mrs. Judge answered. "Hello," he said, "this is Joe Geezre."

"Oh, Joe! Your card was wonderful! I want more."

"That's the only one."

"Where did you get it?"

"I drew it in Judge's courtroom."

"Oh— I'd like lots of them—"

"Take it to a print shop. Have it reduced a bit."

"I will."

"How's Hero?"

"Thinks he's a lion. Stop and visit him sometime."

"Well— I might just do that."

"We'll be here all afternoon. I'm bored. Ah— Joe?"

"Yes?"

"Maybe you'd go to the printer with me?"

"Sure. I'll mosey over after lunch."

Joe had twenty minutes before it was time to put in the biscuits, so he dumped his dirty clothes on the bed and separated socks from underwear. Then he tore down Mary's bed, put on clean sheets, and folded the once-used sheets for their trip to the laundry. He made a salad. He took the kettle out of the oven and put in the biscuits.

Bulldog arrived first, carrying a handful of stolen iris. Joe filled a pickle jar with water and Bulldog stuck the iris into the jar one at a time, carefully arranging them. Woolheater joined the party and Joe brought the iron kettle to the table. When Bulldog asked what it was Joe said, "Dog soup, cooked by Indian Joe." He brought out iced tea, biscuits, jam, butter, and salad. Woolheater asked Bulldog if he was writing anything and Bulldog told him he was researching the hippie tales—stories about war protestors, marijuana harvesters, poets, and the burning of the student union.

"Soup looks good, Joe," Woolheater said. He wasn't reluctant to taste it, proclaiming it delicious. "It tastes like lamb," he said. "Or mutton. Mutton has a dark, rich taste, like this."

Bulldog meticulously buttered a biscuit, put jam on it, and stirred sugar into his tea. He asked Joe, "Why were you reluctant to tell Rachel you saw Phil go over?"

"That's something I'm ashamed of," Joe said.

Woolheater asked, "Who's Phil and what did he go over?"

"Phil's the man who went over the dam." Joe served himself salad in his soup bowl. Like Bulldog he slowly buttered a biscuit, postponing eating the soup. *Woolie's showing off because he's a biologist. Woolie would eat a laughing hyena if you set one in front of him.*

Bulldog said, "Wonderful biscuits, Joe. As good as Mammy's." He served himself a dollop of soup. "Who's Indian Joe?"

"A friend."

"Is he a red Indian?"

"To be sure," Woolheater said. "We sat on a Navajo rug contemplating a buffalo skull. We smoked the pipe."

Bulldog tasted the soup. He said, "Wonder where he got the dog?"

"I don't think it's dog. I think it's beef."

"It's good. If I don't miss my guess there's some red wine in here."

"Do Indian chefs cook with wine?"

Joe's fried eggs and sausage lay heavily on his stomach. He ate all the salad out of his bowl and ladled in some soup. He tasted it and said, "I don't think it's dog. Indian Joe's having his fun with us." He sipped broth until his stomach relaxed. There was no taste of fat. His stomach glowed. His vision sharpened. Woolheater took a refill. Joe reached for the ladle. Spilling some soup on the tablecloth, he wiped it up, licking his finger. Bulldog growled. Woolheater bared his teeth to snarl, "This is authentic dog soup. There's no sham in Indian Joe. I smoked the pipe with him. I know." It was obvious that Woolheater, left alone, would eat the whole kettle.

Bulldog said, "I interviewed the head hippie, Joe. I've run his stories to the ground."

"What's next?"

Bulldog shrugged. He turned to Woolheater. "Know anything about hippies?" Woolheater squirmed, caught out. He looked into his bowl, pushing a round of carrot like a hockey puck.

Joe spotted a hair and discreetly pulled it up the side of his bowl where the gravy ran away from it. The hair was short, white, and springy. Joe searched his bowl for others, expecting to find a black one because he suspected the dog might have been a border collie, a popular breed. One border collie would make several kettles of soup. *Unless it was a puppy*, he thought. *I hope we aren't eating puppy soup. I hope it was an old dog, one that lived a long and happy life.*

Woolheater sucked his spoon clean, rolled his eyes, and said, "Hippies. I can tell you about hippies. My daughter lived with one—a young man with perfect teeth, hair down to his shoulders, and vacant eyes. He had two children when she moved to his farm. Chickens for eggs and goats for milk. He had an organic garden, a wood-fired sauna, a pond. My wife refused to go there, but I went. I took saunas with the hippie men, women, and children—vegetarians, whole-earthers, admirers of primitive cultures." The dog soup had loosened his tongue. "It was easy for me to take off my clothes, but I couldn't change my habits of thinking. So I didn't do much talking. They wouldn't have listened to a professor anyway. Being a hippie, you see, is a head trip, a soft-headed head trip. No experiment was controlled or allowed to run its course, therefore Hippie Hill became littered with failures: solar water heaters made out of steel drums, traps to catch the beavers that were cutting down the willows around the pond. Nobody ever persuaded the beavers to go into the painless traps. And nobody observed that it's natural for beavers to eat willow trees. Expensive looms to weave nobody-ever-decided-what. Veterinary medicine was declared subversive. The hippies smoked tobacco and cannabis and drank Third World beer, but they wouldn't eat a dog. They would gorge on honey, tofu, brown rice, and beans. They massaged one another with scented oils. They were hedonists. They were strong willed, illogical, and opinionated, so I held my silence and let them rave on because I wasn't there to educate them. I was there to save my daughter—by hanging around, by bringing out groceries, Mexican beer, and by holding my tongue while college dropouts lectured me on biology. My daughter chose natural childbirth and I was there standing by with my bourgeois car aimed at the hospital. My grandchild (I didn't know its sex for a week) was born with, according to my daughter, no pain or fear. Mother and child spent hours every day floating in a bath tub where I brought kettles of warm water. Jenny lay on her back like an otter nursing the baby, and I was only allowed to see it that way, with its sex pressed tight against her belly. I think, in all truth, the child benefitted from being suckled like an otter.

"Yes. That summer I spent a lot of time with the hippies. Someone might be playing a guitar or a concertina. Someone else would build a fire in the sauna and we'd go sweat. Then we'd jump in the pond."

Bulldog asked, "What about the child's father? How did you get along with him?"

"I tried not to think about mundane things, such as tetanus. In the fall Jenny left him. She moved in with us, enrolled in school, and worked off her incompletes. Now she's married, squabbling with her sister and sister-in-law over her mother's table settings." Woolheater's tone changed, becoming less matter-of-fact, more personal. "It's all one lovely, harmonious collection of stuff that I hate to see divided. And my son Peter doesn't want to see it split up, so I have a job of diplomacy on my hands. Oh, why can't we all be hippies and eat out of tin plates with wooden spoons?"

"Drink sassafras tea, wild honey and goat's milk—" Bulldog said, smiling dreamily. "And sometimes eat fox soup with the boys."

Beware the sly and vengeful fox!

Joe picked up his mother's bowls and took them into the kitchen. He washed them carefully and divided a can of fruit cocktail three ways. He added maraschino cherries. Joe asked Bulldog if he would see Rachel again. He said he would. It was his notion, based on what he'd learned from talking with Rachel, that Phil was unaware the dam lay close under the bridge, obscured by the bridge. Bulldog theorized that Phil never saw the dam. He was floating with his back to it, looking up at Joe. "Floating down the river on a lazy afternoon," Bulldog said, "he might've thought it was a riffle—or nothing at all." He asked Joe, "Will you go back and search?"

Joe crushed a cherry against the roof of his mouth. The dog soup had made him clear sighted and melancholy. He rolled the cherrystone behind his teeth. "Tell Rachel I'll go this afternoon."

Bulldog smiled. That was what he wanted.

"So what about your book?" Joe asked.   "How's it coming?"

Bulldog frowned. "The material's too thin. No crime, corruption, or pizzazz. I'll leave River City for someone else."

"What about Methusela? Seems you could make a whole book out of him."

"Who's Methusela?" Woolheater asked.

"He's our famous writer. The one you saw buying garlic."

"Oh," Woolheater said, "Bobby. He was in the bed next to me at the hospital."

"I didn't see him?"

"His curtains were drawn."

"Oh—"

Woolheater said, "Wonderfully grouchy old fart, Bobby. What the British call a remittance man. Never held a real job. Reminds me of the hippies. Head full of large ideas, but he won't be pinned down on specifics."

Bulldog asked, "Did he tell you why he lives here?"

"He can walk the streets here without getting killed."

"Why does he buy so much garlic?"

"I didn't ask, Joe. That's kind of personal, don't you think? He was reading the *Egyptian Book of the Dead*, chuckling at the funny parts."

Bulldog made an empty gesture. "See, Joe? That's Methusela for you. Think you could get a book out of that?"

A mood of soup companionship filled the spaces between the men. Finally, after repeated vows to meet again, Bulldog and Woolheater tore away. Joe took a bundle of clothes to the laundry room to meet his female shipmates. The laundry room was deserted. He started a machine and checked his mail. He stuck his hands into his pockets and paced the livingroom. Every time he passed the north window he paused to stare at pigeons atop Whoso Findeth. He returned to the laundry room and, too impatient to wait for his clothes to dry, brought them back to his apartment where he draped them over the chairs, tables, and sofa. Then he changed into the golfer's suit and Florsheims to call on Mrs. Judge.

By coming up the alley and cutting across the back corner of her lot he saw her through the patio door. She sat at the piano. Her posture was good. Her back was straight and her

arms were strong. She played fortissimo. Rather than
interrupt her, Joe returned to the alley. A question teased his
mind. Why hadn't the Judges built a fence between their lawn
and the alley? Houses in other parts of town had privacy
fences, but in the Judges' neighborhood there were none.
Maybe restrictive zoning prohibited such fences. The absence
of fences resulted in a spacious, free atmosphere, but without
fences there could be no nude weddings. And if Judge wanted
to play lawn darts in his robe and wig he would have to wait
until dark. *I'll bet Judge spotted Gigi. Graham is six-five
without heels, and Judge saw him walk to the restroom. Judge
would deduce that a tall woman wouldn't wear heels. Unless
someone advised her to flaunt it. There's always the flip side,
eh?*

A dog picked up Joe's trail. Joe stopped, whistled once,
and squatted invitingly. "C'mere, Alley! Alley Dog, here!"
He snapped his fingers. The dog, a blonde cocker, came
running. Joe rubbed her nape and scratched her rump.
"Where do you live, Girl?" He pulled up her tags and read,
"Missie! You're not far from home, Missie." When he said
her name she wagged violently. "Now you go home, Missie.
Don't be following Joe Geezre! Go home!" Joe knew to be
firm. He didn't look back for half a block and when he did she
wasn't there. As he walked he thought about Saint Teresa. *On
the one hand and then on the other,* he thought. *On the one
hand she is a saint. On the other hand she is a long-dead
sinner.* He thought about Hub. What are the early signs of
MS? Falling? Slurred speech? Impaired vision? And how
will his family live if Hub can't work? Joe approached the
Judges' front door. He guessed she was still playing because
it took her a long time to answer the bell and when she did she
was breathing hard. "Come in," she said. "Where've you
been? I saw you out back half an hour ago?"

"I didn't want to interrupt your playing, so I took a walk."

"Oh, you Walker! I'd like to put on jeans and prowl this
town from one end to the other!"

"Why don't you?"

"Judge's friends might see me."

"So what? Where do they walk?"

"On hiking trails. Or else they do tennis or jog."

"Oh, jog. That's a beast. What were you playing?"

"Nothing important. Give me a minute to change and we're off. Do you have a favorite printer?"

"No. You choose."

"Hero! Hero! Come out and be sociable! Sit down, Joe. I'll only be a minute." She went into the adjoining room looking for Hero. She returned carrying him and set him in Joe's lap. Joe held Hero's collar so he couldn't jump down as she left the room. "Hey, Buddy? What's your hurry? Sniff my fingers. That's cocker you're sniffing there. Missie. Didn't get her last name, but she lives over on Hilltop." Hero sneezed and wagged his tail, wanting down. "Ever eat another dog, Hero? Alpo Alfredo? Here—" Joe set Hero down and he immediately climbed Joe's leg. "No, Boy. Up or down. You can't have both. You're just a doggone dog." Joe strolled into the large room to sit at the piano. Its cover was down, but the bench was warm. He lifted the cover and placed his fingertips lightly on the keys. The ivories were warm. He pressed them enough to feel their action but not enough to make them sound, and he looked out at Judge's potting shed. He wondered if she played well. *Nothing important.* He closed the cover and got up so he wouldn't be caught daydreaming. He tried to interest Hero in a stuffed toy but Hero chose to be aloof. Joe looked at the Judges' art—Chinese paintings and four slabs of polished stone. *The Four Seasons, no doubt. Maybe that's what she was playing.* Joe looked at his silly shoes and thought of Fred Astaire. He was executing some nifty dance steps when Mrs. Judge came back dressed to encounter the world. She told Hero to be a good boy as she and Joe set out for the printer's. That chore only took an hour. When they were finished with it Joe saw that she wasn't ready to end their outing, but dressed as he was he could think of nothing else to do. It was too late for lunch at the Expensive Cafe and too early for the Opera. He said, "Normally I would walk home from here. But I'm wearing domino shoes. Do you mind giving me a ride?"

"Of course not. Where do you live?"

"On the hill. Flattop."

"I've never heard of it—"

"It's across from the chapel. I'd offer you a cup of tea, but I have wet clothes in the livingroom."

"I don't mind a few wet clothes."

Joe directed her to the parking lot and they entered by the lower deck, taking the elevator up so he could check for a Rosealyn letter. There was one. He asked Mrs. Judge to wait in the hallway while he straightened up. He put Rosealyn's letter on the mantle, tossed the damp clothes onto his bed, and filled the kettle. Then he ushered in his guest.

"Lovely place," she said. "Iris!"

"Have my feelers out for chenille bedspreads. Hen and rooster—twin beds. Oh—look at that picture. Tell me what you think of it."

She crossed the room confidently, like a lion tamer. "Nice view," she said.

"*Whoso Findeth Wisdom Findeth Life* is the oldest building around. It was originally a library, hence its motto. And its pigeons are picturesque."

"Lovely," she said, sizing up *Hollyhocks*. "Is this your work?"

"No."

She examined the picture carefully before saying, "Since it's not yours I'll be candid, Joe. It's damned good!"

"I think so."

"What's it called?"

"I call it *Hollyhocks*. I don't know what the artist calls it."

"Who did it?"

"Nikki Wildcat."

"I like it very much."

"Is China tea okay?"

She nodded.

Joe used a tea ball so he wouldn't be tempted to read her fortune. He placed cups, spoons, milk, sugar, lemon, napkins, and the teapot on a tray. *No cookies!* Mannie hadn't been to the cookie store. *Darn!* He served tea on the hammered brass table. Mrs. Judge sat beneath *Hollyhocks*. "I'm moving *Hollyhocks* over there, when I remember to buy a bulldog," Joe said.

"Bulldog?"

"You know, picture hanger. J-shaped metal with a nail through it."

"Oh, yes. Picture hanger."

"You have nice pictures."

"Thank you."

"Who collected them? You or Judge?"

"Consensus—"

"Does Judge have good taste?"

She wobbled a limp wrist and winked. "He can be influenced. Yes. I'd say he has good taste—if I don't rush him. If he has time to think."

"With me it's instantaneous. Yes or no."

"Yes. I know."

Joe poured. He asked, "Do you follow the literary scene? I mean, are you interested in famous writers?"

"No. Except for in the movies. I go to new movies. Do you?"

"Yes." Joe's eyes strayed to the letter on the mantle.

"Well—" Mrs. Judge said, "what have you been doing lately?"

What have I been doing lately? The question hurt Joe's feelings because it sounded—he thought—like she assumed he was lazy—unimaginative. He set down his teacup and spread his arms like a skinny bird attempting to fly. He said, "Oh, just the usual." *Petting alley dogs. Smoking marijuana. Reading other people's prayers. Eating dog soup. Learning to drive. Falling in love. Kissing married women. Dating transvestites. Having my fortune told. Searching the river—*

"Searching the river," he said.

"What for?"

"Rachel's husband. He took his boat to the river and slipped over the dam."

"Oh, yes." Mrs. Judge put nothing in her tea but she stirred it thoroughly. She sipped. "I read about that in the paper. He hasn't been found?"

"No."

"And you're assisting the search?"

"I was standing on the bridge. He looked up at me, and then he was gone. He didn't know he was in danger."

"Rachel?"

"She's a nice woman. No children. I promised her, indirectly, I'd go out today and search."

"How do you search a river?"

"You look at the water."

"Who are you going with?"

"You. If you want to—"

"I'd like that. I'd like that a lot. But not dressed like this—"

"When we finish tea you can change." Joe picked up the phone. "I have to beg my brother to launch the boat for us."

Joe phoned Everett and made arrangements. While he talked he thought about Hub. He thought about Rosealyn getting a job. He hoped he would find Phil's body so Rachel could put some of her grief to rest. He had come to believe that Rachel was the strong silent type.

"What should I wear?"

What you wear to work in the yard, Joe almost said before he remembered that she didn't work in the yard. "Some kind of hat or cap with a visor. Trousers."

She nodded. On her way home she stopped at a sports shop to buy a tennis visor. While she changed clothes Joe took another look at the pictures, especially the portrait of a Chinese woman. Something in it brought Madame Leontyne to his mind. He had always thought of her as being Black. But her daughter certainly wasn't Black. But was the girl with the tight jeans really her daughter? Madame Leontyne was indeterminate, vaguely Oriental. Her face was round and dark. She covered her hair with a scarf. Her eyes were green. A woman of color. Perhaps Creole, or gypsy. Perhaps she wore green contact lenses. The opera singer Leontyne Price was

Black. Perhaps Leontyne wasn't the fortuneteller's real name. Joe didn't know. Mrs. Judge entered dressed for safari. "Sorry to keep you, Joe, but I didn't want to cause trouble later by being improperly dressed. What time will we get back?"

"Maybe after dark."

"I'll leave Judge a note to fend supper for himself." She left the room. Joe stared at her Chinese painting and felt an intense hunger to gaze upon Madame Leontyne's face.

Mrs. Judge followed Joe's directions, parking in front of the weathered shack. Joe suggested that she wait for him, but she would have none of that. She followed him through the maze of parked cars. It delighted Joe to see Preacher even though the chicken gave him nothing but hostility, threats, and assaults—no compassion or understanding. "Get back there, Chicken!" Preacher toed the line, craning his neck and blinking his bright eye—itchy for a fight. Joe knocked, rattling the screen door. Madame Leontyne opened it wide and led the way through her kitchen, beckoning them. As he passed the stove Joe looked at the teakettle. He touched it. It was cold. He said, "I have one question for you."

"Don't be absurd, Joe. You have hundreds of questions. And don't be so hasty. Are you on a rocket-launch countdown or something?"

"Not especially."

"Relax. Be a gentleman. Introduce me to your lady friend."

"Madame Leontyne, I'd like you to meet Mrs. Judge."

"Sit there. Take the loveseat. I'll put on tea water."

Joe and Mrs. Judge sat on the faded burgundy loveseat. Joe watched white cathairs spring from it to his trousers. Mrs. Judge took everything in. He thought it possible she'd never been in such an impoverished room. A clatter of teacups came from the kitchen. Then Madame Leontyne brought in a steaming tray.

"My question is, how do you heat your water so darned fast?"

She smiled, setting the tray precariously on a footstool. She pulled up a chair and addressed Mrs. Judge, "I answer questions for my bread. If I'm in the bank and a teller asks, *Can I help you?* I laugh in his face. *Not for free you can't,* I say, *No free questions!*" By the time she said the word *questions* Joe had taken a twenty from his billfold and dropped it onto her tea tray. "Microwave oven, Joe."

"Thanks."

"Don't mention it. Was that your burning question? My tea water?" She turned to Mrs. Judge, "The last time Joe came here, I feel it's my duty as a sister to tell you, he tried to seduce me! He asked me, a married woman, to go honkeytonking!"

"No I didn't! The last time I was here we talked out at the clothesline!"

"Oh, that time. Well— If you're going to count *every* time!"

"And you said Everett would see Wayne Newton. He did not. And you said he would lose money in Vegas. He did not. So your track record stinks!"

"If that's your opinion, why are you here?"

"That's a question!"

"Okay." She pointed to the clock. "Your sand is running, young man!"

Joe half expected her to bring out the Temptations. He said, "Tell me how to find the missing man. His name is Phil. He's in the river."

Madame Leontyne rose abruptly and turned as compactly as a bullfighter, her large body making her feet small by comparison. She wore purple velvet slippers. "Oh, Joe! This is painful! You're not here on a prank, are you?"

"I'm serious. I want to find him."

"Yes, yes. I see you do!" She ran into the bedroom and slammed the door. Joe heard the bed groan as if children were jumping on its springs or as if Madame Leontyne were lying face down, crying, her body wracked with sobs. Joe wanted to go in and comfort her, but it didn't seem like the thing to do. Mrs. Judge was enthralled. Joe knew she'd never seen

such a display. He lifted his teacup gesturing, *Drink your tea.*
When he put down the cup he saw loose leaves moving in the
bottom. After several minutes he said softly, "I think she'll be
back."

Slow minutes passed, but there was no indication that
Madame Leontyne would return. The bedsprings continued to
squeak. Joe stood, gesturing for Mrs. Judge to follow him.
Quietly, they made their way through the kitchen where a note
was pinned to the screen so they wouldn't miss it. Joe read,
Phil is floating on the water.

When they were in the car, driving across the bridge, Mrs.
Judge asked, "How did she manage to put that note on the
screen?"

"She obviously climbed out the bathroom window, walked
around the house, and put it there."

"She's too large to be climbing out windows!"

"Maybe she got her daughter to do it."

"She has a daughter?"

"I don't think so. Maybe she's not large. Maybe that's all
padding. From the size of her feet she might be skinny as a
rail."

"What do you think of the note?"

"Hogwash. The expanding gases cause buoyancy.
Everyone knows that. I *told* her he's in the river. It's logical
that he's *floating* in the river. But where? See? She left out
the important part. Where?"

"The note said, *Below the bridge.*"

"What?"

"The note said, *Below the bridge.* It didn't say anything
about floating."

Joe directed Mrs. Judge to the plumbing shop where
Everett waited for them, his van hitched to the boat trailer.
Everett placed his palm to the back of his neck as if he had a
stiff neck. In their childhood code the gesture meant, *You're
a pain in the neck!* In this case it could be translated as, *She
is one good-looking woman. What's she doing with a dud like
you?*

Joe and Mrs. Judge rode to the river in Everett's van. Everett launched the boat and helped them get in it, insisting that they take two lifejackets and two paddles. Joe checked the gas. He carefully primed the engine.

"How will you get her back to the shop?" Everett asked.

"If I had a good brother," Joe replied, "he would help me. He would be waiting here at dark. I'd find him by a dot of red light. The glowing ash of his cigar."

Everett shoved them off and said, "Don't hold your breath."

Joe pulled the starter rope several times, adjusting the choke after each pull. When he hit the right combination and the engine coughed to life he steered up to the dam to show his contempt for Madame Leontyne's clairvoyance. He circled the pool, idled the engine, and let the boat drift downstream past a fire department rescue boat. A grim fireman nodded. Joe wondered if he was the one Phoebe Jones slept with. Mrs. Judge asked, "Where's the bridge?"

Joe pointed.

"Not that bridge. That bridge is *above* the dam. There has to be another one downstream."

Joe turned into the current thinking about what she'd said. *She distinguishes upstream from downstream, above from below. She's no dummy.* He looked into her eyes, bright in the shade of the tennis visor which pinned her shiny hair tight to the sides of her head. He thought her face, her entire head, was exceptionally well groomed. She didn't look frowsy and working class, like Pinkie. She didn't look too intellectual to comb, like Paula. Mrs. Judge had the taut rested look of one who has lingered in the spa. To test the accuracy of her observations he asked, "Which way is downstream?"

"Don't be silly, Joe. There's a bridge down there. How far is it?"

"About eight miles."

"That's where Madame Leontyne told you to look."

"Madame Leontyne told me no such thing. She's a fraud."

"Of course. But you paid her twenty dollars—"

"Okay. We'll go." He steered along the south bank, staring at the water. He would return along the north bank. That was the routine. Mrs. Judge saw where he was looking so she turned her back to him and looked the other way, toward the middle of the river. Joe had seen Madame Leontyne's bedroom. There was no exit from it other than the bathroom which had a small, high window. And the bedsprings had squeaked all the time he and Mrs. Judge waited on the loveseat.

"Great blue heron," Mrs. Judge said.

Joe used enough power to hold the boat straight in the river.

"Big bird," he said. As he spoke the bird launched itself. Joe hated making it fly.

"Marvelous!" Mrs. Judge exclaimed. "One of those babies killed a woman in Texas. Drove its beak into her neck."

"Are you a bird watcher?" Joe asked.

"From a distance."

"Madame Leontyne's note said, *He is floating on the water.*"

"No. It said, *Below the Bridge.* You can drift along and watch birds—or you can open the throttle and go to the bridge. Madame Leontyne answered your question. To be fair, you should look where she told you to."

"Okay." Joe steered away from the bank. Mrs. Judge snugged her visor and moved forward to hold down the bow. Their passage made a noticeable breeze, and the engine roared. Joe saw the cottonwood root he had tied to with Bulldog and Graham. He remembered the frozen river—the tree root ripping the ice. He remembered the *Deutsch* boys. The river widened. Joe picked the deepest channel. The hair conditioner Trish recommended held his Unisex in place, nevertheless he longed for his captain's cap to protect the top of his forehead.

When they got to the Hogtown bridge he cut the engine. "Well?" he asked.

"It's your show, Joe. I'm along for the ride."

"You wanted to come down here. That makes it your show."

"I am merely sticking up for Madame Leontyne. Sisterhood."

They saw the hump and they both knew what it was turning in an eddy, stuck there, going nowhere idle and swollen and sodden inhuman. Joe brought the boat closer. It floated face down. Blue shirt, khaki trousers. Leather belt. No shoes. One white sock. One blue-cotton-white foot. Joe measured the depth with a paddle. He felt no bottom. "Can you drive the boat?" he asked.

"Yes, I suppose. Why?"

"We'll have to tow him over to the sandbar. It's too deep here to do anything. If you'll drive the boat I'll hold him."

"I'll hold him."

"No, c'mon—"

"What do you think I am, Joe, a tourist? You drive the boat." She knelt in the bow. "Take me close. More to the left." She gripped the cuff of a pants leg. "Okay, Joe. Slowly, slowly. Back us across!"

"You okay?" He reversed.

"I'm okay. Just go slowly. Oh my god!"

"You could use the boat rope—"

"This'll work. Slowly. Slowly."

Joe crept the boat and its tow across the river. When he felt the nearness of the sandbar he backed upstream letting the bow swing down with the man's body streaming before it. Joe killed the engine. "Hold on!" he said, stepping out on the sandbar side. He gripped the man's belt and pulled the buoyant slippery corpse alongside the boat.

"Sister Leontyne was right," Mrs. Judge said.

"Let's not argue about who was right, eh? Let's decide what to do now."

"Is there any question of what to do?"

"Well— I don't know—"

"Why not put the body in the boat and go back?"

"That would be a grim boatride. Are you up to it?"

"Yes. We'll lift together."

Joe knew getting the man into the boat would be difficult. But she was willing, so he set about the task. "You pull on the pants cuffs. I'll stand here and lift his shoulders." Joe towed the corpse. The shadowy shapes of turtles followed underwater, unwilling to lose it, stalking it like torpedoes. "Ready?"

"Yes."

Joe got a firm grip, flexed his knees, and lifted as hard as he could. He hadn't overestimated the difficulty of lifting the corpse, while standing in mud. It wasn't a pretty job but he and Mrs. Judge managed to drag the dead man into the bow, face up with his arms splayed out of the boat. Then the corpse rolled, tipping the boat hard toward deep water. Joe's shoe, mired in the underwater muck, came off. He stooped to dig for it. The boat, tipping far enough to capsize, drifted broadside to the current and swung beyond his reach. He sloshed after it waist-deep in the river. "Stick out a paddle so I can hold you!" The paddles were pinned beneath the corpse. The boat drifted faster. "Can you start the engine?" Joe yelled.

Mrs. Judge shrugged. She sat in the stern, leaning hard away from the corpse, trying to balance the boat.

"Turn the throttle to START! Pull the rope!" he yelled. The boat drifted faster. Joe stood helplessly watching it go. He saw Mrs. Judge studying the engine. She pulled the starter rope several times. *She's not pulling it hard enough. She can't get leverage. It'll never start for her!* The boat drifted to the bend and Joe watched it turn and slip out of sight. He clenched mud with the toes of his left foot and stared at the cottonwoods crowding the bend. They stood like a filigree of strangers between him and the boat. *How ridiculous! I let the boat drift out of reach. Standing here in one shoe. How ridiculous! This is absolutely the worst thing that could have happened.* He slogged to the sandbar and walked down to where it tailed off, blending into the brushy bank. He stared at the pale cottonwoods, listening, fearing that Mrs. Judge would panic and jump out of the boat. Or the boat might capsize dumping her in the water with a floating corpse. He had neglected to ask her if she could swim. *Maybe she'll drift onto a sandbar. Maybe she'll drift to some fishermen who can start the motor and bring her back.* He listened intently to a

woodpecker rattling a dead limb in the forest.   Far in the
distance, low on the wind, he heard the moan of a coal train
going east. *Coltrane.* What a shock for a fisherman to look up
from his lines and see a boat drifting down, a dead man in one
end, a sobbing woman in the other.   She could explain
everything. She wouldn't be sobbing. She was strong. She
was in control. A kingfisher, flying upstream, screamed loud
and Joe jumped. Harmless birds. But they always startled
him. Kingfishers and tight-holding quail that crouched in the
grass until almost stepped on and then exploded like a nest of
buzzing rattlers. And the barred owl that yelled in the night.
Harmless birds. A corpse is harmless. But few people would
choose to drift with one. *Roll over to the sun a puffy face, salt
white—here I am.* Then, softly, he thought he heard the sound
of Everett's engine. He stared at the bend straining to hear,
straining to see. He held his breath to hear better. There was
nothing. Then there was the moan of an outboard. Then there
was nothing. The shifting wind. The rattling cottonwood
leaves. Then he heard it again and saw her coming up the
river, a lovely swirl of blue smoke fuming the water behind
her. She leaned hard, balancing the boat. The corpse dragged
a hand in the water. She brought the boat alongside the
sandbar. Joe climbed in.

"Do you want to drive?" she asked.

"Not a chance. That's your job." He hunkered forward
and tugged the corpse straight in the boat.

Mrs. Judge opened the throttle. "Keep me in the channel!"
she said loud, over the engine noise.

Joe nodded. He sat cramped, his knee snug against the
corpse, watching the channel, using hand signals to keep her in
it. She wasn't afraid of speed. He liked that. To keep his
eyes off the dead face he stared at the water. His mind swirled
with thoughts of Madame Leontyne and Rachel and Mrs. Judge
and himself. He tried to be glad they'd found the body, but he
could muster no glow of satisfaction for their success, no pride
in their accomplishment. His eyes were irresistibly drawn to
the dead face, but with no power of his will could he attach the
name *Phil* to it. The word *Phil* had abandoned him. He

couldn't remember the Phil whose eyes looked up to him when he stood on the bridge looking down. He took off his shirt and covered the face. He projected their arrival. If they were lucky the fire department boat would still be there. Otherwise he would ask someone to phone the police. He turned to her. Their eyes met. He didn't smile and she didn't smile. He looked back at the channel. Everett's engine hummed as the boat cut a vee that widened into a wake, lapping the banks on either side.

———————

Mrs. Judge and I were both shaken by the experience. She didn't say anything, nor did I when two firemen lifted the body out of Everett's boat. Nor did we speak while we waited for Everett to come. When we were alone, sitting in her car, she said, "I need a drink."

"Okay. Can you drive?" I asked that because her lips were pinched purple tight and her hand was shaking.

"Of course."

"I'll tell you where to go. Cross the bridge. There's a bar."

I directed her to the alley behind the Pentimento Bar and we slipped in the back door, like regulars. I led her to a booth then went to order one installment of Thom's recipe and an onion and icewater for myself telling the bartender to be prepared to bring us two more. *When I hold up my hand it doesn't mean I want to go to the toilet. It means we want two more drinks! Don't make us wait. A man doesn't like to wait for his second drink. Third drink, fourth drink, no big deal. But the second one should be prompt.* I had no choice about the words I was saying. They came from my brother. Words I'd heard Everett say.

"Sure." The bartender nodded. "Gin for the woman. Icewater for the man." He leered. "Oldest trick in the book!"

I carried our drinks to the booth remembering Gigi, statuesque in her red heels, turning heads at the Savoy. I was wearing a white undershirt. My shirt was gone.

"Martini?"

"Yes. I thought I'd try something different."

"Gibson—"

We melted into the decrepit vinyl booth. Neither of us offered a toast. We sat there and coasted. I wasn't compelled to say, *Gee, you did a good job with the boat.* She wasn't compelled to analyze Madame Leontyne's prediction—or question how Madame Leontyne managed to put her message on the back screen. In due course I held up my hand. Later I held it up again. Mrs. Judge said, "That's not exactly true, what I said about the pictures. They're Judge's. He bought them long before we married. I suppose you noticed—we're a June and January couple."

I nodded. *Why did you marry an old man?* was in the front of my mind.

"He'd never been married. He judged my divorce. That's how we met."

"Is he a good judge?"

"He's fair."

The mysteries of marriage teased my mind. Everett and May. Woolheater and his wife. Rosealyn and Hub. Pinkie and Graham. Judge and this young woman. All mysteries. The naked hippie bride and groom. The fruitbats with their crinoline-wrapped balls of long-grain wedding rice. I held up my hand again.

Mrs. Judge said, "If I drink another I'll have to walk home."

"Can you drive now?"

"I can do it. But not if I drink any more."

We left before the drinks came. "What's this place called," she asked.

"The Picture Reconsidered."

"That's appropriate. I'll tell Judge about it. He'd like to wear a disguise and come here and relax, play a few games of darts."

Put on a disguise, I thought, *like Graham putting on a dress.*

"He's terribly isolated. Harassed by defendants—plaintiffs—jurors. They squeeze him into the role of being a judge, explaining the law. You can imagine."

Any judge worthy of the name has enemies. I figured Judge hadn't told her about my harassment. She put her key in the ignition switch but showed no interest in starting the car. "Let's sit here awhile," I said. "There's no need to rush into traffic."

"Good."

"This is nice. We can watch people come and go." Two men climbed the steps to the back door of Pentimento, ignoring Mrs. Judge and me. I thought about Judge being afraid. Like a leper he sought the company of other lepers. *Judge Lebow and Mrs. Lebow.* "He's a leper, isn't he?"

"Who?"

"Judge."

She laughed mightily. "You think my Judge is a leper?"

"Yeah."

"That's hardly a compliment! He has a bell around his neck so people can hear him coming?"

"No. Just the opposite. We all have bells. He's tired of hearing bells."

"Yes! You're right! People adore Judge! It's not especially good for my ego. People are helplessly attracted to him." A new thought overwhelmed her. "Where's your shoe?"

I pantomimed writing. She didn't get it, so I whispered, "Pencil? Paper?"

She found a note pad in her purse. I wrote, *Below the Bridge*.

"Yes, Joe. That's what I said. Where's your shoe?"

There had been no shoe on my left foot for the past hour. I had hobbled around the boat landing, gotten in the car, gotten out of the car, gone into the Pentimento, walked to the bar to order drinks, and walked out of the Pentimento all with no shoe. Why had she just now noticed that I was half barefoot? Or had she not cared to ask about it until now? "I lost it in the muck there, below the bridge, knee-deep in water."

"How can you walk with one shoe?"

"It's not hard. How did you get the motor started?"

"It was easy."

"Were you afraid?"

"Something came over me. Life prepared me to be alone with a dead man, so I wasn't a bit afraid. I was sad. The day was bright and quiet. The river was serene, lovely. I read instructions on the motor. It was easy, but sad."

I nodded. "You did a good job. I'm proud of you."

"Too bad you don't have your shoe. We could walk this alley and sober up before trying our luck in traffic."

"Try our luck! Try me! Not only can I walk with one shoe, *I* can walk with *no* shoe!" I took the shoe off my right foot. "C'mon. Let's walk the alley."

"Be careful of broken glass, Joe."

"And rusty nails. And copperheads."

"Ever been snakebit?"

"Oh sure. Non poisonous."

"Really?"

"In my job I got nipped from time to time. Once by a dead snake." As we passed a dumpster and I tossed in my shoe.

"Hey, Joe! Keep that! We'll go down the river and get its mate!"

"Right," I said. I groped in the dumpster for it. She stood beside me, her elbows on the rim, looking in.

"This is what you've wanted, isn't it? You want to look at trash."

"Uh-huh."

"It's not archaeology. It's the hunter-gatherer urge that makes us crave thrown-away stuff."

"There's an eggbeater. Looks like a good one."

"This is downscale window shopping, Mrs. Judge." I retrieved my shoe from a pile of chicken bones. We walked a ways up the alley.

"Please don't call me Mrs. Judge," she said. "Call me Anne."

"Okay, Anne. Do you feel like driving?"

"I'm as sober as a judge." She giggled. "Let's shop some more."

"If I had my shoes I'd walk your butt off, but—"

"Okay, let's go to the car."

We sat in the car awhile because Anne was in no hurry. Maybe she was a bit dizzy from the martinis. "I really love Judge," she said. "I really do."

"He judged your divorce?"

She nodded. "He was a bachelor. He likes music. He collects Chinese art."

"What were you playing?"

"It's not important. I'm an orphan. My adoptive parents, lovely people, promoted international ice shows and in every country they picked up a curio or souvenir. They got me in Brazil. They took me with them until I was school age. Then they boarded me in the States. I showed aptitude for the piano so they sent me to good teachers. Judge learned all that when he read my divorce papers. He invited me to come play for him. He bought me a grand piano. Isn't that impressive? I'm the only person ever to play it. Except at the factory. I'm sure someone tested it at the factory."

I looked at steps leading up to the landing. A sturdy bannister kept drunks from falling off. It's surprising more drunks don't break their necks, the way they stagger around this town. If a judge takes a flask to lunch does that mean he's unhappy because his wife can't play the piano? How could there be a chunk of ice big enough to skate on in Brazil? "Are you a good piano player?" I asked.

"*No*, I'm not a good piano player. I can't sharpen a pencil until the point breaks off. I can't live in the infinitesimal distance between the fine point and the finer point. I divorced my first husband because I can't play the piano! Judge wants me to play professionally. He wants to be my patron because, you see, I really am an orphan. My mother lived in the street. My father was a tourist. She didn't check his passport. Who were those British women at the Savoy?"

"Friends—"

"I'll bet the tall one's a pianist."

I smiled.

"I knew it. I could tell."

"How?"

"She's burned out from trying to put the finer point on the fine point. She looked strung out, like she might tear off her clothes and run naked through the clam sauce!"

"Of course you're absolutely right about that," I said, knowing it was gin that made Anne talk. Gin and a journey with turtles.

Anne dropped me at Flattop. I rolled up my pantslegs to make it look like I'd been wading creeks, like I had a reason for being barefoot. As I embarked I met two shipmates from B deck. "Ahoy," I said, smiling, but they held stony, grim countenances. I guess they thought I was simple-minded at my age to let my pale shins shine like moons. I held up the wet shoe in explanation, but they ignored it. One muttered, *Another reason to lock the building.* Her companion replied, *That won't keep him out. He lives here!*

I stood in a hot shower nursing my hurt feelings. You could take any tall skinny guy, chop off his ear, steal his shoes, turn him loose on the world, and he'd be a leper. The kind people run from. I turned up the cold water and got angry. I yelled against the stinging splash of the showerhead, "I'd like to see either of you do what Anne Judge did!"

I tuned the radio to *Opera Hobby* and made supper. While the corn casserole baked I washed Indian Joe's kettle. It was a dutchoven with a flat lid that fitted snug so it could be nestled in a bed of coals and covered up. I steeped a pot of weak tea and went to check on Woolie. He was fine, watching the American Kennel Club. As I returned from his place I mused on his crystal and silver and china, his two daughters, and his daughter-in-law. His wife's crystal-silver-china set could live with one daughter awhile and another daughter awhile. What a good plan, until a piece got broken. And son Peter. I'd never met him. He lived in California. I didn't even know his profession. All I knew about him was that he had a wife and his name was Peter Woolheater. After *Opera Hobby* a jazz show came on. There is no other species of music that can be so good sometimes and so bad other times. I switched to the lowbrow AM station and listened to a news reporter say the fire department had recovered Phil's body. Good. They kept our names out of it. I didn't want the world-at-large to know I'd been down the river with Anne Judge. I didn't want Pinkie to know. I drank tea and watched pigeons flutter above Whoso Findeth.

After dinner I phoned Madame Leontyne and told her about our success. *Did you have a nice nap?* I was tempted to ask, but I knew she wouldn't answer a free question, so I said, "I hope you enjoyed your nap."

"Whadda you mean, nap?"

"You left us in cat hairs while you went in your bedroom and wouldn't come out. I presume you were napping."

"No, Joe. You got what you wanted. Don't hurry back."

"I'll return to check you, Madame. Don't you mistreat Preacher. That chicken's not for your pot."

She hung up. I settled under the reading lamp with a plateful of orange sections and Saint Teresa. When my eyelids got heavy I turned out the light and went to bed, but I didn't sleep, because there was something on my mind I couldn't pin down. It wasn't Anne Judge or Phil's body. It wasn't Madame Leontyne or Preacher. It wasn't Pinkie. It was Rosealyn. I'd forgotten about her letter!

Dear Uncle Joe,

Just a note to tell you I'm coming. I'll probably see you the day you get this letter or the next day. I don't know how fast the postal service is between us. Don't say anything to Mom and Dad. I really need a couple of days anonymity—as you suggested.

Love, R.

I settled in to wait out the night knowing I wouldn't be able to sleep—with the knowledge that Rosealyn was coming to visit me.

I wrote notes to Rosealyn telling her my apartment number, my deck, and the fact that my door was open. I taped the notes to the outside hatches, above and below. I turned off all the lights except the small one in the ventahood and drank tea. I thought about my frightened shipmates and the fact that I'd posted notices on the outside doors saying I was unlocked. I wasn't afraid. There's no virtue in being unafraid. The lack of fear has no moral superiority. I remembered my outrageous behaviour with Paula Ramsay, shining my flashlight for muggers when she thought I was a mugger. I said mugger out of delicacy. Rapist was the word behind the word. Who would wander in on me? Woolheater? Paula? Melanie Moore? Pinkie? Bulldog? Graham? Mary Thunder? Indian Joe? Rosealyn? Of all the people who might drop in, one was certainly on her way. Rosealyn. When she ran the path by the river, stopping and turning, I didn't think she would be a dancer. But I didn't think she would marry Hub and become a mother either. I thought she might be a research physician, a rocket scientist, a theologian, or a judge.

I pictured Anne. Her head was hard. Not her mind. Not her personality. She wasn't hard-headed in the sense of being stubborn. Her head was visually hard—in shape and outline. Her hair was crisp and defined. Her lips were painted—lightly. Her eyes were shadowed—lightly, giving her a precise dimension. Her muscles looked firm. She reminded me of a painted Japanese actress. Her chin was prominent. Maybe her eyebrows were tattoos. Or maybe she was totally natural. I would never know. But I knew she yearned to put on jeans, walk the alleys, let her hair down, and take off her mask. I recalled the white terrycloth tennis visor trapping her shiny brown hair tight to her crown. The underside of the visor's green bill. Billiard cloth green. Once I daydreamed of taking Pinkie out in a canoe and floating with her under Japanese lanterns. But in reality, in the hard light of day, it was Anne I took out in Everett's boat. So that night, while eating orange sections, I performed a brutal surgery. I carved Pinkie into a soft-edged, scented, mysterious moonlit night woman and I carved Anne into the seashell cameo of a hard-edged, alley-prowling, day girl. I remembered Pinkie lying on the backseat while I drove to Kansas City—reclining, soft, remote, exhaling formless smoke that covered her face like gauze before rolling out through the mysterious crack in the window. I remembered Anne sitting straight at her black piano. I remembered Judge on his lawn wearing his black robe. I remembered Graham in the Savoy wearing his red dress. I remembered Pinkie asking me for a kiss. I remembered her saying, *If we're going to be friends we have to be wise.* If I had been wise I would have known there was nighttime in Anne and daytime in Pinkie. But I hadn't yet found wisdom.

Wind blew in the window tickling hairs on my leg. I basked in the anticipation of Rosealyn's visit. My chest puffed up at the thought of her coming to my place. I would get the crystal-silver-china set before my sister-in-law got it. I would polish it with a soft, clean cloth. I would ask Rosealyn about Hub's symptoms. He worked at a computer. If his disease confined him to a wheelchair, perhaps he could still work. Rosealyn was the baby of Everett's family. Maybe her brothers and her sister would pool their part of the Vegas wealth, giving it to her. *It's easy to spend other people's money.* I'd heard that many times. I was hungry to see her. I could feed off her intelligence. I could tell her about my two loves—my daytime woman and my nighttime woman. She would understand. I chuckled at the idea of Woolie watching a dog show. Dog on TV. In my mind I said to him, *Hey Woolie! You've developed quite a canine taste, eh?* I kicked the recliner back a notch and closed my eyes. Who knows how much time passed? A spring thunderstorm blew in with lots of lightning and rain. Every flash lit the red tiles of Whoso Findeth. CRACK-BOOM! The tiles flashed silver with rainwater. I didn't have to look to see them gleaming in the darkness. Asleep, I heard someone dripping. I couldn't open my eyes. Softly, I heard Madame Leontyne come into the apartment. She hovered above me, touching my teapot to check it for warmth. I felt hypnotized. She said to her companion, *Sit on the sofa. It doesn't matter that you're wet.* I heard her companion slump onto the sofa and I felt the Madame bending over me, looking down into my face. *Don't open your eyes, Joe. I've brought Phil. You can ask him your questions.* I wanted to know what was on his mind when he looked up at me. Why didn't he see the dam? What made me think he had an anchor tied to his leg? Why did Rachel carry a brand-new green leather billfold? How did Madame Leontyne know his body was down there below the bridge? Did he appreciate being retrieved? Was our finding him an act of love? Did he care? Did he pray? Would he make a wet visitation to Rachel? Those were my questions, but I couldn't wake up enough to ask them. Without opening my eyes I saw him on the sofa. Half sitting, half lying, he was propped there looking dead at the sky. In the lightning flashes I saw his chewed face. It was not the face I saw looking up at me from the boat. Which boat? He was scared and surprised and embarrassed. There had been no time for him to reflect on his error. There had been no time for his mood to change. I smelled Madame Leontyne's perfume. I had never realized it before, but perfume defined her. Perfume was so much a part of her that it went unnoticed—like her corpulence. But I didn't want to think about Madame Leontyne. I wanted to think about Rachel. *Phil, is Rachel a daytime woman or a nighttime woman? Does she love you? Does she care that you're dead? I couldn't see it in her face.* I struggled to ask questions, but my jaw was frozen. Lockjaw. Then a most miraculous thing happened to me—Madame Leontyne, billowy and dark in her muu-muu and gypsy scarves, wreathed in perfume, leaned over and kissed me. Her soft lips were slow. They kissed away my lockjaw. They kissed my eyelids. They were my lullaby. My jaw went slack, my mouth fell open. I snored the raspy sound of a wooden boat chafing a wooden pier. Some time later I awoke. My recliner was dry, but the sofa was soppy wet. My recliner floated beside the open window, between it and the sofa. I heard treefrogs singing. The windowsill was dry in the freshness that comes after a spring thunderstorm. Having watched the sun rise a thousand times I have never seen the night darken before the dawn. All my dawns have lightened gradually. That's why I don't believe homilies. I don't trust conventional wisdom because my bare toes have touched unconventional wisdom. Then I knew why Everett visited Madame Leontyne. I stared out the window. There was no darkness before the dawn. If anything, there was dim light before the dawn. Woolie had awakened me numerous times. He had one coming. I showered, dressed, and went to knock him up.

"No, Woolie, I don't want to go anywhere. I'm expecting a guest. Make us a pot of coffee and bring it to my place. I'll fry eggs. Bacon?"

He gave me a sour nod because there were no pretty waitresses at my place.

"You don't look so chipper, Woolie?"

"The storm kept me awake. The storm and my ribs."

"Your tape is too tight. When do you get it changed?"

"Today. But I want it tight, Joe."

"Yes." I'd heard that one. I nodded, wondering if I repeated myself as much as he did. When I went back into my place I smelled Madame Leontyne's lingering scent. I put large towels on the sofa and pressed them, sponging up water. The sodden towels smelled of river water, filling me with a shameful species of horror. I tossed them in the trash bin and they hit the bottom echoing a mortal thud. I went back for the wet cushions. I washed my hands thoroughly and put a fresh cloth on the table. I poured orange juice and arranged bacon strips in the skillet.

Woolie and I ate slowly. He had an excellent method of making coffee, every bit as good as Thom's martinis.

"Why did you name your son Peter?" I asked.

"Huh?"

"Peter Woolheater. It rhymes. Sounds funny. Why did you name him that?"

"It was my father's name."

"Oh. I suppose I'd have to ask your grandfather why he named his son Peter Woolheater."

"It goes back before him."

"How far back does it go?"

"All the way."

"Dern, Woolie! How far is all the way? You're a geneticist. Does it go back to the first gene, this name Peter Woolheater?"

"Of course."

I looked at the tight man with tight ribs picturing him naked, hunched in a smoky sauna. Someone opened a Franklin stove to toss in firewood and by the orange flames I saw Woolie's chest gleaming wet with sweat. I saw his daughter in a bathtub clutching her child to her breast. I saw all the way back to the first mother with her first child—swimming, clutching. Naked bride and naked groom. Big, fat, and wide. Skinny as a broom.

"Let's go jump in the pond," I said.

"Looks like a good day for it. But I'll buy a paper instead. Had enough coffee?"

"Oh. I could read a *Star* and drink another cup. Before you go, help me move this sofa to the hallway."

"Why?"

"I'm redecorating."

We put the sofa in the hallway. Woolie had gone to buy his paper and I was washing up the eggy plates when someone knocked. I knew by the knock it wasn't Rosealyn. It was a heavy, distempered knock from the manager come to tell me that my lease wouldn't be renewed after the provisional period. Everyone knew a detective had been checking on me. Everyone knew Mary Thunder spent the night with me. I had posted notes on the outside doors advertising the fact that the building was unlocked. And just now I had dumped a wet sofa in the hallway.

"You left out smoking marijuana, eating puppydogs, checking my mail in my underwear, coming in barefoot with one ear! None of those things are crimes!"

"Marijuana?"

"I was kidding about the marijuana."

"You make people nervous, Mr. Geezre. And your little friend with the downturned hat snooped the halls reading everyone's names off their doors. Who's he?"

"He's a celebrity, more famous than Wayne Newton! If those people had recognized him they'd have begged for his autograph! Why the heck do you think he wears dark glasses and a downturned hat?"

"And that Indian. I caught him in the laundry room washing cardboard boxes full of very dirty clothes."

"I didn't give him permission."

"It's your lifestyle, Mr. Geezre. Were you in the navy?"

"No."

"Then why do you say *Ahoy, M'Boy!* to everyone? Women don't appreciate being called boy." He handed me the notes I'd left for Rosealyn. The tape on them was carefully folded down so they wouldn't stick together. He had preserved them with humiliating care as if he expected me to use them again, somewhere else. I felt sorry for him. He didn't have the personality for conflict. So. I had lived up six weeks of my provisional two months. That left a fortnight for this voyage, then there would be a new berth for me. I didn't own many things. I could borrow Everett's van. And I was snug in Flattop for the time being, long enough to receive Rosealyn. Give her a nice vacation. I felt good. I felt generous and free. I smiled at the manager, shook hands, and thanked him. "Thanks, really," I said. "I'm not mad."

Woolie returned with a *Star*. We drank a fresh pot of coffee. I read the comics while he studied the bra ads.

Rosealyn called Joe from the bus station. She told him she had one suitcase, one package, and an AirportRoller which she'd ordered from *TV Guide*. She planned to walk to his place pulling her goods on the AirportRoller, and she invited him to meet her somewhere along the way.

"Sit tight," he said. "I'll be there in fifteen!" He laced on a pair of medium weight Basses and flashed out of Flattop in

high spirits. *Rosealyn in River City!* As he passed the chapel
he saw bushwackers. Two boys and a girl, seven or eight
years old, stood on a redwood bench discussing their attack.
When Joe neared he heard the girl say, "Sean's truck is messed
up. Dad put grease on the *tires* so it won't go." One of her
co-conspirators said, "I hope it's not cooked rice. I hope it's
the hard kind!"

"Wedding's been cancelled," Joe said in passing. "Go
home."

"Huh?"

"Whose wedding are you here for?"

"Sean's."

Joe stopped, feigning concentration. He pulled his chin.
"Sean— Sean— Nope. Sean didn't have enough blood—
wedding's been cancelled!" He turned abruptly and marched
across the boulevard. On a less important day he would have
lingered to attend Sean's wedding. He had been in many
wedding photographs, crowded up on the chapel porch,
grinning, thinking of the day the bride would open her wedding
book and see his mug. But he'd never thrown rice. He left
that ritual to the invited guests. He certainly threw rice at
Rosealyn's wedding. He wore a rented tuxedo, he threw rice,
and he gave Hub a Hoover. But he didn't enjoy it. He
couldn't understand why Rosealyn wanted to marry a computer
programmer and get pregnant. Joe had saved a tidy sum to
kick in, anonymously, on her grad school tuition. It was still
in the bank. He would send it to her at the appropriate
time—when one of the kids needed braces or piano lessons.

Joe cut across campus, walking on the grass. He knew a
professor who suffered from MS. In the early stages of his
disease the professor's wife took out loans and built a new
house, on one level, with doorways wide enough to
accommodate a wheelchair. She installed sink faucets with
easy-turn handles. She enrolled in law school. Joe was
impressed by her providence. If Rosealyn and Hub returned to
River City he could buy them a house. Rosealyn could enroll
in graduate school. He cruised alongside the stadium
daydreaming of football crowds swathed in earmuffs, scarves,

and feather coats. He dreamed of a skull-tight aviator's helmet with fleecy earflaps swinging loose like ears. But that's not the kind of hat Trish had in mind. She was thinking of a trilby. He wondered if Trish was married. She didn't wear rings. Perhaps she removed her rings to protect them from haircare chemicals. He thought of Rosealyn's red hair. He quickened his pace.

Rosealyn stood behind the bus station. He gave her a swirling airport hug. "Rosie!"

"Josie!"

"So this is the roller, eh?" He hefted her suitcase.

"Yeah. I can pull it myself, but I have this other package." She pointed to the bundle at her feet. "What have you done to your hair?"

"It's a long story. Has to do with Trish."

"Who's this Trish?"

"I'll arrange for you to meet her."

"What are you doing?"

"Taking the roller off. I'll carry your suitcase."

"It's too heavy. And I have this package."

"I can manage. We'll cut up the alley. Save time." He started walking and Rosealyn skipped at his side to keep up, lugging the package.

She said, "I can't wait to see your place. You're living right on campus. You must feel like a teenager? Mom said your apartment's big, two bedrooms, and nice?"

"The apartment's snug, Rosie. The location is perfect. I'm right in the middle of the action. A cafeteria, art museum, library, concert hall, chapel."

"What's wrong with it?"

"Nothing."

"Something's wrong."

"I said it's perfect didn't I?"

"When you said *perfect* there was an unspoken *but* in your tone. *It's perfect but* is what you said."

"I did, eh?"

"Yes."

"What'll you tell May if she catches you in town and you haven't called her?"

"She won't catch me if we stick to the alleys. Unless we run into Dad's truck."

"That won't happen. He's retired."

"What!"

Joe nodded, thinking, *If Rosie doesn't know Everett's retired it certainly isn't my job to tell her.*

"Dad retired?"

"Back to my question. If they catch us, what do we say?"

"I'll say I came to see you. Back to my question. What's wrong with your apartment? Are you lonely there?"

"Lonely? Don't make me laugh. Let me tell you about my friends. I have lots of friends."

"Tell me."

"I don't know where to begin. Wait until we get you unpacked and brew a nice pot of tea."

"Still drinking tea?"

"Sure. What's wrong with that?"

"What's wrong with your apartment?"

"Won't you leave it alone?"

"I'm not the kind of niece to leave things alone, Josie. I'm a bulldog."

"We already have a Bulldog. And a Pekinese. You can be the rat terrier."

"Okay. I'm a rat terrier. What's wrong with the apartment?"

"I got my eviction notice this morning."

"Eviction? You just moved in."

"Seems I've failed to be a model tenant. There's a two-month period during which the landlord can cancel the agreement. No questions asked."

"Baloney. Questions can always be asked. It's fascist to say no questions."

"The rental agreement doesn't say no questions. It says something like—*Without being required to show good cause.*"

"Why haven't you been a model tenant?"

"I threw a Native American and Indian party. I got in trouble with the law."

"Uncle Joe!"

"True." He grinned, shifting the suitcase to his other hand.

"That's too heavy for you," Rosealyn said. With her free hand she tugged at the suitcase handle. "Here. I insist! Put it down!" Joe set the suitcase at her feet.

"It's heavy."

Rosealyn maneuvered the suitcase onto the wheeled frame and strapped it in place. "C'mon. I'll pull it a block. You pull it a block. Here. Carry your housewarming gift." She handed him the bundle.

"Heavy—" Joe said.

"Yeah. It's a pot for your begonia. I decorated it with oystershells. Very beautiful. Housewarming gift."

"I don't have a begonia."

"Get one."

They mounted the hill alternating the tasks of pulling the suitcase and carrying the oystershell pot. They passed the museum and crossed the street to Joe's apartment. He saw that the outside door hadn't yet been fitted with a lock. He held it open for Rosealyn to pull the suitcase through. "Go around that sofa. I'm the next door on the left."

"Whose sofa?"

"Mine. I threw it out."

"It looks better than mine."

"It got wet."

"Wet? Did you pee on it?"

"I did not *pee* on it!"

Woolheater looked out his door.

"Woolie! C'mere! Meet my beautiful niece!" Woolheater pulled his head back. Joe knew he had gone to comb his silver locks and brush his moustache—freshen up his cologne. "Rosealyn, enter."

Rosealyn was impressed, remembering Joe's dingy rooms in her grandfather's house. "Give me the tour!"

"To your right, cleverly concealed behind a room divider and breakfast bar—is the kitchen.   Refrigerator, range, dishwasher, counter, sink, cabinets—basic kitchen. Clean, eh?"

"Spotless. Do you have a maid?"

"Nah. Just Mannie. Here, this large area where we enter is the livingroom. Sparse decor, the way I like it. North-facing windows. There's the dining area, with a good view. To your left, three doors. One to your bedroom, one to the bathroom, and one to my bedroom. There's not much close-ette space, but I don't have much close. Get it?"

"Yeah. But I don't like the idea of you having to move."

"Forget about that. I'll find a better place."

Woolheater knocked. Joe introduced him to Rosealyn. Woolheater, smitten, shook her hand. Joe half expected him to unbutton his shirt when he said, "I'm on my way to see Joe's nurse."

"Nurse? Is this Trish?"

"British nurse," Woolheater said, smirking. "Trish is his American hairdresser."

Joe said, "Pinkie. I know her and her husband. We'll have dinner with them."

Woolheater chimed in, "We will?"   Emphasizing the pronoun to include himself. Joe stared at the fresh-scrubbed, pink-eared, silver-haired professor and conceived his grand idea. Woolheater departed. Joe made a pot of tea which he served on the brass table while Rosealyn unpacked. "Let's drink it with milk, okay?"

"Fine." She handed Joe the bedspreads. "I hope they'll do?"

"They're lovely!"

"This place is perfect for you, Joe, like a dream. I can't see you leaving it."

"I'll get revenge. If they think I've been troublesome up to now—they ain't seen nothing! I just conceived a grand idea! I'm going to throw you a big, loud party. A blowout."

"Oh, boy!"

"Tell me all about Hub and the kids?"

"The kids are fine. Hub had a scare. That's why I'm so exhausted." Rosealyn sat in the overstuffed chair and stuck out her feet, propping them on the brass table. Her posture looked uncomfortable, and Joe knew she'd propped up her feet out of nervousness, trying to appear relaxed. "Here, take this recliner before you kick over the teapot."

"I won't usurp your chair."

"Of course you will, Rosie. We don't play games, you and me. We go back as far as snake guts."

"Okay." She moved to the recliner.

"Lean back. Back. Back! Get comfortable."

"Back any more I'll be in psychoanalytic position."

"Maybe that's the idea."

"Okay, Dr. Geezre. I'm on your couch."

"Tell me about Hub."

"He might have MS. He went to Atlanta for tests. Our doctor advised us to prepare for the worst. Seems the tests might not tell much anyway."

"If he has MS, how will you manage?"

"I've been worrying about that. From Jackson to Memphis, that's all I thought about. At a little town in the Bootheel a woman got on. She was afraid the earth would split open and swallow us, bus and all. She could die in her house with no regrets, but being entombed in the belly of a Greyhound terrified her. I held her hand and told her about Hub, she calmed right down. Seems she's experienced with that particular calamity. Then," Rosealyn giggled, "this is the funny part, she asked me to pray with her!"

"Did you?"

"Well of course. I'm not a pagan!"

"Did it help?"

"Enormously. When I got to St. Louis I called Hub and told him he doesn't have MS. I told him to get that shitty idea out of his head."

Joe nodded.

"I'll bet you could march out of this academic hothouse and never look back."

"Of course. In two weeks I shall. But Rosie, while you're on my couch you must listen to me."

"Okay, Dr. Geezre."

"I lived in two rooms in my father's house. I spent nothing on wine, nothing on women, nothing on song. No rent. No car payments. I purchased no gasoline. I put my money in the bank."

"It's nice to know I have a rich uncle. But say no more, please."

"Okay."

"The warm milk makes me sleepy."

"Go cuddle under that little hen."

"I think I will. I couldn't sleep on the bus."

"Do it. I'll make arrangements for your party."

Rosealyn pulled herself up from the recliner, and Joe went to the breakfast bar to compose his guest list.

Pinkie	*Anne*
Graham	*Judge*
Paula	*Woolie*
Bulldog	*May*
Phoebe Jones	*Everett*
Phoebe's cook	*Indian Joe*
Madame Leontyne	*Mary*
Daughter?	*Melanie Moore*
Trish	

Pinkie and Graham hadn't left for work when Joe called. They were delighted by his invitation. Pinkie offered to bring something—make it a pot luck. What to bring? Saturday night. Eight o'clock. Joe called Anne. She said she would bring Judge. "But," she said, "don't tell anyone he's a judge."

"Anne, he's up for election. He might need the votes?"

"Why not make it a costume party, Joe? If Judge came dressed as a plumber nobody would pester him."

"My brother would ask him about toilet wax, flusher diaphragms, ballcocks, nipple valves."

"Then Judge can come as a sportscaster, wear a check jacket, bow tie, microphone—"

"If he did that, who would you be?"

"A bag lady! I'll bring a grocery cart of things I've found in the trash."

Joe called Bulldog, who liked the idea of a party. "A masked ball," he said, "A costumer!"

"Who will you be?"

"Errol Flynn, at it again!"

"Will you please invite Phoebe's cook for me, and Phoebe?"

"Sure. Phoebe loves a party. She'll come as a distinguished poet." He laughed at his joke.

"Her cook?"

"Lloyd. I'll make him up as a London bobby. He has the accent. If I had the costume I'd make him a Beefeater!"

Joe crossed names off his list. He phoned Everett who said, "Hey, Bro. What's going on?"

"I'm inviting you to a costume party. Saturday night. Eight o'clock."

"Housewarming?"

The word reminded Joe of Rosealyn's housewarming pot with oystershells. "Not exactly," he said. "It's a party for my lady friend."

"Are you having booze?"

"Only if you bring some. What are you doing right now?"

"Nothing. I'm retired. Haven't done anything all day."

"Help me haul off a sofa."

"Okay."

"Don't knock. My lady's sleeping."

"That Englishwoman?"

"She's American. Just like you and me."

"Joe, act your age. What are you trying to prove?"

"This woman's nice, Everett. Don't get any wrong ideas."

"Nice? Is she a looker?"

"She looks a lot like you."

"If she's good looking why's she sleeping in your place?"

"C'mon, Everett. I have lots of calls to make." Joe tried Mary's number in Topeka and got a message that her phone was no longer in service. He called the Pentimento Bar. Mary hadn't been there. He called Firm But Fair and got Detective Bradley. Joe said, "There's an Indian woman, Dick, Mary Thunder. She has a father named Indian Joe. I want to invite her to a party but I can't find her."

"I'll put you on hold."

Five minutes later Dick came on the line. "Try the Salvation Army Shelter. Joe, the blotter says you found the body?"

"Yes."

"Did my hypnosis help?"

"No. My fortuneteller told me where to look."

"Uh-huh."

"The party's Saturday night. I'll be honored if you came?"

"Saturday nights are busy."

"It's a costume party. If you're undercover, stop by for a few minutes. You'd be welcome."

Joe took a seat beside the chapel to wait for Everett. He wondered if the greased tires had slowed Sean's escape. He remembered seeing *Blood Wedding*. That was years ago, and it terrified him. He made a note to ask Paula if virgins suffered an inordinate fear of blood. Maybe someone had written a book about virgins and blood. If so, he wanted to read it.

Everett parked at the curb after using his Chancellor's House ruse to get past the traffic guard. Joe stared at the van's obsolete *Geezre Plumbing* while Everett lit a fresh cigarillo.

"Unnecessary precaution," Joe said. "There's no stink in this house."

"Where's the cushions?"

"I put them in the trash."

"Why? This thing is brand new?"

"It was wet."

"Wet? Let's get the cushions. I'm not taking a new sofa to the landfill."

Joe led Everett down to the trash bins. Sacks of garbage had been piled on the cushions. "They're under that garbage."

"See? I always know when to light a cigar!" Everett climbed into the bin and started digging. He handed out a cushion. "One." Then another, "Two. Three! Let's drag 'em out in the light and see how they look. Not bad garbage, eh? Old folks are tidy. They've got nothing else to do."

Joe bristled, "That's me and my garbage you're talking about!"

"Myself included," Everett replied. "I'm retired." He put the cushions on the sofa. They were clean and dry. He said, "Joe, you're crazy. There's nothing wrong with this sofa."

"I know I'm crazy. That's my specialty. I got a crazy idea about my zebra—that it might cause Woolie some harm. But he managed to have a wreck without it. Then I got a bad feeling about this sofa—"

"What's your bad feeling?"

"A ghost sat on it. Let's go to the landfill."

"If you think they'll bury this sofa, you're crazy. Those dozer boys will take it home."

"I'm afraid for anybody to use it—"

"Look, Bro. Put it in the van. I can get it sanitized."

Everett drove fast down the hill, squealed into traffic on the one-way, and turned sharp into the parking lot. "C'mon," he said. "Let's negotiate." Joe hadn't been there since Rosealyn's wedding. Subdued, he walked a step behind Everett, craning to look up at the glass. In the sanctuary Everett collared Father Butler, a teenage priest. "Come out to the parking lot, Father. Bless my van."

"What's this?" Father Butler asked, fumbling an orange.

"I've cursed this goddamn van every goddamn day for as long as I remember. Now I'm selling it, so I want it pure for the next owner."

Father Butler winced with each *goddamn*. Joe introduced himself. Feeling awkward because of Everett's irreverence, Joe said, "I've been reading the *Life of Saint Teresa*. Are you familiar with her?"

Father Butler blinked. "Which one?"

"You mean there's more than one?"

"There's Saint Teresa of Avila. And there's Saint Thérèsia. And Saint Teresa Margaret of Italy." The priest tapped the toes of his black Monopoly shoes.

"Which one said *More tears are shed over answered prayers than unanswered ones*?"

Father Butler pursed his lips. "Come in my office. I have a book of Catholic quotations."

Joe followed the young man, leaving Everett standing in the hallway. In Father Butler's office Joe avoided the eyes of a familiar face—a photograph of old Father Booger, the spooky priest of his childhood. The young priest searched his book but couldn't find the quotation.

"Is it bogus?" Joe asked.

Father Butler shrugged. "It's hard to prove that someone *didn't* say something, especially if the someone happens to be a saint."

As Joe followed the priest to the parking lot he reflected on all the Fruitbats over the years who had said Comanche was Custer's horse. *If you say something often enough, that makes it true*.

"Have you been comforted by Saint Teresa?" Father Butler asked him.

"No," Joe replied. "I can't say that I've been comforted. But I find her descriptions of rapture fascinating."

"Yes—" Father Butler said, his eyes twinkling. "And her parable of the Four Waters."

Joe had many questions for the priest—for another day—in privacy—when he had an appointment. He waved and said to Everett, "I'll mosey on."

"Don't you want to watch him bless the van?"

"I'll take your word for it." Joe walked east toward Madame Leontyne's fortunetelling parlor. Along the way he passed a house being gutted for renovation. A pile of lath and plaster had been tossed onto the lawn. He selected a cross of lath which he carried, tapping the brick sidewalk, walking with his eyes closed. *Nobody knows how to plaster anymore. It's all drywall now,* he thought. The phrase stuck in his mind. For several blocks he repeated, *It's all drywall now. All wall. Now dry, how dry, cow dry.* He used the cross for a sword, fencing his way through Madame Leontyne's parked cars. Then he used it to fend off Preacher. Within the scope of Preacher's tether he sat down, thinking Preacher would feel less threatened at chicken level. "C'mere, Fella. Let's have a crowing match! How many girlfriends do you claim? Me? Oh, I'm not in your league. I'm no loverboy."

Preacher stalked Joe, ruffling his hackles.

"Are you jealous? You think I'm keen on Leontyne?"

She came out her back door screaming, "What in the hell are you doing sitting right where I throw my dirty water? What are you telling my chicken?"

Joe rolled onto his back, holding his paws in the air. He whined like a puppy. Madame Leontyne kicked him hard. "Come on, Boy! Get up from there! Somebody'll see you acting crazy! What are you trying to do? Get a free ticket to the loony bin?"

Joe stood, towering above her. "I once read a book about wolves," he said. "I was demonstrating typical wolf behavior, to show I'm not threatening. You didn't feel threatened, did you?"

"Uh-hum—"

"I know why you throw your water here. To mark your spot. Typical wolf behavior."

"I throw my water here because it's as far as I can pitch it without coming out in my panties!"

"Ah yes, but you *could* pour it down the sink. You don't have a clogged drain, do you?"

"I throw it out the door because my grandmother threw hers out the door!"

"Live modern! Your grandmother lived in olden times!"

"Did you come here to argue with me?"

"If I'm in a bad mood it's because you and that ghost kept me awake last night."

"Boy, you are too much!"

Joe slipped his arm around Madame Leontyne, hugged her, and whispered in her ear, "I want you to come to my costume party Saturday night. Bring your daughter, if you have one."

Madame Leontyne pushed him away. "Of course I have a daughter. Spookie saw you out at drivers' testing."

"She acted like she didn't recognize me."

"It's not her job to recognize you."

"I can't argue with that. Are you Black?"

"That's a question, Joe. No free questions. Besides, that one's personal, like asking a lady's age."

"How old are you?"

She laughed. "Come in the house. Sometimes I find myself in a generous mood."

Joe went straight through the kitchen to sit on the cat-hair loveseat. He resolved not to ask her if she had visited him during the night or how she got the note on her back screen or even what was written on the note.

She brought two cups of tea. Lipton tags pursued the cups like moths. She offered no milk, lemon, or sugar.

"I've never seen your cat," Joe observed.

"I don't have a cat. I use a chicken."

"Cat died, eh?"

"Ran off."

"Gotcha!" Joe leaped up and danced around the room. "You answered a free question!"

"I'm weary, Joe. Drink your tea. I mean to tell you, I'm sick and tired of peddling information to people who have no earthly idea what it is they want to know. But you. You're different."

"Yes'um."

"You're full of questions. Still a virgin, at sixty-two. That says it all."

"What does it say?"

"You're one of those trees that flower in the fall. Trees are supposed to flower in the spring, but some of you get it backwards."

"I'm backwards?"

She nodded solemnly. "You blossom in October."

"How long have you known Everett?"

"He only had two children the first time he came here, that's how long. The twins—Lucille and Lewis."

"So you and Everett go way back."

"Oh yes."

"His youngest daughter, Rosealyn, is my best friend."

"She's in River City, but it's a secret."

"You know everything, don't you?"

"No. I get hunches, that's all."

"You make intuitive leaps."

"Huh?"

"My neighbor, Dr. Woolheater, was married. He got used to being around a woman's intuition. But I never got used to it."

"And now, at this late date, you're getting horny ideas."

Joe nodded. "Married women."

"Because they're safe. Every schoolboy starts out with a crush on a married woman."

"Yeah. And Rosealyn. She's kinfolks."

"She's the blood daughter of your twin, which makes her very close. You know about blood?"

"Well sure, Dr. Woolheater—"

"You and Rosealyn have the same blood. That's why you think the same way."

"We don't always think the same way. I thought she would go to graduate school. But instead she got married and got pregnant."

"And how old was she? Twenty-three? When you were twenty-three you weren't biting your wrists looking for a place to put it. So how would you know anything about anything?"

"Put it?"

"Ying-yang, Joe. Doodlebug. To get that wisdom you keep harping about you'll have to switch things around.

Rosealyn didn't get married and get pregnant. Turn it around. See? When she was twenty-three, moaning in the moonlight, she certainly didn't let on to her old-maid uncle!"

Joe settled into the cat hairs and drank deep from his tea.

"Let's get this straight, Joe. You lived in River City sixty-one years and during those sixty-one years all us women left you strictly alone. But now you have five or six girlfriends. Why?"

"That's the question I'm asking you!"

"You pretend you don't know?"

"I'm not a smarty-pants like you."

"It's as plain as the nose on your face. After your mother died you didn't trust women. But that was fifty years ago. Now you've started asking women questions. It's written all over you. Basic, hungry, curiosity. You have a titty fixation. You're a six-foot-five-inch sixty-two-year-old baby crying for titty. Your begging eyes and your dumb questions fire up the mother-lust in women."

Joe flushed. He couldn't breathe. His hand shook, spilling tea. *She caught me with her temptations!*

"Are you all right?"

"Shortness of breath. Allergic to cats. I'm a dog man, myself."

"They's no cats in here."

Joe swept his hand across the loveseat, ploughing up a windrow of white hairs. "What's this, ghost dandruff?"

"Oh, that came with the sofa."

"Yeah. Well, it's stuffing me up."

"But are you getting any smarts?"

"I'd say you gave me a full adult dose. It'll take me a week to figure this all out."

"You'll never get it figured out. We are alone, Joe. A man and a woman. Ying-yang. Are you thinking about my bed in the next room?"

"When I came here drunk your bed was the magnet that drew me."

"What made you think I was available?"

"I've always thought so."

"That's a disrespectful thing to say, Joe. You thought I was a whore?"

"I didn't say that—"

"Sex draws everybody to the fortuneteller. Women. Men. They think they want a better fortune—more money or a better job, but what they really want is better sex." Joe blushed. "You're getting your color back."

"I'm sorry—"

"The egg has a membrane around it that the sperm must penetrate. Find the membrane—and you find the meaning. Membrane explains everything. It's everywhere. You still have questions, Joe, but I see by the whites of your eyes that you want out of here. I hope you don't feel seduced."

"Seduced?" He reached for his billfold.

"No. Don't pay. You broke me down. Made me your friend. I can't take your money. But the next time you see Spookie go a little bit out of your way to be nice to her. Don't treat her like a whore's daughter, okay?"

"I never would—"

"I know. Sure, Joe, we'll come to your party. Look for the membrane."

Joe stood. Madame Leontyne remained seated. He walked out through her kitchen and headed north hungry for the creosote smell of crossties and the glint of sunlight on the rails. He followed tracks thinking about the membrane enclosing his brain, the membrane around his stomach, the membrane around Earth. He remembered riding up the river in Everett's boat—Anne watching his hand signals. He had nothing to watch except the dead face facing him. No membrane of skin contained that face. It had no aura of life. *Death has no membrane* came into Joe's mind. He repeated it as he goosestepped on the crossties, altering his stride to their interval. When he got to Dead Man's Curve he left the tracks charting a course for Flattop, and as he walked he made an inventory of his guests. So far he'd invited Everett and May and Madame Leontyne and her daughter and Bulldog and Phoebe and Lloyd of London and Pinkie and Graham and Anne and Judge and Detective Bradley. "It will be a standup party," he announced to the red light, "I only have five chairs." The light changed as he stepped into the crosswalk saluting the light walking man, his double, the okay guy who said, by his cheery presence, it was safe for pedestrians to enter the street. *Did Madame Leontyne make a pass at me?*

———————

I walked slowly giving Rosealyn plenty of time to finish her nap. I stopped at a grove of flowering trees, their blossoms losing prominence to transparent green leaves, and I sat in their shade. The apple trees were flowering uniformly making it impossible for me to pick one that might be an October bloomer. Late bloomer. Madame Leontyne brought me up short. Whenever I've tried to make her kind of intuitive leaps I've fallen on my face, like mistaking Paula for Kimberly. It would be interesting to put Paula and Madame Leontyne head-to-head and let them duke it out in a psychological slugfest. I have a number of personal questions for Madame Leontyne. One: Why is your daughter so lightskinned, whereas you are so dark? Two: Why do you keep all those cars parked beside your house? Three: Same thing for the dead refrigerator on your front porch. Four: If I moved to a house with a yard would you sell me Preacher? I promise I would take good care of him. Feed and water him, get him a coop of hens, too. I'd invite Woolie over for eggs. Supermarket eggs are infertile but in my youth, before henhouses became factories, a premium was paid for infertile eggs. I never knew why. Perhaps it was because people didn't want to eat chicken sperm. Or it might have been because people thought of fertilized eggs as embryonic chickens. Or maybe fertilized eggs began mitosis and spoiled quickly, in the days of muggy iceboxes. Why, Madame Leontyne? And there was a premium on brown eggs. Why? And did Coca-Cola really contain cocaine? So I'm a fall bloomer, am I? In that case I'll buy myself a hotrod and a gross of rubbers. Maybe I'll buy myself a big house with room for a garden and chickens, close to the schools so if Rosealyn needs help later, if she needs a place to live, I can take her in. Her kids and Hub too. Wheelchair accessible. A big house on one level with wide doors.

Stinging insects mazed above my head, their loud humming making me yawn. If I were Phoebe Jones perhaps I would write a poem about crabapple trees and wasps and bees. If I had been Everett I might have followed Madame Leontyne to her bedroom. Thank God I kept my hands off Anne Judge when she was three-martinis tipsy, eyeshopping the trash bin— *Oh, there's an old eggbeater!* Of course at that moment I remembered snuggling Mary Thunder in the trash corral. Eggbeater. And I remembered Everett climbing in the trash to dig out my wet sofa cushions. And I remembered ripping the zebra skin and stuffing it into a trash bin. I remembered trying to kiss Mary Thunder. That was my first adult kiss, and I didn't desire it. Ah, here's a distinction. Here's a membrane of meaning. A kiss is good only insofar as one desires it! My first kiss with Pinkie didn't work. I got my face slapped. But our second kiss was bliss. Lucky for me I didn't grab Anne Judge and hop around half-shod like a one-legged stork. I might have gotten fresh and then what? She would have had to slap me. Hero would have had to pee on my foot. Judge would have had to crack my skull with his gavel. No more croquet for me. No piano lessons. No blue birds over— The white cliffs of Dover. No melted icecream staining the seat of Woolie's car because I would be under the jailhouse because that's where Judge puts barefooted fellas who alley-smooch his orphan Annie. A honeybee landed on my bare arm and crawled, tickling, stumbling through the hairs.

Well yes, Madame Leontyne. Maybe you're right and maybe you're wrong, but one thing's certain. You haven't begun to crack this egghead because if you could see inside here you'd know I'm certifiably crazy. What are the odds of a man being blasted by a plastic champagne cork dead center in the naked hole of his starboard ear? What kept the concussion from rupturing my eardrum? Eh? There's a membrane for you. If we didn't have membranes in our heads we couldn't hear. Hymen, of course! Rubber balloons. Hot water bottles. Bags of blood. Blood-brain barrier. The membrane of self-preservation that kept my hands in my pockets instead of gripping Anne Judge's enticing shoulders. We must be vigilant— We must be valiant— I am beginning to feel waves of sympathy for my brother. Poor sod carried our hod sixty odd years. When the dogwood pink of May is repeated in October how can a man stay rational and sober?

The honeybee nibbled my skin. "Crazy me? Ha-ha; ha-ha; HA! You bet your stinger-ee, Bee!" I spoke too exhuberently, producing a startled skip-step from the fruitbat who happened to be flitting past. He stopped, spotting me among the flowers. He wore a tennis visor much like Anne Judge's except it was red with Greek letters embroidered on its sweatband. His shoes were first-rate Adidas. His faded jeans he had deliberately torn at the knees. His blue sweatshirt bore the design of a mythical bird's beak and eyes. He looked at me, his cheeks as clear and soft as Rosealyn's before she got pregnant and married Hub.

"Hello?" he said.

"Hi," I replied.

"Stingeree-bee?"

"Huh?"

"Did you say stingeree-bee?"

"I certainly did!"

"Hey," he stepped forward. "That was my favorite thing to say when I was a kid. For a whole year I said stingeree-bee. I thought it was so cool."

"Me too! I said it when I was a kid. Still do."

"Cool!"

"Frigid!"

"Yeah. What're you doing?"

"Taking a sit. Earlier I took a walk."

"You walk a lot. I've seen you all over town, man. I mean, everywhere."

"Yeah."

"That's cool—"

"Good day to you, Stingeree-bee," I said.

He trudged away and I felt a surge of affection as I watched him walk down the hill because I knew he carried the

meaningless phrase inside his head. I went home to roust out
Rosealyn.

She was awake when I got there. In fact she had made
a pot of coffee and was sitting at the breakfast bar drinking it,
snuggled up chummy with Bulldog as if they'd been friends
forever. I changed from my walking shoes to slippers and
eavesdropped. She was telling him hot gossip from
Mississippi. He soaked it up, taking mental notes. She said
Hub had joined the country club which she described as being
a tin-roofed warehouse—formerly a cotton gin. I fancied that
Bulldog would write a play, "Damper Down," about a
Mississippi couple swinging to a country-club band. Sure,
"Damper Down" would have a love triangle. The woman
would be Rosealyn's age, the mother of two, her yearning heart
tortured with lust for a highschool band director. Her husband,
confined to a wheelchair, would be impotent. The hairy-
chested, blueblooded, baritone director liked her company,
having purchased a treasure map to her mines of sensitivity and
intelligence. But, alas, the baritone had no appetite for her
body. And that was precisely what she found appealing in him.
He, unlike her other suitors Wilde Turkey and Jackie Daniels,
did not bruise her flesh with his eyes. Oh, Baby! Tree-top
tall, won't you kindly turn your damper down! And then, dig
this! This is what makes it a drama, the woman realizes that
the only thing in the world that could possibly make her happy
would be for Mr. Baritone to bruise her flesh. Love wounds.

I padded into the kitchen, hefted the pot, and poured
myself a cup of coffee.

"Joe," Bulldog said, "I'm in love with your niece!" To
Rosealyn he said, "Joe told me all about you. He's very proud
of you."

Rosealyn demurred.

"Have a nice nap?" I asked her.

"Sure. Where did you sneak off to?"

"I invited Madame Leontyne to our bash."

"Bash, eh?"

"We're gonna rock old Flattop like she's never rolled before. A costume party so people can cut loose and have a good time."

Bulldog giggled. "Will you hire a band?"

"A steel band. Y'know, Caribbean cats wailing on oil drums. I'll audition the Salvation Army drum and tuba corps."

"Something tells me this is gonna be a loud party!" Bulldog smiled. He tipped his barstool, balancing at a devilmaycare angle with one foot on the breakfast bar, one foot on a rung of Rosealyn's barstool.

"Loud and proud!" I said, and the idea came to me to slip invitations under Flattop's cabin doors. Why not invite the entire crew?

Rosealyn said, "Uncle Joe, if you rock this joint there's no telling what they'll do. They might elect you president of the Birthday Committee."

"Eh?"

She handed me a flier. "This came while you were gone." The flier named those shipmates whose birthdays fell that month. Clearly it was the captain's practice to call musters in celebration of birthdays. I might have found that practice interesting, if I hadn't been told to vacate in two weeks.

"Who's coming to your party?" Bulldog asked.

"Phoebe and Lloyd, I hope?"

"Sure. They accepted."

"The party's for Rosealyn, so she'll be here. Her parents. Maybe the woman who sold me *Hollyhocks*, if I can find her. And Madame Leontyne."

"Want me to bring Methusela?" When Bulldog said that he pushed against Rosealyn's barstool, rocking back like a kid riding a bicycle no hands. Bulldog had exceptionally good balance. He liked showing off.

"Methusela?"

"He finally returned my call. As a matter of fact, I'm going shooting with him this afternoon. If you want me to I'll bring him."

Impulsively I said, "That would be a coup. Two famous writers attending my rock-and-roll. Maybe I'll invite Mr. Man from the *Journal*."

"No, Joe. Don't make it public. Keep it an intimate costume affair. What about your transvestite friend?"

"He's invited."

"His wife?"

"Sure. She's a nurse. And Rosealyn's father is bringing the booze."

Bulldog grinned. "I'll finally get to see the locals let their hair down. This party has the makings of a lease-breaker!"

I bounced on my toes, getting fired up in a party mood. I was content to forget Madame Leontyne's theory of membranes for a while. I said, "There's no lease to break. I've been evicted!"

Bulldog's barstool reared like a stallion. I perceived Rosealyn had already told him about my eviction because I saw an informed, defiant gleam in his eye. He patted her hand and said, "Don't worry about your Uncle Joe. We'll fix it so he isn't kicked out!" Bulldog's fondness for Rosealyn illuminated his face. She glowed. I saw by the sparkle in her eyes that I was a rich uncle indeed. I would throw a party more interesting than anything she'd seen at Hub's country club. I asked Bulldog, "You're shooting with Methusela?"

He nodded. "Come along."

"Do you enjoy shooting?"

"Heavens no! This will require a nifty bit of acting on my part. How about you? Can you shoot guns?"

"I'm hare-brained and army trained," I said, grinning, knowing for sure I hadn't uttered those dumb words since my army days.

"Do you have a gun?"

I had given mine away but I feared Bulldog would lose confidence in me if I said that, so I lied. "Sure. What kind do you want? Shotgun? Rifle? Pistol?"

"Do I need one?"

"Let's think this through. If someone invites you to a poker party they expect you to bring your own money, eh?"

"Exactly."

"But if someone invites you for a ride on their yacht they don't expect you to bring your own boat, do they?"

"No."

"So, is Methusela's invitation more like yachting or more like poker?"

"He wants *me* to watch *him* shoot."

"We'll come along and feed you clever comments so he'll think you give a rip. That is, if Rosealyn wants to?"

"Oh sure. I need a he-man story to take back to the Cotton Gin. I can't let Mr. Daniels and Mr. Turkey think I spent my vacation with opera buffs and fairies!"

"Right," Bulldog barked, "you tell them Miss'ippi peckernecks they's some he-men in Kansas! Me and Meth and Joe and Woolie!"

"We don't have a car," I observed. "The gun club's too far to walk. Woolie's off in his Chrysler getting his ribs taped. Phoebe? Would she take us?"

Bulldog shook his head. "She calls him *El Misogynist*. She'll have no part of Meth."

"Simple." I flipped the yellow pages. "I'll rent us a car. A big black one to make us look important!"

"And phone the deli. Cheese, fruit, cold-cuts, wine. We'll need something to sit on."

I thought of Indian Joe's Navajo rug. It would have been perfect. Then I remembered the chenille bedspreads. Rosealyn went to get them. I ordered a rental car delivered to Flattop, port side aft. Our expedition took shape.

"Think of it as Ascot," Bulldog said. "You don't have to be a jockey to go to the races."

"If he's *El Misogynist* I won't be welcome."

Bulldog pinched her cheek reassuringly. "Don't you worry, my Turtle Dove! We don't trim our sails to Phoebe's distinguished inaccuracies. She thought Joe was a plumber!"

The woman who delivered our car drove us back to her office to sign a contract. That was fine with me because I hoped to learn something. I sat beside her. Rosealyn and Bulldog were in the back. I overheard him tell Rosealyn stories about Marlon Brando and Gore Vidal. I felt great. She was having a good time, far away from Hub and her children. She told Bulldog, knowing I could hear her, that she'd made a big mistake by passing up my offer to help with graduate school. I saw that the car had power steering. That scared me. Neither Graham's Ford nor Woolie's Chrysler had power steering. I feared making a fool of myself. Or—I might ask Rosealyn to drive.

While we waited at the deli we drank coffee and ate cheesecake. "If you were planning to shoot you wouldn't do this," I told Bulldog. "Caffeine helps with concentration but it makes your finger shaky on the trigger." In due course we loaded our provisions and Rosealyn wheeled us toward the gun club driving well, proving by the science of genetics that May's good driving genes were dominant over Everett's bad ones. Bulldog sat up with her relegating me to the backseat, like a little family going on a picnic. Mommy and Daddy in the front. Junior in the back. Bulldog had purchased three bottles of wine, so I mused if he offered me wine with lunch that would indicate we were a French family. If he didn't offer me wine we would be a Kansas trio. I toyed with the wine bottles, happy that they didn't have plastic corks.

As Rosealyn drove she told Bulldog about a picnic she remembered from childhood. She said the occasion was her tenth birthday when I took her to the river. As she recalled, we each packed our favorite food—peanutbutter/jelly sandwiches for her, bologna/cheese for me—fig newtons for my dessert, jawbreakers for her—iced tea for me, orange crush for her. "And—" she said with heavy emphasis, "Uncle Joe made me hold a snake's tail while he sliced its belly open! That's the day my two most disgusting words came together—*snake* and *guts*! We pulled apart every dead rabbit and turtle we found. And we didn't wash our hands before lunch. So if I'm a slob now you can look to my uncle for the cause. I told Mom. She said, *Pay attention to your uncle. He's trying to make you a doctor.*"

I interrupted Rosealyn's story to give her directions.
When she parked at the gun club I explained our mission to the
caretaker who assigned a cadet to guide us. Meth and two men
waited at a range table. They sat on folding canvas stools.
The cadet scurried to get more canvas stools. The writers had
never met, but they were both famous—a tall skinny guy and
a short fat guy—so they recognized one another. Bulldog
shook hands with the Old Man and introduced Rosealyn and
me. Methusela introduced Doley, his literary adjutant, and
Tommy, his shooting buddy. I took an instant liking to Meth
because my mother taught me to respect my elders and I
figured him to be a decade and then some older than me. We
didn't shake hands. He was obviously shy. Tall and gaunt, he
wore a tan fedora, a belted shooting jacket, an orange silk
scarf, military-creased twill trousers, and sturdy, scuffed boots.
He didn't say much. His eyes were bright. He was
memorizing us like a kid learning his geography lesson.

Bulldog also was dressed for photographers—who were
painfully absent. If anything remarkable transpired it would go
unrecorded. Bulldog stood beside Meth, grinning. I thought,
*Here we have the long and the short of it. Sit up on your
haunches, Literary America, and howl!* Methusela dismissed
the cadet with a gruff, "That's all, Buster!" Assuming the role
of host he directed us to sit in a circle. He said, "I brought
schnapps. It's strictly forbidden on the firing range, but we're
beyond the law." Tommy produced a crystal decanter, a silver
tray, and six glasses. He filled them and passed the tray.

"I hope you work up a good appetite," Bulldog said.
"We brought a picnic."

Methusela nodded, saying softly, "Superb!"

I looked at two police targets, black thug shapes set at
pistol range, while Bulldog carried the conversation. I came to
understand the thing he'd told me earlier about him and
Methusela paddling back-to-back in the literary canoe. He was
unable to stir up any literary gossip with the Old Man.
Methusela wouldn't talk. I had a lot of questions, but I hadn't
read any of their books. Neither Doley nor Tommy wanted to
talk. Tommy busied himself with preparations. I'd heard

stories about him. Sort of a genius, he'd filled Christmas tree ornaments with paint and presented them to Methusela. Geriatric therapy. Strange fellow, Tommy. He wore a Gary Gilmore teeshirt. Doley toyed with his Swiss army knife, and Rosealyn drank it all in. There were no other shooters in sight. From the skeet range we heard the random popping of shotguns. "What kind of guns did you bring?" I asked.

Meth cracked a tight smile. "Betsy!" he said, as if that answered all questions. He wet his lips and shook his empty glass. Tommy stepped to fetch the decanter.

I waited for more information. Finally Doley said, "Betsy is his big-bore. Elephant gun." That didn't tell me much about the gun, but it told me something about Methusela. Tall Man had chosen a hard-recoil rifle for his rendezvous with Elf. *Mano a mano*. Hand-to-hand. Man-to-man. *Hombre hombre*. The silhouette targets were pristine. I observed, "You've put the targets at pistol range—"

Methusela growled, "Ever been charged by a musty elephant? That's the distance right there where you drop the sucker, or become Afroburger."

Mano a mano. I felt Methusela sense my horror that he was going to drink schnapps and blast targets at close range. Tommy said, "There's no fun shooting if you can't see the damage." Shooting close targets with a big-bore rifle would be like dropping grenades down a toilet. I tried not to show disapproval. I was a guest.

Bulldog asked to see Betsy.

"No," Methusela said. "The targets are at pistol range. We'll shoot damned pistols." He squeezed his empty glass. His knuckles were white. "Shall we, Mr. Geezre?"

Tommy, Doley, and Meth leered at me. Six baleful eyes challenged me to a shooting match. Of course I remembered my last athletic contest, playing croquet with Judge. Judge worked with a gavel every day. His muscles were toned to it. A croquet mallet is merely a gavel with a long handle. His tool. His backyard. His wife. Her dog. His cheering section. Peaches. I had that experience to build on. A loss builds character. And I had been shot in the ear by Chinese and likewise by a fruitbat named Harry, so I was tested under fire. I figured I could take Methusela. "Sure," I said. "What are the stakes?"

Bulldog grinned. I remembered the time I saw him come out of Phoebe's bathroom with a towel draped around his neck. My first impression told me he was a boxer. He easily maintained his balance in Everett's boat and he could ride my barstool no-hands. So I figured he could shoot pistols with Methusela. All he needed was a little coaching.

"A bottle of Russian vodka," Methusela said.

"You're on." I stood, for emphasis. "I'm not familiar with your pistols, so I get twenty practice shots."

"Agreed!"

"Make it five bottles of Russian vodka?" I said.

"Agreed!"

"C'mon, Bulldog," I muttered. "Let's pop a few caps!" I took him aside and said, "Let me do the talking. You're going to wax Methusela!"

"Me?"

"You've got the eyes for it, Bully Beef. And a steady hand. But I wish you'd left that darned coffee and cheesecake alone!"

"Nah, Joe. Not me, you."

"Trust me, Bully." I led him back to the group. Doley opened a velvet-lined pistol box revealing a pair of twenty-two target pistols, identical except for their serial numbers. Our choice. I picked up one and some empty magazines. My adrenalin was pumping. I tried to hide it from Bulldog. "Relax, be steady," I whispered.

"You relax your own self," he said. "You're shaking like a damned leaf."

Doley handed me a box of ammunition and I walked Bulldog to the firing line. I put him in a solid stance, showed him how to align the sights, and told him how to breathe. "Squeeze the trigger," I said. "Hold the pistol gently. Don't grip it. Hold it exactly where you want it and squeeze the trigger. You should be surprised when it fires." I put him to squeezing off dry shots while I loaded magazines. On his first shot with live ammunition he didn't flinch. He was fierce. In fact, after watching him empty the magazine in a tight pattern I suspected he knew more about pistols than he let on. "Take your time," I whispered. "Make him shoot first."

Methusela came to the firing line. He kicked gravel, dug in, and jerked off a few practice rounds. I sensed overconfidence. We checked the pistols for safety before Tommy set up fresh targets. Then Bulldog and Methusela stood to fire. They stared at one another, both wishing for a *Newsweek* photographer. Methusela took off his hat and tossed it to Doley. He pulled a long woolen muffler from his pocket and tied it across his ears, knotting it under his chin. He looked like Scrooge with a toothache. Bulldog turned up the brim of his panama. This was serious business. The shooters toed the line and commenced firing.

Bulldog was steady like a rock and as cool as a deep-water carp. None of his shots strayed out of the eight ring. Methusela wobbled. He'd had too much schnapps, or not enough. When all the shots were fired it was clear, without toting up points, that Bulldog had won. Methusela sulked.

Rosealyn gave Bulldog a peck on the cheek and asked, "Where did you learn to shoot?"

"At a dude ranch in Colorado. The cookie taught me. We set up chili cans behind the cookshack and blazed away with his six-shooter. I got quite good."

Tommy unzipped a leather gun carrier and reverently removed what I took to be Betsy. She was a 425 Westley Richards Magnum. She had a Monte Carlo stock, open iron sights, and a Mauser bolt action. She was a beauty. Tommy took her to the firing line where he presented her to Methusela. Methusela lasciviously chambered a cartridge, raised Betsy to his shoulder, and took deadly aim. I figured he would receive a dislocated shoulder or a broken hip when she kicked. Methusela fired. The elephant gun belched a cloud of smoke and cut a large hole in the target. But the report was hollow, not as loud as I'd expected. I looked at Tommy, who gave me a sly wink.

It was Bulldog's turn to fire Betsy. Seeing him take the rifle gave me cotton mouth and sweaty palms. He aimed quickly and pulled the trigger, suffering no ill effects. Tommy smiled at my anxiety. He leaned close and whispered, "Smoke and mirrors. I hand-load the Old Man's cartridges. Cut back the gunpowder so he won't get hurt. And I add lampblack to make smoke."

"Does he know?"

Tommy shook his head. "As long as he can drag his carcass out here and shoot Old Betsy he thinks he's fit. He sleeps with her."

Methusela respectfully placed Betsy on the gun table and went to inspect his target. "Look at that elephantine hole!" he chortled. "And those twenty-two wasps circling it like Saturn and Jupiter and Mars swishing around the Sun. Very artistic arrangement, quite by chance."

"Saturn and Jupiter and Mars?"

"Yeah. Most of the planets are queer."

Bulldog took Methusela's target from the frame. "I'll keep this," he said. "It's art."

Doley put up fresh targets and Methusela generously offered me and Rosealyn turns with Betsy. I declined for both of us, "No thanks! That big gun is too much for me, and I won't allow my niece to risk it!"

"Here," Tommy said, producing a box of Christmas tree ornaments. "Try these!" As he spoke he tossed a silver ball at a target. It hit and shattered, releasing a cascade of red paint. "Toss a few," he said. "Make a picture. Red and yellow—orange. Yellow and blue—green!"

Rosealyn and I plinked away with Christmas balls while Methusela and Bulldog retired to the beach umbrella for more schnapps. They thought they'd fired elephant loads, and they felt good about it. Male bonding.

Methusela and his boys stayed on the range, declining the picnic which Bulldog and Rosealyn and I unpacked on the hilltop between the clubhouse and the parking lot. Rosealyn spread the hen and rooster beneath a large oak. Bulldog panicked when he discovered that we had no corkscrew. He was ready for wine, feisty because the schnapps had whetted his appetite, so I used my pocketknife to drill the corks. I poured up two glasses of white Italian wine, pheasants on the label. I couldn't read the Italian words, but they looked significant. We were a Kansas family. Being the child, I amused myself playing mumbly peg with my knife while Rosealyn matched Bulldog glass for glass and he told yarns about movie stars and rich people. He said he would return to New York in a few days, and he described his apartment, every detail of it. He invited Rosealyn to go with him. It was obviously a real invitation, one he expected her to accept. Rosealyn was tipsy and relaxed and thoroughly captivated—having a picnic she would remember for the rest of her life. She was a beautiful woman, healthy and full of wit, good humor, integrity, and potential. I watched Bulldog fall in love with her. Not that I thought he wanted to be her lover, he wasn't that kind, but he definitely had a crush on her. He wanted to take her to the opera and New York literary parties. He wanted to be photographed with her cheek-to-cheek in an ice cream parlor. Of course Rosealyn wasn't accustomed to drinking Italian pheasant wine, certainly not glass-for-glass with a man of Bulldog's experience. Of course she over-drank. She removed her shoes and danced barefoot with a technique that hadn't changed since childhood. Bulldog applauded. Then he took it upon himself to give her instruction. He showed her how to run in choppy steps and leap like a Russian. That boy could really jump! They were dancing full tilt when Methusela stumbled down the trail followed by Tommy and Doley carrying heavy burdens of firearms. Methusela stopped, spreading his arms stiff and important like Christ of the Andes. When Bulldog and Rosealyn, winded, paused in their recital Methusela threw them kisses. Tommy and Doley, unsure of how long Meth might stand there, sat down. I got glasses and poured wine for the shooters.

"Superb!" Methusela exclaimed. He quaffed his wine and dropped his glass to the ground. "That's quite a frog-sticker you've got there, Sonny," he said, reaching for my knife. He tested the blade with his thumb. Rosealyn and

Bulldog joined us. She was flushed. Her curls stuck to the sweat of her brow and a thousand photographers missed that opportunity to capture a truly beautiful woman. Tommy and Doley gulped their wine and threw down their glasses. Monkey see monkey do. They lifted the firearms and shuffled down to the parking lot, following their leader who counted cadence—*hup one, two-three! Hup one.*

We packed the remains of our picnic. I tossed wine bottles into a trashcan, to which Bulldog added Methusela's target. "I thought you were going to frame that thing as a work of art?"

Bulldog shrugged, his face beautifully serene, without a trace of malice he said, "It never hurts to tell an old boy what he needs to hear."

Rosealyn clearly was in no shape to drive so I crawled behind the wheel and took Bulldog to Phoebe's. From there I drove Rosealyn and myself back to Flattop. In addition to drinking all that wine she was tired from her bus trip. She hit the sack and I opened a window to let in a nice breeze. Then I tried to read a few pages of St. Teresa, but I couldn't concentrate. My mind wandered from pillar to post. My imagination was definitely overstimulated. *Of all the crazy things Madame Leontyne could come up with,* I asked myself, *how did she ever think of membranes?* Judge hadn't begun to give me any insights comparable to the membrane theory, and he had an extensive network of informers—bailiffs, patrolmen, detectives, prosecuting attorneys, district attorneys, chancery clerks, justices of the peace, nightwatchmen, coroners— All Madame Leontyne had was an ad in the *Trader*. Her clients came around to her back door, told her what they wanted, and she told them how to get it.

"Mannie!" I croaked softly not to awaken Rosealyn, "pull up a chair, Dude. Let's discuss this concept of membranes."

I prefer to stand, Sir.

"That's a membrane right there, Mannie. The separation of master and man. You have your dignity. Nobody cracks jokes while Methusela shoots Betsy. Rosealyn spins a prayer cocoon around Hub's illness putting transparent words between him and his disease, eh Mannie? A scab on the wound. Everything sensible has its boundary—"

Yes, Sir. If that's the way you see it.

"Mannie, sometimes you're a pain in the neck!"

Sir Joseph, sometimes you lose your grip.

"On reality?"

Precisely.

"Do you think I should invite Paula to the party?"

Not a half-bad idea.

I didn't want to disturb Rosealyn by talking on the telephone so I slipped out the hatch, walked over to the Flagship, and took the stairs up to Paula's high office. Luckily she was in. I'd feared she might be off teaching a class. She sat me on a comfortable sofa and smiled, open and relaxed, because she was in her place. It didn't take a psychologist to figure that one out. She had shelf upon shelf of books and through her window, tiny on the horizon, I saw the ammunition factory. Her diplomas were prominently displayed. I saw her Ph.D. sheepskin from Columbia, a school named after Christopher Columbus who was, in turn, named after Christ. My mother named me after St. Joseph. Paula was named after the Apostle Paul. I mused on those religious matters, but I didn't express them to her. She had no desk in her office. She sat in a cozy chair beside me—turned at an angle, three-quarters facing me. Her hair was brushed nicely. Maybe she was scheduled to attend a committee meeting or a dissertation defense. She said, "I'm glad you dropped in because I have something to show you."

"I didn't drop in, I climbed up. What is it?"

"Can't you guess?"

I had no idea what she was talking about until she lifted her feet and danced them in the air like puppets.

"New shoes! I bought a pair of English walking shoes."

Sure enough. They were a popular style, ugly enough to be comfortable. "They look okay."

"Indeed they are."

"Let's test-walk them."

"Right now?"

As we left Paula's office an intriguing thought occurred to me—we would be seen together, man-and-woman, on campus. It was one thing for her to receive an oddball character in her office. Maybe she had no choice there, no say-so. Any kook might traffic in a psychologist's office. But it was quite another thing for her to stroll across campus with me. We went to the fountain where some ecology major had thrown laundry detergent. White suds frothed in the churning water and the breeze blew bubbles into the boulevard. No way to clean up the river—putting soap in it. I led her from the fountain down a steep grassy hill under the trees saying, "Let's put those Clarks to the traction test on the downslope."

"I've already tried them," Paula said. "They grip pretty well."

As we approached the pond from its upstream end where the brook feeds it a bell in the tower clicked off chiming three times. "Sit on the grass?" I asked.

"Sure."

I picked a sunny spot. "You're invited to a costume party at my place," I said, "tomorrow night."

"Thanks."

"It's to honor my niece, visiting from Mississippi."

Paula nodded.

"It's a costumer so people can wear masks if they want to—enjoy themselves."

"Your niece lives in Mississippi?"

"Yes. She's at Flattop sleeping off too much wine. We went to a macho literary event where an old man shot his rifle, which he calls Betsy. What do you make of that, Doctor? What could possibly be inside his head?"

"Joe, my name's Paula, not doctor. Who cares what an old man calls his gun?"

I smiled mischievously remembering basic training, *This is my rifle, this is my gun. This is for shooting, this is for fun.* "How's Melanie Moore?"

"Still upset about her little trick?"

"She's a snot, but I forgive her."

"Forgiveness is good for the psyche."

"How's she getting along? I want to invite her to my party."

"She got accepted in my alma mater."

I nodded.

"My work on the prayer book dried up. People stopped writing entries. Except you, of course."

"Get your students to fake some."

"Thanks, Joe!"

"Maybe you hexed it by tampering with it."

Paula looked at the ducks on the pond. "I'll bet you're superstitious?"

"I've seen things I can't explain."

"Such as?"

"I ate a shaman's soup and my vision became so keen I could see the pores in the soup bowl. It's one of my mother's bowls. I have three of them. They were cheap to begin with and over the years they've gotten stained. No amount of bleach or Bon Ami will make them white. But when I ate that soup I saw the bowl new, as it was on her wedding day. I saw a tight young lady, a judge's wife, grab a putrefied corpse and take it away from turtles. She didn't have to, but she did. Why? Where did she get the courage? I have a friend who is teaching me about membranes."

"What are membranes?" Paula asked.

"Surely you know what a membrane is?"

"Of course. But I don't know how you're using the word. What do you mean when you say membrane?"

"Some are containers— The yolk sac of an egg. Others are frontiers— The place where one thing stops and another thing begins."

"Always arbitrary," Paula said.

"Maybe that's what Madame Leontyne is trying to teach me." I looked in Paula's eyes. They were sympathetic and warm. *In a pig's eye* she'd said to me. I doubted she'd ever looked into a pig's eye. She'd used *pig's eye* as an example of a paltry thing, but pigs have beautiful eyes. All dogs have the same eyes. You can be sixty-two years old, stop a cocker, look into her eye, and see what you saw in Rambler's eye when you were eleven. Pigs, however, differ one from another. There's something unique, like humor, in a pig's eye. "For the past nine years I've thought my favorite niece got married and got pregnant, betraying me, abandoning the plans we'd made. We never spoke those plans, but we both knew what they were. Can you guess the answer?"

"No."

"My niece didn't get married and get pregnant. She did it in reverse order."

"That's too simple, Joe. Anybody could guess that."

"I couldn't. I had nine years to figure it out—but I couldn't."

"Nine years. Nine months. Are you telling me you didn't count months from the wedding day?"

"No."

Paula laughed. She looked fondly at me and said, "Joe, you are a wonder. Your favorite niece gets married, has a baby six months later, and you didn't count the months."

"How did you know it was six months?"

"Arithmetic. It takes a month to find out, a month to think about it, and a month to plan a wedding."

"I guess I'm dumb."

"I guess you are." Paula's tone undercut the words as if there was a double meaning, as if she meant the opposite of what she'd said. There's always the risk of being in error, but I thought Paula was warming to me. I stared at the unnatural ducks. If I taught myself to discern every membrane, to reverse every proposition, to search out every yin-yang—maybe I would gain wisdom or maybe I would simply lose what little sense I had. Maybe I was sitting on thin grass. Walking on green glass. Bust my skinny ass. "Take for instance," I said, "those ducks on the pond. They're not natural."

Paula said, "They swim, they quack, they chase one another."

"They are Easter toys that got dumped here. They couldn't survive in nature. They don't reproduce. They don't have the instinct to migrate. They don't winter here."

"Really?"

"Yes'um."

I felt something coming from Paula. I had felt it from Pinkie moments before she asked me to kiss her. Don't tell me an old dog can't learn. I crowded Pinkie in her kitchen, grabbed her across her table, and kissed her. Got my chops slapped. But I felt her wanting to be kissed. That shift, that change of desire, once learned, I won't forget. Madame Leontyne shifted the shift when she said, *Are you thinking about the bed in the other room?* And Paula was shifting the shift. In the springtime it's common to see fruitbats entwined on the grass. I looked deep into Paula's eyes, smelling a trace of her scented shampoo or perfume. It would have been inappropriate for her, a psychology professor, to entwine on the grass with me, a sixty-two-year-old Walkman, a recently retired virgin.

She smiled as if she knew what I was thinking. "This is nice," she said. "But it isn't walking."

We went down the hill, looped around the stadium, and at the Flagship took the elevator to her office. I stopped at her threshold. "What time's your party?" she asked.

"Eight. Come in costume. Who will you be?"

"I won't disclose that."

I nodded and took off, certain that none of my guests would be able to disguise themselves enough to deceive me. They didn't all know one another, but I knew them. If Indian Joe were to wear milkman's whites and hawk an Igloo of Eskimo Pies, would I not know his nose in a thousand? If Judge were to put on a wig of braids and eagle feathers, would I not know his walk, his thoughtful manner? Would I not know Madame Leontyne's girth or Paula's eyes or the thing in Pinkie that made my icecream melt? Of course. Would Everett come as a riverboat gambler? May as Mario Andretti? Mary as an apache dancer? Graham as Margaret Thatcher? Bulldog as Sugar Ray Leonard? Nobody would come as Joe Geezre because nobody would slice off an ear for authenticity. Not in a pig's eye. Pigsty.

As I walked past the chapel I remembered the prayer book. Perhaps Kimberly, responding to my note, had left me a message. I checked the book. There was nothing there, so I wrote:

> Dear Joe,
> I'd love to walk with you.
>
>   Kimberly

I let myself into Flattop quietly. Rosealyn was asleep. I stood in the kitchen staring at jars of spaghetti sauce, cans of tuna, quick rice, cornflakes— I had frozen corn and frozen lima beans, but none of it seemed good to me. I wanted to cook supper for Rosealyn, but it's hard to cook when you have no hunger for food. I figured I'd lost my appetite by falling in love with Paula. People stricken by love can eat only a grape or two, weak tea, perhaps a bite of cheese—an olive. I liked the idea of being in love with Paula because that took the pressure off Pinkie and Anne, both married women. Jealous husbands. But being in love with an unmarried woman carried a different, more intense, danger. It was like stepping onto the high wire without a net. There was no trampoline of protection between Paula and me. No membrane of marriage. I was still staring at dull food when Rosealyn wandered sleepily into the kitchen.

"Have a nice nap?" I asked.

"Super. I feel groggy, but human. Whatcha doing?"

"Saying hello to my friends. The Quaker man, the Bon Ami chick, the Arm and Hammer."

"Mr. Peter Pickle?"

"Sure. Mr. Peter Pickle. What do you want for supper?"

"Joe, I'm not hungry. If we get hungry we can go to a restaurant."

I closed the cabinets.

"Let's walk. I want to see the river where we used to hang out."

I snapped up her offer. As we cruised out of Flattop I kept my mouth shut, letting Rosealyn think her own thoughts. River City was her hometown too. She had private memories of its out-of-the-way places. She had known lots of River Citians I never knew. She had walked with them and talked to them. She had ridden the streets in their cars. As we sailed up Massachusetts I nodded to the golfer and asked Rosealyn, "What do you think of that guy's suit?"

"It's wrong for golf," she said. "Too tight in the shoulders."

"He's not a golfer. He's a dope."

"Right. It's a nice suit. Do you like it?"

"Sure. What do you think of those ducks?"

"They're silly. Mom said you looked good at your retirement dinner."

"That dinner seems years ago. I looked like a jerk."

"Yeah, Mom said you did."

"You said she said I looked good!"

"White lie."

"You go to hell for white lying."

We walked on. I wondered if Rosealyn was using birth control. More membranes. I said, "The blood-brain barrier isn't physical. It's chemical. It keeps toxic chemicals from swimming through your brain, making you crazy."

"You should be a professor."

"No. But you. It's not too late."

As we crossed the bridge I looked for Fritz the Cat. When he came in sight I put my arm around Rosealyn and hugged her, turning her toward me so she wouldn't see his obscenity. Safely past him, I stopped and put my hands on the rail. Looking down I said, "A man died here. Madame Leontyne told me where to find his body."

"Some of my high-school friends thought she was genuine. But of course I never visited her."

"She sure was wrong about Everett."

Rosealyn laughed.

I've let the cat out of the bag! I had no business telling Rosealyn about the Vegas money. *Time to throw up a smokescreen.* "When I was a kid the man next door had some extra kittens. He put them in a bag and dropped them in here. He told me they would grow up to be a catfish."

"She was wrong about Dad—"

"She said he would lose money in Las Vegas."

Rosealyn smiled wistfully. "You don't know, do you? Dad always went to her before his Las Vegas trips."

"I know that."

"He gave her his money. He'd stash Mom in a floorshow and go drop a few nickels in the slots. Later he would tell Mom he'd lost big at poker."

"Why?"

"That's how he supported his illegitimate daughter. You're his twin brother. How could you think he was dumb enough to keep throwing his money away in Las Vegas—year after year?"

I saw my twenty being folded three ways and tucked into the extra-tight hip pocket of Rosealyn's half sister. "Uh-huh," I grunted. "Spookie."

"Uh-huh. Mom's not supposed to know, so keep it under your lid."

"Uh-huh."

"So Dad finally won a pocketful of nickels, eh?"

"He won big. But I don't think I was supposed to tell you, so keep it under your lid."

"If we stand here long enough he'll drive by and see us."

"Yeah."

We crossed the bridge and cut down to the river bank. "How did you find out about your half-sister?"

"He told me. Kinda funny, eh?"

"How do you mean?"

"I mean I'd expect him to put that burden on his eldest son, not his youngest daughter."

"He put the burden on his youngest—"

"She's eight years younger than me."

"I know where she works."

"Where?"

"At the driver's license factory. Saw her when I took my test."

"Say, you looked cute driving that big car!"

"Think so?"

"Yeah. This is what I was hungry for. My old uncle and my old river."

Old Man River, I thought unhappily, knowing I would have that dreadful phrase in my noggin for the next hour. *He don't do nothing.* "C'mon," I said, "Let's walk. Work up an appetite." *He just keeps rolling.*

Rosealyn used her young legs to set a fast pace. We didn't talk, and after half an hour I felt us moving close to one another's blood-brain barriers. I was thinking about Hub's MS, Everett's illegitimate daughter, Madame Leontyne's membranes, the backwards bareback horseman, Paula, Peaches, and the thimbleful of libido that had come my way too late to be anything more than an embarrassment—when Rosealyn took off running. She ran about fifty yards, stopped abruptly, turned, and ran back. She fell down crying. I knelt beside her and, without knowing why, I began crying too. I felt as low as I would have felt if my own heart had died. After a while Rosealyn stopped sobbing and grinned through her tears. I suppose I looked pretty funny to her with big tears on my cheeks and snot running to my chin.

"You're a chameleon," she said, "you don't even know why you're crying, do you?"

"Nope. I'm a dope."

"Why don't you run for Congress?"

"Why don't you eat do-do?"

"Why don't you?"

"Well, let's make up some story," I said, "to explain why we're crying."

Rosealyn found a wadded tissue in her pocket and blew her nose. I used my sleeve.

"Joe! I spank my kids for doing that!"

"You're a mean mother, ain't you?"

"It's a hard job, being a soft mother."

"Why did that backwards man on a dumb horse make you think of me?"

"Since Jennifer was born I've used birth control, Joe."

"Oh—"

"I refused to have any more of Hub's kids. I refused to live with him."

"Oh—"

"I planned to move back here. Then he came down with MS. So now I'm a monster. Maybe this year of bitching is what caused him to come down with the disease. Ain't that a bitch!"

"Oh—"

"So don't feel like the Lone Ranger, Joe. You're not the backwards bareback rider, Hub is. And I'm his goddamned horse!"

"Rosealyn, don't use such language!"

"In sickness and in health."

"Rosealyn, baby—"

"And to top it off, Joe, I've rubbed a goddamned blister on my goddamned heel!"

"Let me see. Take off your sock."

"Florence Nightingale."

"Shut up. I'm a darned good foot doctor."

Rosealyn rolled the sock over her heel, uncovering a water blister. I touched it with my fingertip and said, "This thing is bad only if you break it. If we can avoid breaking it the fluid will re-absorb and it won't get infected. But no matter how careful we are, it'll probably break. So the next best thing is to drain it and put on a bandage."

"If I walk my shoe will break it."

"Precisely."

"Are you prepared to *carry* me back to civilization?"

"I'd carry you to the moon if necessary. In this case, I'm prepared to walk over to your mom's house and ask her to come give us a ride."

"Blow my cover?"

"I'll explain. She'll understand."

"We'd look like bad kids who tried to run away from home. Think of something else."

"Okay. How's this. You wait here. I go get the car. I take you to my place, sterilize a needle, poke a hole in this blister, drain it, put on a bandaid, and you're okay?"

"Fine. I'll wait right here."

I stood, feeling my knees creak. I started walking slowly because my legs had stiffened. Each step put more distance between Rosealyn and me. When I'd gone a hundred yards I turned and waved. Then I picked up my pace, wanting to increase the distance. *I'll put a membrane between us so I can think about you. Such a sad state of affairs.* I did the kind of solitary walking I'm capable of. When I get my long legs moving I can cover some ground.

Woolie met me in the passageway and I told him about being evicted. He offered to argue my case but I told him to save his breath because I was already out of Flattop, in my head. He asked where I was and I told him I didn't know. "But don't fret, Woolie, I'll find another lilypad. This old frog knows how to jump. Someplace to plant corn, tomatoes, okra. I'll get my feet in the dirt. Maybe I'll keep a few chickens. You'll make the coffee and I'll fry the eggs. We'll have breakfast club twice a week. March around the table."

Woolie nodded, stroking his chin. "Sounds like a hippie dream."

"No. It's a sailor's dream."

Woolie grinned. He was a lovable old guy. It would be fun cooking breakfast with him, but I figured him to marry soon and be too busy running errands to visit me. I invited him to Rosealyn's party.

I fetched Rosealyn and treated her blister. We drank iced tea listening to radio news, and I was tempted to ask her about the membrane between herself and Hub. But I didn't. I figured it was none of my business. Instead of prying into her personal life I told her about Mary Thunder and Indian Joe. I told her about Comanche's tailbone and the Navajo rug and the dog soup.

Rosealyn phoned home.   She gave me the phone. Jennifer had a scratch on her nose. Daddy had taken Taxi to the barbershop and gotten his hair cut short for the summer. Michael had been fishing with Daddy in the new boat. They'd caught a mess of fish.   Hub asked how I was enjoying retirement, inviting me to teach him to fish. I told him Everett, not me, was the fishing twin. Nobody said anything about MS. I was tempted to ask him how he felt. I searched my mind for a way to apply the membrane theory, but I found none.   I thought about the earthquake that would someday swallow New Madrid. I thought about moonshine and weddings in the delta. I thought about leg braces, crutches, and a wheelchair for Hub as we talked about fishing and his new boat.

"Promise you'll come down, Joe.   Now that you're retired you have no excuse."

"I will," I said.   "I'd like to see the South again."   I meant it. I would go visit them—if Rosealyn stayed there. If she left him and moved back to River City—that would be a different story. I looked at her sitting in my recliner, lit by my reading lamp.   She had picked up a volume of Saint Teresa. She and her brothers and sisters had been taken to church every Sunday, so I wondered if she was still religious.   Maybe, like me, she only remembered the windows. Her face looked calm in the lamplight.   She had opened the book without comment as if it were something she expected to find in my house. I rattled ice and smiled at myself for being dumb.   I'd forgotten her younger sister. Had Everett's youngest daughter been taken to church every Sunday?   If so, which church?   The Church of Hoo-Doo?   The Pagan Denomination?   The Weeping Onion? Rosealyn, hearing the ice, looked up.

"What do you make of that book?" I asked.

She shrugged, closed it, and put it aside.   "I haven't read enough to get a sense of it.   All I know is—I'm certainly not a saint.   When Jennifer Bighead was born I said some profane words."

"You remember what you said?"

"I'll never forget. Saint Teresa talks about mental prayer. It's interesting— Maybe I'm praying in reverse when I think long strings of profanity."

"If Hub gets healthy you'll divorce him. But if he becomes an invalid you'll stay with him, eh?"

"That's about the size of it."

"So when you prayed for him not to have MS you weren't praying for him. You were praying for yourself."

"Exactly. But give me credit, Joe. I *knew* I was praying for myself."

"You're a good woman."

"I'm not a shit. Have you ever been in love, Joe?"

She looked at me in a new way. There was something in her eyes I'd never seen before, something pulling us into a deep conversation. I wanted to slow down, backtrack, but I couldn't. To stop talking would have been a betrayal. I could think faster than I could form words, and my thoughts ran to maintain the rhythm of their flow. My thoughts pulled words out of my mouth as if the words had been strung together for me, before I even thought of them. "I loved my mother and I loved my dog and I loved you and I loved myself, but I've never been in love."

"Never in love?"

"No. But Rosie, things are changing. I've begun to feel tremors. In the last week I've kissed two women."

"Who?"

"First the Native American woman. I felt nothing. Then a married woman. I kissed her and felt a rhumba. Now I know why people bother with kissing."

"Good for you, Joe."

"Today I sat on the grass with a psychology professor. She wanted me to kiss her."

"She makes three."

"Yeah. And Madame Leontyne gave me the rolling eyeball."

"Four! You are River City's most eligible bachelor. What caused all this?"

"Membranes."

Rosealyn knitted her brows, waiting for an explanation.

"In the old days before synthetics our Boy Scout troop had a cotton tent. In the rain the tent would turn water until you touched it. But wherever your fingertips touched drops would form. And those drops would grow fat and drip in your face while you tried to sleep. We all knew it was folly to touch the tent. But we couldn't resist. Sooner or later some boy's hand would scout up in the candlelight and touch that canvas membrane."

"That's it, Joe! That's exactly it. I can crochet. I can sew. I can knit. I can comb the baby's hair. But sooner or later I know I'll reach up and touch the tent. I've got to get myself a man."

What's wrong with the one you have? was screaming inside my head, but I refused to speak the words. The faults of Hub were none of my business. If Hub were to take me out in his boat and if we were to fish ourselves into a state of exhaustion I wouldn't expect him to tell me secrets about Rosealyn. *Vice versa.* But I wouldn't soon forget Rosealyn's saying, *I've got to get myself a man.* I remembered looking out the window and seeing Paula grip the iron fence, catching her breath. I thought she was Kimberly needing help to pay her phone bill. And I remembered finding her alone in the Palm Tree eating veal. Overweight. Middle-aged plump. And in her spare time she was learning to fly. I wondered how many times she had said, *I've got to get myself a man.* And I remembered the combined smell of lilac blossoms and skunk musk when I stood in the bushes illuminating my silly face for her. I remembered the smell of her fragrance as we sat by the pond, when I felt that bittersweet tremulation right where I was supposed to feel it, in my chest. In the membrane of my heart. Maybe her heart had been broken. Maybe she was hard up, to take an interest in an old river like me.

I enjoyed looking at Rosealyn's profile as it was lit by the reading lamp. She had her father's nose. I remembered hearing Madame Leontyne say, *She's the blood daughter of your twin, which makes you very close.* Now I knew about Madame Leontyne's daughter who was also my niece, also the blood daughter of my twin. *Madame Leontyne is my extra-legal sister-in-law. I'll ask Judge about that sometime. What is my legal relationship to Spookie? Am I her step-uncle? Is Madame Leontyne my half-sister-in-law?*

Rosealyn picked up the book to read it in the lamplight, so I got a pad and pencil and drew her. Maybe she knew what I was doing. Maybe she was lost in the life of St. Teresa. Or rapture. Or the Four Waters of Prayer. Maybe she was pretending to read.

Time passed. "Have you ever met your half-sister?" I asked.

"No."

"Salvation Army time. Put on thick socks."

"We're going to the Salvation Army?"

"To invite Indian Joe and Mary Thunder to the party."

But they weren't in the shelter. I cruised by Pentimento looking for them. Then I parked at the Brewery and, with Rosealyn leaning on my arm, we slowly made our way to the camp under the bridge where we hobbled up to the fire, casting our shadows on the concrete abutment. Two men shared a carseat. I knew better than to ask them questions. That would have been inappropriate. There was no pot cooking on the fire. There was no smell of food. Frogs sang from the grass near the water. Rosealyn settled in as if she would spend the night. I sat beside her.

"You got any smokes?" one of the men asked.

I shook my head.

"Feed the far," the other man said.

I shrugged.

"Yeah! Feed the far! Take a hike. We burnt all the brush wood."

Rosealyn stood to give me a hand. Of course the men didn't know we had a car. We climbed the embankment. "I hate to leave," she said. "Those guys are hungry."

I drove to a fast-food store where I bought a sack of hamburgers and fries. I bought cigarettes from a machine.

Then we cruised North River City picking up scrap lumber. We returned and settled in. Rosealyn passed the hamburgers. I opened the cigarettes taking out one as if it was something I did every day. I used a coal from the fire to light it. The men were eating, so I didn't offer them smokes. I took shallow puffs, feeling the nicotine march into my bloodstream, crash through my blood-brain barrier, and make me dizzy. I turned my back to the fire watching my shadow dance against the abutment. One of the men asked for a cigarette, and I gave him the pack. "I'm gonna quit," I said. "You keep 'em."

He looked at me suspiciously. "You went and got these," he said, "now you're quitting?"

"I just wanted one," I said.

"You running from somebody," the other man told Rosealyn. She took the cigarette and puffed it. We stared into the orange-and-blue flames as the black circle closed in tight around the campfire shrinking the light. I felt very much like her rich uncle. I didn't know what she was feeling. When cars crossed it, the bridge hummed above our heads. The man smoked vigorously.

"Who you looking for?" the other man asked.

"Native American Mary and Indian Joe," I replied. "I want to invite them to my place tomorrow night—tell them if you see them?"

The man didn't speak or move. His eyelids were hooded against the bright firelight, or perhaps against the smoke. I felt transported to the time before telephones, before writing. *Grapevine. Call them on the grapevine.* I gazed at Rosealyn in the flickering light. *My child, running to dance. What passion roils your guts, woman?* I stood and, like an amateur hobo, I saluted the men at the fire. They ignored me.

Rosealyn and I went to the car. It was dark green, not black. The rental agency owned no black cars. I unlocked Rosealyn's door. As I walked around the car I caught sight of her through the window staring at the brightly lit Brewery. I looked and saw a crowd of people her age, wondering if she wished she were shut of her old uncle so she could go there and be a woman alone, incognito. I opened my door and said,

"You drive the car home. I need a walk, and you've got a blistered heel."

"Okay."

I handed her the keys and struck out, but half a block down the street I stopped in a doorway. She sat in the car. *She might drive back to Flattop. Beat me home,* I thought. *She didn't bring a purse, so she's not touching up her face. Does she wear makeup? I smelled no scent of it. If she has no purse she has no money. Unless there's a thrice-folded twenty tucked deep in her pocket. Mad money.* They used to call it that. Money for a taxi if you got mad at your date. And there was pin money—to buy pins and gaudies. And there was egg money—the Mercury dimes a woman earned. If there was a premium on infertile eggs, why would a woman keep a Preacher in the yard? Yardbird? Because everybody knows hens lay better when there's a cock around. Membrane. A woman's eggs. Charlie Parker. Peaches. Eggbeater. The dome light glowed in the rental car and I remembered Pinkie covering hers so the neighbors wouldn't see Graham in his dress. I remembered hearing Pinkie and Graham make love, and I remembered sitting on the cat-hair loveseat with Anne Judge—hearing Madame Leontyne's moans from the peacock throne. Those sounds activated my hormones. Slide trombones. Rosealyn crossed the street. She went into the Brewery. *Some uncle I am. Dutch uncle.* As I walked up the hill I talked with my troubled conscience. *Contributing to the delinquency of a niece.* Was I seeking revenge on Hub because he took her away from me? Is that why I led her into temptation and turned her loose outside a tavern? Or was my giving her the car keys an act of love? I didn't feel good. But I didn't feel bad either. When I got home I took a long shower. That's one thing about Flattop. She has an abundance of hot water. I brushed the tobacco off my teeth, put a fork in the door, and crawled between cool sheets.

8

Glue

Joe heard Rosealyn creep in. The soft click she made shutting the door awakened him. He listened intently. He heard no other sound. Perhaps she was in her bedroom turning down the little hen, undressing, closing her eyes. Dawn broke the night into palms of rosy shadow. Wide-awake robins whistled in hackberry trees above which Joe saw Whoso's roof glow as if it were floating on a luminescent cloud. *Times have changed. No committee these days would inscribe such profundity on a mere library.* Joe sat drowsily watching Whoso's pigeon flock comfort itself by crowding together.

Then a falcon dropped from the dawn, seized one of the pigeons, and tore it away from the flock. The falcon's bones, talons, muscles, and feathers moved aerodynamically, attempting flight as the pigeon, its heart and lungs pumping, its eye-membrane flashing, resisted the attack by rolling off the edge of the roof. The falcon extended and beat its wings to stop their fall and together they rose, climbing toward a gray patch of sky between the buildings. The pigeon was being hauled upsidedown with its tail to the wind. Its feathers buckled and ruffled, dragging in the air as it flapped violently trying to pull free as the locked birds merged into a single two-headed, four-winged bird, alive-in-death, struggling against itself.

Joe had constructed a museum exhibit to demonstrate streamlining. In the background he'd painted a heron eating a fish—head first. He molded a bullsnake in the act of swallowing a rat. Head first. *An old man being born leads with his head. The yin-yang streamlines two yolks. My eggs are curved.* The falcon's labored wingbeats rattled empty windowpanes and in the space between the buildings the predator had no time to readjust its grip. It banked sharply to avoid hitting a treetop. Then the pigeon, dying, flogged so violently that the falcon had to drop it or crash into the museum. The limp pigeon fell between a lilac bush and the sidewalk, where a snowstorm of white downy feathers hung in the still air.

Joe heard no sound from Rosealyn. He presumed she was in bed. Where had she spent the night? Perhaps she'd driven someplace in the rented car. Joe knew of insomniacs who drove through the tunnel of their headlights. Maybe her blistered heel healed. He imagined her dancing all night in the Congo. Maybe she'd met a juke-joint junkie wearing a heavy gold chain and Rolex teeth. Joe remembered childhood mornings when Everett awakened him by climbing through their bedroom window.

He dressed quietly and slipped down the hall. "Woolie, let's go to breakfast. My treat."

"You driving?"

"Sure. I'll drive."

"Where to?"

"Your choice."

"The Big Flag. What about Rosealyn? Isn't she hungry?"

"She was out late."

As Joe drove south on the one-way he chewed his lip, deep in thought. Woolheater bided his time sensing that something was brewing. He figured Joe was angry about being evicted. Like any novice driver, Joe leaned forward keeping his eyes on the road. He gave wide berths to the parked cars and he watched side streets for tomato-sign runners. He was especially cautious as he pulled alongside a bicyclist. Woolheater said, "Thirty pounds of bicycle, one hundred and thirty pounds of young flesh, and she thinks she can mix it up with a two-ton car!" Joe watched Woolheater gaze hungrily at the woman's legs. For a moment, as the car passed her, Woolheater could have reached out and patted her tanned knee. He obviously had that notion under his pile of gray curls.

"What is sex drive?" Joe asked.

"Huh?" Woolheater pulled his eyes off the bicyclist.

"Libido. What is libido?"

"Do you mean, seriously, what is libido?"

"Yes. Explain it in terms I can understand."

"It's a chain of golden pleasure—the links of which are fairy-spun. It connects a man's genitals to his brain. When he stands erect the chain of libido holds him together but when he goes horizontal, locks his arms around a woman and tumbles down the meadow of desire, then the golden chain hangs slack, kinks and loops entangling his guts, his heart, his liver and onions. It flails those organs generating sparks of sensation and flashes of pleasure too wonderful to describe!" Joe's foot involuntarily pressed the accelerator. The car took gas smoothly. Woolheater glanced at Joe. "Slow down, Hotrod, you'll get a ticket."

Joe lifted his foot, popping their necks. He asked, "So that's how it is?"

"That's how it was in the beginning, that's how it is now, and that's how it is in the end because if it weren't for being whipped by the golden chain— Did you ever see a firehose turned on with no firemen present? Can you imagine such an amphetamine-engorged python? Such writhing and slashing and tangling— That's how the golden chain whips through a man's viscera—that's libido, Joe. If it weren't for libido no animals would copulate. *Ho hum. What a bore*, said the bear. *How bothersome*, said the beaver. If our fathers hadn't been beaten by the golden chain—"

"That's real scientific, Woolie. Thanks."

"No charge."

"Do women feel it?"

Woolheater held his hands palm up and shrugged. Joe paused in the turn lane, his left indicator flashing. As he swung into the parking lot he watched the twenty-foot flag snap to a fresh southerly breeze. *Yankee Doodle.*

"There, Joe! There's my parking place right by the front door. Aw hell, you passed it!"

"That's a handicapped place."

"Nah. I park there all the time."

"I know you do."

When Joe got out of the car he felt wind in his earhole. He waited for Woolheater. "How's your ribs?" he asked.

"They're cracked, Joe. Like my ass. I don't see any damned handicapped sign?"

Joe gripped Woolheater's hand, leading him like a child. The flag whipped above their heads. "There," Joe said, "painted on the asphalt. See?"

"Oh, on the ground? I never look at the ground."

When they were settled in Sarah's booth Woolheater asked, "Why did you ask about libido?"

"I'm making a survey."

Sarah approached—cream in her left hand, coffee in her right. As she poured coffee Joe asked, "Sarah, do you have time for my survey?"

"I always have time for you, Lover. What's on your honeydripping mind?"

"Libido."

"Is this a joke?"

"Probably. What does libido feel like?"

"Darned if I know. What is it?"

"Sex drive. It makes girls and boys chase one another. What does it feel like?"

"You're pulling my leg—"

"I'll pull your leg," Woolheater quipped, reaching.

"I'm serious," Joe said. "My brother woke me up crawling in the window. He told me he'd spent the night in a naked woman's bed. I wondered why he did that."

"Uh-huh!"

"And this morning his daughter came in at dawn. I didn't ask where she spent the night. It wouldn't be appropriate for

me to question her. But I'm wondering if there might be a
genetic connection here."

Sarah shifted her weight and looked at the slick scar on the
side of Joe's head seeing a pattern of white scar-dots where
stitches had been. Her eyes followed the hole curving into his
head. Joe imagined her saying: *You have a hole in your head,
Mister. Some men don't know how to tell a joke.*   "Yeah.
Well—" she said, waving to a customer. "I'll come back for
your order."

"She thought you were telling a joke," Woolheater said.

Joe went to the restroom dreading the Penis Boy graffiti.
But there was none. The bathroom was fresh painted. He
mixed hot and cold water and lathered his hands, luxuriating in
the rush of warmth, remembering Trish's fingers scrubbing his
head. He cupped water, lifting it to his face. To avoid waking
Rosealyn he'd crept out of Flattop foregoing his morning
splash. He shucked paper off a roll and dried his face. *I asked
a scientist. He told me it's a golden chain. I asked a sexy
woman. She took her pot elsewhere.*

"I ordered for you," Woolheater said.   "Sausage and
eggs."

"That's fine. I don't suppose your busted ribs feel like
walking home?"

"Sure. I don't walk on my ribs. Why?"

"I want to return that car. Get it out of sight out of mind."

"Suits me. Then what?"

"Oops! I'd better keep the darned thing. I have to get
grub for the party. Onion dip, horseradish sauce, carrot sticks.
Then I'll start rounding up my costume."

"What's your costume Joe? More libido stuff?"

"I'll get a painter's smock, rub orange paint in my hair,
wrap gauze over my earhole, and be Van Gogh."

"Joe Van Gogh. That won't fool anybody."

"I'm the host, Woolie. It's good manners for the host to
let his guests know who he is."

"Yeah. I reckon."

"Who will you be?"

"Wilt Chamberlain. You remember him, nice fellow, athletic—"

"You don't have the skin."

"No. And I don't have to tell you my costume either."

Sarah, returning to their table, eyed Joe. "Refill?"

"Just scare it," Joe said.

It was Woolheater's turn at the restroom. When he pushed back his chair Sarah moved making room for him, but she didn't leave the table. After he was gone she told Joe, "When I pull the day shift I adjust the window shades to keep out the glare. As the day passes, everything moves. The light changes. Things change. The breakfast crowd ain't the lunch crowd, know what I mean? A little professor comes every afternoon. Last week he proposed to me. Said he wants a warm body waiting when he comes home. I told him to buy a dog. My kids are grown. I haven't got any savings. I've got big feet. Sure, I'd like a little pecker. A quiet man so smart I wouldn't have to pretend to listen. But I won't marry that one—because of lido. I've got it. He ain't."

"Why don't you marry Woolie?"

Sarah looked back toward the restrooms, making sure Woolheater couldn't hear her. She said, "How can a man his age have all that thick, wavy hair? It's natural, too?"

"Genetics. Does he have lido?"

"Nah. He talks too much."

"You mean Woolie is short in the lido department?"

Sarah tore a guest check off her pad, nodding. "But when Joe Geezre wants something Joe Geezre knows how to get it."

"Huh?"

"You and me and the mulberry tree, Joe!" She handed him the guest check, smiling warmly. He felt her magnetism. *Nonverbal communication*, he thought. When she turned and walked away he observed a distinct, jaunty, slow-rolling movement in her hips. She'd never bothered to walk that way for Woolheater. She turned the corner and Joe saw the fulsome points of her breasts. Feeling a tremulation of fear in his diaphragm, he fingered the billfold from his hip pocket and opened it to count out money. *I won't lay down an obscene tip, the way Woolheater would. I won't encourage her.* He turned over the guest check. There was nothing on it but a phone number. Joe wadded it. When Woolheater returned he found Joe sitting there, holding his billfold, staring morosely at the traffic.

"Put up your money, Joe. You drove, I'll buy."

"I invited you. I said I'd pay."

"Yeah," Woolheater chuckled, "but you can't pay if you don't have a check." He waved to Sarah. "Chick! I need the check!"

She cruised to their table deliciously, rolling, like a ship in the tropics. She smiled. "I gave it to Joe."

"I lost it."

She inventoried their breakfasts, naming every item as she wrote it down, *eggs, sausage, juice, extra toast, coffee—* Then she tore it off and handed it to Woolheater. She gave Joe a provocative stare and whispered, "Confucius say, *Man who lose key to Sarah's apartment get no new key!*"

Woolheater laughed, but Joe didn't catch the joke. Woolheater laid down a large tip. He went to the cash register and Joe, ill at ease, stood beside him staring at pastry in the display case, his eyes drawn to a cinnamon roll glazed with caramelized sugar. Perfect pecan halves encrusted it like ears. Cinnamon outlined a spiral edge coiling deep into it. *Like a seashell*, Joe thought. He remembered Anne Judge contemplating her navel. He was filled with a curiosity about navels, wondering if they descend like corkscrews threading left or right. He wondered if his earhole looked like a navel. He bought the roll.

"Granola Joe! Have you lost your mind? What are you doing with all those empty calories?"

Joe grinned sheepishly, holding the roll at arm's length. Already it had printed a grease stain on the white paper bag. "I drank too much coffee," he said. "I feel stupid and jumpy." Sarah brought an armload of menus to the hostess station. Joe saw her smile and wink. Outside, he looked up at the flag while Woolheater fumbled coins into a newspaper vending machine. Joe asked, "Topeka or Kansas City?"

"*New York Times*, Joe. Think big."

Woolheater helped Joe carry the food into Flattop. When Joe made room on the breakfast bar he found a note.

Dear Uncle Joe,
I was out late and thought I'd sleep till noon but some
bird kept banging on the window. I'm off to find my
costume. *Party time!*
                                        Love,
                                        R.

He spent several hours cleaning house, scraping carrots, trimming radishes, and chopping cauliflower. Then he set up his easel near the north window, clamped a canvas in place, and unpacked a palette, paints, and brushes. He loaded the palette and spent an hour painting a sketch of the street, the oval iron fence, and the limestone wall beyond it. He used short Van Goghesque brushstrokes. Then quickly, jabbing, he painted in the two-headed, four-winged bird. *It ain't art*, he thought, *but it rounds out my costume.* Joe spoke aloud the names of his guests, counting them on his fingers, asking the old question, *Will anybody come?* Afraid his party might flop he sat at his phone, ate the cinnamon roll, and called a few more people.

A skunk in the lilacs smells the dead pigeon. She is cautious. Shadows fill the space between the buildings but it's not yet dark enough for her to venture out. Blossoming redbud trees are of no interest to her. A large Black woman, having climbed the steps from the street below, crosses the boulevard and walks toward the chapel but before getting there she turns toward the flat-topped building. She wears a red gingham dress and over it a white serving apron. Her head is tied in a

headrag. She carries a chicken tucked casually under her arm.
She enters the flat-topped building and makes her way down the
hall, stopping to study nameplates on the doors. At the end of
the hallway, as she peers at a nameplate, a door opens abruptly
putting her face-to-face with an elderly white woman who holds
a clothes basket. "Where yo' takin' dem clothes?"   Aunt
Jemima demands.

"I'm— Going to the laundry room!"

"Gimme dat heah!"   With her free hand Aunt Jemima
grabs the woman's basket. "Show me yo' machine!" she
commands.

The white woman, frightened, steps into the hallway and
leads Aunt Jemima to the stairs and down them to the laundry
room while Aunt Jemima scolds her, "Heah now! What do a
fine old frizzled-up white woman be messin' with my work fo'?
Git on back to yo' soaps an' let *me* take ker dis! What do dis
washing' machine take, two-bits a lick?"

"It's free."

"Hummm. Dat's good. I gonna wash yo' dirties lack dey
ain't never been washed!"   She dumps the clothes into a
machine.

"But they're not separated! The whites and the colors!"

Aunt Jemima says, "Woman! I gonna separate you frum
yo' eye-whites, you don't git me some two-bitses!"

The woman turns and makes for the stairs. Aunt Jemima
leans on the machine breathing hard, smiling.   Black
greasepaint glistens her forehead. She returns to the top floor
and walks the hallway until she finds Joe posting notes on his
door. "Here's your little-bitty friend," she says. "I brought
him to stay with you."

"Preacher! Hey there, fellah! How're you doing? But—
I can't keep him here."

"Castro did. He kept lots of chickens in hotel rooms."

"C'mon in. I'll have to change the beds."

"What for?"

"If I put Preacher in my bedroom he'll fight the cock there,
so I'll put that one in Rosealyn's bedroom and put the hen in

my bedroom. And I'll hang a don't disturb sign on the doorknob."

Aunt Jemima looks Joe in the eye and nods, wondering what he is trying to say. She follows him and watches him switch bedspreads. Then he puts a pan of water beside his bed and a bowl of dry oatmeal on the window sill. She sets Preacher on the window sill and says, "You be a gentleman chicken. Don't dirty the bed. You gonna dirty, do it on the floor." To Joe she says, "I know I'm early. I can help you lay out food. What have you got to drink?"

"Icewater. Hot tea. Everett might bring some booze."

A compact woman stands at the trunk of her car, parked on the building's lower level, south side. She wears blue overalls cinched with a leather bricklayer's belt and a long-sleeved red teeshirt. She clamps a firm two-handed grip on the toolbox in the trunk. Her hair is tucked at her nape under a black bowler. She tugs mightily. Lifting the toolbox to the lip of the trunk, she sets it on the ground. She wears clown-white makeup, white gloves, black eyebrows, and a tidy black moustache. Her toolbox is filled with styrofoam blocks painted pink to look like bricks. Also in the box are spray cans of shaving cream and a trowel. She closes the trunk lid and, gripping the car for balance, begins a stretching routine. Squatting deep she rises looking serenely supernatural as Melanie Moore, wearing her black mortarboard and gown, flits behind her. Melanie carries a rolled diploma which she lifts like a telescope, checking apartment windows.

Joe Geezre drives into the parking lot maneuvering his Ford between a pair of white lines. He gets out and stands straight—tall. His hair is long and stringy and he wears an electric blue suit. He also wears a black hat which, too small for him, sits high on his head with its brim curled upward in the style favored by Shanghai theatre managers. His wife, struggling to escape the car, turns sideways and pulls against the doorpost. But she can't lift the weight of her enormous abdomen. Joe Geezre goes to her assistance, pulling her from the car. She is in the last days of pregnancy, perhaps she is overdue, and she wears an enormous blue polyester dress speckled with white dots. In a fit of whimsy she has sewn on a red bow which rides high atop her tummy as she walks slowly, leaning back on her heels with her legs wide and her toes turned out. She blots perspiration with a dainty white handkerchief and leans on Joe Geezre's arm as he, with short steps and slow, leads her to the sidewalk. "We'll take the elevator," he says. "If there is one."

"Oh gawd yes! I can't climb a stair," she groans as they pass the athletic bricklayer. "Gimme another Nicorette, Gigi!"

"Evening," Joe Geezre says to the bricklayer, tipping his Shanghai hat.

The bricklayer cocks her head, framing her clown-white face with her hands as if to say, *Surely you see I'm a pantomime artist!* She smiles and nods, tipping her black bowler.

"Cat got your tongue?" Joe Geezre quips.

The bricklayer immediately drops to her knees, lifts a paw, and meows silently like a kitten begging favor.

"Speak and be spoken to," Joe Geezre says gruffly. "That's my policy."

"Maybe she's here for the party," Joe Geezre's wife whispers. "She might be in costume."

"Maybe she's a rude mechanical!"

The bricklayer nods, closes the trunk of her car, lifts her box of bricks, and marches toward the Geezres saying in pantomime that she will accompany them in the elevator. She holds up three fingers. No sooner are the Geezres and the bricklayer in the elevator than it lurches and Mrs. Geezre accepts a violent kick from her baby.

"Is it time!" Joe Geezre yells, gripping his grandfather's gold watch. "This old ticker might be slow!"

"No, no. Not yet," she says smiling, pale and clammy. "Just a kick. I do hope there's a phone to call the hospital and alert them—if the baby starts coming!"

"I'm sure there's a phone," Joe Geezre replies with the hollow conviction of a father-to-be. "And I'm sure a nurse will be at the party."

"There's a comforting thought," Mrs. Geezre replies. The bricklayer caresses her box of bricks, rocking it in her arms as if it were a pink baby.

The elevator stops with a lurch equal to the one with which it started. "You should fix this thing!" Joe Geezre snaps. His wife endures another baby kick as the bricklayer uses the heel of her trowel to rap soundly on the door until it opens. The bricklayer moves quickly. Holding her arms wide, gesturing vehemently for her companions to remain in the elevator, she points to the indicator light.

"Two," Joe Geezre says. "This is only two."

"Maybe its says two," his wife replies, "but it's actually one."

"Doesn't matter," Joe Geezre says. "We want three." He presses button three and the doors close. The elevator descends. The doors open and Joe Geezre stands face-to-face with Indian Joe. Indian Joe looks at the people in the elevator, not recognizing anyone. He wears the rug shawl-like around his shoulders. An eagle feather hangs limp behind his ear, and there are daubs of red warpaint on his cheekbones. He steps past the pregnant woman and stares at the indicator numbers ignoring the white-faced bricklayer who grimaces, smiles, and frowns attempting to snare his attention. Joe Geezre presses button three again, hard, but as the doors close a delicate hand slaps the rubber safety lip and the doors reopen.

"Room for one more?" a glamorous woman asks. Without waiting for a reply she tries to enter the elevator but as she steps across the threshold her dog darts between her feet wrapping its leash around her ankles. She screeches, pitching forward into the elevator.

"Lady with a baby!" Joe Geezre says, stepping between the falling woman and his unborn child. The glamorous woman's dog, pulled by its leash, follows her. Her ostrich-plume hat falls off, and Indian Joe, solid as an oak tree, grips her shoulders to keep her off the floor.

"Thank you," she mutters, regaining her feet. The bricklayer ceremoniously hands her the ostrich-plume hat. "Truffles," she says, pulling the leash. She stoops for her dog. "Come to Mummy, Truffie. Mummy will hold you." She wears bright red lipstick, a paste-on mole, and a frizzy platinum-blonde wig.

"Miss Monroe?" Indian Joe asks.

"Ooooh yes!" she gushes.

"I admire your pictures!" he says sincerely.

"And I yours I'm sure!" she replies. "I've seen you fall off your pony numerous times!"

"Yes," Indian Joe nods gravely. "Always a pinto. It's in my contract. I've been shot off my pinto by many white male actors, Mr. Cooper primarily. Hi, little fellah." He scratches Truffles' head. "What's your breed?"

"He's a half-breed," Marilyn replies.

Indian Joe looks at her stonily.

"He's half cocker and half poodle."

"Cockapoo—" Indian Joe proclaims.

"No. The other way around. His mother is a cocker and his father is a poodle."

"Oh yeah?" Indian Joe continues to scratch Truffles' ears. "I like his spunky spirit. He'd be good."

"He *is* good!" Marilyn Monroe coos. "He's Mother's Angel!"

The elevator ascends and the bricklayer taps the alarm button shave-and-a-haircut. No one is amused, so she donates them an imbecilic downturned smile which says, *I'm sorry*. The elevator stops and its doors open to reveal Melanie Moore, who has flown up the stairs, reading the notes on Joe's door:

> Come In! Make yourself at home!
> Captain Geezre has departed for
> France having sub-let his apartment to
> Mr. Joe Van Gogh. Manager, more
> shaved-ice for snocones, when
> convenient. No rush thanks, Capt.
> Geezre.

Melanie Moore grips the doorknob attempting to turn it, but it is locked. The door at the end of the hallway opens and in walks Cowboy wearing his black trousers and shirt, spurs, and sombrero. He carries a box of Mexican food. "Is this where Joe Geezre lives?"

"Yes. But he's enroute to France," Melanie Moore says.

Joe Geezre looks at his pregnant wife and shrugs. "News to me," he says.

"Have a nice trip," his wife says. "Write me a French letter."

Indian Joe recognizes Joe Geezre and, gripping him by the shoulder, shakes him fondly, "Joe! Joe Geezre, Old Buddy! Good to see you!"

Melanie knocks again. The door opens and the guests are greeted by their host. Beaming, obviously delighted to see them, he says, "I forgot to put a fork in the door. Come in! Come in! Ah! Mr. Cowboy! You brought some of your exquisite, greaseless food!" Uncle Sam peers over Joe's shoulder.

"Yessir, Mr. Geezre. Potato chips, red sauce, and guacamole dip."

"Put it here, *Muchacho*!" Joe Van Gogh bows low to Marilyn Monroe, who he doesn't recognize, and he looks long at the bricklayer trying to figure who she is. Joe Geezre shakes hands with Joe Van Gogh. The pocket of Joe Geezre's blue ruffled shirt bristles pencils and ballpoint pens.

"I'd like you to meet my wife," Joe Geezre says. "She's expecting."

"Expecting what?" Joe asks.

The pregnant woman grips her false abdomen, leans on her heels, and shakes it at him. "A baby!" she says. "You *do* know about babies, don't you? Where they come from!"

"Yes, of course."

Marilyn Monroe heads for the window to check the view, and the bricklayer falls to clogdancing. She grabs Joe, trying to get him to join her. "Have we met?" he asks. The bricklayer stops dancing, lifts her toolbox tight to her chest, and looks warily left and right, having caught sight of a frightful mummy leering over Joe Van Gogh's shoulder, its rotten bandages parted slightly at its eyes, its mouth taped shut. Joe shakes hands with the mummy as Sigmund Freud sidles up alongside Marilyn Monroe to help her observe the view—the street descending the hill, the limestone wall, and Whoso Findeth Wisdom Findeth Life. The bricklayer scurries around until she locates the bathroom. She settles in its doorway and squirts a layer of shaving cream across the doorsill. Then, using styrofoam bricks and shaving cream mortar, she begins bricking up the bathroom doorway closely observed by the pregnant woman and the mummy.

An automobile salesman lights his cigar with Monopoly money. He then tries to extinguish the money by blowing on it, but his puffing only makes it burn faster. The flames singe his bushy white eyebrows, and he manages to put the money out by stuffing it into a Cadillac brochure. "Great Caesar's Ghost!" he exclaims, turning the sooty, smoldering, pages, showing car photographs to anyone who will look. "Whadaya make of this one, eh? Ain't she a beaut? Sedan DeVille. Enough discreet horsepower here to pull anybody's ox outta de ditch, eh? And hey, howabout dis Eldorado? City of Gold. Girls love it!" His last remark catches Uncle Sam's attention. "Buy the convertible, Uncle, let the wind blow your whiskers!"

Joe Geezre finds the telephone. He lifts the receiver saying, "Hullo, hospital? Progress report. All calm. She's dipping guacamole. Stand by." He hangs up the phone.

Joe Van Gogh, his apartment rapidly filling with guests, moves the easel aside to make room. Indian Joe helps him saying, "Hey, be careful! This paint's still wet. Nice picture, Joe. Thunderhawk?"

"Scottish Rite. Is Mary coming? Did she get my message?"

"What message?"

"To come to my party."

"What party?"

Joe Van Gogh shrugs. "How's your tailbone?"

"It thrives, Joe. Where's your neighbor, the cooker of good coffee?"

Joe Van Gogh points to the man wearing the red-white-and-blue suit. "Uncle Sam Woolheater. False beard and sideburns, but his white hair is real."

Indian Joe nods, saying, "If you don't mind I'll ask him to brew us a pot?"

"I'm sure he'd be honored," Joe replies, "but he might require you to dance *America the Beautiful* in return."

"I'd dance *Nutcracker* naked for a good cup of Java. Say, did my soup do anything for you?"

"It strengthened my sight."

"It's about time for another batch."

"Where's Mary?"

Indian Joe pulls a long-stemmed pipe out of his sleeve. Lighting it with the BiC he says, "Don't ask me. She's free, red, and twenty-one." He strides forth to negotiate with Uncle Sam. On the way he encounters Aunt Jemima and circles her in a flamenco gesture. Then he borrows one of Joe Geezre's pens and writes:

> My Dearest Uncle,
> Brew a strongpot of coffee and in exchange I will willingly and forever give you the City of Chicago containing limitless meadows of Wild Onions.
> Chicago Owner,
Joseph Thunder

He folds the note, slaps it in Uncle Sam's palm, and pursues Aunt Jemima with a libidinous gleam.

A short but well-dressed General MacArthur inspects the bricklayer's work. He wears sunglasses and a khaki uniform which displays many brass ornaments—monkey balls, ruptured ducks, campaign ribbons, Hershey bars, and medals of occupation. There are stars on his collar and scrambled eggs on his hat. He puffs a corncob pipe saying, "See here, young man, you have cut off *la trine*, the piss trench, the latrine! Where will my GI's go—"

The bricklayer replies with a shrug.

"Come now," General MacArthur says in his high-pitched military voice. You've P.O.W.ed the only damned pot in the house!"

The bricklayer stands. After using a kerchief to wipe flecks of mortar from her hands she says something that looks like, *That's not my problem.*

General MacArthur turns on his heel and bumps into Sherlock Holmes who is identifiable by his deerstalker, calabash, and magnifier. His face is distinctly African and he uses his magnifier to peruse the general's campaign ribbons before announcing in a British accent, "Sir, these are in wrong sequence, different to what they should be. You are not whom you appear."

The pregnant woman, hearing Sherlock's British accent, parts the crowd with her paper-mache tummy. "Fee, fi, fo, fum! I hear the voice of an Englishman!" Upon seeing his black face, however, she stops short. He turns his magnifier on her and after a careful examination says, "You, Madam, are in a family way. I hope this news is welcome."

She bumps him with her paper-mache. "It doesn't take Sherlock Holmes to see this!"

"Not your masquerade, Madam," he pats her hollow tummy. "It would deceive few fools. I'm speaking of the *aurora natalis* flush in your cheek. Quite apart from your spotty rouge, this flush is characteristic of lower-class Middlesex girls who find themselves compromised. You, My Dear, are conceived."

"Of course, you newt! I wouldn't wear this getup if I wasn't."

"Married?"

"Cheeky bastard!"

"Picked a name yet?"

"Josephine for a girl, Joseph for a boy."

"Look at that one over there! I believe he *is* an Indian. A red Indian, I mean." Sherlock points with his pipe and the pregnant woman turns to see Indian Joe dogging Aunt Jemima. "Gotcha!" Indian Joe yells, grabbing her apron strings. "Hold up a minute. Let's play Doctor. Lawyer. Indian Chief!" An oily Wayne Newton squeezes past them on his way to flirt with Marilyn Monroe.

Mary Thunder enters, searches out Joe, and thanks him for her invitation. He welcomes her with a peck on the cheek. She hands him the silver flask saying, "I forgot to give this back. I refilled it with scotch. Good scotch."

"Oh," Joe says, "Give it to that man over there. The fellow with the singed eyebrows."

"Lawdy, Lawdy, Lawdy," Aunt Jemima says. "I done plumb give out runnin' from you." She knuckles Indian Joe in the breastbone and says, "I don't dig redskins, Kaw-Liga. Get yourself a better costume."

Indian Joe stares at her. "Costume!" Then his dark face melts into a network of smile lines and wrinkles. He flashes her a grin saying, "C'mon, you knows you likes Indians! Everybody likes Indians—we're akin to whales in that regard. And elephants. Ever hear of anybody who didn't like elephants?" But Aunt Jemima has dissolved into the crowd. Indian Joe bumps elbows with the Mexican food purveyor and says to his tray of *hors d'oeuvres*, "No thanks, Cowboy. Onions make my urine stink!"

Marilyn, retreating from Wayne Newton, turns her attention to Indian Joe. "Don't feel bad. *I* like Indians! Thanks for grabbing me in the elevator!"

"Shhhht!" Indian Joe hushes. "Somebody might take that the wrong way! Will you let me hold Truffles?"

Joe catches Marilyn's eye and shakes his head. She thinks he's trying to warn her that the bathroom is unavailable. As she hands Truffles to Indian Joe she says, "I *know*. No powder room! What are we going to *do* as the evening wears on?"

"We'll kick that flimsy wall down," Joe replies, wondering who she is.

"No violence," Indian Joe counsels, "it's better to negotiate." Carrying Truffles tenderly, with Marilyn Monroe tethered by the leash, he makes his way to the bathroom door and says, "How, Paleface? Is this a brick wall?"

The bricklayer nods emphatically.

Indian Joe's pipe has gone out. He shifts Truffles to the crook of his left arm and relights his pipe. "I see. It seems you've taken the john off the reservation."

The bricklayer nods.

"Why?"

The bricklayer pantomimes frantically riding a horse, looking over her shoulder.

"That means, in your language, *John-run-away-from, no-john,* or *non-john*?"

The bricklayer nods.

"John Wayne," Indian Joe explains to the bystanders. "She's afraid of John Wayne." He flashes a volley of Indian signs, but she can't read them so he says, "There are a number of persons in attendance this evening who would prefer to see you say *yes-john* or *some-john*."

The Cadillac salesman, attracted by Indian Joe's gesticulations, sidles in close, as does Uncle Sam who rubs Truffles' nape saying, "Hi, Bow-wow. You look good!" He gives Indian Joe a meaningful wink.

"Tell you what," says Indian Joe. "Take down your wall, give us visitation rights in the Pasturelands of the Toilet, and we'll cede to you the state of Oklahoma henceforth and forever. Now isn't that a fair trade?"

The bricklayer shrugs, pulling out her pockets.

"You're telling us you're in no position to bargain?"

The bricklayer nods brightly. Indian Joe turns to Uncle Sam and says firmly, "I thought I asked you to make coffee? Hot. Strong. Black!" He shifts Truffles to his right arm and scans the room for Aunt Jemima.

Uncle Sam backs off. The bricklayer nods, accepting Oklahoma for the toilet as Aunt Jemima, having undergone a sea change, materializes beside Indian Joe pulling his arm, turning him away from Uncle Sam. "It's okay, Joseph. He'll make coffee and Paleface will let us use the pot to put it in. You're one hell of a negotiator."

"Yeah. Instead of piddling around with linguistics I should have gone for a whole-hog M.B.A."

The bricklayer begins dismantling her wall, scraping off mortar with her trowel. Having no other place to put the mortar, she piles it on Melanie Moore's graduation hat.

"Let's go get some fresh air, Joseph."

"Ugh," Indian Joe replies. "Truffles needs a walk." He winks at Marilyn Monroe, but she is mesmerized, staring at the fortuneteller. Indian Joe unsnaps Truffles' leash. As he and Aunt Jemima make for the door they work their way around a card table at which the fortuneteller, a veiled gypsy woman, is dealing blackjack.

"Twenty-one!" she tells Marilyn. "You're going to take a trip and meet an honest well-digger." Marilyn, delighted, wiggles. The gypsy advises her, "Stay out of strange bedfellows, Babyface." Marilyn, her red lips parted, stares intently into the gypsy's veil. She doesn't notice that Truffles' leash, looped around her wrist, has gone slack. "Pick a card, Babyface!" The gypsy fans the deck. Marilyn puts a finger to her lip. "I know you," she says distinctly, not in the voice of Marilyn Monroe but in her own voice. "I know I know you! Who are you?"

The door opens and in walks Methusela. In his right hand he holds Betsy, leaning on her as if she were a staff. In his left hand he carries a Gigolo's shopping bag in which clink five bottles of Russian vodka. Behind him are the Pleiades, seven virgin widows all wearing white masks. Methusela stands face-to-face with Sigmund Freud, staring at her as if they harbor a grudge. The famous writers exchange curt nods and Dr. Freud says, "Vell — Ve half de neuro-seas and vee half de psycho-seas, and now vee half one of *dese*!" He jabs his cigar at Methusela's gun.

"Betsy," Methusela says. "She goes where I go."

"Lovely name, Bet-sea. Let's see, Bet-sea? Wager ocean!"

The elephant gun's muzzle shifts slightly when Betsy hears her name. Joe squeezes through the crowd to greet Methusela, "I'm delighted you could make it."

"I lost the wager. Fair and square." Methusela indicates the sack of vodka which he has lowered gently to the floor.

"Oh. Good! Let me summon the general to receive his spoils." Joe weaves through the crowd looking for the short man. Marilyn fills his place beside Methusela. She flirts, twisting, smiling, and jiggling. Sigmund observes Methusela's reaction to Marilyn. Methusela's knuckles grow white gripping Betsy's muzzle.

"I don't believe we've had the pleasure," Marilyn purrs. "I'm Miss Monroe. Have you met Herr Doctor Freud?"

Methusela nods. "I can play a Nazi war criminal, a mad scientist, or a writer underwater."

"Oh! Herr Doctor Freud, vat do you tink about dat, undervater vriter?"

Sigmund wags her cigar and gazes around the room as if she'd rather be Groucho Marx. Carrie Nation, hatchet in hand, enters the apartment shouting, "Where's the booze!"

Wayne Newton corners Joe Geezre and confronts him. "Say, Mr. Geezre. I understand you've been looking for me?"

Joe Van Gogh returns with Douglas MacArthur and the bricklayer's toolbox. He sets the toolbox in front of Methusela and holds the general's hand while he mounts it. MacArthur, now at eye level with Methusela, salutes him as Methusela formally presents the Gigolo's sack. Joe and Marilyn Monroe clap hands, and the crowd picks it up. There is loud applause, but most of the guests don't know why they're applauding. MacArthur, hugging his Gigolo's shopping bag fondly, announces, "The Russians are here!"

Leaving the dog free to explore the lilac bushes, Indian Joe hustles Madame Leontyne out to the redwood bench beside the chapel. He lights his calumet and they toke it back and forth awhile in the twilight. "Crepuscular," he says. "This is quite nice and crepuscular."

She nods, saying, "Eleven letters down meaning twilight."

He looks beyond the boulevard, his eyes attracted by a blur of white and black movement as the skunk drags its pigeon into the bushes. Truffles sees the skunk and gives chase. "Look at that dumb puppy," Indian Joe muses. "He doesn't know about skunks."

"Nice party," Madame Leontyne says.

"Wonderful party."

A battered van turns off the boulevard, jumps the curb, and stops in front of Flattop. Painted on the van is *Sand Rats*. Scrawny rat-like musicians crawl from it and commence wheeling speakers and keyboards toward Flattop.

"Looks like we got outta there just in the nick," Indian Joe says to Madame Leontyne.

"Yeah."

"You run a fortunetelling shop, eh?"

"Why haven't you been to see me?"

"Because I'm in the same racket. If you're a good girl I'll show you my Comanche tailbone."

Madame Leontyne slaps him, smearing his warpaint. He grabs her in a headlock and pinches her cheek, scooping off a glob of blackface which he holds to his nose, smells, and licks. "Chocolate or licorice?"

"Lemme go! You heathen cannibal sonofabitch!"

He holds her tight. She kicks, punches, and pulls free. There are tears in her eyes. "God help me," she says. "I came awful close to eating a Preacher."

"Are you sane?" Indian Joe asks.

"Of course. Preacher's a chicken Joe Geezre fell in love with. I almost killed him for supper last night. Some Benevolent Spirit stayed my hand."

Indian Joe uses his handkerchief to wipe tears from her eyes.

Truffles doesn't receive a full blast of skunk spray. Much of it is deflected by the lilac bushes. He only gets a mild application, enough to make him interesting and distinctive when Madame Leontyne and Indian Joe take him back to the party. They enter the building holding hands. The Sand Rats have set up in the hallway, and the Pleiades Widows are returning from their apartments bearing extra glasses and ice.

Methusela's vodka bottles stand on the breakfast bar, awaiting the Pleiades.

Mary Thunder unties her braids, brushes out her hair, and puts on Joe's grass skirt. When she lifts her arms in the hula everyone can see she is authentic, wearing nothing at all but the skirt. Rosealyn and her half-sister Spookie sit crosslegged in a corner holding hands. Judge stays in costume. Sipping from his flask, he inspects the vodka bottles which Bulldog has uncapped and lined in a precise row like transparent soldiers. The Sand Rats open with Joe's request—a medley of Taj Mahal favorites. Melanie Moore, her mortarboard piled high with shaving cream, says yes to Mary Thunder's invitation to dance. They are joined by Rosealyn and Spookie. Joe, knowing he is a woman, asks Dr. Freud to dance. He takes her in his arms and they two-step. Anne Judge removes her bowler, shakes her hair loose, and pulls Judge from the shadows to dance a slow samba. The crowd falls back, admiring their graceful ballroom technique—the Cadillac salesman man and the white-faced woman.

Indian Joe stifles the band to announce his engagement to Madame Leontyne. She pokes him in the ribs and says it will be a cold day in hell when she marries a redskin. Retired Professor Woolheater serves hot coffee. Phoebe Jones reads a poem about fearing the Timberwolf—accompanied by the Sand Rats singing *a cappella*. Graham uses his wig to unscrew lightbulbs so he and Pinkie can dance in the dark. The party grows mellow. Bulldog and Methusela, ignored by the philistines, stand near the framed photographs, catching light from the open door. Bulldog explaines the significance of Comanche. "General Custer's mount. Survived the battle."

"Damned rare chunk of horsemeat."

"Grew fat and shaggy in his old age. Seventh Cavalry mascot, until he died."

"What's this?" Methusela uses Betsy's muzzle to flick a plastic cork across the carpet.

"Bubbly, I suppose."

"Didn't hear it pop. Cheap bastards opened it before we arrived."

"More tears are shed over answered prayers than unanswered ones."

"What the hell does that mean?"

Bulldog tosses off his glass of vodka and says, "Obviously—"

"Obviously hell! You've been running around saying that for the last twenty goddamn years! You've about worn it out. Tell me what it means?"

Bulldog makes himself another drink. The single light burning above the breakfast bar illuminates pink scalp beneath his thin hair. His eyes are puffy. His facelift has slipped. He is drunk. Methusela jabs his fist-and-glass in Bulldog's face, demanding a refill. Bulldog obliges him without offering any fresh ice. Then Bulldog leads him to the limelight near the open doorway. Mellow Sand Rats music drifts into the room, washing over him and Methusela. "It means we're standing here visible and alone. Is this why we wrote a million words, to come to a Kansas party and be ignored?"

Methusela, also drunk, nods soberly as he blinks to see the dancers' faces passing through the patch of light. Phoebe as Amelia Earhart, May as a mummy, Spookie the gypsy, Rosealyn as Marilyn Monroe, Trish as Carrie Nation, Cowboy, Aunt Jemima, Indian Joe—

Joe leads Paula into the bedroom where Preacher sleeps on the chest of drawers. Paula unwraps his bandage. He turns out the light and pats Little Hen for her to sit down. She steps in Preacher's water bowl.

"C'mere, clumsy," Joe says.

"Shall I leave it on or take it off?"

I'm really having a date, Joe thinks as she peels off the moustache and sticks it, like chewing gum, on the wall above the bed. He takes her in his arms and pulls her down. Her soft mouth is flavored by the sweetness of Dr. Freud's moustache glue.

———————

Rosealyn's party ends like a warm accordion being nestled into its velvet case. The Sand Rats, who never actually cranked up their full volume, roll speakers and keyboards down the hallway and out the door to their van. The Pleiades, leaving their glittering glasses in the darkness, go back to their apartments. Graham and Pinkie give Bulldog and Methusela rides home. The rivals weigh down Graham's Ford, sitting together but distinctly apart like grim-faced heads of state. Indian Joe takes Madame Leontyne to Red's Place, a subterranean nightclub. Rosealyn walks Spookie home. They take turns holding the poocock's leash down the hill, telling one another about themselves. They have both danced with their father, Wayne Newton. "He held me close," Rosealyn says, "trying to feel my breasts."

"Yeah. Me too."

"You too?"

"Sure. He couldn't see my face through the veil and he whispered, *You're the prettiest girl here.* I whispered back, *I'm not a girl, Pops.* That really stirred up his curiosity."

Rosealyn laughs. "Kinky!"

"Was your mother there?"

"She was the mummy."

"She didn't recognize you?"

"No. She had no reason to think I'd be me. I'm not arriving until tomorrow."

"Want to spend the night at my place?"

"That would be an improvement. I spent last night under the bridge."

"Why?"

"I fell in with two guys who had a carseat and a fire. Frogs were singing. I stared at the fire and got enchanted by it, couldn't leave. So I stayed there until the sun came up. Why did you dress like a gypsy?"

"To have a veil so nobody would know who I was. Why did you dress like Marilyn Monroe?"

"I wanted to be a blonde and act sexy—swing my hips."

"Dad went for you in a big way."

"Yeah. Don't ever tell!"

They stop at the park to sit on a bench and let the dog run. "Stay away from skunks!" The dog noses a toad under the

light. The bench is out of the light, back in the shadows, and
when a swing-shift jogger pads by on his air-soles he studiously
avoids making eye contact with the flashy blonde and the veiled
gypsy.

———————

Anne and Judge walk arm-in-arm up the boulevard. They
stop at the fountain to look at stars reflected in the water.
Anne is thinking about getting home to feed Hero. Judge is
thinking about his docket. A car driven by Phoebe Jones
circles the fountain. Lloyd tips his deerstalker to the Judges.

———————

Cowboy and Mary Thunder are the last guests.
Woolheater has long since gone to his apartment. Mary puts
a fork in the door.
"What's that for?" Cowboy asked.
"To keep it from locking. That's the way Joe does it."
"Why?"
"He's like those monks that sleep in coffins. Like, if
somebody wants to break in he says, *Welcome.*" She goes into
the bathroom to take off the grass skirt and put on her clothes.
Cowboy hangs around thinking he might get lucky. When she
comes out of the bathroom they disembark together, his heels
ringing loud on the polished deck. When they get to the dark
museum Mary steps into the lilac bushes to give him the slip.
He waits half an hour before realizing what she'd done. It
doesn't occur to him that she's used the fork so she can get
back into Joe's apartment and creep into the guest bedroom.

———————

Joe feels warm breath on his face. He clenches his eyes
tight and fights hard to stay asleep, but like minnow bubbles his
mind shimmers up to consciousness. He listens to her
breathing, reluctant to move for fear he will wake her.
Starlight illuminates her moustache clinging to the wall above
them, its wings drooping like a moth. Joe feels warm and

happy and scared. *This is wonderful,* he thinks, *thank God I didn't pray for it!*

THE END